An Orphan's Wish

BOOKS BY LIZZIE PAGE

Lizzie Page

An Orphan's Wish

bookouture

Published by Bookouture in 2023

An imprint of Storyfire Ltd.
Carmelite House
50 Victoria Embankment
London EC4Y 0DZ

www.bookouture.com

ISBN: 978-1-83790-712-0
eBook ISBN: 978-1-83790-711-3

To children in care and to those who were in care.

Twinkle, twinkle, little bat!
How I wonder what you're at!
Up above the world you fly,
Like a tea tray in the sky.

PROLOGUE

Ivor never told Clara what he had gone through in the war, and Clara didn't ask. You didn't. People had different reasons not to talk about it. For some, it was too raw, too painful. For others, incredibly, the war might have been the first time in their life they had freedom or a sense of purpose, and no one wanted to hear that! Clara suspected Ivor's reasons – wanting to give privacy to his dead comrades, not wanting to relive the time he lost his arm, and a wish to put it all behind him. Each one of these reasons was strong enough on its own. He still had nightmares about it, she knew that. She had seen him sweating, tossing and turning in his sleep.

In the autumn of 1952, Clara had found out some of what Ivor had experienced. Mr Dowsett, the local librarian, had seen a newspaper article mentioning an Officer Delaney of Suffolk and asked Clara if she wanted to take a look.

He was at Dunkirk, which she knew; he had led his troop, which she didn't. They were under fire on the beaches, and they were loading up the boats with the injured to evacuate, and he went back for more people time and time again – with no care for himself, not a thought for his own safety, he went back to pick up more. He was told to stop, yet he continued. It was a nightmare mission. Sergeant Jack Robinson said, 'If I saw him again, I would buy him a whisky, a double or even a triple. If it weren't for him, there's no doubt I would be getting eaten by maggots in a French grave. It was like he was possessed, he was determined to save us all.'

Clara never told Ivor what she had learned, but she was proud of how brave he was. And she thought how lucky she was to be engaged to him. A good man like that! It was second time round for her – and she was grateful to get another shot at love.

She wouldn't have imagined that was possible.

At other times, she found herself going over that sentence 'With no care for himself, not a thought for his own safety, he went back...' and something about it made her feel uneasy in the pit of her stomach. It was only a few months after reading that article that Clara was able to work out why.

1

It was January, 1953, and it was the children's first day back at school. As usual, Christmas had gone on far too long, and Clara was secretly relieved it was back to business.

She had a very important day ahead of her.

The evening before, all five of the children in the home – Jonathon, Peg, Gladys, Frank and Trevor – had gone to sleep promptly, and that morning they had set off brightly for their respective schools: Peg, Gladys and Frank to Lavenham Primary, Jonathon and Trevor to the High School. No one had tooth- or tummy-ache, no one claimed Stella the cat had kept them awake and no one demanded a day off.

So Clara had no excuse not to go to her meeting.

Not that Clara was looking for an excuse. She had spent a lot of time planning what she would say today. Ivor – her neighbour, boyfriend and, more recently, fiancé! – had been helpful too, showing a new side of himself yet again. While he hated public speaking, he was good at challenging Clara to make her speech the best she could: *What is it you want to say? What is it you want them to feel?*

But now she was here, Clara felt wobbly. It was a full

council meeting – they called it an *extraordinary* meeting – and there wasn't an empty seat in the chamber and the public galleries were also packed. They weren't all here to see Clara, probably, but for the controversial motion just after her, which was about a new bus route 'set to slice Bury in half like a corpse'. The mayor had to tell the public gallery to quieten down a few times, and he had thumped down his gavel more than once.

Clara was giving an update on: *The State of Suffolk's Children's Homes – An Insider's Perspective.*

Clara hadn't chosen that title but she rather liked it. The word 'state' was layered, of course, and 'insider's perspective' made her sound rather like a spy, or a mole, infiltrating the service to report back, when in reality she was a permanent fixture, a housemother, and this was the only perspective she had.

That she had been invited to take this slot was also perhaps extraordinary, but Mrs McCarthy, the leader of Suffolk County Council, had invited her and you didn't say no to Mrs McCarthy. She was the only woman in the country in her position and you didn't get to where she was without 'stepping on a few toes'. She took children's care seriously and had been one of the few councils to race to implement the findings of the government's Curtis Report on childcare.

People in the public galleries had taken off their winter coats, rolled up their sleeves and loosened their ties. Some were picnicking. One woman in the gallery was knitting, which reminded Clara of the French woman, Madame Defarge, who they say knitted at the guillotine.

Clara talked about life at the home in general terms at first. And the audience looked underwhelmed, but maybe that was because it was bus wars that had brought them in, not 'an insider's perspective' on the state of children's homes. Clara talked about how she had five children in her care right now, but it was an ever-changing number: sometimes more, sometimes fewer. Privately she thought five was optimum, and these five were optimum in particular, but she didn't say that.

Then, Clara talked about some of the problems she faced at the home. She had to be selective; she wouldn't achieve anything by bombarding anyone with unpalatable facts.

It was like looking after children really: you have to choose your battles. You don't tackle nose-picking, hand-washing *and* tooth-brushing all at the same time, otherwise they lose interest. You have to break everything down into small manageable steps.

'A parent came to us recently and their child was missing in the system. The child was in our care, my care, but we didn't know where or when or what had happened to her previously. This is completely unacceptable. We need careful documentation. For us simply to "lose track" is bad for the children and bad for the parents.'

This was Florrie. Florrie had recently left Shilling Grange to go and live with her father. He had found her after spending several years looking for her.

The audience nodded at that. Hard not to. Clara looked up from her notes. Knitting lady was still knitting. Picnickers were still picnicking. The mayor was still playing with his gavel.

'Some parents wish to be reunited with their children. It is not good enough to say we have lost touch with them or we no longer have them on our books. We need to support parents of children in care far better, so that if at *any* time they want to come back, if they are ready, they can. Many mothers and fathers have given up children for reasons outside of their control: a sudden turn into poverty, a bereavement, homelessness. We need to make sure there is a route back for them.

'I currently have a child in my care who hopes her mother will come and get her – perhaps the mother is out there looking for her. The thing is, we don't know where she is – and we *should* know.'

This was dear Peg Church – the child who'd been with Clara

the longest. Peg didn't speak but she wrote nineteen to the dozen. Carefree Peg, Clara's little drummer girl, who enjoyed skipping and shells. She also loved going to Sunday School, and she had adored Mr Newton, Clara's late father.

'I also have in my care a child who was separated from her siblings.'

This was Gladys Gluck. Gladys loved games – everything had to be decided by 'Rock scissors paper'. They played the alphabet game so often that Clara swore her gravestone would say: *Antelope, Ant-eater, Ant. Malta, Monaco, Morocco*. And Gladys would spend hours over a jigsaw. She also had a sweet singing voice and was learning the flute with Anita.

'Again, nobody knew quite where the siblings were. Worse, nobody cared where they were. Children are being split unnecessarily from their families and then lost track of. This is bad for everyone.'

Clara had managed to reunite Gladys with her brothers, Trevor and Frank, last year. They had been living with a foster family who treated them terribly. Aeroplane lover, spider collector, habitual hat-wearer Frank got nits and stomach aches, knee-ache, hip-ache and toothache so often that Clara found she was taking him to Dr Cardew's surgery every week. Also, A. Frank was a Dr Cardew fan and B. Dr Cardew was a Frank fan.

Trevor was more interested in his friends, cycling and chess than either Clara, the home or his brother and sister, but he was a cheerful, hard-working lad and the reports from his school were glowing: 'If Trevor continues in the same vein, he will be prefect or head boy.'

No child from the home had ever been in such a responsible position – even academic ex-resident Alex – and Clara was immensely proud.

'Well-being increases when siblings are placed together. It's crucial,' Clara said. When she had rehearsed this, she had thumped the kitchen table, but it seemed inappropriate now. 'Vital and it's not even that difficult to organise!'

At the front of the room, Mr Sommersby, the head of children's services, was shaking his pen. Clara noted the blue stain shapes on the paper in front of him and tried not to be distracted by them.

'All the children come from troubled backgrounds. I haven't met any who didn't need extra care and support.'

Childcare officer Miss Webb always said that as long as the children had clean faces and clean hands, then not to worry too much about 'their inner worlds', but Clara always did.

'They might not appear to want anything, but any child with us has experienced difficulties and needs extra help going forward.'

This was Jonathon Pell. The son of war hero Maurice Pell, he was probably the child she had most concerns about at that moment. Jonathon was polite – he was the only child who stood up when an adult came into the room – but he was monosyllabic. The good manners couldn't hide the fact that he was constantly sad.

Clara watched as Mrs McCarthy rose to her feet. In some ways, with her walking cane and frosty hair, she seemed old-fashioned, like a relic from a different age; and yet in other ways she came across as someone who was ahead of her time.

Mrs McCarthy spoke. 'What I like about you, Miss Newton, is that you are a problem-solver. So if these are some of our problems, how do you propose we solve them?'

Clara nodded, for this part too she had rehearsed with Ivor.

'We need to remember the children are young people who deserve kindness and respect – and family, if or when that's appropriate. This means greater support for parents too – birth parents, foster-parents, adoptive parents.'

'And practically?'

'Siblings should never be separated. This is the least we can do. I would like a system whereby parents can get back in contact with the children in care whatever has gone wrong before. I would be happy to see open adoptions.'

Ivor had said: 'Remember Churchill's speeches? He always says things in three. It's a thing with the great orators,' so Clara continued with that in mind.

'To summarise: I would like to see better communication, increased support and much greater transparency. Thank you for listening.'

Relieved it was over, Clara smiled around her, before suddenly remembering something else.

'Oh, and then there's bags.'

'Bags?'

Clara felt emotional, remembering the way various children had transported their belongings from their previous home to hers. Staggering into the house with splitting paper bags, or things wrapped in a towel, or clutching just a book, a pen or a shell – it wasn't right.

'There must be a way we can transfer the children and their few belongings with more *dignity*.'

Mrs McCarthy clapped, but she was the only one.

The mayor called for a ten-minute break and, as Clara got up to go, it all felt slightly anticlimactic. He wouldn't have done that to Churchill, Clara thought. He wouldn't have done that to the people fighting against the proposed bus route.

Mr Sommersby and Mrs McCarthy remained inside the council hall. Mrs McCarthy might have waved goodbye, or she might have been stretching her arms. In the long narrow corridor outside, Clara buttoned up her coat and put her gloves back on. Ivor had offered to come to meet her but she had told him not to waste his time.

The wall-light flickered suddenly. If the children were with her, they'd have said it was ghosts. Clara felt like she had exorcised a few ghosts in there.

Over the years, she had taken on the council several times, and won. She had taken them to task over their plan to unfairly fire her, she had stopped children from being sent to the Christian Brothers in Australia, she had stopped the home from being sold off, she had insisted children should see their notes – she had done plenty. She knew her strengths.

Clara wasn't a person who generally felt pleased with herself – she was always looking for the next problem to solve or going over what she'd done wrong. But now for a very small moment she let herself bask. She'd got her point across. She had said something. Even if nothing ever changed, even if nothing ever improved, at least she'd done her bit, she'd done her best.

And now she could get on with organising something else – something far more exciting.

Things to Do for the Wedding (in no particular order)

Set a date
Organise the party
Buy a dress
Book a photographer
Order flowers
Choose bridesmaids, best man, pageboys, etc.
Decide on hairstyles C + I
Think about the honeymoon
Write the guest list
Send invitations!!

2

Clara had told the children she and Ivor were engaged last Christmas. It was at dinner, and the branches of the tree were heaving with gold ribbons and red tissue paper. They had pulled the crackers and were groaning over the jokes. Clara had won a pink toy ring and whispered to Ivor, 'You can have that as a wedding ring.' The children had heard, and squealed and clamoured over each other and Clara, and she dropped it in the excitement.

'It's like *Romeo and Juliet*,' commented Trevor, who was being dragged through the text at school and was playing Mercutio.

'Except it's not going to end in a double suicide...' Ivor joked.

'Hopefully not,' said Trevor ominously.

Gladys and Peg were both over the moon and, although Clara kept trying to bring them back down to earth – 'It's going to be small, girls, no fuss' – they kept going off on their own flights of fancy about being flower girls, bridesmaids and so on. They wrapped the tablecloth round themselves and kept grabbing the pink toy ring from the cracker and pretend-marrying each other – although Gladys would shriek, 'I do,' and Peg would shake her head as though saying, 'I don't!' and then they would both collapse in laughter.

Maureen wasn't there for Christmas Day, but she and Peter came to visit on Boxing Day. Maureen had brought Clara a terrible tea tray with a portrait etched on it. 'It's supposed to be the Queen and a dog!' she explained helpfully. 'You hate it, don't you?' and Clara quickly promised to use it every single time they had tea. Maureen had actually cried when they told her the wedding news. 'It's just so romantic. It's like something out of *Woman's Weekly*.'

Clara didn't understand how both of these sentences could be true at the same time. Nevertheless, she was moved by Maureen's heartfelt response.

'You're my two most favourite people in the world – of course I'm happy!'

Peter also had been surprisingly emotional. He shook Ivor's hand and called him Sir. When he and Clara went outside for their customary cigarette, pretty snowdrops pushing through the frozen ground, he said how happy he was for her, and that he hoped he and his girlfriend Mabel would, one day, tread that same path.

The marriage really meant something to them; Clara hadn't realised just how much.

Then when she next came to the home mid-January, Maureen had asked, 'You know the wedding – am I invited?' Her face was screwed up like she didn't dare take in the answer.

'Of course you are, Maureen! In fact, I want you as my maid of honour!'

Maureen blushed. 'It's just I haven't had an invitation yet, so...'

She was purple-cheeked. Maureen was like a pendulum – sometimes her self-esteem was off the scale, other times it was non-existent. Today it was the latter.

'But no one's been invited yet,' Clara reassured her. 'There's so much to organise. But I will send out the invitations as soon as I can!'

The next morning, Clara and Ivor were sitting in his workshop, which was across the road from the Grange. His daughter Patricia was with the Norland Nanny, who was also looking after Patricia's best friend, (Baby) Howard Cardew.

They weren't entirely alone: Clara's cat, Stella, was here. Recently, Stella was more often at Ivor's than she was at home. Ivor was blasé about the cat, which, curiously, she seemed to respond to.

Today, finally, they were organising the wedding together. Clara tried not to, but sometimes when they were planning she remembered planning her wedding to Michael, ten years earlier. Back then, they had a guest list of no more than six. They were going to borrow witnesses off the street. The cake would mostly be cardboard. The dress would be made from parachute silk. She shook herself – times had changed, thank goodness, and this was all going to be very different. Indeed, she had recently done a 'What kind of wedding suits you?' quiz in *Good Housekeeping*.

a. A romantic and intimate gathering

b. A family-party affair

c. An elopement to Gretna Green

d. A fete-like community occasion

She had not told Ivor her answer: mostly D's. 'For you, a wedding is an event to bring everyone together' because she had a feeling Ivor was a mostly B's: 'Nothing makes you happier than being with a few select loved ones'.

Still, they would meet in the middle – they always had so far.

Ivor set two mugs of coffee on his worktop and offered her a plate of shortbread. Clara opened her notebook to the right page and marvelled at her new Bic crystal pen. The adverts said it would revolutionise writing, and Clara, who was probably the customer of their dreams, would agree that it had.

'So you're happy with the venue now?'

'Very.'

It had taken ages to decide where to marry. Clara would put her hand up to that. That was her fault.

Church held negative connotations for her, so she had been scrabbling around, looking for an alternative. There was a registry office on the ground floor of the council building, but she could not imagine marrying at the council offices, where Miss Webb pored over folders or Mr Sommersby presided. It would be a busman's holiday. All the bunting in the world couldn't fix it.

She couldn't imagine marrying in London, where she had been an unhappy child, bitterly spending her childhood evenings and weekends in places she didn't want to be.

Back in November, Mrs Horton had suggested, 'somewhere meaningful to you both,' and Clara had pondered that phrase for a while. Her home – Shilling Grange was historical; it had been the home of the poet Jane Taylor, centuries stamped into its walls – but it was also damp and had a smell of socks and mice and children. Ivor's home? She adored his homely workshop with its rolls of material, its machines, its staplers, but it was no place for entertaining.

Maybe, at a push, the Royal Festival Hall?

Mrs Horton had suddenly had an idea. 'Didn't Ivor ask you to get engaged by the sea at Hunstanton?' she'd said, and Clara had grimaced.

Hunstanton wasn't the place. Clara still felt awkward about that entire episode. That beach was the place of many doubts, the place where she had turned him down. She would say 'postponed' him.

Maybe they just weren't *meaningful place*-type people?

And then, some time later, Clara had banged into the vicar of St Peter and St Paul – literally banged – she definitely got him on the toe and her elbow caught him in the ribs. It was a terrific coincidence – if she were religious, it would have felt like divine intervention.

Once they'd both collected themselves and he had resettled his collar, he said, 'Ah, Miss Newton, congratulations. I hear you're engaged.'

After she'd thanked him, Clara asked, 'How did you hear?'

'Little chap with the planes told me.'

'Frank?'

'That's it. He said, 'A. My housemother is getting married. B. To the man who darns my pants.'

Yes, that sounded like Frank.

'So congratulations are in order. Shall we have a celebratory smoke?'

Clara shook her head in pretend despair, 'Any excuse.'

They had sat on the bench outside the church. The grass was still frosty, like a sprinkling of icing sugar over a Victoria sponge, and she knew it would make the back of her skirt damp. The sun was behind a cloud and if you listened carefully, you could catch the melodic strains of St Peter and St Paul's choir warming up.

'So do you want me to do you and Mr Delaney a simple ceremony here?'

'Oh, I hadn't thought,' admitted Clara, honestly. 'Can you really do that?'

'A ceremony in the church but without too much churchy stuff?' He grinned at her. 'I'm sure we can arrange something.'

The vicar stubbed his cigarette out on the ground and then picked it up. 'Mrs Dorne goes mad...'

There were a few early buds pushing through the mud but the

trees were still empty of leaves and some looked like massive dandelions. It was lovely here even in the depths of winter, and Clara knew it would be beautiful in spring or summer. This meeting with the vicar felt serendipitous, but old habits die hard, and Clara was still slightly resistant.

'You sure you won't do too much of the...'

'Of the boring old preaching? No, Miss Newton.' He smiled at her. 'I know you.'

You couldn't offend the vicar. He was one of the most thick-skinned and good-humoured people Clara knew.

So *that* was a tick off the list.

'Now how about dates?' Clara asked Ivor, since that was next on her list. Nailing down the day felt like chasing after a sheep that kept veering towards the edge of a cliff.

'Doesn't that depend on what the vicar says?'

'He said May is all quiet on the wedding front.'

When they'd discussed it before Christmas, both she and Ivor were keen on June. June bride and all that, plus Lavenham was at its best then. The fields, the sunflowers, the berries. There was something about the way the sun dappled, and the colours of the houses against the blue sky.

But Clara also wanted Marilyn to be there, and she was booked to visit Lavenham in May. Marilyn was Michael's mother and lived in America, and she and Clara were great friends. She was also Clara's landlady, since she owned the Grange and leased it to the council.

The trouble with May was there was a lot of other stuff going on. Was it too much to shoehorn a wedding in? There was the school fete, which might see Peg crowned May Queen at long last. Ivor had a trade fair that he had to go to, since he had given up the markets to concentrate on these exhibitions. And there was a half-term holiday in May – was that good or not?

But then, just when she'd proposed the one day that fell on none of the above (14 May), Ivor, his face perspiring, said, 'Ah, wait, that's actually Ruby's birthday...'

Why did he have to tell her that?

'Is it a problem?'

'I don't want to think of her every time we celebrate.'

So he thought of her on that day?

'And I want many years of celebrating with you,' he continued obliviously.

'Is Ruby going on your guest list?' Clara asked in a sing-songy I-couldn't-care-less voice. Ruby was Ivor's ex-wife. She had left him for another man and, when she became pregnant with Patricia, she'd asked him for help. Ivor, being Ivor, had agreed.

'No way. She is the last person I want anywhere near us, Clara.'

Ivor's tone too had changed, only his had gone from featherlight to brick-house heavy. He had said it before too: he had no interest in Ruby now.

'It's you and Patricia I want in my life.'

'Okay,' said Clara, trying not to be downcast. 'I suppose other weekends in May are available.'

So they decided on 30 May and Clara wrote it down.

'So that's everything settled?' Now Ivor sounded relieved.

'We've only just started, Ivor!' Clara laughed, consulting her list and tapping her new pen. 'Are you happy with the Cloth Hall for the party? It'll be expensive.'

Ivor didn't like dancing 'in public', but he did at least accept there was a need for a celebration after the ceremony. And they'd budgeted – he had savings, she didn't, but she was careful with money, and neither of them were spendthrifts.

'You only get married once,' he'd said, then, realising, looked embarrassed. 'Or twice.'

That was another thing Clara didn't ask him about: his first wedding. She really didn't want to know.

Not true. Clara did want to know – she wanted to know it was *bad, bad, bad* – but she didn't want to risk that it wasn't.

'I'll book it then...'

'Want me to come with?'

At the outset, Clara had been delighted at Ivor's interest in wedding planning. He really was a 'new man'. One of the things she both adored and found frustrating about him was his interest in all the tiny details.

'No.'

Ivor laughed. 'Let's hope the date fits.'

'It will.'

'How do you know?'

Clara winced. 'Because I already checked what dates they had available.'

She had gone yesterday. The usual gentleman was away, and she was greeted by a shiny man in a shiny suit who asked too many questions. He wanted a deposit the next day at the latest.

Clara remembered her dear friend Judy arranging her wartime, make-do-and-mend wedding, and Mrs Horton arranging her own –second chances wedding – and how both grooms had stayed out of it. Not Ivor. The one good thing was he always seemed to think of things she hadn't thought of.

'What about food?' he said now.

'Food?' scoffed Clara. Food was nowhere on her list.

'We have to feed the guests, don't we?' Ivor said. He might look delightfully kissable when he crinkled his face up like that, but Clara was determined to keep on track. 'Can you imagine Anita if we didn't.' he continued, putting on Anita's distinctive accented voice. '"Eight hours they kept us locked up and not a finger sandwich!"'

'Then I'll do the usual, I suppose. Spam or cress. Cheese for Mrs Horton. Cake. I might do a jelly,' Clara said ambitiously. She spun her pen and then wrote down *raspberry jelly*. Then paused. Was Ivor trying to stop himself laughing?

'Maybe I'll attempt that trifle again. You liked that, didn't you? I'll wait for it to set next time.'

Now he was making a decidedly anti-trifle face. 'You want to do it all yourself?'

'Well,' Clara said, 'not particularly, but why not?'

'I don't think that's a good idea.'

This annoyed her. They weren't made of money and she would prefer the limited budget went on something else – anything rather than seeing townspeople she hardly knew stuffing their faces (which was why perhaps a 'family affair' wedding (B. In the *Good Housekeeping* quiz) would have been a better idea for her too).

'We'll see...' Clara muttered under her breath, before adding *decide about food!* to her list. 'Let's move on. I thought Joyce could take photographs.'

Ex-Shilling Grange child Joyce was turning into an artist. Collage was now her favourite medium but she was an excellent photographer too.

'As long as she doesn't cut our faces up,' mused Ivor after Clara had described Joyce's portfolio.

'If she attaches mine to the body of Sophia Loren, I don't mind.'

'Good, ask her then.'

In fact, Joyce had already been asked and Joyce was delighted. So delighted that she said Clara could even have a discount. Clara, who had imagined she wouldn't be charged since this was Joyce's first job and because she was doing the eleven-year-old a favour, was a little taken aback. She would pay for the materials, agreed.

'We'll use the Garrards for flowers?'

The local florists, the Garrards, had done the beautiful and much-praised flowers for Clara's father's funeral.

'Naturally,' said Ivor, which was good because, once again, Clara had already asked them and they had already agreed.

'Right – hair?'

There were probably better hairdressers springing up all over Suffolk now, hairdressers who didn't leave you with a faint smell of burning, who didn't blow smoke in your dry eyes, and who didn't leave you with a rock-hard helmet head, but Clara had to stay loyal. Beryl of Beryl's Brushes had been if not a rock, then certainly scissors, and sometimes paper, throughout Clara's difficult times.

In the few months since Clara's father had died at the Farnborough Air Show, Beryl had reframed their landlady/lodger relationship into a doomed love story: Antony and Cleopatra had nothing on them.

'Beryl is going to do mine and she can do yours too.' Clara quickly ticked 'Hair' on the sheet in the hope that it would quell opposition.

Ivor scowled. 'I will go to my own barber's, thank you.'

'The Ivor Delaney Chops place on the high road?'

'Exactly, it's good. Nice people. Very reasonable too.'

'I think you might try—'

'No.'

'Fine.'

For the honeymoon, Marilyn was going to treat them to a couple of nights away. Clara had set parameters – parameters that she hadn't told Ivor about but she felt he'd agree to: somewhere within two hours by train and not full of poshys. Nobody was better equipped for that task than Marilyn.

'Goodness only knows where she'll send us,' Ivor questioned out loud.

'I'd just like to go somewhere simple. Maybe Brighton,' Clara mused. Somewhere she and Ivor could hold hands and promenade. Dip their toes in the sea, eat a buttered teacake. It didn't have to be warm, it didn't have to be glamorous. Somewhere, anywhere they could watch the world go by. She didn't ask for much – just being alone with Ivor was enough. Although, she thought, Peg would love to go to the sea and dig for shells – all of the children would.

'Next is music,' Clara told him. 'And Anita said she would never speak to me again if she wasn't in charge.'

'Oh, of course.'

'We're to leave *everything* to her. The music in the church. Music at the party. She wants to control the whole lot.'

Ivor grinned. 'Do you know, it's like you collected all these people around you purposely so that each would have a job at the wedding.'

'Ha,' Clara said. If only she had had the foresight to do that: she could have gathered someone to do the speeches and the invitations.

There was one thing Clara didn't have to worry about – the wedding gown – because Ivor was making it. Maybe it was unconventional for the groom to provide the bride's dress, but she trusted him. She trusted him about everything. He knew how she wanted to look probably better than she did.

'I've ticked off bridal dress.'

He grinned. 'I haven't got started yet, but...'

'How long do you think it will take?'

'About fifty hours.'

'Fifty?!' Clara screeched.

He shrugged. 'I want to do a good job.'

'Are you sure you'll have the time?'

'My first gift to my wife? I'll make time.' He looked up from his work and winked.

Wife – the word gave Clara a frisson that was not altogether a good frisson *yet*, but it wasn't a bad frisson either. It was just weird. Some words took practice. A title change took a while until it became familiar. It didn't mean you were against it, it just meant you were acclimatising. It was like getting the children ready to go to 'big' school.

'What are you getting me then?' Ivor asked.

Pretending to examine her notes, Clara laughed. 'There is nothing on my list about a present for you.'

'I see...'

The sewing machine whirred into life again, making it clear that the planning meeting was over. But now Clara was beginning to doubt herself on this too.

'Do I *have* to get you something? Is it a tradition?'

'You don't *have* to do anything...'

'But I should get you a present, yes?'

He shrugged. 'I always love presents!'

'But you're so difficult to buy for!'

'That's because you don't know me as well as I know you...' He winked. He was joking – or was he?

She wrote *Ivor present?!* on her list.

'We need to do the invitations this weekend.'

'What's the hurry?' Ivor counted on his fingers – 'February, March, April, May – four months is plenty.'

'Otherwise, people will be worried they're not invited,' said Clara, thinking of Maureen's quiet sense of exclusion. 'Or they might be busy!'

Mrs Garrard had intimated that she and Mr Garrard were planning to go to see cousins in Ambleside. Mrs Horton had said there was a summer bowls tournament and bowls tournaments were unmissable. Sister Grace, who sometimes came to look after the children, might be in Scotland. Even Anita had said, 'I have to have a confirmation soon, Clara, or the choir might have an obligation.'

'That'll be good though, no? I thought we had too many?'

Clara shook her head. 'I want the ones I like to come!'

'What about the ones you don't like?'

'I hope they stay away. Obviously.'

Sometimes, she wondered if Ivor was quite all there.

'You could trim your list,' he said, as though it were as easy as hemming a skirt.

'We could, but no. And I haven't even seen yours yet!'

He sighed. 'I'll have it ready for the weekend, Captain.'

So, that was settled: Saturday 30 May in the Church of St Peter and St Paul. And as soon as it was decided, a flood of relief. Yes! They were at the starting gate now. It was really happening. And they had better get a move on!

.

3

It was dinner time the same day and the children were trying to avoid the lumpy bits in the mash. Frank was flying his tin plane over his plate and dropping bombs on it when the telephone rang.

Clara was waiting for Miss Webb to arrange more children coming to the home. Two had come last year, but neither stayed more than a couple of weeks. When she had complained to Mrs Horton that there didn't seem much in the way of traffic, she'd said children were a bit like buses.

'You wait ages and then three come along at once.'

Clara had shaken her head, thinking of the council meeting. 'Do not talk about buses to me.'

The telephone continued to ring. Someone was determined. Clara knew if she left the room the children's mash would magically disappear into the food caddy, the plates scraped clean; but the call might be important. It could even be wedding news! Reluctantly, she left the room to answer the call.

'Shilling Grange,' she said as she finally picked up the phone while trying to keep one eye on the children.

'Is that Miss Newton?' asked a hushed young man's voice, a voice that Clara didn't recognise.

Funny how, straight away, you get a feeling, even when nothing has been said. She didn't know who the bad news would be about, but she knew it was bad. The young man's voice was terse.

'It is. May I ask who—'

'Clifford asked me to call,' the young man interrupted urgently.

Clifford?

'He said to tell you they're treating him like a prisoner.'

Clifford had been at the Hunstanton Reform School for Boys since spring last year. Clara remembered the bars at its windows and the bust in the hallway with the inscription SPARE THE ROD, SPOIL THE CHILD. She remembered the horrid feeling it had given her. It was a far cry from Clifford's old life, strutting around Lavenham like he owned the place.

'He's frightened. He wants you to help.'

And yet Clifford was not beyond pranks, obnoxious pranks. He was the type of boy who would tell you something like this, you'd panic, you'd hurry, then you'd get there and he'd be lying on a couch, eating grapes, 'Surprise! You didn't really believe all that, did you?'

'He's been locked in. He's in isolation. He's not been allowed to communicate with anyone for days.'

'What did he do?' Clara finally managed to ask.

'He tried to escape.'

'How do you know all this anyway? I mean if he's in isolation...'

The young man whispered impatiently, as though amazed at her stupidity.

'We have ways. Don't tell them I called.' He spoke even faster now, and Clara thought she heard footsteps his end.

'I won't. Who is this anyway? What's your name?'

But the line was dead.

Back in the kitchen, just as she feared, every child's plate had been miraculously swept clean. Peg and Jonathon were grinning conspiratorially.

'Thank you, Miss Newton,'

'De-licious,' said Gladys.

Trevor actually rubbed his tummy. 'That's great, I feel like a champion.'

Only Frank didn't play along. 'A. I think you could mash it more. B. I think we should have it less.'

It was a mystery. Clifford could be a nuisance. He could even be dangerous. But then people in charge could be cruel. She had seen it with Frank and Trevor's foster family, she had seen it with Sister Eunice, she knew it happened. Nice people find it hard to believe what not-nice people are capable of, but when it came to children no one should be naive. These were extreme cases, but Clara understood that her role was to acknowledge those extreme cases, not to pretend they didn't happen.

Poor Clifford.

On the other hand, and back she returned irrevocably to it, perhaps this was just a nonsense. Clara was a master at sniffing out a prank by now; they came round like the seasons. At the moment the younger children were going through a 'made you look, made you stare, made you lose your underwear' phase.

Maybe this was Clifford's equivalent?

After the rest of the dinner things had been cleared up, Clara had a quick cigarette outside the back door and tried to make sense of what she'd heard. She didn't smoke often, and especially not in front of the younger ones, because they not unreasonably struggled with the distinction between things adults were allowed to do and things children were allowed to do.

The children were polishing their shoes for tomorrow and Jonathon was scrubbing the bathroom sinks – he was a good boy, you knew where you were with him. She left it five, then ten minutes before nervously calling back the Reform School. An older man answered after two rings.

'Oh, good evening! My name is Miss Newton and I'm calling from Shilling Grange Children's Home in Lavenham.'

'Ye-es.'

'Would it be possible to speak to Clifford Harvey, please?'

'He's in bed,' the man said without a moment's hesitation. 'Only call between seven and eight a.m.'

And then he hung up, leaving Clara even more concerned than ever.

The children did their reading or spellings at the kitchen table and then retired upstairs. Clara mopped the kitchen floor and wiped the surfaces. She thought about cleaning the oven – it would need to be done some time soon for cooking all those wedding foods – but she couldn't face it.

By the time she went up to the boys' room the younger boys were asleep but, oddly, Jonathon was out of his bed and rummaging in his wardrobe.

'Just looking for something,' he whispered, but his face was scarlet and, if he were one of the naughtier boys, she would have thought he was up to something.

She told him she was nipping over the road to Ivor's workshop – she'd be two minutes, no more – and he promised to keep an ear out. Something made her pause, but she didn't know what. And her mind was on Clifford.

'You are all right, aren't you, Jonathon?' she asked uneasily but, ignoring her, Jonathon climbed into bed and closed his eyes.

She thought of his father, the highly decorated war hero Maurice Pell, and thought, *of course he is.*

Clara told Ivor about the mysterious telephone call and he was immediately concerned. The possibility that it was a joke didn't even occur to him. She felt slightly guilty that that had been her first reaction. Part of her had hoped Ivor would dismiss it and reassure her it was nothing to worry about.

'What will you do? Tell the council?'

'They won't do anything. You know what they're like.'

The most Mr Sommersby would do would be to write a letter explaining how difficult things were (for him). He wouldn't send it until the end of next week. And then, most likely, he would be fobbed off. Clara wasn't sure whether it was because Mr Sommersby was incompetent, or lazy, or if he fundamentally didn't care, but whatever it was the result was usually the same: inaction.

No – if something had to be done, it had to be Clara.

'Then I'll go tomorrow,' Ivor said.

Or Ivor.

Clara did try to call the Reform School in Hunstanton the next morning within the narrow window of time she had been given. This time, a woman answered her call. Possibly it was the same woman Clara had met last year; she had never found out her name.

'Clifford? Oh, he's in lessons.'

It was too early for lessons, wasn't it?

'But they told me to call now. Could you ask him to telephone me?'

'It's up to him who he calls.'

'But you will tell him I have been in touch?'

Again, the pause went on too long.

'I shall. Goodbye.'

Clara hadn't even told her who she was.

Clara didn't like it one bit. She was glad Ivor was going to investigate further. Even if he didn't find out everything, he was good at disarming people (no pun intended).

Gladys stood halfway down the stairs. Clara trotted up to her.

'Can we play Newmarket, Miss Newton?'

'Maybe later,' Clara said as the little girl wrapped her arms round her to be carried down. 'Now, porridge or toast?'

The children were the perfect distraction that morning. Frank and Trevor were arguing about who had the worst teacher. Jonathon was dealing out the plates and bowls with a determined look in his eye.

Clifford would be all right, he had to be. She had to focus on taking care of the ones who were in her care now. But as she did the cleaning, Clara worried some more about Clifford – he may have been one of her most challenging residents, but the thought of him in distress was pulverising. She told herself not to over-think it. Clifford was generally difficult and it seemed more likely he was the boy who cried wolf rather than the boy eaten by a wolf. And yet...

A few minutes later, Peg thumped in the kitchen, bleary-eyed and hair all over the place. She handed Clara a note.

'Bad dreams?' Clara knelt so she was at Peg's eye level. 'Not those clowns again?'

Peg hated clowns. It wasn't *completely* irrational – a little while ago, a couple who were both clowns had wanted to adopt her and Peg hadn't liked them at all.

Peg nodded fiercely, seeming annoyed at her own treacherous imagination. She put her cheek next to Clara's. And Clara felt her heart melt. No one moved her like little Peg, who had been aban-doned on a church doorstep as a baby and who never said a word.

'You'll never have to live with clowns, darling, I'll make sure of that.'

Peg didn't look mollified. She scribbled some more. 'Or jugglers?'

What exactly Peg had against jugglers, Clara wasn't sure. She read a lot; maybe there were nasty jugglers in her *Five Find-Outers* series?

'Or jugglers,' Clara confirmed. 'Or even tightrope walkers.'

Peg shrugged. She wrote that she didn't mind them.

'Or lion tamers?'

Peg's eyes lit up. She wrote that she'd like to live with lions and lion tamers.

Peg worried a lot about being adopted, but Clara thought it was unlikely. All the prospective parents seemed to skate over her as if she were invisible rather than silent; or those who did wish to adopt her, like her old teacher Miss Fisher had, were not considered appropriate.

Miss Webb complained that it was 'a buyer's market' when it came to children. The prospective parents had hundreds to choose from. Was it any wonder that some of them were like children in a sweetshop on a Friday afternoon, selecting all the toffees and lemon sherbets, leaving the aniseed until last?

The children noisily got ready for school, Clara reminding them to take their coats, their hats, their bags. Frank was clutching two broken aeroplanes and Trevor his brand-new compass for drawing circles.

'Not to be confused with a compass for exploring,' said Clara, laughing, as she hurried them out of the door.

'I never would,' Trevor responded indignantly at the idea.

Jonathon was lugging a heavy schoolbag and a heavier sports bag.

'Do you have PE today?' Clara asked him, trying to make conversation – he was always so quiet.

He blushed. 'Just rugby.'

'I'm sure you play well,' she said, watching him as he bit his lip.

'I don't,' he said before adding, 'But my father did.'

Clara watched them all dash into the street, still calling out reminders. 'Peg, don't forget the letter for your teacher! Frank, your shoelaces!' before finally shutting the door. The house was always suddenly so quiet without them.

Soon after, Ivor came over, swinging Patricia's hand. Patricia was now clutching Poppy, her latest favourite bear. She had given up on her mallet (which was a relief) and replaced it with a cardboard tube.

'You're with me today.' Clara told her.

'I know you're going to be a good girl for Aunty Clara,' said Ivor.

Patricia tilted her little chin, if not eagerly than certainly with more enthusiasm than she used to muster.

When Patricia saw Stella the cat sitting on Trevor's jumper under the kitchen table, she burst into song: 'Ding dong dell, pussycat's in the well.'

Clara looked at her nervously. It wouldn't be beyond Patricia to put Stella in a well, if they had a well – which fortunately they didn't. Patricia was turning into quite a forward child. Clara sometimes admired her, sometimes was intimidated by her. As Mrs Horton said, 'The spirited ones make lovely grown-ups.'

'And difficult children,' Clara had said with a laugh. 'I know.'

In May, Patricia would become Clara's stepdaughter, another word that had a lot of baggage and gave Clara a frisson. Stepdaughter and stepmother. Perhaps 'step' actually meant 'not'. Stepmothers in fairy tales were horrendous. Cinderella's stepmother, Snow White's stepmother, even Hansel and Gretel's stepmother! Leaving the children to roam around in the woods – hadn't she let them wander for miles to be cooked and eaten by a witch? But then, Clara rationalised, it wasn't as though housemothers in stories were any better! Look at the Miss Hannigan in the American cartoon *Little Orphan Annie* that ex-resident Peter sent for the children from his job working on comics in London! She was a fright.

Patricia was not exactly wild, but she was not calm either. Clara thought she was like a whirlwind; she was a hoot, she was a blast. She didn't listen – or rather she pretended to listen, and then she went off and did exactly what she liked. Clara was slowly working her out. She felt that, in the end, she and Patricia would do better than all those fairy stories. Love was love, and Clara would win over Patricia one day. And, until then, she would just have to wait.

Since he was taking the 8.45 train, Ivor couldn't dilly-dally. With a bit of luck, he'd be in Hunstanton by eleven and be with Clifford not too long after. Clara wished she had a muffin or a bun or something to give him to sweeten the journey. All she had to offer was a bruised apple. Laughing, he declined.

'Don't worry, I'll find out what's going on. The kid needs an advocate, that's all.'

He kissed his little girl and then he kissed Clara on the cheek.

'I'll be back by five, six at the latest. You can serve me up some of your delicious tomato soup.'

Clara looked at him dolefully. 'The one you liked is Mrs Horton's soup.'

He chuckled. 'Tell her it's lovely – oh, and don't forget: food for the wedding.'

'And you'll do your guest list – and we'll get the invitations done this weekend?'

'Come hell or high water.'

Clara would remember that phrase for a long time.

4

'I've got lots of jobs to do today,' Clara warned Patricia, as she did whenever the little girl came over. 'But after they're all done, we'll have some time to play.'

'Playground!' yelled Patricia.

'We'll have to see,' Clara said, smiling, not wanting to over-promise when she knew how much work she had to get done.

First, she did the sheets. There were zero bed-wetters at the moment, which was a bonus. Peg made trips to the lavatory three or four times in the night, but what an advance that was. Under Sister Eunice's fierce regime, the littlest resident had been a frequent bed-wetter – and who could blame her? Frank had gone through a wetting phase too, after coming from such a terrible foster home, but he seemed to be over it now.

Some sheets and pillows hung out to dry. Others ironed. Clara was tempted to skip the ironing, but Mrs Horton had somehow found out and had been severe with her as a result.

'The ironing kills all the fleas and the lice. You must iron everything, Clara! Do you want to be bitten to death?'

When she came back into the kitchen, Polly-the-bear was riding Stella and Patricia was shouting 'Gee up.' This was something Patricia had been told several times that she was not allowed to do.

'Please leave the cat alone, Patricia,' Clara pleaded with the little girl. Imagine if Stella turned on her and scratched her eyes?

Clara set Patricia up at the kitchen table with some paper and crayons. Patricia didn't like that the paper already been drawn on but Clara explained she didn't have any fresh and, finally, the girl settled down.

With the beds made and Patricia occupied, Clara allowed herself to enjoy a minute's peace in the parlour, where she found herself considering Ivor's wedding present. Her favourite-ever present had been a collection of Jane Taylor poetry. It was a shame that it was a gift from Julian White, local solicitor and one of Clara's former suitors, but it was the thought, not the person that counted. But she didn't think Ivor would like a book.

A bicycle then? But Clara decided he didn't actually need a bicycle – he could always borrow hers.

Mrs Horton said Mr Horton was the same but at least Mr Horton liked playing bowls and there were a surprising number of bowls-related things you could choose as a gift. And Anita said Dr Cardew was also similar but Dr Cardew did at least like books, and he loved music, or medical things.

Every Christmas and every birthday, Clara struggled with presents for Ivor, and now she had to show once again that she knew him. And she did know him – but Ivor could still be an enigma. Other men liked hip-flasks; Ivor didn't drink except on special occasions. Cufflinks? Ivor didn't like wearing his suit. A wallet? But he had a wallet; what would be the point of getting him another? A photo frame? She could spirit Patricia away to a photography studio, or maybe she could even get herself done, perhaps in her favourite silk nightdress that Anita had given her. She reddened. Ivor would probably only laugh.

When she came back into the kitchen, Patricia had drawn the usual houses and suns and flowers. But she had also done some elephants. Clara told her that she was good at drawing, but Patricia screwed up the paper in disgust.

'NOT elephants, they are horses!'

Clara spent the next few minutes apologising for her dreadful eyesight.

The weather grew windier as the morning went on. It was a proper January day. Clara thought sympathetically of Jonathon battling in his sports lesson as she went to collect the pillowcases that had been blown from the clothing line and were strewn across the lawn.

It was just gone eleven when Clara answered the door to Mrs Horton. Her friend was looking for Ivor about cushion covers she had commissioned for Mrs Horton senior, her mother-in-law.

'Brass monkeys out there,' she said, rubbing her arms. 'Now where on earth is Ivor? He said he would be home.'

Clara explained that he had gone to Hunstanton to try to find out what was happening with Clifford. Mrs Horton was unimpressed.

'Why on earth did he do that? If Clifford is in trouble, it's council business, Clara.'

Clara blushed. Mrs Horton didn't disagree with her often, so when she did it stung. She explained that it felt as though time was of the essence and, anyway, Ivor and Clifford were close, and Ivor was happy to help.

'Clifford needs a...' She forgot the word Ivor used. Not a lawyer. What was it?

'Oh yes, ambassador,' she said, although that didn't feel right either. 'Someone to represent his interests. Ivor can do that. And quickly.'

Mrs Horton was not mollified. 'Racing off like Keystone Cops.'

Clara snorted. Ivor had in no way resembled a Keystone Cop. He didn't even like them.

'Ambassador? What a ridiculous idea.'

'You know Clifford. Trouble follows him. Anyway, it's no big deal. Ivor wanted a change of scene, I think. He's been working so hard lately.'

Mrs Horton pursed her lips.

Clara tried to divert her with talk of wedding plans. Mrs Horton nodded at the church as the meaningful place, 'quite right', and she nodded at the Cloth Hall as the venue, 'of course'; but, when Clara said she was thinking of doing the food herself, she hooted.

'It's a wedding, not a funeral.' This didn't make sense as a joke, but Clara understood Mrs Horton's intention.

'Well, what do you suggest?' Clara asked, exasperated. It occurred to her that what she most wanted was for Mrs Horton to say was 'I'll do it.' That's what a mum would say, and Mrs Horton was *quite* like a mum.

'Didn't Julian White have a lady who caters?'

Clara sighed as she realised Ivor might be right, again: they were going to have to pay for someone else to cook.

'Where are the invitations then?' Mrs Horton asked, moving on from the food.

'We'll get them out this weekend,' Clara snapped back. Come hell or high water.

'About time too,' said Mrs Horton. She really was in a filthy mood. 'You know how complicated it is with Mr Horton and his bowls schedule.'

'I do.'

'And Clara, have you decided what you will be doing *after* the wedding?'

Clara clammed up. Not this again. Everyone had an opinion.

'Workwise, I mean, because I don't understand how you can

blithely just carry on here when you will have marital responsibilities elsewhere.'

Clara nodded. She knew Mrs Horton couldn't understand
what she was going to do next although to be fair, Clara didn't
know what she was going to do either. A resolution to that tricky
problem hadn't occurred to her yet.

At the door, as Mrs Horton left, Clara said, 'Oh, that was it!
Ivor will be Clifford's *advocate*. Not ambassador.'

But that didn't cheer up Mrs Horton.

5

As soon as Mrs Horton had left, Clara took Patricia out. Patricia refused to use her pram any more and Clara had forgotten how slowly she walked, especially today when the wind was up and they were against it. Patricia stopped to peer at the cracks in the pavement and to look at a tree. She stopped to gaze at the bricks in the wall and the grouting between the bricks. Her cheeks were red with cold. Clara didn't want to return her soon-to-be-step-daughter with chilblains or some preventable disease. Nor did she want to be late for the other children, who would be coming home for lunch.

They were making their way to the post office, since Clara had letters to send to ex-residents Rita in Switzerland and Alex in Oxford. When they finally arrived, Clara bought stamps and chatted to the postmistress and the postmistress's assistant (who she realised might have to go on the guest list). She asked Patricia to post the letters in the slot in the pillar box, which Patricia enjoyed doing 'again, again!' She would have posted her mittens in there too if Clara hadn't stopped her.

On their slow march back in the drizzle, Clara saw Julian White stepping out of his office into the overcast day. He cut a smart figure. He held on to his bowler hat with one hand and clasped his coat to him with the other. Patricia pointed at him. If Clara had been on her own, she would have been able to hurry past, no problem, but there was no hurrying Patricia. There were always car tyres or wobbly paving stones to obsess over.

Clara suddenly realised Julian might expect to be invited to the wedding. Actually, she feared it was such a small town that *everyone* in Lavenham might expect to be invited.

After they exchanged greetings, Clara made a big fuss of Bandit, Julian's lovely dog, and Bandit made a big fuss of her – Clara hoped Julian wouldn't confuse her delight at seeing the dog with delight at seeing him.

'Why are you always with this girl?' Julian smirked, looking at Patricia like she was a Christmas tree up in October. 'She's not a Shilling Grange child now, is she?'

'I'm not *always* with her.' Clara couldn't help being offended. It was the way Julian said things. 'And no, of course, she isn't.'

'Ohhh, it's Mr Delaney's lovechild, isn't it? I remember now.'

Julian took obvious pleasure in saying *lovechild*. Clara knew she shouldn't let him wind her up.

'If you say so.'

'He's got you right where he wants you. How convenient he found a mother figure for her so quickly.'

Clara scowled. In fact, turning Clara into a 'mother figure' was something Ivor had resisted – not that she would tell Julian that. You couldn't give Julian an inch. He was one of those people who twisted everything. She asked him about his woman who cooked, Mrs Wesley from the next village. Clara would never forget the delicious Scotch egg she had once made her. In truth, Clara liked anything she did not have to cook herself, but this had been off the scale.

'I might have a job for her,' Clara said, hoping Julian wouldn't realise the nature of the job – she didn't want to discuss her nuptials with him – but of course he did. He was uncanny like that.

'The wedding is happening at last?' His face seemed oddly immobile, waxy, like a candle. She could have sworn he was about to either laugh or cry. 'Margot fired her and I don't know where her contact details are.' Posh Margot, with her thousand-yard stare, and too-long nails, was his girlfriend. She was the type to fire everyone. Clara thought Margot and Julian made a good match.

'That's fine then, don't worry. It was just a thought.'

Julian made an expression like she'd asked him to roll a huge rock up a steep hill.

'I suppose I'll find it, if it's that important.'

'It's really not a problem.'

'Oh, it's no problem,' he echoed, but his sigh made it clear it was. 'So, who will take over Shilling Grange – or whatever you're calling it these days – once you've left?' Now, he had the tone of a disappointed head teacher.

Clara had only changed the name of the home once. Just because his law firm Robinson, Browne and White had been called that for centuries and had their own coat of arms. It was just like Julian to have a little dig. Two digs in one sentence, though, was impressive even by his standards.

'No one. I'll still work there for the time being. I'm getting married, not...' Clara searched her brain for an appropriate analogy. 'Emigrating,' she chose eventually. This was true; she was not emigrating. Why did everyone think they had a say in her business? No one was coming after Ivor asking him what he planned to do after he married.

Julian pulled another face. He was less chirpy than usual, she thought. He seemed to have aged suddenly. He was twenty years older than she was, although it hadn't seemed like such a gap in the past. Thank goodness she was with Ivor, she thought.

'I'm looking forward to seeing how that works out.'

What he meant was: *I'm looking forward to seeing how that falls apart.*

'What about you and Margot? Will you be tying the knot any time soon?'

Tying the knot, that's what her father used to say. Julian brought it out in her.

'Uh, no.'

As soon as Clara said it she realised she hadn't seen Margot around lately, and she felt rotten for bringing it up. She shouldn't stoop to his level.

'Bit awkward actually. Margot decided to take her chances elsewhere.'

'Ouch.'

'Yes. Well... I should have realised I was on a hiding to nothing. There aren't many gals left like you.'

Clara bristled. It was Julian's joke to pretend he was still in love with her. He probably never had been – the only person Julian had ever loved was himself.

'Do you have any spinster friends, darling? You know I do like female company,' he asked with a smarmy smile.

If I did have, I certainly wouldn't pass them on to you, was Clara's immediate reaction.

'I will give it some thought,' she lied judiciously. You didn't want to make an enemy of the most connected man in Lavenham.

Patricia loved Bandit as much as Clara did, and in the end, Clara had to drag her away from the dog, shrieking. It was as undignified an exit as any and Julian was shaking his head, exasperated, as they went.

'Me want dog,' Patricia demanded as she stamped her feet.

'We all want dog,' said Clara through gritted teeth. As usual, seeing Julian had discombobulated her. It wasn't that he was right – mostly he was wrong – but it felt unfair that he had these opinions of her (and Ivor) and nothing she could say would make a difference.

6

The children were due home for lunch and Clara was washing up the breakfast pans when Ivor called. She ran for the telephone, soap bubbles glistening on the back of her hand. He must have arrived in Hunstanton, but she doubted he had got all the way to Clifford's school yet.

'Don't be alarmed,' he said, which was instantly the singularly most alarming thing she had ever heard. 'I found Jonathon at Lavenham train station.'

'Jonathon...?' Clara heard the name coming out of her mouth, but it didn't sound like her.

The bubbles on her hand, little blue lights, popped.

'What was— he's supposed to be at school.'

Ivor cleared his throat.

'I think he was running away.'

Oh goodness. Clara should have known something was wrong! It had been a difficult half year at the home for Jonathon and on top of that, he had been especially upset about the air-show disaster – he thought had he been there her father might have survived – but to run away? She hadn't foreseen that – and she should have. Perhaps if she hadn't been so wrapped up in wedding planning, invitations and Scotch eggs, she might have. Keeping the children safe was her job.

Ivor was still talking. 'I couldn't just send him back, so I persuaded him to come with me. He was in a bit of a state but he's calmed down now. He said he'll talk to you when we're back – to explain.'

Clara leaned against the bannister, her hands still damp. She didn't understand it. *Jonathon* was running away? It wouldn't be the first time a child from the home had bolted. Denny had somehow got all the way to Southend Pier. And Maureen had, devastatingly, disappeared for weeks. Even Peg had once packed up and threatened to run off to be a shell-collector in Margate. But Jonathon? He was so timid. He wasn't brave enough or selfish enough to do that sort of thing.

'Where are you now?'

'We're in Old Hunstanton. He's in a tearoom, wolfing down a slice of fruit cake. Don't worry, I'll look after him. We'll find out what's going on with Clifford and then we'll be back before you know it.'

The children blew in at lunchtime, a riot of colour and noise. The girls were excited to see Patricia was still there and made as big a fuss of her as she had of Bandit. Patricia let them pet her and then bared her teeth and told them to go away when she had had enough.

Peg wrote that she had scored ten out of ten in her spellings, or 'spells', as she called them. Gladys said she had been asked to sing a solo in the school choir.

'I might not bother though,' she said, popping a carrot in her mouth.

Only Trevor asked where Jonathon was, and he didn't pursue it when she said, 'With Ivor. They'll be back tonight.'

They had Mrs Horton's tomato soup and crusty bread. Gladys

and Frank played the alphabet game – countries beginning with S. Sweden, Switzerland, Spain. Peg played with her shells and tried to defend them from Patricia.

'Chess club is cancelled this afternoon,' Trevor said. This seemed to have put him in a bad mood, although he was also annoyed since couldn't find his school tie and had had to borrow one.

'Why?'

'Headmaster said everyone needs to get home early today because of the bad weather.'

'Bad weather,' Frank scoffed, which was exactly what Clara was thinking. It was unnerving how often her thoughts went along similar lines to those of a scruffy eleven-year-old.

Clara was relieved when the children went back to school for the afternoon, the door slamming wildly behind them. Her head was crammed full, worrying about Clifford and now Jonathon as well.

But first she had to deal with Patricia.

Ivor was vague on the afternoon nap-question – sometimes Patricia napped, sometimes she didn't. Clara regretted not taking Patricia to the Norland Nanny, who had a sing-songy voice and a never-ending stream of games up her sleeve. Howard was the most stimulated baby in the universe. Everything was jolly there and when she was with her, Patricia napped without question. The nanny was religious about cot-time and worshipped routine. After spending time there, Clara always resolved to be more disciplined. And every time something cropped up to throw her off course.

When Clara suggested Patricia was tired and might want to sleep, just for five minutes, Patricia howled as if Clara had committed some kind of crime. However, two minutes later, she fell fast asleep on the sofa. She was still holding on to Peg's shell, which she must have stolen from her room. Clara sighed. She was looking forward to Ivor's return very much.

With Patricia finally asleep, Clara hurried up to the boys'
room to see if there was anything there that could help explain
Jonathon's secret flight from the home. She tried to remember
Jonathon at breakfast time, at tea last night... She'd had a long chat
with Jonathon the other evening, but it had been the first time in a
long while. It would be fair to say he kept himself to himself. He
performed tasks around the house impeccably – you didn't have to
ask him twice – but he rarely volunteered to spend time with any
of them. He was concerned – overly concerned – about what job
he would do when he left school. It seemed like he thought it
would be revealed to him one day, come down in a clap of
thunder.

They had been tidying the parlour; he was polishing and she
was dusting.

'I didn't know I wanted to be a housemother,' she had tried to
reassure him, 'I never knew such a job existed. And now I
wouldn't want any other job in the world!'

'Ivor told me that he knew he always wanted to work with
fabrics.'

'Did he?' *Unhelpful!* 'Ivor doesn't know everything.'

Jonathon had shivered.

'Have you considered...' Clara looked for alternate ideas. 'The
military?'

'I'm not brave enough for the military.'

'There are many options, Jonathon,' she had told him. 'You
could go to university.' She added quickly, 'And you *are* brave
enough for the military.'

She remembered visiting Victor – another of her suitors – at
his lecture theatre at Oxford and how impressed she'd been with
it all. All those brilliant young faces getting educated. Ex-resident
Alex was going to go to university. Evelyn might too.

Jonathon had carried on polishing, avoiding the compliment.

'Or you could be an athlete. Or a job associated with sports.
Sports teacher?'

Jonathon had nodded, but looking back, it was clear this nod was a let's-end-the-conversation-yes rather than a real yes.

Now, searching in and under the bed, the pillows and the drawers, Clara found nothing. She didn't know what exactly she was looking for, and she felt bad for invading his privacy, but the urge to protect him was stronger and it was propelling her to search. She wasn't a great believer in her own housemother instinct – it had failed her too many times, but she had to try.

At teatime, Gladys dropped her plate while she was taking it over to the sink and the children roared as though they were in the school canteen. Patricia screwed up more drawings and cried for Ivor.

'Daddy will be home soon,' Clara explained, but soon wasn't good enough for Patricia. She was very much a *want-it-now* child.

Clara made them do extra chores to help pass the time, although Peg slunk out to the shed to play her drums. The children needed occupying. Blowy weather often made them behave worse. Miss Fisher used to say that some children were particularly affected by the wind and the moon's phases: 'It can be catastrophic.'

About six, Maureen called to say she was not coming on Sunday because of the bad weather. Clara never wanted her to feel that she had to come and see them, but she was disappointed all the same.

She was keeping an eye out over the road for Ivor and Jonathon's return when the telephone rang again.

Clara grabbed the receiver. 'Have you changed your mind then?'

'What about?' an amused voice said. It was Ivor.

'I thought you were Maureen,' she explained.

If he was calling her, he wasn't on his way.

'They won't let me see Clifford,' Ivor said.

'Oh no,' Clara said quietly, hoping the children wouldn't hear the concern in her voice.

'They were quite aggressive about it, so we decided we'd try again tomorrow.'

'But why?' Clara was starting to panic. Why wouldn't they let them see Clifford?

'No, not aggressive, more... defensive? We will stay over at the Ocean Breeze tonight.'

'Is Jonathon all right with that?'

'Maybe a change of scene will do Jonathon some good.' Ivor paused and Clara felt that he was about to say more about Jonathon – but instead he changed tack. 'How's my little girl?'

Clara paused, scratching her arm. She could hear Patricia screeching at Peg, 'I will tell Daddy of you!'

'Same as ever!' Clara said, trying not to sound as anxious as she felt.

'There are storm warnings,' Ivor said wearily. His rumbling voice was like a storm itself. 'I'd better go. Keep yourself safe.'

'And you.'

As she hung up, Clara closed her eyes and wished all three of them were home with her.

7

That evening, the wind was so loud that the windows clattered. Peg appeared like a ghost at Clara's bedroom door, but Clara led her back to her own bed. She couldn't have this for the next five years! Clara checked the other girls were settled. Gladys was snoring, surrounded by discarded clothes, which Clara picked up. Patricia was face-up, her mouth set like she was contemplating future adventures. Clara didn't dare go near her. She was the lightest of sleepers – Ivor said she could hear a pin drop in another street. As she eased the door shut, she heard one of the girls let out a grumble.

She peeped in on Trevor and Frank and they too were fast asleep. Frank had made something out of papier mâché at school and it was on his bed. It was a desert island, apparently, but mostly it resembled a newspaper mulch. Carefully, Clara placed it on the desk, where it wouldn't be trodden on. While she was doing that, she spied Trevor's brand-new compass peeping out from under the chair.

The rain was coming down outside, but inside these children were safe, they were warm, they were loved. It was a good feeling.

Satisfied she wasn't needed, Clara sat down at the kitchen

table with a cup of tea to go over the guest list again. Anything to distract her from her worries about Clifford and Jonathon – and Ivor being so far away.

Every day she meant to cut the list down but instead it grew. What about Maureen's ex-beau, Joe? And did she have to invite Julian? He wasn't a friend, but would it look odd if he was excluded?

As she worked through the names, Clara found herself missing her mother. At key moments in her life – when she met Michael, when she lost him, when she got her job, when she met Ivor – she missed her and the grief came back, fresh as daffodils in spring: *We are here, you thought we'd gone, but we were just under the surface all this time.*

Clara often wondered how different her life would be if her mother were still alive. One word occurred to her – a selfish word – it would be *easier*.   ·

A mother to sew that button back on, to nip into town with, to drop by for a hot drink, to take that parcel to the post office.

Not *just* easier, more enjoyable too.

Sometimes she saw women in town, pottering about on the high road, about the same age her mother would have been now, and it never failed to move her. A certain type of coat, a certain type of hairstyle, a certain type of shoe would bring pieces of her mother back to her.

She missed her father too, but in a different way – he'd lived a longer life, and she'd known him in a way she'd never got to know her mother. Her mother never got to know the adult Clara had become, and the adult Clara never got to know her mother.

But Clara knew she'd had her mother for years longer than the children at the home had theirs. She hadn't had it bad compared to most. She supposed her grief gave her a tiny insight into the children's turmoil, although it was nothing compared to what they'd gone through – and yet still those children got up bright and early (too early!) and still wanted to play Newmarket.

She would visit her mother's grave in Africa one day – it would be the trip of a lifetime – with her husband by her side, and she would not weep too much; she would honour her. She would live and love to make her proud.

Saturday morning came round and it was too cold to play outside. The children were stuck in the parlour or in their rooms and they were like prisoners denied visitation rights.

Peg and Gladys included Patricia in their games, which was kind because Patricia was not particularly cooperative. When Clara popped in to check on them, Stella the cat was wearing white socks on her front paws.

Trevor was trying to teach Frank to play chess. However, Frank was easily distracted and not a great student. Nor was Trevor a great teacher.

'Don't be afraid to retreat,' Trevor was explaining as Frank rolled around on the floor, pulling at his hat.

'It feels like going backwards.'

'It's not though – it's doing what's necessary.'

And then a little later: 'No, you can't have two on one square at the same time.' Trevor was bellowing now.

'Why not?' Frank bellowed back.

'It's not allowed. It's the rules, that's why not!'

There was a sound of pieces dropping onto the floor.

'Right, that's it...'

This was followed by the noise of a punch maybe, and then a squeal and then a wail.

'Misssss Newton, he hit me.'

Clara tried not to wish away the hours until Ivor and Jonathon were home but, as she did the washing that morning, part of her couldn't help wishing it was already evening. She put the wireless on as she made lunch.

Car Ferry Disaster. Princess Victoria. *Scotland to Northern Ireland*.

There might be orphans, was Clara's first thought as she heard the dreadful news. There would be children this evening finding out they were all alone in the world. Telegrams and telephone calls. Tender words – and harsh words too. Some children would be cuddled by grandparents and fussed over by weeping aunts. Others would be told to get on with it with no explanation, just a 'they've gone. Go to school.' But there would be good people out there, good people who would help.

Throughout the war, they'd seen the worst of humanity and the best of humanity – for years, Clara had waited for an equilibrium to return, so people could just be. Now she realised there was no equilibrium – there never would be and there probably never had been. It was either a figment of her imagination, or the naivety of youth. She simply hadn't known what was going on in the world.

The wireless crackled, whimpered, then gave up the ghost. Clara wasn't upset. What with this and the trial of Derek Bentley – a young man with learning difficulties who was found guilty of murdering a policeman and had recently been executed – the news recently had been dismal. There was nothing she could do about it though, so there was no point getting down about it.

Clara took Patricia to Anita Cardew's after lunch. Anita answered the door with Baby Howard at her knees. He blew a raspberry at them and got roundly told off.

'What if it were someone important, Howard?' admonished Anita, and then laughed at Clara's expression. 'You *are* important, darling, but you know what I mean.'

Patricia and Howard clutched hands, best friends, happily reunited.

'Choir is cancelled,' Anita said, clearly unhappy about this turn of events.

'Oh no. Why?' Clara asked, knowing how much Anita adored her choir.

'Lots of the singers come from the coast and this ghastly weather means they can't get here,' Anita explained.

'Oh, what a shame,' Clara said, nodding indulgently. Weather talk bored her, it always had.

Maybe Howard felt the same, for he blew another raspberry and was scolded again.

Anita ushered them into the living room and immediately wanted to talk about music for the wedding. Today her idea was for The Children of Shilling Grange Orphanage group to reunite. In theory, it was a wonderful plan, but practically it was unworkable, since it was unlikely that most members of the group, like Clifford and Denny and, especially, Rita, would be able to make it.

'Haven't you invited them?' Anita pressed.

'No one's been invited yet,' said Clara a little nervously. 'We're doing the invitations this weekend.'

'Surely Rita will come?' Anita asked.

'I doubt she'd come all the way from Switzerland just for a wedding.'

'Just for a wedding?' shrieked Anita, then laughed. 'Don't you realise? This is the Wedding of the Century!'

8

_____

It was still bucketing down when Clara left Anita's an hour later. It was like the weather was confirming everyone's prejudices of January as the longest, bleakest month. Clara was relieved Patricia was out of her hands for the afternoon so she could catch up with her chores. It wasn't always true that the younger they were, the more attention they demanded, but in Patricia's case it definitely was.

Back home, Gladys declared that God must be angry about something, while Frank repeated the same joke he had told hundreds of times: 'It's probably God doing wee-wee.'

Just darting to and from the shed, Gladys and Peg got so drenched that Clara had to hang their clothes on the clothes horse, making the house smell even damper than usual. By coincidence, Peg's 'spells' were all about weather phenomena. (Fortunately, 'phenomena' was not on the list.)

Typhoon. Earthquake. Tornado.

Frank had given up chess, because 'A. It's stupid and B. I hate you,' so Trevor had moved on to teaching Gladys. Clara liked listening to Trevor's instructions. 'No, it has to be like this.' There was a debate about something called castling, which turned out not to be small castles at all.

'You have to protect the king.'

'Why?' asked Gladys.

'Because he's your most valuable asset.'

'Is he?'

While he was short-tempered with Frank, Trevor was patient and older-brotherly with Gladys.

'You have to think ahead. Strategy, long-term planning.'

Maybe she would get Ivor a chess set as a wedding present, Clara thought as she washed the towels.

She was returning clothes to their rightful drawers when Frank came upstairs to find her.

'Here,' he said, stuffing a card into her hands.

To Frank

Please come to my Birthday Party on Saturday 31 January from 3–5 at Old Longford.

Love from

Lester

Mum says don't worry about a present!

'But that's this afternoon!' Clara exclaimed, horrified. It was already half past two, although it was so dark, you might think night was falling. Ivor and Jonathon could be back at any moment and she wanted to make sure she was home to welcome them, find out about Clifford, and then talk to Jonathon.

'Yes,' said Frank enthusiastically. 'It's today!'

'But... but why didn't you tell me before?' Clara asked, doing a poor job at hiding her frustration.

'I did!' said Frank, screwing up his face. 'Didn't I?'

Clara would have remembered. And the reason she would have remembered was because the children from the home – Frank in particular – were rarely invited anywhere. They might be popular in school but the leap to crossing over a threshold was something few Shilling Grange children had achieved. There was a certain image the town had of Shilling Grange children that Clara hadn't quite yet managed to change.

'Who is Lester anyway?'

'He played Joseph in the nativity,' Gladys, who had run in looking for the playing cards, prompted helpfully. 'He forgot his lines.'

And then a fight had broken out, Clara remembered. She slammed the drawer shut. Was this a way out?

'You hated him then!' she reminded Frank.

'Don't now,' Frank explained airily. 'He's my best friend.'

'But do you really want to go?' Clara asked, for the wind was howling, the rain was bouncing off the paving stones outside and she wanted to stay home.

'I told him yes,' Frank answered, shocked she'd even ask such an outrageous thing.

The *Don't worry about a present* in particular had sent Clara into a tailspin.

'But it said don't worry about a present,' pointed out Frank, alarmed at her alarm. 'I thought that meant A. don't worry and B. about a present.'

'It means *do* worry,' explained Clara. Oh Lord. What was she going to do? This was the first time a child from Shilling Grange had been invited to a birthday party and she didn't know what was an appropriate present to bring. Had they put don't worry because they knew he was from the home, or did they write it for everyone?

It felt like an alien world. She didn't want to get it wrong for Frank. What if they teased him? Children could be merciless. Everything was so expensive. Clara didn't have a budget for spending on the children's friends.

. . .

Clara finally admitted to herself that there was no way out of going to the party, and she and Frank braved the elements. Clara was holding a paper bag of crayons she had found. They were not new, but they looked – mostly – unused. She hoped no one would think they were babyish.

The wind made their umbrella turn inside out. Frank had his hat and Clara had tied a scarf round her hair, but by the time they got there they were drenched through. Lester's house was one of the pink and crooked ones that were centuries old. Through the window, she could see five or six boys cross-legged on the floor, listening to someone. There was a table pushed against a wall, full of sandwiches and one of Frank's (and Clara's) favourites, jellies.

'Don't go,' he said, gripping her hand tightly as she went to knock on the door.

'I have to get back,' Clara said, gently extracting her hand from his wet one. 'Here's your best plane.' She pushed his Tiger Moth into his hands. 'There.' But Frank merely dropped it to the ground.

He was making a scene and one thing she hated was a child making a scene. Usually the children were good at not doing that. Peg because she didn't speak, Gladys because of her sunny temperament, Jonathon because of his will to please, Frank because he was so easily distracted by military aircraft and Trevor because of his general disinterest in Clara. But now Frank was, unusually, edging towards a drama and Clara didn't know how to stop him.

No other parents appeared to be staying. Some of them didn't even walk up the path but handed their child a present at the gate and waved a goodbye. Some of the children came on their own, pushing past Clara and Frank to let themselves in the unlocked door. 'Please stay. Please,' Frank begged as the door opened to a woman smiling at them in a dry party frock. Clara, in her sodden shapeless sack, felt underdressed immediately. She started to smooth Frank's hair down and felt wet wool instead.

'You must be Frank.' The woman smiled at Clara. 'Do you want to come in too?'

'I couldn't possibly intrude '

'YES!!' bellowed Frank. 'Yes, she does.'

'It's no intrusion, honestly,' the woman said, giving Clara no choice but to stay. 'I'm Mrs Greene, how do you do?'

Inside, the house was cosy, the leaning walls felt protective and, most importantly, it was dry. A small ginger boy raced up to greet Frank. Clara didn't recognise him from the nativity, but then again, all the children had been disguised in tea towels. She wished she was wearing a tea towel right now.

'We're going to play some games – my husband loves musical beds,' said Mrs Greene.

'Sounds like every day in my house,' Clara joined in nervously. And everyone looked at her quizzically.

The first game was sleeping lions.

'The first one who moves is out – and then so on,' Lester's mother instructed enthusiastically.

'Of course,' said Clara. This was such an excellent idea for a game that she could have kicked herself that she didn't already know it.

The children lay down and Frank insisted Clara join in. Of course she was the only adult lying down since she was the only adult still there. And she wasn't even a parent. She could have predicted that Frank couldn't do it, and within ten seconds he sat bolt upright and grinned around the room.

'You're out,' bellowed a short dapper man who Clara presumed was Lester's father, but Frank ignored him and lay down again, close to Clara. He didn't get the rules.

The game eventually finished, and Frank went spinning around the room.

'He's, uh, never been to a children's birthday party before,' Clara explained to Mrs Greene apologetically. And nor had she. It felt like a foreign country. They do things differently here.

'I'm going to go now, Frank,' she said to him in a do-not-question me tone. 'I really have to collect Patricia.'

And she wanted to get ready for Ivor and Jonathon's return. Maybe they were already home, wondering where she was.

'Please.' Frank's cheeks were bright red. 'A. I want you here.' He leaned into her and his breath smelled of rice pudding as he whispered. 'B. I don't know how to do it.'

Clara was about to reassure him when Lester came over and both boys decided it would be a great plan to fly around the room like aeroplanes. The short dapper man came over to her.

'I'm Lester's father, Mr Greene.'

Clara put on a smile. She felt torn between Frank and the children at home who were expecting her back. It was a ridiculous dilemma.

'Frank's your son?'

'Uh, not quite...'

His wife put her arm through his as though he were the village idiot. 'Frank is at Shilling Grange,' she told him. 'You know that.'

Shaking her head indulgently at Clara, she said, 'He never listens to me.'

'I do,' he protested.

'You don't,' she told him. 'He doesn't,' she insisted to Clara, rolling her eyes for emphasis.

'Shilling Grange is the children's home,' Clara clarified, since Mrs Greene seemed determined to avoid the word.

'Oh yes, the orphanage. Frank goes there?'

'Yes. No, he lives there. With me.'

'You live there too? You don't want children of your own?'

'I don't,' Clara said simply. She always tried not to bristle when asked this, but bristling was her first reaction. She *was* asked it an awful lot, when she herself would never presume to ask it of anyone. Why couldn't people keep their noses out of other people's business?

'Don't blame you,' agreed Mrs Greene. 'I never got my figure back after Lester.'

'You never had your figure to start with,' the father said, and then he poked his wife in the side. 'Just kidding, you look like Greta Garbo to me.'

'I'll help with the squash, shall I?' Clara interjected, keen to escape this domestic she had somehow found herself embroiled in.

She and Frank played musical bumps and pass the parcel. Clara almost won pass the parcel, which would have been dreadful, but she just managed to throw it to the girl next to her. The girl next to her was not grateful – in fact, she looked quite put out and then, after she unwrapped the parcel to find a pack of liquorice, turned up her nose. Then she and Frank played musical statues and Frank at first seemed to have got the idea of this, but, when he was told he had moved and was out, he carried on playing, which irritated the other children.

A dog slunk in and Clara was relieved, because it diverted attention away from Frank. The dog was golden brown, with a delightfully long sad face and it was skinny except for its huge tummy.

'This is Suki,' said Mrs Greene. Clara crouched down to stroke her and the dog's dark eyes on her were trusting and sweet. Frank also knelt down and so did Mrs Greene.

'You've got a way with her,' she told Frank, as he tickled Suki's belly. Clara appreciated that, because Frank didn't seem to have a way with anyone today. He was being particularly tiresome.

'Suki won't let just anyone touch her, especially now,' Mrs Greene went on. 'She must like you.'

'Hear that, Frank?' said Clara, because his mouth was hanging open.

'Is she poorly?' asked Frank.

'Nooo – oh you mean... no.' Mrs Greene laughed. 'She's expecting puppies, Frank. God help us!'

Frank and Clara stroked Suki some more and she licked Clara's fingers. Clara thought she was every bit as lovely as Bandit – and Bandit set the bar high.

'You wouldn't be interested in one, would you?' Mrs Greene asked.

'One what?'

'A puppy.'

'Please!' squealed Frank.

'No,' said Clara automatically.

But then she had it. The wedding present – or the damn present, as she had renamed it. It was simple. It was staring her in the face. She could imagine it perfectly: a little dog for Ivor, she and Patricia to enjoy together. Pets bring you closer. Pets weren't strictly allowed at Shilling Grange, but Mrs Horton had wangled it so that Clara could have Stella for Rita, and Stella was easy. Yes, a puppy would be harder work than a cat, but what lovely work! And it would live at Ivor's anyway.

She pictured Patricia's joy. How she loved the dignified Bandit. How she loved Bertie, the Garrards' yappy dog. How it would be killing two (or more) birds with one stone (what a horrible analogy that was). It might even make Jonathon happier, and Peg, and – perhaps most of all – herself, because she would be able to tick the damn present off her list.

'On second thoughts,' Clara said, 'Maybe? But Frank, you have to promise me you won't say anything to any of the children – or to Ivor.'

'This is the greatest day of my life,' Frank announced.

9

It had stopped raining finally, yet it was perhaps even windier on the way home. The cold air wrapped around Clara like a clutch from icy arms. She and Frank clung together and she imagined him blowing away.

Whatever was wrong with Clifford at the Reform School for Boys, Clara was now convinced, she shouldn't have sent Ivor charging in there – this was council business. This was not their problem. They should have kept their noses out. But Ivor would have done his best and, if it was in vain, on Monday they could go and sort it all out through official channels.

She was looking forward to seeing Ivor again. And Jonathon. She would try to get to the bottom of his unhappiness. It was vital he felt safe in his own home; why had he run away?

As they battled homeward, Clara realised she had some more people to add to the wedding list now – Lester and Mr and Mrs Greene, seeing as they'd been so kind as to invite Frank to his first party and were responsible for the present for Ivor!

Even the branches on the trees were wobbling as the wind whipped through them. A paper bag flew past them, and Frank yelled. His hand in hers was cold but he shouted that it was fun because... She heard him say 'A' and 'B' but couldn't hear his reasons, but she laughed anyway.

As Clara held the puppy secret to her too; it was making her smile. A puppy. She remembered telling the children the difference between good secrets and bad: a good secret is like if you get a good mark from school but don't want everyone to know because you are modest. A bad secret is like smoking.

A puppy was the best kind of secret.

Clara and Frank made it home at half past five and Clara noticed that Peg and Gladys were in almost exactly the same positions as they had been when she had left them three hours earlier. After all her worry, they hadn't even noticed she and Frank had gone. They were on the floor, doing a jigsaw that Marilyn had given them for Christmas. Marilyn had a remarkable hit rate when it came to presents but this, considered Clara, was a miss; it was of the *Titanic*. Why someone had put that ship on a puzzle was a puzzle. Why Marilyn had sent it was another puzzle.

Before she'd left, the girls had emptied out the bits all over the rug; now it was nearly all done except for the ragged-edged hole in the middle. Peg got up and danced around the room.

'Has Ivor been in yet?' Clara asked. She was looking forward to a cosy evening. There was something lovely about being inside while a storm raged outside. But he should have been back by now. The trains were still running, weren't they? She wondered if that was what Anita had meant when she'd said earlier that people couldn't make it to choir.

'Is Jonathon home?' Clara added more loudly, to get the girls' attention.

'He's not here,' Gladys said, looking around her lazily before turning her attention back to the puzzle. 'Look, Miss Newton, there's a tiny orchestra.'

Clara knew that showing interest in the children's hobbies

was important – *who else would?* – so she examined the several little figures in dinner suits playing piano, cellos and one man in a bow tie might have been playing a tiny violin – all while their majestic ship went down, and she said how interesting it all was, how clever, but her mind was elsewhere, worrying about Ivor and Jonathon.

The Norland Nanny kindly delivered Patricia back. She was on her way out, she said, as she departed.

'In this?' said Clara. It was bucketing down again.

'I know!' she said gleefully. 'Nice weather for ducks!'

The nanny had only just left when the telephone rang. Clara hurried to it. Ivor's voice was distant and she gathered immediately, disappointingly, that he was still in Norfolk.

'You're not getting back today then?' she asked flatly.

'We wanted to,' Ivor explained. He sounded so sorry for himself that Clara almost forgave him. Plus, she reminded herself, it *was* mostly her fault he was there. Ivor had no news about Clifford. He had knocked at the door of the school and been sent away again. This time, the people there were less polite. They even accused Ivor of harassing them – 'They said you were harassing *them?*' repeated Clara in a high-pitched voice. The cheek of it!

Then Ivor said he had seen a group of boys, absolutely drenched through, coming back from God knows where, and he asked them; they confirmed it – Clifford was indeed being punished by being kept in confinement. One little one chirped up before the others shushed him, 'Brutal confinement, we call it.'

Clara gasped. *Brutal?*

'We're going to have one last try tomorrow and then we might have to get the police involved.'

This was worse than she had anticipated. Horrible to contemplate. She wouldn't let herself imagine it...

'What about Jonathon?' she asked. 'Has he opened up at all?'

Ivor cleared his throat, which told her that Jonathon was there, within earshot.

'He's as you'd expect...'

The rain was still crashing down, sounding like a mop sluicing around the floor. She wished desperately that Ivor weren't so far away. It felt like a fool's errand. It felt like they had travelled away from the direction they should have been travelling in, and she was uneasy in a way she hadn't been for a long time. And all for Clifford – who not only was no longer one of the home's children, but probably wouldn't be thrilled to hear they were involved either.

'How's Patricia?' Ivor asked.

'The Norland Nanny said she had a long nap,' Clara said, choosing to focus on the positives.

'Have you had weather warnings there?'

'No such thing as bad weather,' she said, which was something Ivor himself liked to say. 'Just bad equipment.'

He laughed but he didn't sound happy.

'You will be back tomorrow, won't you?' Clara asked, willing it to be true. And then she wanted to say something light – to cheer him up. 'Those wedding invitations aren't going to write themselves.'

He laughed again, but this time with feeling. 'Of course I will,' he said. 'I miss you, Clara.'

'I miss you too.'

They had spam and fried potato for dinner, then the children cuddled up on the sofa under a blanket. Clara read them 'The Wishing Chair' by Enid Blyton. In this story, the children could go anywhere they wished to go.

'Where would you go if you could go anywhere?' she asked them.

Trevor wanted to go to play chess in Russia with the greats. Frank wanted to go to the playground down the road. Gladys wanted to go to London to see the Queen. Peg wrote down 'seaside', reminding Clara that she hadn't taken her to the sea yet.

Patricia just said, 'Daddy.' It reminded Clara of ex-resident Rita's single-minded 'Mama'.

'Daddy be back soon,' Clara reassured her.

The wind was wild, it rattled the doors and the locks. It sounded like someone was trying to get in. Clara thought of ex-resident Florrie and her love for the wild storms in *Wuthering Heights* – and Heathcliff. 'He's bashing his head against the wall!' she had said, startled. She thought of poor Clifford perhaps trying to call for help or panicking about being confined and alone. No, she couldn't think about that. And Jonathon and Ivor would be fine. At least they were together.

Once the children were in bed, Clara put away the abandoned toys and got going with her wedding planning. She liked the parlour at night, with its doilies and antimacassars perfectly in position. It was her place of sanity.

By the time she next looked up from her lists, it was gone eleven o'clock. The wind was still making the window frames creak like old ships, and as she gazed out of them, Clara noticed the moon was hiding behind the clouds. After a short while, she left the room.

Moving around the house restlessly, she felt like she was hunting something but didn't know what. In the boys' room, they were both snoring lightly, Trevor flat on his back, Frank on his side still wearing his hat and, once again, his papier mâché creation on his bed.

In the girls' room, Gladys and Peg were sharing one bed and Patricia was curled up in another with Polly bear, her roll of cardboard and her old mallet. When she was awake there was often something poised about her, yet when she slept, she looked like she was fighting demons, her sheets all screwed up, her mouth wide open. Clara hoped she was not frightened by the howls of the wind. While it was fun in the day, it was altogether a different experience at night. Lightly brushing her cheek, Clara whispered 'Goodnight,' but this was a mistake – Patricia sprang awake and burst into song.

'My Bonnie lies over the ocean. My Bonnie lies over the sea. My Bonnie lies over the ocean. Oh, bring back my Bonnie to me.'

'Who's Bonnie?' Clara laughed. She loved Patricia's little theories about her rhymes.

'Daddy,' she said.

'He'll be home tomorrow, darling,' Clara whispered as Patricia fell back asleep.

CLARA'S GUEST LIST / DRAFT SEVEN
– in no particular order

Mr and Mrs Horton and Mrs Horton senior?

Harris and Sons. The twins.

Judy's parents and brother

Mr and Mrs Dowsett

Billy and Barry Coulson and Aunt and Uncle

Joyce and her family

Terry and her family

Alex. Victor. Victor's wife and sister and Bernard!

Mr and Mrs Garrard – Bertie?

The postmistress and the new assistant. Whatever her name is. FIND THIS OUT!

The milkman, his wife and the milkman's boy.

The butcher and his boy

The petrol station man

Dr and Mrs Cardew, Baby Howard. EVELYN

Rita and her mama

Miss Cooper? – NOT if Mrs Mount is coming.

Denny and his parents

Joe and his wife and baby Vincent? Check with Maureen.

Beryl and Doris
Farmer and Mrs Buckle
Miss Webb plus one
Norland Nanny plus one
Mrs Dorne plus one
Sister Grace plus one?
Miss Fisher plus one
Sir Alfred Munnings and family
Mr Sommersby and wife? NOT if Miss Cooper is coming.
Mr and Mrs Greene plus Lester

10

There was no word from Ivor in the morning and, despite wanting to, Clara was too busy to sit around waiting for the telephone to ring. When he'd gone away with Ruby that time, she hadn't heard from him for months, and when he worked in London or Norwich she didn't hear much from him either. This was different, though – she had Patricia and he had Jonathon. It was, she decided, a measure of how much Ivor now trusted her with Patricia that he wasn't checking in every five minutes.

Try to smile when a child walks in the room, Clara told herself; she didn't want them to know how stressed she was. Miss Webb thought that if you were nice to a child then they would erroneously expect the whole world to be nice. Clara didn't agree with this theory. Nevertheless, it was sometimes tiring to be nice all the time. She grinned at Frank as he wandered into the kitchen.

'What's the matter with you?' he asked, perturbed. 'Your face looks like the wind changed and you got stuck.'

They had porridge for breakfast and some of them had bread and honey too. They were all hungrier than usual; it was that kind of day. Clara chopped carrots and turnips for the stew they would have for lunch. Since it was Sunday, they would eat dinner at lunchtime and have something lighter in the evening – crackers and cheese, probably.

The air was still thick with the threat of more rain; there were so many dark grey clouds it felt like it wasn't yet day. Patricia fell off the kitchen bench, giving everyone a fright, but she wasn't hurt. Gladys had put her pullover on the wrong way round, and Peg was crying because she only had one page to go in her notebook.

'I'll find you a new one, Peg.'

Clara knew how important the notebook was to her. Peg gave a watery smile. On her last page, she wrote – 'where is Ivor?'

Clara realised the tears were probably about that. She remembered Peg had been planning to help Ivor with 'some scissoring' today.

'He'll be back soon, darling, and you'll have a lovely day today, I'll see to it.'

Trevor was frustrated that his only chess opponents in the home were too weak.

'Maybe I could play?' Clara offered, but Trevor refused, shaking his head so his hair covered his eyes. 'You're all right.'

Frank stared out of the window, a plane in each clenched fist. It was a gloomy view out there.

'I didn't sleep,' he said suddenly. 'It was too noisy. I thought I heard howling. It felt like people were dying out there.'

'Don't be silly,' Clara said. She felt strangely unsettled. 'It was just the wind in the trees.' What she didn't tell him was she also didn't get a wink of sleep; she was too busy worrying about her three boys.

Clara chivvied the children along to Sunday School. If they hadn't wanted to go, she wouldn't have sent them, especially on such a bleak day as this, but the children saw it as a magical kingdom and hated to miss it. Peg and Gladys especially loved it. Quietly spoken Sunday School teacher Mrs Dorne was some kind of miracle worker, Clara thought. She envied her. She was one of those effortlessly likeable people.

Today, Clara was glad of her wool coat and that Patricia was dressed sensibly too. You could say that for Ivor's little girl – she always looked impeccable. She didn't jump in muddy puddles – or, when she did, she somehow came off without looking as though she had. Peg used to be the opposite. She'd see a muddy puddle and there would be filth all over her cheeks. Some children only had to so much as peek outdoors and they would be covered in leaves or mud or unknown things. Not Patricia; she had something fastidious about her that reminded Clara of her dear friend Anita.

The wind whipped icy against their cheeks. There were already deep and wide puddles collecting in the road and Trevor and Frank went straight for them.

'You'll be cold all morning,' Clara pleaded with them, to no avail. And Frank had holes in his shoes that Miss Webb hadn't allocated money in the budget yet to replace.

You could see their outlines reflected in one of the puddles, and then bosh, Gladys jumped in.

'Noooo, Gladys!' Clara shrieked, failing to sound assertive.

And then Frank, then Peg, then Trevor all piled in.

'It's a river!'

'A canal.'

'An ocean.'

'The Mariana Trench.'

Once the children had finally decided they had had enough fun, Clara hurried them along. The water was up to their ankles in some places. The grass was sodden; it was like wading through marshy bog. Clara's stockings were wet through and she was worried she'd lose her shoes. She picked up Patricia and carried her on her hip. Patricia thought it was hilarious to poke Clara's face.

It's odd – there are no tales about evil stepdaughters, are there?

Mrs Dorne was waiting at the foot of the church steps. Nothing much about Sunday School warmed Clara's cold agnostic heart, but the sight of Mrs Dorne almost did. She said her hellos in her cheerful little voice and clapped her big navy mittens together. They had a string attaching them like a toddler's. She was wrapped up – and she did not cut a slender figure even without her winter coat. One push and she might have rolled away.

Mrs Dorne asked where Jonathon was and Clara gulped then managed to say that he was away with Ivor, as if it was a planned trip.

'I hope they're safe,' Miss Dorne said, a worried look suddenly crossing her face.

'Absolutely,' Clara responded, stomping from side to side to keep warm even though the wet leaves made her afraid of slipping.

'You haven't heard the news?' Miss Dorne pressed.

Clara wracked her brain – news? – She wouldn't be talking about Derek Bentley's trial and the capital punishment, would she? That was days ago. Clara decided she must be talking about the ferry.

'Terrible,' Clara agreed. 'It must have been dreadfully frightening.'

'You wouldn't think it would happen in this day and age, would you?' Miss Dorne said, shaking her head, before being distracted by the arrival of more boys and girls.

One was Lester – and Frank tore after him. When Lester saw him, they hugged. Trevor, however, dallied, and Gladys pulled at Clara and whispered, 'Don't say anything but he's waiting to see his girlfriend!' She giggled.

'Oh goodness!' said Clara, slightly thrown by this development.

She thanked Mrs Dorne, took Patricia by the hand and left. She suddenly couldn't wait to catch up Ivor with all the goings-on. It was only a couple of days, but it felt as though he'd already missed a lot.

A car went by and would have sprayed Clara with puddle water had she not leapt out of the way. Clara was about to shout after it when it pulled to a stop ahead of her. It was Anita. She wound down the window, her face grim.

'There've been floods all along the coast. Canvey was hit badly.'

Clara noted that Anita did not apologise for the splash.

'Canvey?' she asked.

'Yes,' said Anita, nodding. 'It's an island in Essex.'

'Right.' Clara didn't know Essex had islands. *You learn something every day,* she thought.

'I will come over if you like, later,' Anita persisted.

'Why?' Clara asked, confused.

'Clifford lives along the coast, doesn't he?'

Anita had always had a soft spot for Clifford, her little song-bird. Clara could never really get her head around it. They were like chalk and cheese in every other way.

Clara laughed. 'They're not in Canvey.'

Anita perked up. 'Phew!' she said, and before she drove off, she made Clara promise to pop in to see her soon for more wedding music discussions.

11

Clara and Patricia trudged their way to the library, where Clara had a meeting with Mr Dowsett, the librarian. If Mr Dowsett had reservations about a three-year-old gatecrashing their meeting, he was kind enough not to express them. The library was shut but he unlocked the door and welcomed them in. They gratefully took off their coats, which were dripping.

'New Jane Taylor fans are always welcome!' he said, and Patricia gazed at him like butter wouldn't melt in her mouth and then began reciting:

> *Twinkle, twinkle, little bat*
> *How I wonder what you're at.*

'That's not the one we learned,' Clara pointed out. Patricia stuck her tongue out at her.

Mr Dowsett, who always looked on the bright side, said, 'Isn't it beautiful that our Jane Taylor inspired not only small children but other writers too?'

> *Up above the world you fly*

Like a tea tray in the sky.

Gosh, Patricia loved the limelight. Usually Clara's children, while assertive at home, were quiet as mice out of it, and she had to encourage them forward. Patricia definitely didn't need any encouragement!

Before she could launch into the next verse, Clara interrupted: 'Shall we get going?'

Clara had taken over the running of the Jane Taylor Society and next week she would be conducting her first meeting. She had been reluctant to go to the Jane Taylor Society meetings at the library but Mrs Horton and Ivor had persuaded her – they both thought it would strike a chord with her; and, to her surprise, it had. It wasn't just Jane Taylor's poetry that Clara had fallen for, it was her story of quiet perseverance. Her older sister, Ann Taylor, was the more outspoken one, out there in the world with her newspaper articles and speeches and a husband and a large family. By contrast, younger sister Jane was the more solitary one, writing rhymes for the children she never had and poems that she would never be acknowledged for. Somehow, Clara could relate.

Mr Dowsett gave Patricia a thick black marker pen and told her to draw on some coloured paper sheets he produced. (These had *not* already been drawn on, so Patricia was delighted.)

Clara had never held a community meeting before, never mind an academic talk, and she wanted to go over the agenda she had prepared to check it would be up to standard. Mr Dowsett sat with his hands on his knees and waited.

'Welcome is to welcome everyone...' she explained nervously.

'I thought it might be,' Mr Dowsett replied, hiding a smile.

'Sorry, yes... and introductions are for the people who don't know me?'

'Not many of them!'

'The apologies are for absences,' she continued.

'I guessed.'

'You think the subject matter will be all right?'

'What I think doesn't matter, it's your event now. You're the president.'

'Yes, but...'

Mr Dowsett pressed his hands together. 'I think it's excellent.'

Mr Dowsett had to be positive, she thought – it was his idea she took over the society – but 'excellent' was high praise. He followed up with, 'Just what we need.'

'I'm not sure about the Q and A – what can I possibly answer?' Clara asked.

Mr Dowsett smiled wryly. 'Anything I can't answer, I say, *"you can read about it here."*'

Clara laughed. 'I can always show them my special book, can't I?' It was a rare person who wasn't impressed by the first edition Jane Taylor anthology.

'Wonderful!' Mr Dowsett declared, standing to signify he thought they had covered everything they needed to.

Yet despite his reassurances, Clara still found the prospect of the meeting terrifying. You would think giving a talk to the council would be worse, but Clara knew what she was talking about there. The children's welfare was her job; Jane Taylor was just a hobby, and a fairly new one at that.

'The Society is in safe hands,' Mr Dowsett said, taking her hand between his papery ones. He had such a kind face. And he had been ill last year. She wanted to do him proud.

'I hope so.'

Patricia refused to give back her pen. Cajoling, pleading and threats didn't work.

'Okay, keep it then,' Mr Dowsett said, pinching her cheek. 'What a bundle of fun you are!'

Patricia ran rings around everyone. Clara sighed, thinking she needed some of Patricia's energy.

12

Clara and Patricia met the children from Sunday School, and they all walked home together. Frank said they had been looking at 'A. The Ark and B. How did Noah decide which animals to save?'

It seemed to Clara there was a straightforward answer to this, and a more profound one. 'They just got two of each of them,' she said, deciding, as she always did, on the straightforward.

'A boy and a girl to do the reproduction?' Frank asked, and all the children went silent and looked at Clara expectantly.

'Do the reproduction,' repeated Patricia with that incredible sense children have for something slightly taboo.

'Why not ask Mrs Dorne next week?' Clara suggested. Clara herself did the birds and the bees talk once a year, and today was definitely not that day. Like talking to the council or the Jane Taylor Society, it needed a lot of preparation and a certain amount of bracing herself.

'I did,' said Frank, 'she said to ask you.'

'I'm sure she did. How about we go to the playground later?' suggested Clara, deciding that changing the subject completely was her best approach.

As they rounded the corner to the home, Clara saw a car

parked outside, then Miss Webb at the door and another woman who she didn't recognise. The other woman was wearing a wool coat and a patterned headscarf tied under her chin. They went to the back of the car, opened the boot, then lugged something from it and set it on the pavement. A wheelchair. Then a man emerged from the passenger seat and manoeuvred himself into it. He seemed to be resisting their help. The woman offered him a blanket and he shook his head angrily. He wheeled himself towards the path and both women followed him.

In among all her concerns about the council, Clifford, Jonathon, Ivor, the cold weather, the invitations and the Jane Taylor Society meeting, had Clara managed to forget Miss Webb was visiting with prospective parents?

No, she hadn't. Miss Webb hadn't told her about any visits.

Clara approached. 'I wasn't expecting you,' she said, smiling, aware that whoever these people were, they were guests, and she always wanted to give the correct impression of Shilling Grange.

Miss Webb made a pout and then, in a girlish forgive-me voice, said, 'Didn't I mention it?'

'No, you didn't.'

She was just as bad as Frank and his parties.

'I meant to,' Miss Webb said, baring her teeth. If she was trying to be contrite, she wasn't doing a great job. 'But it doesn't really matter, does it? – you're here.'

'This is what I mean when I talk about better communication, transparency and the thing is, Jonathon is not here,' Clara said, under her breath so the couple wouldn't hear her.

To her surprise Miss Webb shook her head and muttered, 'They're not here for him.'

Clara was surprised. 'Then who?'

The couple had reached them now.

'Come in, welcome!' Clara said automatically.

The house looked a mess but, worse than that, none of the children had been prepared.

'We've been looking forward to see you,' Clara lied. 'Sorry, children, change of plan. No playground today.'

'For Chrissakes,' yelled Frank, to the visible shock of the visitors.

Miss Webb was flustered. 'We don't say that,' she said.

'He just did,' said Trevor, grinning.

Clara tried to settle them. 'Children, behave. These people are here to meet you to see if—'

Patricia interrupted. 'Are you going to do the reproduction?'

Miss Webb's face was scarlet. She opened her mouth and closed it like a fish.

'Patricia!' said Clara, but she too could think of nothing else to add. She tried once again. 'Gladys, Trevor, Frank – I need you three to wash, tidy yourselves up and then come into the parlour. The rest of you – to the kitchen, please.'

Miss Webb grew even more flustered. 'No, Miss Newton, that's not it at all.'

'What then?'

Clara hung up her coat, and the children's. She felt increasingly annoyed.

Miss Webb had a rictus smile on her face as she spelled out the words. 'You've misunderstood. These people are here for Peg.'

Peg?

Clara tried to think on her feet but for once she couldn't. They were here for Peg? This felt impossible. *No one* came for Peg. And if they were – obviously, that might mean Peg would leave? Not her Peg, surely? Joyful, lovely Peg.

'The other children may go but we need Peg here, Miss Newton. MISS NEWTON? Are you listening?'

Clara shook herself.

'Ah um, okay, everyone, can go to the playground after all...'

'What?' chorused the children, united in confusion.

'Yes, uh, coats back on...' Clara tried to organise her thoughts. 'Oh, but not you, Peg, and no, not you, Patricia. You're too little.'

Peg didn't like being singled out like that. She stormed upstairs, leaving Miss Webb open-mouthed.

Frank, Trevor and Gladys pulled at their outdoor clothes and then tore away, Gladys apologising and blowing kisses. They left the door wide open.

Patricia remained, the last child standing. And then she started howling too.

Miss Webb would have preferred them to gather in the parlour – she thought it was more 'respectable' – but Clara led them into the kitchen. She still felt dazed. These were potential parents for Peg? She remembered that Peg's shells and her skipping rope were in her handbag in case of emergency. She had a note under her pillow from her that read, *Mama Newton.* Peg called her different names all the time, and each one of them was charming.

Fortunately, the Easleas were a docile enough couple and they didn't seem bothered by the chaotic welcome. They reminded Clara of a pair of guinea pigs the Lavenham primary school kept. At going-home time, the children had lined up to hold them and Peg had nearly dropped one when it was her turn.

The Easleas whispered to each other and Clara wished she could hear what they were saying.

'If you could take care of the tea, Miss Webb,' said Clara. Miss Webb had thrown them in it, she could blooming well pull her weight. 'I'll go up and speak to Peg.'

Miss Webb looked shocked at the request, nevertheless she agreed.

Tentatively, Clara went into the girls' bedroom. She knew she had to put her own feelings about this behind her and do what was best for Peg. But the prospect of Peg leaving felt like a knife to the heart.

'How are you, little Peg?'

'What they hear for?' Peg scribbled, her face was worryingly mutinous.

'Miss Webb thinks they might be a match for you,' Clara tried to explain gently. She told herself she mustn't sound sad – that would make it even harder.

'Why?' Peg immediately wrote in reply.

'So you can be a family together?' Clara said, forcing her voice to burst with cheer.

More scribbling.

'Are they my mum and dad?'

Clara's heart sank even more. Did Peg think the couple might be her real parents? Oh God, this was what happened when you didn't explain things properly.

'No,' Clara said quickly, too quickly. 'They're from Chichester.'

Why that should rule them out was ridiculous.

'I mean, no... They are hoping to adopt you.'

She remembered Peg's peaky little face, and the shadow that seemed to appear over her eyes, when first Evelyn's mother appeared, and then Rita's mother.

She had been waiting all this time for her own mother.

Clara knew she had to do better.

'Isn't that a wonderful idea!' she continued, but Peg looked as unsure as ever.

'Away from here?' she wrote slowly. Clara could only bring herself to nod.

'Away from you?' She underlined the 'you'.

Clara gulped. If she had had time she would have prepared Peg – and herself. Miss Webb shouldn't have sprung this on them; but, even as she blamed Miss Webb, she knew it was her fault too. Peg should never have been allowed to think she was going to stay at Shilling Grange forever. And Clara should never have let herself think it either.

'I can't divide myself into two,' Clara said, forcing a laugh.

How good would it be if she could! If she could have Clara 1 living a conventional life with Ivor and Patricia, and Clara 2 in the Grange. Why stop at two? Clara 3 could be swanning around with Peter in London!

'Away from Miss Fisher?'

'We'll be able to visit.'

Clara shifted uncomfortably. She knew a visit was a drop in the ocean.

'I wanted to go to the high school next year.'

Peg had never mentioned this before, but Clara supposed she did. She had seen lots of children go there before her.

'You'll go to a high school near them...'

Peg nodded thoughtfully. She looked less upset now.

Clara wondered what was happening downstairs. Probably Patricia would be prancing around, performing. Hopefully Miss Webb was making tea and unearthing some biscuits.

'What about the wedding?' Peg suddenly scribbled urgently, as though this was by far the most important consideration.

At this, Clara smiled; she couldn't help it. There was something lovely about how important the wedding was to the children.

'We'll see what we can do about that, Peg. Nothing is set in stone.'

'What's wrong with that man?'

'Uh... he can't walk.'

More scribbling. 'Why?'

'I don't know why – some people can't.'

'Like Joyce?'

Joyce, who had childhood polio, had lived at the home for a short while until she was adopted.

'Yes, although Joyce could walk sometimes, couldn't she?'

It was another unsatisfying answer, Clara knew that, but Peg pursed her lips together. She wrote again.

'You SAID everything would stay the same. When you told us you were getting married, you said, nothing would change.'

She pressed hard on the paper.

'I said...' Clara had to choose what she said next carefully. Peg had a habit of never forgetting a word out of place. 'I *said* I was not leaving the home – and I'm not. That Ivor and I would continue as we are. But you getting sent to a real family was always a possibility – that hasn't changed.'

Despite Clara's best efforts, Peg still wouldn't come downstairs. She folded her arms and pulled her blanket up higher. Which was exactly what Clara would have done too if she could have.

Clara decided that she would get to know the couple and let Peg cool down for a bit. Peg wasn't wrong, though: the fact that the man was in a wheelchair was unexpected. Silly really – she got annoyed when people were surprised by Ivor's disability, and yet here she was. But Peg was a child of many needs, and she found herself wondering if Mrs Easlea would have the resources or the strength to deal with both of them.

A stupid question, one part of Clara said. An *insulting* question, even. But it still hovered. It still existed; it still begged an answer.

Back in the kitchen, Patricia was prancing around as Clara had anticipated, while the Easleas watched and Miss Webb made the tea.

'She looks like you,' Mrs Easlea said, and smiled.

Clara found it strange when people said that: they said it a lot though.

'Thank you,' Clara said awkwardly. 'I don't know how, though – Patricia is not my daughter.'

Ivor got it a lot too. He said children often grow to take on features of the people they share time with – just like dogs and their owners.

'Oh.' Mrs Easlea looked mortified. She had a pleasing accent, a hint of West Country maybe. 'I'm sorry...'

'No need,' said Clara, trying to sound more forgiving than she felt. She felt a rising antagonism to this pair of strangers in her kitchen. The country was full to the brim of children left shattered by a six-year war. You couldn't open a newspaper without reading about a child orphaned in a house fire or a road accident. Councils were constantly juggling children and adoption and fostering and goodness knows what. Surely Peg wasn't the only girl who fitted the bill? There would be other nine-year-olds desperate for a home like theirs. Why did it have to be her Peg?

'I thought this home was for older orphans only,' Mrs Easlea said, watching Patricia now squeeze a doll's tummy in the hope of getting it to squeak. 'Six and above, they told me?'

'Oh? Well, yes, Patricia doesn't live here. She's...' Now Clara couldn't bring herself to open the can of worms that came along with the word 'fiancé'. 'She's my neighbour's child.'

'You all kind of muck in together?' Mrs Easlea asked, clearly delighted at the idea.

'Something like that,' Clara replied tersely.

Mrs Easlea nodded approvingly. Mr Easlea had some scissors and was expertly cutting little hand-holding figures out of paper. He held them up and Patricia grabbed them and shouted, 'Mine!'

'Thank you,' prompted Clara.

'You're welcome,' said Patricia. Miss Webb, Mr Easlea and Patricia went to the parlour to show Mr Easlea the *Titanic* jigsaw. Mrs Easlea stayed behind to talk to Clara.

Mrs Easlea tilted her head. 'He fought in the Dardanelles,' she said in a low voice. 'In case you were wondering. They didn't think he'd make it – but his squadron saved him.'

Clara didn't want to say that that wasn't the bit she was wondering about.

'We've been together since we were sixteen,' Mrs Easlea said proudly. 'Love at first sight.'

At this Clara smiled. She was struck with love-story fever. Recently, she wanted to ask everyone about their weddings. Did *they* have caterers? How long did it take them to get the invitations out?

'He was devastated for many years. Nothing changed in how I feel about him but it's taken a long time to get to this place.' She looked like she was about to cry. 'What a pretty tea tray,' she said as she took a minute to gather herself.

'I wanted to be a mother more than anything in the world,' she went on. 'I know – we women have more opportunities than before. We can be what we like.'

Clara disagreed with this. The pressure on her to stop working after her wedding was crushing her. Sometimes, she felt like a creased shirt – about to be ironed flat whether she liked it or not. If she had a penny for everyone who asked her what she would do once she were married, she would have over a pound. But she didn't, and she couldn't say anything to Mrs Easlea. She wasn't here to argue about her views of society.

'But it was always my dream to be a mother,' Mrs Easlea went on. 'Once we got married, I was just waiting. We even named them, the children we were waiting for.'

'What did you name them?'

Mrs Easlea blushed. 'Sid for a boy and Margaret after my mother for a girl.'

Margaret – Peg was often short for Margaret. Clara wondered if the Easleas had made the connection too.

Mrs Easlea continued. It seemed she didn't often get the chance to talk about herself and now she had the opportunity, she was going to run with it.

'And then he had to go to fight. And then he came back like this. And Sid and Margaret stayed up here' – she pointed to her head – 'or maybe in here.' She clapped her hand over her heart.

'I wasn't... I didn't. They don't have to be Sid and Margaret, you know. Of course, I had dreams – Sid might like fishing, and Margaret might like baking, but I never... I never thought they had to. My dreams are' – she coughed – 'flexible.'

As much as she hadn't expected it to, Clara's heart went out to her. She had taken eight years to convince him. They had been together six years before that. This family was a long time in the making.

'And Mr Easlea does want to adopt now?' Clara asked, remembering Mr and Mrs Mount, who had gone through the entire adoption process only for philandering Mr Mount to devastatingly change his mind at the last minute.

'He wants me to be happy.'

And Clara thought, *is that enough, is that a good enough reason to have children?*

And once again it struck her how this was all an imperfect process, one that made it hard for some and easy for others, but what was the alternative? It would be a good enough reason for people to have children naturally. 'We wanted someone we could make a real difference to. Like Peg. Do you think she could possibly be happy with us?'

Silly tears were threatening again. She didn't know where they came from. Clara blinked them back and smiled at sweet Mrs Easlea.

'I'm sure,' she said, hoping that Mrs Easlea didn't notice how shrill her voice was. 'More tea?'

13

The Easleas and Miss Webb were still there when there was a loud thump at the front door. Clara's heart started to race again. Finally! Ivor and Jonathon were back. What a day!

Apologising, Clara hurried to open it, but her heart sank when she saw it was neither Ivor nor Jonathon. Instead, it was Mrs Horton, and she marched inside, carrying a large saucepan with a lid. Her sense of proprietorship annoyed an already tense Clara.

Mrs Horton was wearing a bright rainhat and a large sou'wester, and large rainboots. She made a comical sight, like a dejected fisherman.

'Any news?' she asked urgently.

'How do you mean?' Clara asked, closing the door behind her.

'From Ivor?' Mrs Horton responded, and her tone said, *obviously!*

'Uh no. Not since yesterday,' Clara replied, thoroughly confused as to why Mrs Horton was concerned. Were those cushion covers that important?

'No need to panic,' Mrs Horton said, although Clara thought this was rich; there was one person here who was panicking, and it wasn't her.

'I'm not. I've got people here,' she said in her best warning voice.

'Oh Lordy, already?'

'How do you mean? They're prospective parents. For Peg.'

Clara could see light slowly dawn on Mrs Horton's face, but she still was no further along to understanding why the woman was in her hallway with a saucepan.

As Mr Easlea wheeled into the hall, Clara found herself holding her breath. How did he navigate through all the narrow rooms and hallways in life? Mrs Easlea followed him, her face anxious.

'These are Mr and Mrs Easlea,' Clara introduced them to Mrs Horton, 'they came to see Peg.'

Somehow Mrs Horton managed to act like everything was normal. 'Oh, Peg is a splendid child, very special indeed!' she said throatily. She had put down the saucepan on the telephone table and now she took off her rainhat and hung it up. 'Miss Newton has worked wonders with her.'

Mr and Mrs Easlea looked awkward.

'We haven't actually met her properly yet,' Mrs Easlea said, looking from Clara to Miss Webb.

'Oh my,' said Mrs Horton. 'That's... unfortunate, I see...'

Clara was just going to run upstairs to try to persuade Peg to come down to say goodbye, when there was a noise and Peg tiptoed down to the bottom step.

'At last!' shouted Miss Webb, super jolly. 'We've been waiting for you!' Clara was glad that the Easleas said nothing but smiled at Peg and gave her time. They were patient people.

Peg handed the Easleas a piece of paper. It was a pencil drawing of shells. She had got skilful at that recently. She managed to capture the lines, the curves, the timeless quality of them.

At this, Mr Easlea's eyes welled up and he clearly couldn't speak. Clara found she couldn't either. Sweet girl.

'We'll treasure that, Peg!' Mrs Easlea said in that soft accent she had, but it was all too much for Peg, who fled back up the stairs.

The Easleas promised to visit again soon, and then Miss Webb left with them. As soon as the door was shut, Clara turned to Mrs Horton, who was now trying and failing to light the hob.

'What on earth is going on?' Clara snapped.

'We'll have stew. And I have cheesy dumplings.'

'But why?' Clara pressed, becoming even more frustrated.

'I thought you'd need something hot. And I know what you're like. Mr Horton will be here any minute.'

'Mr Horton?'

'They're doing the new registration for next season. He couldn't get out of it, I'm afraid.' She clapped the oven gloves together. 'Bowls – the bane of my life. You do it.'

Clara lit the hob for her. 'No, I mean why is Mr Horton coming here?'

'He's great in a crisis,' Mrs Horton explained patiently, as if Clara was stupid.

Crisis? What crisis? Clara threw up her hands. This was exasperating. 'What. Are. You. Talking. About?' she said, louder than she had intended.

'Oh, Clara,' said Mrs Horton. Now she was shocked. She brought the oven glove to her mouth and it concealed half of her concerned face. 'You haven't heard? Hunstanton is under water.'

BBC NEWS

Sunday 1 February 1953

East Anglia suffers worst losses

With the death toll steadily mounting, over 130 people were known last night to have died in the flood-stricken areas of east and south east England Many more were still unaccounted for.

At Brightlingsea many boats sank in the harbour; others were smashed to pieces in the shipyard.

At Woodbridge, more than 8,000 gallons was pumped out of one building.

Many Suffolk farmers lost livestock in the flood. One suffered the loss of over 200 sheep and 60 cattle.

At Lowestoft, boatmen rowed into a church to rescue 40 children sheltering there.

A state of emergency was declared in many parts of south-west Holland and north-east Belgium. The city of Rotterdam was partly submerged.

East Anglians, whose long sea-line has witnessed so much of triumph and tragedy, were kept awake by the great wind that raged through the night, most of them doubtless bearing in their thoughts those in peril on the deep.

We in East Anglia can again record with thankfulness that those who man the lifeboats of our coast, like their brothers elsewhere, were not found wanting.

14

Mr Horton arrived just a few minutes later. He switched on the kitchen wireless and it let out its usual coughing sounds like a death gargle. There was a faint man's voice and then the disconcerting toot of a trumpet.

'It's a bit temperamental,' admitted Clara.

She was struggling to take this in, and she couldn't understand why. She had turned sluggish suddenly; maybe she was coming down with something. Everything seemed foggy, not just outside but in her mind too. Mr Horton groaned theatrically, which Clara thought was over the top. It was only the wireless.

'How the heck are we going to hear the news?' he asked urgently.

Mrs Horton didn't stop her husband from swearing either. Things must have been serious.

Clara began. 'I've got Friday's newspaper – there was nothing in that. It was all about the execution of the Bentley boy.'

'The floods happened last night,' Mr Horton explained gently, obviously realising this was a lot for Clara to take in.

'Oh.' Clara felt like she was doing a slow dance to a jive. She was not usually slow mentally. Floods? It felt like she was trudging through mud herself.

'What's happening?' she asked again, and then, realising she wasn't being clear enough, she asked, 'Do you mean this could be really bad?' and they looked at each other.

'We're not quite sure,' Mr Horton finally said, which Clara understood to mean, yes,

it could be really bad.

Clara pulled herself together. 'There's a wireless that works properly in Ivor's workshop. It's nearly brand new.'

He had bought it so Patricia could sit and listen to the children's shows upstairs. Did Patricia sit and listen nicely? No, she did not. Nevertheless, Ivor had got into the comedy shows, and he and Clara listened to *The Archers* occasionally.

'Do you have the key?' Mr Horton said, again with uncharacteristic urgency in his voice.

Clara had felt honoured when Ivor gave her his spare key. It seemed another sign of commitment. It was under the toby jug in the kitchen. Now she held it out to Mr Horton reluctantly.

'I'm not sure if he'd—'

But Mr Horton grabbed it from her palm and was already half-gone.

While he was out, Frank, Trevor and Gladys came back from the playground, and they were shivering and drenched right through. Even their shoes squelched like squeaky toys. Although Mrs Horton was preoccupied with the floods and the wireless and the stew, she still managed to convey her disapproval.

'Why did you let them out in this weather? They'll catch cold. Or chilblains. Or piles.'

'It was brilliant!' said Trevor, hurriedly pulling off his coat. 'I'm going to play chess now.'

'It was A. cccccold,' admitted Frank, and his voice was thick and muffled, 'and B. I hid in a mulberry bush and they couldn't find me for ages.'

'Where's Peg?' asked Gladys. 'Can we play in the shed?'

'Not now – just go upstairs, please,' Clara said, suddenly glad of this momentary distraction.

Frank, Clara noted, was also limping, but she prayed it was just one of those things. When it came to him, it usually was. Clara unravelled the younger ones from their sodden coats and scarves. Gladys's nose was bright red, while Frank's lips were blue. Mrs Horton shook her head but for once she didn't say anything.

After seeing that the children were warm and dry, Clara suddenly had an idea.

Why didn't I think of it before?

She would call the Ocean Breeze hotel, where Ivor had said he and Jonathon would be staying and where they had stayed last year. She pictured its fashionable rock garden and the dining hall that doubled as the breakfast room, the kindly Italian waiter and the sweet old couple rhapsodising about 'young love'. She faintly remembered the bedroom, but she remembered the beach more clearly, the quiet one, where he had asked her to marry her – and where she'd fatally said, 'I don't know,' and regretted that answer for a long time.

The manager would help her, of course. She dialled but there was no ringtone, just a foreboding beep. She'd know if something had happened though, wouldn't she? She'd feel it in her bones.

'Nothing,' she told Mrs Horton. 'But I just remembered – the American Air Force are stationed right near there.' Men like Michael – golden hunks of men. Strong men with discipline. They'd come to everyone's aid.

'It's the American Air Force that's been badly hit,' Mrs Horton explained. Clara was about to respond when she noticed Peg was sitting halfway up the stairs, sobbing.

Clara went up and took Peg in her arms. 'There, there, darling, it's been a long day, hasn't it?'

The Easleas' visit had obviously taken it out of her.

Peg sank her face into Clara's shoulder and then pulled out a note from her dressing gown pocket. 'I don't want to leave.'

'We'll cross that bridge when we come to it,' Clara told her. Her head was pounding. She always had to be careful not to make promises she couldn't keep.

Trevor ran past them in a rage, declaring his compass had gone missing. Apparently, his maths teacher would make him write lines about it if it were lost.

'It's on your desk,' Clara called. 'It was on the floor, I put it there the other night...'

'Jonathon said he would help me with my homework today,' Frank said, but he was pleased, she knew, that he didn't have to do boring old spells.

Mrs Horton wouldn't meet Clara's eye. Clara was feeling increasingly overwhelmed. She often had the urge to be alone, but this was more powerful than usual. She tried to slip out the house unobtrusively, but Mrs Horton caught her at the back door.

'Where are you going?' She looked worried sick.

'Just need some air...' Clara said before opening the door to the freezing wind.

She didn't know where she was going, she just knew she had to get out. To stop having to parent for five minutes. Mrs Horton nodded. 'Go then,' she said. 'We're fine here.'

For once, Clara didn't even care if she had permission or not, nor even if they were fine. Her head was spinning. She dashed out like she had been released from a cage.

Away from the home, though, she wandered aimlessly. She had nowhere to go. First, she went down the high road. It was colder than she anticipated, and she realised immediately that she wasn't dressed for it. She should have borrowed Mrs Horton's rainwear. The shops were shuttered except for one where she could see her reflection in the window. Her face looked old and haggard suddenly, and she was stooped like her mother used to be. This wasn't helping. She walked on through one puddle and then tried to avoid the others. A small dog barked at her but even that didn't make her smile like it normally would. Then someone said, 'Good evening, Miss Newton,' but she kept her gaze on the paving stones, the lines between them, and she did not step on them, for that would be bad luck – no, not bad luck, worse luck.

She saw the light of the church of St Peter and St Paul and felt herself inextricably drawn towards it. The vicar was in the central aisle talking to a group of people, who were laughing and agreeably disagreeing with him.

'You would say that, Vicar, but you'd be wrong.'

Clara paused self-consciously as the vicar nodded over, acknowledging her. Only as she drew closer did she realise they were talking about his favourite subject, cricket. Eventually the crowd left and the vicar turned his big smiley face towards her. She used to dislike men of faith, but this man was different.

'More wedding planning, Miss Newton?' he asked cheerfully.

'No, it's...' She must have been more worried than she realised; her voice was trembling and it came out shrill in this place of many echoes. There was always something listening in here.

The vicar's expression changed. He looked troubled and she couldn't stand it. She shouldn't burden people with this, not before she knew what *this* was...

'It's silly – the children are misbehaving,' she said quickly in an attempt to brush off his concern.

'Yes?' he said, but she could see he was thinking, *is that all?*

She shook herself. 'Like children tend to do.' She gave him a wry smile.

'You're a fine housemother, Miss Newton,' he assured her as he took her hands. She apologised – hers were icy; she hadn't realised until she compared them with his, which were warm and soft, like sinking into a feather pillow.

He said he would light a candle for her. He asked if she would like him to pray for her and she surprised herself by saying, 'Can't hurt, can it?'

And then some more people came in – a tiny well-dressed old lady and her middle-aged daughter perhaps – and they looked distressed, and the vicar looked torn between them all. Clara said, she would go home now, 'please, not to worry.' And she strode past them, head held high, her inappropriate shoes clacking on the cobblestones. By the time she got home, she told herself, there would definitely be news.

15

When Clara arrived home, the children were sitting around the table in the kitchen and Mrs Horton was standing at the stove. Mrs Horton appeared to be trying to get them to say grace before eating. Frank and Trevor were responding by bellowing 'grace!' and 'Tuesday's child is full of grace. Wednesday's child is full of woe,' and Mrs Horton did not like that one bit.

'Does Miss Newton let you get away with this kind of behaviour?' she asked. Clara could see she was at tether's end.

'Miss Newton's behaviour is worse than ours...' said Trevor mutinously, and Clara wished she had stayed away for longer. Mrs Horton had confirmed as soon as Clara walked through the door that there was no news yet.

Peg started sobbing again into her bowl – or maybe she hadn't stopped sobbing all evening – and Gladys and Frank were shrieking that she was a weeping willow.

'Leave it, she's only a baby,' Trevor defended her, but Peg didn't like that either.

'I'm not a baby,' she scribbled. 'I don't want to leave.'

Usually, Clara would have sat Peg on her knee and cuddled her for as long as it took, but she couldn't today; she didn't have anything left to give, not until she knew Ivor and the boys were safe. She felt topsy-turvy and upside down. Her head was aching. Even the smell of Mrs Horton's stew made her nauseous.

'Peg, love, there's nothing to worry about. Please eat up, everyone.'

But there was some news. Not the news Clara was waiting for, but some progress at least. Not only had Mr Horton brought over Ivor's wireless, which was working marvellously, but he had fixed her wireless too. It was only a fuse, he said. More importantly, he had discovered a few radio groups and somehow he was making contact with someone in Hunstanton right now. Someone who might have information about the whereabouts of Ivor and the boys.

'Radio groups?' Clara asked, unsure exactly what that meant.

'Shhh,' Mr Horton said, then he addressed the radio receiver, 'Hello?', he said, making his voice as loud and clear as possible. They all breathed a sigh of relief when they heard a tinny voice reply. Mr Horton then shushed them again before he exchanged strange names with the voice. He was BowlGreen5 and the other man was ShabbyHut.

The man sounded jubilant as he said, 'It's diabolical here,' but Clara wouldn't judge. She knew that feeling of euphoria when you've been through something hideous yet made it out alive. She remembered the hot flush of survival she had after the air disaster.

'Right. I know the Hunstanton Reform School for Boys was evacuated quite early on, but it wasn't badly affected anyway,' ShabbyHut went on. Hearing that Clifford might be safe made Clara feel like she was melting with relief.

'I'm in the old schoolhouse, we're up the road – a mile or so. You wouldn't think it would make much difference, but it does. All the people down there – it was horrendous.'

Clara swallowed. If this was her knight in shining armour, then they were going to have to shine up his suit a bit.

'They've converted it into a shelter,' the man said. 'It's up a slope. I had to wade through filthy water just to get here and my boots are too tight.'

'I see.' Even Mr Horton, who was probably five hundred times more patient than Clara, clearly couldn't care less about his boots and was now looking frazzled. 'And is there a list of all the people at the hall right now?'

'I wonder if there is...' the man asked himself. Clara was becoming more and more frustrated with this ponderous voice on the other end of the wireless.

'Could you perchance go and look?' Mr Horton politely suggested.

ShabbyHut said he would and they agreed to communicate again once he'd seen the list. Mr Horton put the receiver down and making an exasperated expression at Clara, he said.

'I suppose it's good to have a contact on the ground, as it were...'

Clara leaned against the kitchen counter; if it weren't there, she might have fallen down. She closed her eyes and thought of the boys: Of Jonathon's timidity and the sadness he seemed to carry with him. And she thought of Clifford, who was loud, brash and confident and the opposite of Jonathon in many ways. But what they had in common was how much she cared for them.

She could not, she would not let herself imagine them all flailing around in the murky sea, calling for help, perhaps even crying for her. Clifford wouldn't give up; he wasn't built for giving up. Clifford would clamber and fight and resist.

Jonathon might not though. Jonathon was not a fighter, Jonathon was a runner, Jonathon could win any race he put his mind to, he could get away from anything. If there was a storm, and then a flood, he would flee from it while Clifford would punch it into pieces.

And what would Ivor do? Sew it up, stitch it up, listen with that gentle look on his face and tell it, hey, it's going to be all right?

No, Clara reconsidered with burning cheeks. Her man was a war hero. Whatever he did, he would be trying to make a difference.

How the time passed, Clara didn't know. The children had their chores and their Sunday-night baths. Gladys suddenly produced times tables that should have been done on Friday, Trevor found his compass but was looking for his school tie. And then, an hour later, the man on the wireless was back.

'I've found a list!' he said breathlessly. 'I'm looking at it now. Let's see.'

Hallelujah! Clara would put him on her guest list, she was so happy! *List-makers of the world unite*, she thought, *we have nothing to lose but disorganisation.*

'What are the names you are looking for again?'

Mr Horton shook his head and told him for a second time. Clara had never seen mild-mannered bowls-loving Mr Horton this aggravated. She had a new respect for him.

There was a pause, and then a witch-like cackle came through the wires.

'Yes, I've got a Jonathon Pell on the list,' he finally said.

The relief that rushed through Clara was powerful. Oh, now she could have hugged Radio Operator man. He was a knight; no, he was a king. He would, Clara decided, be at the wedding, guest of honour, and he would get a special mention in the speeches. 'If it weren't for ShabbyHut from Hunstanton, I wouldn't have known—'

'I hope you don't mind me asking, but he's not related...?' the voice continued.

Clara couldn't help laughing now. She knew *exactly* what he was going to ask.

'Yes, he is – Maurice Pell's son!' she answered, feeling pride swell through her now alongside the relief.

'Well, well, well,' he said, 'I'm a great admirer of his father. What bravery – extraordinary.'

Mr Horton made a noise with his throat, making Clara jump and reminding her that they still needed news of the others.

'And a Clifford Harvey?' she asked quickly.

'Who the hell is Clifford?' Frank whispered.

'No.'

Oh God. Oh no.

'No, wait, I've got a Cliff H. Could that be the boy?'

'Yes, that will be him!' Clara said, clasping her hands together, feeling overwhelmed with joy. Even Frank started prancing around, delighted to be a part of the excitement.

'He's here somewhere, probably getting a hot meal—'

Clara couldn't stop herself from interrupting. Could it be, could it be possible that all her three were safe and sound?

'And the last name – it's Ivor Delaney. D.E.L.A.N.E.Y.'

The line went silent. She could imagine the man scanning his paper up and down. Was it typed? Unlikely – it would be pen; perhaps it was smeary, perhaps it went on to two pages. Or perhaps it was in pencil and fading fast. She racked her brains – what else would Ivor call himself?

'Or Humphrey?' She was nearly laughing through her tears. 'He might have put that as a joke,' she explained. 'It's a private thing. Some people say he looks like Humphrey Bogart,' she added, although no one had asked why.

'I don't think so,' the voice in Hunstanton said apologetically.

'He will be there,' said Clara confidently, choosing to ignore his last comment. She could imagine Ivor in an evacuation centre vividly now. He might be the one checking people had blankets and pillows. He might be the one distributing food. He probably didn't have time to put himself on a list. He wasn't a petty bureaucrat – he hated pen-pushers.

'Keep looking. Try Lavenham. Upholsterer. Man with one arm – anything like that,' Clara added, just in case.

ShabbyHut seemed to understand he was about to suffer a sudden fall from grace. He had gone very quiet. But then, after a silence that seemed to last a lifetime, he said something. Perhaps he had found him at last.

'Are you still there?' Clara called desperately. 'I missed that. Can you still hear me?'

This time his voice boomed around the walls of the house. 'I said, he's definitely not on the list.'

16

Clara's heart was broken. Nevertheless, she forced a smile on her face for the sake of the children, and especially for the sake of Ivor's child.

'Everyone, this is a good start... A great start,' she repeated before sending the children to bed, trying to act as though it was an evening like any other.

Was she lying to them? Kind of.

The older ones said they'd read to the younger ones. The younger ones said they'd listen nicely and yes, they had washed their hands and brushed their teeth and their hair.

'Look!' Patricia bared her baby teeth at her. Clara smiled weakly. 'Wonderful. To bed.'

Back in the kitchen, Mrs Horton was cleaning in silence, those tucked-away spots that Clara had missed, and the shelves, and the cutlery drawer.

'Try to keep things as normal as possible,' she advised.

What was normal? What was possible?

And then, after another useless hour of tea, 'and no thank you, Mrs Horton, I couldn't possibly,' over the stew, the telephone pealed. Clara ran.

'Uhh, Is that Shilling Grange?'

'Jonathon!?!'

And like that the children, who should have been asleep, were up and out of bed and down the stairs like jacks-in-the-boxes. All of them, even Patricia, even Peg, who was a tyrant if she had less than ten hours' sleep.

Oh, but Clara had never been so happy to talk to anyone in her life. The boy was safe. Dear sweet Jonathon. Who shouldn't have even been there in the first place. Anger and concern and love and fear mingled interchangeably.

She heard him take a breath. 'Miss Newton?'

And it was then she began to better understand the extent of the calamity. She heard the anguish in his voice right away. What had she been expecting? She should have gone up there today. She should have been able to put a blanket around him, to tell him it was okay.

His voice was wibble-wobbling and everyone in the kitchen was shouting. Frank and Trevor were whooping. She wanted him, Clifford and Ivor back home safe. She would do anything for that.

'Tell him there's stew,' Frank was calling out. 'And Mrs Horton made it – not Miss Newton!'

'Tell him we miss him,' Trevor shouted. She could hear the relief in their voices. Perhaps the older ones knew what was at stake even if the younger ones didn't seem to.

Gladys called out, 'I love him.'

Peg came over with a note. 'Jonfan is best runer in the word.'

Clara shushed them. She had to hear what he was about to say. She put her hand out but they carried on yabbering.

'Stop!' she called, firmly now. 'I need to hear.'

'Miss Newton,' Jonathon said, a strained voice from the neighbouring county, 'I lost him, I lost Mr Delaney.'

'It wasn't your fault, dear,' she told him, trying to hide her horror. 'You didn't lose him.' She wanted to ask a million questions but right now, Jonathon needed reassurance and she gave it the best she could.

She told the children to go back to bed and helpfully, Mrs Horton hustled them upstairs so Clara could devote herself to the poor boy.

As he told her what had happened, she could hear he was trying not to cry. That brave, brave boy, who wouldn't even let her hold his hand.

Jonathon explained that the three of them had been stranded on a roof for some time when a girl in a rowing boat, a teenage girl, Mona – no, what was her name...? – came along.

'Go on,' implored Clara.

'We took the rowing boat three times. We picked up other people from other roofs. The boat was big enough, but only just. We had to go backwards and forwards. It was pitch-black.' Jonathon spoke almost as though he still couldn't believe it. 'Freezing. We couldn't see the water for the sky. And then we said we'd have to stop, we were all exhausted, but...' Here, his voice trailed off.

'Carry on,' Clara said. 'Please.'

'But Ivor said he'd go one last time – for a dog.' Jonathon took a deep breath and then finished. 'He told us to wait but we waited and waited and he didn't come back.'

A dog, a silly dog. He had gone back for a dog. Of all things.

'He'll be cuddled up somewhere safe, don't you worry, Jonathon,' Clara told him, yet even as she was saying it, she thought, *I have no idea what's happened to Ivor. I have no idea what's going on there or how terrible it is.*

'What was he wearing?' she asked, suddenly alert to how cold Ivor might be.

'His big coat,' Jonathon said, sounding as though his own teeth were chattering.

'Well then,' Clara said, like that proved something.

But then she heard Clifford's voice from further away. 'No, he gave his big coat to me, didn't he? He's only wearing a jumper.'

She couldn't get any reassurance from this.

'Go and get something hot to eat,' she said. Jonathon sniffed, said there was potato soup. She knew it wasn't a favourite.

'Stay in touch. Ivor will... be fine.'

How do you keep something like this from the children?

You can't. On the upstairs landing, Patricia was sobbing. Peg was stroking a shell like it had magical powers. Gladys put her arm round Patricia. 'I love you!' she told her.

Frank and Trevor were staring at Clara, wide-eyed.

'What's happening then?' asked Trevor.

Frank summarised for his older brother: 'A. They've found Jonathon but B. They haven't found Ivor yet.'

Clara remembered how these two boys in particular had endured much in the past and she told herself she wouldn't let this break them. It wouldn't be the final straw – they wouldn't suffer from whatever this was. They had suffered too much already.

'Boys! Clifford and Jonathon are safe! This is excellent news! And we'll hear more soon,' she promised. 'Now hop-skip to bed.'

They looked at each other, unsure whether to resist or not.

'Things always look brighter in the morning,' Clara continued briskly. 'Night, night. Sleep tight.'

'Don't let the bedbugs bite,' they chorused.

She thought they might realise that her heart had broken, but they appeared not to.

17

Downstairs, Clara drank a glass of whisky with Mr and Mrs Horton, who had brought two bottles. Her teeth were chattering like wind-up toy ones from a Christmas cracker. She couldn't help but think how she had been in this position before; she had once been waiting for news about Michael – but surely this couldn't end the same way, not again?

'Ivor will be all right,' Clara whispered, more to herself than the Hortons.

'Course he will,' Mr Horton said, heartily. He had taken the back off the wireless again and was peering into it. 'Does he swim?'

Does Ivor swim? For Christ's sake!

'Uh, not well – he hasn't since... his arm.'

Mr Horton spoke into the box. 'I'd forgotten that. He copes so well, doesn't he? It's almost like he's got four limbs.'

Clara thought of the freezing temperature of the water.

Clara needed something to do. Nothing that involved thinking – not letter-writing or reading – perhaps it was time to start crocheting or knitting? She should do something with her hands to keep them busy. Was it her old friend Nellie who had suggested that Clara was afraid Ivor would die – like Michael had – and that was why she'd taken so long to accept his proposal? She hadn't been, at least not consciously. The world was a different place now; she couldn't fail to notice that. Ivor was a different man to Michael, and she was different to wartime Clara. It also seemed like Ivor had already had his own magnificently awful brush with death at Dunkirk – hadn't he done enough for one lifetime?

She *hadn't* suspected he would die – but now it occurred to her that perhaps that was why this was happening. She hadn't been suitably grateful, careful or superstitious. She hadn't knocked on enough wood or kept her fingers crossed.

She had thought they would get married and love each other forever; only now did she dare consider that that might not happen.

'I'll take Ivor's wireless back to the workshop if mine's okay now,' she told the Hortons after they'd all finished their whiskies. She wished their expressions were a little less alarmed.

'I won't be long,'

'There's no hu—' started Mrs Horton.

'I want it to be perfect for him. For when he gets home.'

She saw them look at each other as if sharing an unspoken agreement: *Best not to argue.* Really, she needed to get out of the home again, with its pressing air of dread and her feeling of being trapped.

She took the key from the toby jug and walked over the road. She let herself in to what she'd come to regard as her 'other home'. They had shared many times here, loving times, funny times, bad times too, she was not ready to accept it might be over. Ivor was not lost, was he?

The telescope was in its usual place at the back wall. This cosy area with its curtains and cushions where they sat, sometimes

still glowing with intimacy. She unscrewed the end of the telescope – she had become adept at it – and looked out. Focus, unfo-
cus, blurry, unblur. It was like memory, perhaps.

Clara imagined Ivor was with her, guiding her through the
night sky as he had done all those times before. As she stared at
the shining lights she thought for a moment, *Ivor might be
watching them too*, which gave her comfort if just for a moment.

We are tiny, we are stardust.

Only next week, she would talk about this with the Jane
Taylor Society. Oh God, she should cancel that, shouldn't she?
No, she couldn't cancel. Ivor wouldn't want her to cancel. She
didn't want to cancel. She had to occupy herself – she would go
mad otherwise.

She put the end on the telescope before tidying up a little – a
mug here, a thread of cotton there. Ivor was not messy but not tidy
either There was a yellow cardigan of Patricia's knitted by Mrs
Horton, a train ticket, a drawing.

Then she saw it: a piece of paper with a handwritten phone
number on it. She knew she couldn't take it, shouldn't take it, but
she did memorise the number. It was easy enough to remember:
58 – her father's age when he died, 40 – her mother's age, 34 –
Ivor's age.

There was no name – but the absence of the name told her
exactly whose number it was.

18

Before long, Clara was back at Shilling Grange and Mr and Mrs Horton were waiting for her in the hall. In their winter coats, hats and scarves, they looked like scared refugees waiting for resettlement. She felt terrible for making them wait for her and ashamed for how snappy she had been with them. They weren't the bad guys here.

Mrs Horton senior couldn't be left for long and they had had to arrange a neighbour to come in to see to her and feed her supper. 'She doesn't eat a lot...'

'I'll be back tomorrow morning, Clara,' Mrs Horton added gently.

'There's no need,' Clara responded mechanically before saying, 'Thank you, though, thank you, you've been most kind.'

'I'll help with the children,' Mrs Horton added.

'They've got school,' Clara continued, but Mrs Horton seemed to ignore this.

'Obviously, if you hear anything, call us, any time, day or night.'

'I will,' promised Clara.

And...' Mrs Horton took a breath. 'You need to rest – go to bed.'

Clara wasn't going to bed; she didn't think sleep would come tonight. Her first thought was, bizarrely, to tidy up the shed; but then, she mightn't hear the telephone out there so she tidied up the parlour instead.

And still the telephone did not ring again.

Finally, settling in the armchair, she took off her shoes. She was that exhausted, she couldn't bring herself to put the shoes away just yet. Her stockinged feet looked strange. Then she realised she had her usual Sunday night to-do list to make for the week ahead. It usually made her feel in control but it didn't today. Yet she would still do it, of course she would. Obligations were made to be fulfilled.

It felt like she was trying to remember something, but she didn't know what exactly. She wrote down the number she'd found. She didn't want to put a name to it yet. Focus. Refocus. She felt like she was trying to pick out the best shells on the beach but the only ones she picked up were too cracked or weren't even shells at all.

She remembered saying goodbye to Ivor on the telephone, so casually.

And then there was the question Mr Horton had brought up. Could Ivor still swim? Rationally she knew it wasn't just about swimming – it was the cold that got you, or getting tangled up in something out there – but still, before he lost his arm, he could swim so...

The question reminded Clara about a mission she had started last autumn. She had read a news story: how few children could swim and what a disgrace that was 'for an island nation'. She had taken all the children to the lido in Ipswich and watched as they lined up, goosepimpled, before someone blew a whistle at them. Frank couldn't stand to be shouted at – and Trevor, who loved a bath, couldn't bear to be the weakest at anything. And Gladys and

Peg had woollen costumes that retained all the water. But she had stuck at it until they could at least all doggy-paddle.

She couldn't bear thinking about Ivor out there all alone. Was he stuck in a car in a flooded street, trapped in a room as the water rose? She imagined his lovely body floating in cold water, some upside-down world of broken furniture and parts of cars, and she pictured his beautiful watchful eyes now blankly open, seeing nothing.

And if the worst had happened, what might his last thoughts have been? This she knew. In fact, she was unshakeably convinced: Ivor would have thought of her and Patricia. He had loved them both dearly.

About one in the morning, Clara was still not asleep when she heard a cry from the girls' room. Peg? No, this time it was Patricia. Clara ran in to soothe her before she woke the others up. Children *sense things*. They just do. You can try to fob them off but they get a feeling when something's wrong.

Stella knew too. For once, she was sleeping curled up like a cinnamon bun on the end of Peg's bed. Clara sneezed. Oh God. She didn't like her being in the bedrooms usually, but tonight was anything but usual. Eventually Patricia settled and Clara snuck away.

She must have fallen asleep because, the next thing she knew, Peg came into her bed and wrapped herself around her. It was four in the morning. She had to get some sleep, or she would be a disaster tomorrow. One night's poor sleep was fine, several in a row was not.

He couldn't possibly be dead.

Clara was back, back in time to Christmas Eve 1944. Memories of the night Michael died. Well, the night she was told he was missing. It was around six o'clock, but it had already been dark for two or three hours. It was the time of year when it feels darker for longer than it is light; and it also felt like it had been dark for years. Things were run-down, people were run-down, but still they persevered, and little things made a difference. A candle. A rose. A soft pair of gloves.

The thing she never told anyone was: Even before the telegram came – she knew it. She already knew it. She was supposed to spend the next day with Judy and her family. She loved Christmas with Judy's family. Her parents were sweet and interested. Her brothers were fun and charming. The food was out of this world.

She didn't tell them why she wasn't coming; she pretended she was poorly. But she just wanted one day by herself to process the news. She knew the next day all hell would break loose. She needed to acclimatise. Everything had been taken from her, and it was agony.

Now here she was less than ten years later and she had lost another man. Or had she? She didn't know it for sure now like she had then. With Michael, she had filled in the spaces like putting down the letters in a crossword – she had worked out that impossible but definite answer. This was abstract: Ivor was missing, unaccounted for. Did she and Ivor not have the same connection or had she missed a sign? Why didn't she know?

EASTERN DAILY PRESS

Monday 2 February 1953

Survivors' Stories

Many of the families whose children would have been at the party lived on South Beach Road, Hunstanton, which initially bore the brunt of the water.

Although Mr Quincy's house avoided the worst of the flooding, his wife and three daughters still needed rescuing.

Mr Quincy, who had been working, made his way to the lower part of the town where the 67th Squadron were already on scene, trying to help.

He managed to get on board a rescue vessel.

'It was pitch-dark, gale blowing, the spray from the waves was like a handful of shingle in your face,' he said.

'All of those who died were dead by eight o'clock that evening.'

As the rescue boat reached Mr Quincy's bungalow, it was swamped by a wave, but he and the crew jumped to safety.

Mr Quincy, his wife, two daughters and nine-month-old son were eventually rescued by US Airman Reis Leming, who helped 27 people from the floods that night.

'I owe a debt of thanks to all of those people,' said Mr Quincy. 'We were the only complete family that survived.'

19

For a blissful half-second when Clara woke up, it was a beautiful day, a better day. A diamond-sky morning, a day you would want to get your teeth into. And then she remembered, leaping out of bed as she did: she had to find Ivor.

'I don't want to go to school,' Peg wrote, yawning at the kitchen table.

'You are going to school,' Clara said as she put breakfast in front of all the children. She needed them out of the way more than ever before.

Even Frank was crying over his bread. 'A. I feel sad. B. What is happening?'

Clara couldn't handle him now. But she had to.

'Don't feel sad,' she reassured him.

'Nothing's happened.' Trevor said. He wouldn't meet Clara's eye.

She burned the porridge and Gladys refused to eat it. Clara wanted to throw down her spoon too. She had no patience for this!

Clifford and Jonathon were all right. She had to be grateful and pleased for that. But Ivor was still unaccounted for. Unaccounted for meant nothing. You try 'missing in action'. That's the bad one. 'Unaccounted for' means no one's counted you.

She listened to the fixed wireless as she cleared up the half eggshells, the ends of the toast, the crumbs.

A rising toll of numbers of dead? It took her back to the war.

The Queen had expressed condolences. The prime minister was deeply saddened. One mayor was angry about sea defences. One mother said she was lucky to be alive. Tilbury had it bad – roads turned to rivers. Lowestoft got off lightly, the presenter said. There was no mention of Hunstanton yet, but she couldn't bear to listen any more. She turned off the wireless and the room was flooded with silence.

Clara decided she would walk the younger children to school and then, when she got back, there would be news. A watched kettle never boils. There was no point waiting for it.

At the school gates, no one looked at Clara strangely or asked if things were all right. The Lavenham grapevine clearly hadn't kicked in yet, which was a relief. Clara knew she'd burst into tears if anyone mentioned anything to do with Ivor or the flood.

One mother said that the drains had burst, and Clara made a sympathetic murmur. Another said that her girls had chilblains and she wished the school wouldn't let them sit near the radiators. Miss Fisher came out and clapped her hands. She looked severe as ever and she didn't give Clara a second glance: she hadn't heard.

Patricia was singing, 'Jack and Jill go up the hill to fetch a pal of water...'

'Pail,' corrected Gladys.

'I said that,' insisted Patricia. 'What's a crown?' She tugged on Clara's sleeve.

'Head.'

'Why she tumbling after?'

Clara took a breath. If she could get through this morning, then all would be well. 'She was worried about Jack, I expect.'

She must not fall. She must not tumble.

Peg, Gladys and Frank eventually sauntered off. Frank and Gladys were gassing as usual.

'Did you hear about the floods?' A scrawny boy ran up to Frank, who responded by pushing him in the small of his back and replying, 'Aston Villa. Aston Villa.' Clara couldn't help but have mixed feelings at how quickly children appeared to move on.

When Clara got back home the telephone was not ringing and the light in the workshop opposite was not on. Might he have got home and be sleeping, with the light off? She went over there – let herself in, called his name out, just in case.

She touched the surfaces he touched; she washed up the cup he drank from. Nothing. Not yet. That paper with the number on was still in the drawer, like a siren calling to her, a mermaid that might dash you against the rocks.

She thought about taking Patricia to the Norland Nanny's but they weren't expecting her, so instead she set the girl up in the parlour with some marbles. Before long, Patricia was lying on her front, telling off the marbles for being naughty.

'You think that's acceptable, do you?' Then in a softer voice she said, 'Too many cooks spoil the broth. Aunty Clara, what's broth?'

Patricia was oblivious to what was going on, thank goodness. Sometimes she burst into rhyme about blind mice or trips to the Queen. Clara's heart ached at the thought of the maelstrom that might be heading her way soon – and might last for the rest of her life. *Might.*

The telephone rang. At last, surely, this was Ivor telling her he was safe and that she had been silly to worry. She raced for it; but it was only Mrs Horton.

'Any news?' Mrs Horton asked before Clara had even breathed a hello.

'Please don't ask me, I'd tell you if there was,' Clara said flatly. The disappointment was immense, shattering. She had been certain it was Ivor. She was going to scold him. *I told you, you shouldn't stay!* Had she? She might have said it in passing, but she hadn't made a thing of it.

'I should get off the phone,' she said weakly. 'As soon as I hear something the whole world will know, I promise.'

Poor Mrs Horton sounded guilty when she said, 'Sorry, I won't call again.'

And then Clara told her. 'Mrs Horton, I-I think I'm going to tell Ruby that Ivor is missing...' She was nearly tripping over her words.

'Ruby?' Mrs Horton said loudly, clearly shocked. 'But why?'

'Because if he's... if he's not coming back then she needs to know.'

Patricia was not hers. It wasn't coincidence she had found the note. It was a sign from the stars. Clara knew it was the right thing to do.

'Where do they stand legally? Ivor and Ruby, I mean,' Mrs Horton continued.

'I have no—'

'I just expected... If anything happened to him you'd take Patricia on – no, I mean – I think he'll be fine. It's only been...'

'Thirty-six hours,' Clara said, aware of every minute that was passing.

After she'd hung up, Clara thought about having a cigarette, then decided to wait until she got the call to Ruby over with. The cigarette would be her reward for doing so. And she would do it now, before she changed her mind.

585434.

Clara finally dialled – and when the person picked up, her suspicion was confirmed. When it came to Ruby, her instincts were invariably correct. Ivor never talked about Ruby. He hated talking about her. She was a dark shadow that followed him around; in some lights you couldn't see her, but in others she was bolder and bigger than anything that was real; she was his other life. His early life, the ties that pulled you back. Children in care may have especially strong bonds with each other, the experts said.

Sometimes Clara sensed Ruby was there in a room with them. He had loved her once. For a long time. Love like that makes an impression, an indentation on your skin. He had loved her twice. He never said he loved Clara more than Ruby. He never claimed he loved Clara first. He never said he didn't love her best. She wasn't jealous – usually.

But this was not about Ivor. This was about Patricia.

The voice that answered was a posh woman's voice – it didn't sound how she expected, but still Clara recognised it.

'Ruby?' she asked quietly, as though she was scared someone might hear her saying the name.

'Who's speaking, please?' said the voice, less upper-class now, more guarded.

'It's Miss Newton from Shilling Grange, it's about Ivor. Ivor Delaney,' she added, as if there was another Ivor in their worlds.

The line went silent and then sounded muffled, as though Ruby was covering the receiver with the palm of her hand. She was telling someone in the room with her that the call was a mistake. A wrong number. And then she was back, speaking into the receiver, clear as cut glass.

'There's no one here by that name, thank you,' she trilled, but, before Clara could say anything, she added in a low voice, 'I'll call you back.'

20

Clara washed up the bowls of porridge and scrubbed at the burnt saucepan; if she'd dealt with it sooner, it would have been easier – there was a lesson in that, she thought – and then went up to check the beds.

If Ivor called now, she would never again complain that he worked too much. If he called now, she would resign from the home. She would be like Mrs Horton, she would run around with cake tins and saucepans of soup. She would be a mentor to the new housemother. She would be the most devoted wife in the world. She would not let Ivor out of her sight ever again.

And if Ruby called now, she'd just stick to the facts. Thirty-six hours. Thirty-seven hours and a half to be precise. *Unaccounted for.* Make of that what you will. Clara wouldn't tell her what to do or what to think.

She discovered that Peg AND Frank had wet their beds. She always asked them to tell her in the morning – she wouldn't be angry – but they never did. Frank's pyjama bottoms were screwed up down one side of the bed, and Peg's nightdress was under hers.

The telephone rang and Clara ran for it. It still could be Ivor... but that dream was dashed as soon as she picked up.

'What do you want?' This time Ruby sounded entirely different. She sounded like a young woman from a Suffolk orphanage.

Clara took a while to reply. There was time to change her approach; but she had decided on this:

'It's Ivor.' She took a deep breath. She hadn't imagined Ruby would call back. She hadn't ever imagined talking to Ruby.

'And?'

'He's missing.'

'What... what kind of missing?'

Were there different kinds of missing? Yes, she supposed there were. Serious missing. Not really missing.

She didn't know the answer. 'In the floods. In Norfolk.'

'I'm sure he's fine.' Ruby sniffed, and the sniff said everything.

'He might not be.'

Cats have nine lives – humans don't. People who haven't lost someone struggle to understand this.

'I don't know why you called,' Ruby said, sounding frustrated.

'I just thought you should know.'

Could the woman not read between the lines? Her daughter, *her* daughter was here. What was supposed to happen to her if Ivor didn't come back?

'He is still unaccounted for.'

There was something about the cold bureaucracy of the statement that she felt suited Ruby more.

There was a pause. When Ruby spoke again her voice was shrill. 'What was he doing there then?'

'He was helping me,' Clara said. She would not cry with Ruby, she wouldn't. 'One of my boys was in trouble.'

Only Clifford was not even her boy, was he? He hadn't been her boy since last year. If she'd cut the apron strings, then none of this would have happened. If she hadn't gone poking around in other people's business, Ivor wouldn't have been dragged into this.

'That's not his job, is it?' Ruby asked, seeming to pick up on Clara's guilt.

Clara noticed Patricia standing in the doorway. She was looking over at Clara curiously. She had a great sense for anything out of the ordinary. Her eyes narrowed.

'No, it's not his job.'

'Why are you telling me this? I've got a new husband. He knows nothing about my old life, the baby. And I want things to stay that way.'

Not all people are up to being mothers.

'I don't know what you want me to do with this information.' Ruby sounded exasperated. As if she were a teacher and Clara was a student who had let her down.

Patricia opened her mouth wide, then launched into song: 'One, two, three, four, five. Once I caught a fish alive.'

'Ssshh, not now,' Clara said.

'What was that?' Ruby asked, suddenly sounding softer.

'Nothing,' said Clara. If she could go back in time, she wouldn't have called. 'I just thought you'd want to know,' she repeated. Patricia continued singing.

'Six, seven, eight, nine, ten. Then I threw it back again.'

Clara wasn't going to spell it out for the woman. Didn't she see? If Ivor was missing, truly missing, Patricia was hers.

'Why did you let it go? Because it bit my finger so.'

'I'm sure you know, Ivor is one of life's great survivors,' Ruby said resentfully. 'He knows how to save his own skin. We both do. Growing up in Shilling Grange tends to do that to you.' She said that in such a cold and brittle way.

'Which finger did it bite? This little finger on my right.' Patricia finished triumphantly.

Clara didn't know what Ruby meant but she knew it was a howl of rage at something.

'Anyway, I'll get there when I can,' Ruby said breezily. She sounded like she was making a casual arrangement to go shopping, not to see her abandoned daughter.

Clara felt herself retract. *Don't be afraid to retreat*, she remembered Trevor saying. But this *was* a mistake. This was a wrong number.

21

After lunch, Clara took Patricia to Anita's house. The Norland Nanny had her hands full with Howard, who was shrieking about a tree or perhaps a treat. Patricia took the nanny's hand and walked away with her to the playroom. It was odd how obedient Patricia was with her, as though she recognised the young woman's authority in a way she didn't recognise Clara's.

Clara would have liked to have dropped and run but Anita called her in. She was in her lounge, at the piano, and she wanted to talk wedding music. Had Clara decided anything yet?

Clara replied truthfully that she hadn't had a moment to think.

'I do think Evelyn should play the violin at the church or at the party – I know she's shy, but it will help bring her out of herself.'

Clara nodded. She wasn't taking it in, she was replaying the conversation with Ruby in her head: '*I don't know what you want me to do with this information.*' Ruby was a cold fish and no mistake. No wonder she and Ivor hadn't worked out.

'Anything wrong, Clara?' said Anita, suddenly concerned. 'You're paler than usual. And your hair!'

Clara pressed a hand to her hair. Yes, maybe it was more dishevelled than usual. She couldn't tell Anita about Ivor yet. She wasn't ready to tell – it would make it even more real.

'Just worn out,' Clara said, hoping to end the conversation there.

Anita clutched her arm. 'You haven't got the wedding jitters again, have you?'

The way she said *again* hurt.

Clara hurried home. She wanted just a little more time before everyone knew. A few more hours of normality before the circus descended. And it would – she knew it would.

But perhaps there was a chance Ivor was all right? She would wait to hear. She hadn't even had time to unbutton her coat when the telephone sang out just as she had begged it to, but again it wasn't Ivor – it was Marilyn's voice, Marilyn with her fortnightly call. Marilyn liked to keep up with all Clara and the children's escapades.

The surge of disappointment that went through Clara was so powerful that this time she couldn't hold back the tears.

'Oh, Marilyn,' she whispered. Here was another woman who knew grief, their shared grief. 'I can't go through this again.'

They spent ten minutes on the telephone, maybe more: several times the operator asked her if they wanted to extend the call, and each time Marilyn said she did. It must have been a shock to her, but she recovered quickly, and said many supportive things. Talking to her, Clara felt she was rebuilt from the foundations up. 'Take all offers of help,' Marilyn advised. 'Don't be too proud.' And Marilyn was right – whatever would be, would be, and she would cope, she absolutely would.

. . .

There was no other news. The unaccounted-for hours were stacking up, blocks into tall shaky towers. They were approaching forty now. When Clara came back from school with the children later that afternoon, Maureen was in the kitchen. *Maureen!* She had put the kettle on and was peeling potatoes, her face shiny with tears.

'How did you know to come?'

Maureen wiped her cheeks. 'Mrs Horton called me. Sister Grace is away so I said I'd help instead.'

'She shouldn't have. You shouldn't have! What about your studies?'

'It's fine,' she said briskly; everything was fine with Maureen until it wasn't.

Maureen's hair was bleached white again – and was it Clara's imagination or had she grown taller and bustier? She wore outfits that were both fashionable and expensive-looking, thanks to Ivor. They made her seem more confident than she was.

What would Maureen do if she didn't have Ivor as her personal dressmaker?

Clara asked, 'You'll be able to catch up?'

'I'm advanced in typing,' Maureen said, and she wasn't boasting, she was just being matter of fact. Young women often were nowadays, Clara found, and she found it refreshing. When she was young it was all deportment, holding yourself back and 'nobody likes a show-off'.

It was important to blow your own trumpet, especially if you didn't have a family to do that for you. And Maureen certainly didn't. Her mother was dead, and her father was in jail for killing her. You didn't get much more of a troubled start than that.

'And I'll never be skilful at shorthand, it's like a foreign language, so I'm not worried about that.'

'Then thank you, Maureen.'

'I'm here to keep the children occupied until...'

Maureen seemed to realise that 'until' was a road to nowhere, so she muttered something and then busied herself with the potato skins and the caddy.

Clara thought for a moment and then got the tea tray out – the present from Maureen – and it worked; Maureen was delighted to see it. 'I'm glad you use it.'

'Use it? I love it,' said Clara sincerely.

At five, Mrs Horton was at the front door with another dish. This time it was macaroni cheese, and Clara felt nauseous at the smell of it. This was food for invalids.

'You didn't need to – the children have already eaten. Maureen...' She trailed off.

'It's for tomorrow,' Mrs Horton said. 'I can't stay – Mrs Horton senior is distressed by the floods.'

Then, 'Clara,' she went on in a low voice so no one else could hear, and Clara realised that what she was about to say was the real reason she had come, not the hastily whipped-up dish.

'I don't think you should get in touch with Ruby. I think you should wait, at least. There is no point inviting trouble in, as it were. I don't think Ivor would want that either – you know how he feels about her.'

'Mmm,' said Clara, turning away. She didn't deliberate for long about whether to tell Mrs Horton she already had. She was feeling exhausted again. 'I get your point.'

Not long after Mrs Horton had left, the Norland Nanny brought Patricia back. The woman stood on the doorstep, even more sombre-faced than usual, and Clara instantly knew that she knew. The nanny muttered that she was 'awfully sorry to hear the news...'

So the Lavenham Grapevine had sprung to life and she had

heard Ivor was missing, which meant Anita would have too, which meant Clara could expect a visit from her soon.

'Bad news travels fast.'

Clara thanked her.

'I always say *no news is good news.*'

'Of course you do.'

'Can I do anything to help?'

Tempting as it was to beg her to look after Patricia, now, again, forever, Clara just shook her head. 'We're managing, thank you.'

'Many hands make light work,' the nanny offered, her eyes lowered.

'That's right...' Clara was thinking, thank goodness for Maureen, who was now letting Gladys and Peg climb all over her while Gladys recited countries beginning with F. 'Finland, France,' and 'if Fingamijig isn't a country, it jolly well should be.'

The nanny said she'd see Patricia at eight in the morning, which was a relief; but, as she was closing the door, Clara realised she didn't know how she was paid – could she afford her? – and called out.

'It's all right, Mrs Cardew is covering it, until...' she said, then looked awkward, realising she didn't know how to finish the sentence.

'I see,' said Clara. Another until. 'Thank you.'

Then Miss Webb arrived, and it seemed it was in a friend capacity rather than a professional capacity, although you could never be sure with Miss Webb. She had brought dessert grapes, which, while delightful, gave Clara more of that *invalid* feeling. Miss Webb said she had been to church, lit a candle for Ivor and said a prayer. Although the vicar had said yesterday that he would do that, that was his job, and Clara couldn't help but feel Miss Webb was overstepping slightly. Ivor is not dead, she wanted to say, but Miss Webb didn't mean that; she said God would save him.

Clara felt grateful that the evening fell early, putting an end to such a miserable day. Miss Webb wanted to drink tea but Clara was too much on edge to sit, so she left her in the kitchen and went to help Maureen organise the children. It was while she was doing so that, out of the landing window, she saw what she had been dreading.

There was a police car outside.

22

The children leapt to the front window and Frank started nee-nawing and zooming around the room like his pants were on fire.

Clara hoicked Patricia up onto her hip and went to open the door, with Maureen close behind her. Miss Webb was a sentry next to her. Clara could feel the tension of the women around her. Miss Webb was laughing softly to herself. Clara knew that she laughed when she was nervous – a defence mechanism – yet she still found it hard to hear.

Two police officers stood on the orphanage steps, both tall and imposing. One of them was PC Banks, who Clara had had deal-ings with last year and had hoped never to see again.

'Miss Newton?'

He took his helmet off and put it under his arm – it reminded her of a picture of a ghost with a ruffle but without a head in another of the children's picture books – but Clara wasn't watch-ing; her eyes were on the car. A figure was emerging from the back. Then another.

Jonathon.

And Clifford.

She had thought Jonathon might be brought back soon, yet

had not expected Clifford. But then he could hardly go back to the Reform School, could he?

Both of them were in fuzzy blankets and odd clothes that didn't hang right. Jonathon was holding a brown paper bag. Clifford was clutching shoes. His hair was slicked back, oily – he'd never looked more like a gangster – while Jonathon, oh, poor Jonathon, looked like he'd just been hung out on the line to dry.

Sweeping past the policemen, Clara rushed out and hugged him. 'Thank heavens you're safe.'

'They're okay,' called the policeman who wasn't PC Banks. 'Only mild hypothermia. They insisted they didn't want to go to the hospital.'

Jonathon shrugged. He didn't look like a boy who would ever insist on anything. Clara thought of him running away. That would all have to be dealt with at some stage but not now. She would have hugged Clifford, but he stuck his hand out for her to shake instead.

'Can't get rid of me, can you?' he said with a shy grin.

'I'm pleased to see you,' she said, and she meant it – until just moments later, when she saw him eyeing Maureen up and down with that all-too-familiar smirk over his face.

Clifford never changed.

Okay, there was a spare bed in the boys' room – Clifford could go in there.

'Did they tell you what happened?' the other policeman asked. He told her his name several times and on the final attempt, she understood he was Sergeant Worsley. PC Banks was in the parlour, talking in hushed tones with Miss Webb.

'Not everything, no,' Clara said, searching her memory for her conversation with Jonathon on the wireless, which felt like years ago, not just yesterday.

It seemed that a girl in a rowing boat came along and, rather than go to safety themselves, Ivor, Jonathon and Clifford took it in turns to rescue several people – they saved up to four families who were waiting on roofs to be rescued. And then Ivor went to look for a dog.

'Do you understand what this means?'

Clara didn't. Jonathon did one of his Jonathon shrugs. The children all looked at him expectantly. No, not all of them – Clifford was pontificating loudly to Maureen: 'I'm not joking, it was like a wall of sea, like a monster. And I thought I was going to die.'

Was he spicing it up for her? No, for once Clara didn't think he was exaggerating.

'It means they're heroes!' exclaimed Sgt Worsley. He clapped Jonathon on the back – Jonathon shrank under his ministrations – and then the sergeant did the same to Clifford, who nodded, even more pleased with himself than usual.

'He said it,' Clifford said, and grinned at Maureen and then winked at Clara. 'Can't argue with the Old Bill.'

Gladys and Peg squealed and hugged Jonathon and he let them, laughing nervously. Clara felt a lump in her throat. Amazing news – but what about Ivor? Had everyone forgotten him?

'This calls for more tea!' she managed.

She put Mrs Horton's macaroni cheese out on the table and the boys tucked in like they'd been famished. Sgt Worsley looked at it longingly, so she told him to help himself.

'Shouldn't,' he said.

But PC Banks came in and dished himself up a large serving.

'You're a woman of many talents, Miss Newton,' he said, and Miss Webb giggled.

'I don't think anyone has said that about your cooking before, have they, Miss Newton?' She couldn't help herself.

Later, Clara left the room and PC Banks followed, grabbing her by the elbow.

'What on earth was Mr Delaney doing there?' he whispered.

She was taken aback by his ferocity. This seemed a cruel question: it wasn't Ivor's fault.

'He went back to...'

'Stupid thing to do. That's *our* job.' There was something about the way he said it that made him sound almost envious. 'But I mean what was he doing in Hunstanton anyway?'

'He was helping Clifford,' Clara said, a flush spreading all the way through her.

'Clifford isn't one of yours.'

'He was...'

It wasn't even her job. Oh, Ivor.

'Mr Delaney shouldn't have been there,' PC Banks said as though Norfolk was out of bounds for Ivor and as though he alone were the final authority on the matter. 'He's only got one arm.'

It was on the tip of Clara's tongue to say something sarcastic – 'Has he? I thought he had six,' – but she didn't.

'He created more work for us professionals.'

Later, as usual, many excellent retorts came to her. She was spoilt for choice, but right then, she was more concerned about getting away from him. Her first impressions of PC Banks had been correct.

'Thank you for your concern... Do you mind?'

He took his hand from her elbow, shaking his head disapprovingly.

Sgt Worsley had some paperwork he wanted to go through with Jonathon. He had already seen to Clifford.

'So it's Jonathon without the H? Let's have your surname then.'

Clara liked him more than she'd thought she would. He was nothing like his colleague.

'Pell. P.E.L.L.,' Jonathon spelled out automatically.

Sgt Worsley laid down his pen and gave Jonathon the reaction that Clara had seen many times before.

'Not Maurice Pell? The two-time Victoria Cross winner?'

Jonathon nodded.

'Well, well, well... The apple doesn't fall far from the—'

'Sometimes,' interrupted Clara briskly. She thought of Alex. And Maureen. 'And sometimes it falls miles away.'

Jonathon looked up, crestfallen. How stupid was she? Quickly she patted his arm, 'I didn't mean you.'

Sgt Worsley turned the page of his notebook. 'Forget about the apples. You did a great thing, son.'

The doorbell rang again and, just like that, Clara's hopes rose, even as she tried to be realistic. Miss Webb squealed, 'I'll get it,' but Clara was already there, Maureen right behind her once again. A man she couldn't quite place was on the step. Brylcreemed hair, bow tie; he was as shiny as a coin with the new queen's face on it.

'Miss Newton?' There was something about the way he said her name that she didn't like. Maybe the way he made it sound like Nuuude-ton. 'You came last week about hire of the hall? For a wedding?'

Maureen looked stricken. Clara opened her mouth, but nothing came out.

'The deposit was due on Friday.'

Clara could feel everyone behind her waiting for her reaction: Maureen, Miss Webb, Jonathon, Clifford, even PC Banks.

'I forgot. Can I bring it in a few days?'

'Not really,' he said, looking around him. 'Lot of people here – you having a party?'

It was Maureen who spoke first. 'Is it refundable?'

Brylcreem man didn't seem to like that. The grin disappeared fast as a rabbit down a burrow. He spluttered a moment and then said, 'It's a deposit, we can't just...'

Clara felt sorry for him. After all, he didn't know what he'd just wandered into.

'Yes, of course, we'll pay.'

'Miss Newton,' warned Maureen. 'But what if...'

Clara was already galloping upstairs, heart pounding. She unlocked and opened the safe and took the money out. She and Ivor had budgeted for this, and this was something she could do. There weren't many things she had power over right now, but she had power over this. This was an act of faith. This proved that Ivor was coming home. They would be married at the end of May, come hell or high water.

She came back, buoyant, and counted precious pounds into his outstretched hand.

'One, two, three...'

'We'll need full payment by the end of the month.' He sniffed, although he seemed much cheered as he stuffed the notes in his wallet.

'Fantastic,' she said, her heart sinking. Who knew what her life would look like then?

'Next time you have a party,' he said, winking at her, 'give me a call.'

23

The policemen and the man from the Cloth Hall hadn't been gone long and it felt like Clara had no time to draw a breath before Anita turned up. She looked dramatic in fur coat and mannish trousers and, as always, with the string of pearls peeping out her blouse, and something about the whole glamorous sight of her annoyed Clara.

'We were at the theatre – I just heard – why didn't you tell me before, darling?'

Anita hugged Clara, engulfing her in her sweet perfume. Clara closed her eyes. She was so weary she could have fallen asleep there, resting her head on that fox fur or whatever it was.

'Ivor will be all right, Ivor is strong,' Anita crooned.

Clifford appeared at the top of the stairs and Anita let go of Clara.

'Sweetheart!' she called, opening her arms to him. He ran down, Anita further remonstrating that she should have heard earlier. Clara only then noticed that Evelyn was behind Anita. Evelyn was also dressed up, and she didn't look like her usual down-to-earth self but a far more sophisticated version. But then she gave a kind of helpless shrug, and that was the Evelyn Clara knew and loved, and then Evelyn took Clara's hand and squeezed it. That squeeze was everything. In fact, it was better by far than all the verbal reassurances Clara had received.

Clifford and Anita went into the kitchen and the rest followed. Clifford was rambling – it was the story he had told Maureen, only he changed some of it, so the flood was even worse, or he was even braver, and Anita gasped.

'Clifford, I am not surprised that you saved people. I always knew you were destined for greatness.'

And Clifford flushed right down to his spotty neck and said, 'Thank you, Mrs Cardew, that's high praise, especially coming from you.' And he was as meek and mild as anybody ever was.

Anita asked if Clifford was still practising his singing and he apologised, he hadn't really; and if it were anyone else, if it were Evelyn, Clara, Rita or Peg, she would have tsked and said, 'How do you expect to become brilliant?' Yet somehow, with Clifford, Anita was full of understanding.

Anita then insisted that Clara have a bath. She simply must. It would be beneficial for her. Miss Webb joined in, even though Clara had assumed Miss Webb had left. She was losing track of who was coming and going in the home.

'A few moments just to yourself!' Miss Webb piped up.

'It's a madhouse, darling, you won't regret it,' Anita trilled.

And then, when Clara demurred, since there was something about this enforced rest she didn't like, Anita backtracked. 'I don't mean madhouse in a bad way, Clara, I simply mean it's evident you need to rest.'

Clara finally submitted, and sank into the tin bath in the basement. It wasn't like the pristine modern bathroom in Anita's house. It wasn't at all comfortable and she didn't trust the lock on the door and there was no way she could really relax while the house was abuzz with people like this.

The only person she wanted to talk to now was Ivor. There was such a lot of news she wanted to tell him. All the stories were piling up, little observations or anecdotes that were waiting to be told, backed up, making him further away than ever: That Peg had prospective adopters who reminded her of guinea pigs. That they had secured the Cloth Hall – obnoxious greasy little man – all booked. (You do not want to know how much the deposit was, Ivor!) Clifford and Jonathon were unlikely heroes – although he'd already know that. Patricia was winning over everyone. Frank had been to a party and had a best friend! Trevor would lose his head if it wasn't screwed on, but was also experiencing his first crush.

And God, how much she missed him. He is only 'unaccounted for', Clara reminded herself as her fingers became creased or, as Gladys would say, 'raisiny'. Unaccounted for was nothing. Weren't we all unaccounted for at some stage or other?

He'd better not be gone, or she would kill him.

When Clara came back in the kitchen an hour later, in her dressing gown and with damp hair, Anita and Miss Webb were so deep in conversation that they didn't at first notice she was there. They were talking about her.

'Her mother. Then Michael. Then Judy—' Anita was counting on her fingers.

'I don't know about Judy,' Miss Webb interrupted.

'She was her best friend.'

Clara thought of Judy's sweet face. She *was* her best friend. She remembered laughing with Judy in her living room in London, falling asleep by the bars of her gas fire. She thought of Judy reassuring her that she was well-suited to working with children.

'Then her father in the air tragedy last year.'

'Of course...'

'And now Ivor...' Anita continued.

'That's a lot,' Miss Webb agreed.

'How do you recover from that?' pondered Anita.

Clara had heard enough.

'Recover from what?' she said loudly.

They both turned around with expressions as though they'd been caught red-handed, which they had. Clara scowled at them. She felt like a huge wall had suddenly gone up between them. Anita and Miss Webb were on the side of sanity and 'everything's all right' and 'can't complain', while here she was, stuck on the other side in a desolate land of terribleness.

'I thought you said Ivor would be all right. Ivor was strong, you said that...'

They looked frightened of her fury just then, but Clara couldn't help herself. She was enraged with everyone and everything – the storm, the flood, PC Banks – and, in that precise moment, she had never felt more alone in the world.

24

Shortly after Miss Webb had left, Dr Cardew had come by, briefly, to walk Anita home, and he had handed Clara some dusty white tablets in a tiny brown bottle, which were to help her sleep. Clara – torn between wanting to sleep until Ivor returned and never sleeping again – had declined them, but he had pressed the container into her palm.

'They're just in case, Miss Newton.'

Maureen washed up the cups and then made the beds up. Now Anita had left, Clifford was back to trying to impress her again. Clara worried. Maureen *wouldn't* be impressed by him, would she? She was older than him for a start – not that you could tell; Clifford looked mature for his tender years.

Clara also wanted to talk to Jonathon without the police there, without all the noise, without Clifford and his crowing. Jonathon said he wanted to go upstairs, and she walked with him out to the hall.

'Wait a moment,' she pleaded. 'You said – what happened with Ivor – the last time you...?'

'Ivor said he heard a dog. I couldn't hear anything though. Nor could Clifford.'

The damn dog he went back for wasn't even a real dog?

'We shouldn't have let him go back,' he said, 'but it was like he was possessed.' His face fell. Jonathon had never been a carefree boy but now he looked as worn as an old man. It was like he was possessed? Clara racked her mind – where had she heard that phrase before?

'You were courageous,' she said presently. She couldn't imagine the terror of it. 'I want you to know that – to remember that always.'

If he could hang on to that, when everything else was dark, it might make such a difference. Her children, the children of Shilling Grange, were nobodies' babies – it meant all those encouraging words, those reassurances were harder to find.

'Mr Delaney said the world is alarming and that all you can do is carry out acts of love and it's not right or wrong, it just is...'

'Ivor said that?' Clara responded, confused. Why would Ivor have said all this?

'It was the last thing he said to me.' Jonathon swallowed. It clearly made sense to him. Clara felt his pain. His foot was already on the bottom step when she asked what she had planned to ask him.

'Jonathon, wait; has this got – why did you decide to run away?'

He paused, the world on his narrow shoulders.

'I just didn't want to be here any more.'

There was more to it, she knew that, but Jonathon was slippery as an eel on this. He yawned and said could he please go up to bed.

The conversation with Jonathon wasn't the only one Clara kept repeating to herself later that evening. The conversation she'd had with Ruby was also whirring around in her head. What had she called Ruby for? She couldn't understand it. Why hadn't she stopped herself? Ivor would have stopped her...

Just twelve hours earlier she was absolutely certain that contacting Ruby was the right thing to do – the righteous thing – but now she knew it was wrong. It could not have been more wrong.

She was immersed in fear for Ivor and now it felt like a thick different layer of dread was also washing over and around her. It was like an inch of stupid shame covering every part of her. No one could see it, she was the only one who knew about it – but it was there.

Gladys and Peg were on the stairs, waiting for her to go up to bed.

'Miss Newton?'

'You two should be asleep.'

They handed over a picture of two figures. She knew one was her by the apron, and her hair, pulled back, with the fuzzy bits at her forehead. She was not that big-bosomed or wide-hipped – they had given her an actress's hourglass figure – and the picture-Clara was smiling. And she knew the other one was Ivor, for there was an absent arm and he had a big smile too, and his thick hair and his braces, and it was lovely.

In the picture, the sun was shining in the sky – it was a thick yellow circle with ray-like tentacles – and there were cotton-wool clouds and trees brimming with leaves. Only a few weeks ago, Ivor had taught them that you can draw a flying bird with just two lines only, a big flat M.

'We did it together,' Gladys said, while Peg nodded vigorously.

'You are too sweet.' Then Clara said it was bedtime again, but they didn't go but stared at her. Then Gladys nudged Peg and Peg flicked open her notepad.

'Is it are fault?'

Our?

'Why do you say that?' Clara asked. She didn't understand.

Gladys whispered, 'That Ivor is missing. Is it because we don't pray enough? We should pray more. Maybe Jesus forgot about us.'

'Jesus doesn't need you to remind Him about Ivor,' Clara said, and Gladys clearly thought about that, and then clutched Clara round the waist.

Peg was writing fiercely. 'Why does everyone we love die?'

And Clara could neither write anything, nor say anything to that.

Four tired little-girl eyes blinked at her.

'They don't,' was all Clara managed to say as she clutched both girls to her. 'I'm still here.'

<u>REPORT 17</u>
Ivor 'Humphrey' Delaney

Date of Birth:

Not sure.

Family Background:

Ivor is a foundling. He remembers being in Shilling Grange from the age of three or four. There are no notes from earlier.

Health/Appearance:

Handsome. Stocky. Dark hair. Dark eyes. He denies he looks like Humphrey Bogart but there is something there.

He only has one arm but he has the strength of three men.

Food:

Ivor's favourites are marble cake, coconut ice and broken biscuits. He doesn't like margarine but will eat it.

Cottage pie. Mrs Horton's tomato soup. Roast chicken.

Hobbies/Interests:

Ivor loves sewing, mending, rebuilding and fixing.

Other:

Oh, Ivor – I have loved you from the moment we met.

25

After an hour of tossing and turning in bed, Clara decided to take one of Dr Cardew's sleeping tablets, and was soon adrift. How many should she take? She was never good with medication. She even shied away from taking aspirin unless her monthly headaches were really bad.

Were you supposed to take two at a time? She took another one, just in case. She knew she should have eaten something today.

Soon, her mind started to wander – there would be a funeral to organise. So soon after her father's... Ivor had helped her with that and he wouldn't help her with this one – well, obviously. Who would have thought that only four months later she might be back to bury her fiancé? Who would have thought it wouldn't be a wedding at St Peter and St Paul's this spring, but a funeral?

There was a knocking at the front door. *Was it Ivor?* It didn't sound like his knock, and wouldn't he come to the back of the house? – but it could be. She was feeling woozy as she stumbled out of the bedroom. This was odd. She touched her face and realised she had cold cream on it. It was only eleven o'clock, but it felt much later. She passed a barefoot Gladys on the stairs.

'Is it him?' Gladys asked, rubbing her eyes.

'I don't know... Back to bed, sweetheart.'

Aware of every step on the floorboards – she knew which ones shrieked and which ones stayed silent – she made her way to the door. She was feeling most peculiar.

It must be. Ivor had come home. Ivor wouldn't care how she looked. Ivor was back. It felt like it took forever to unlock the front door, then she swung it open. 'I've been worried sick—'

It wasn't Ivor. It was Julian White, and, despite Clara's fuzziness, she could see he was drunk as a lord.

'I've got the address you wanted.'

'Oh, Julian, for goodness' sake,' she blurted. She couldn't hide her disappointment that it was him.

'What? Mrs Wesley from the next village. I thought you wanted to get in touch with her?'

'You haven't heard?'

Julian always knew everything.

'That you're getting married? Darling, believe me, it's the talk of the town.'

Clara's sigh was louder than she had intended. She stared up at Julian's familiar yet uncomprehending face.

'That Ivor is missing. In the floods.'

She could see horror creep across his features like a shadow.

'Nooo. I hadn't heard anything. I'm sorry. Let me in, Clara. I'll get frostbite out here.'

Clara stood in her flannel nightdress; her feet were cold on the doormat. She had, she thought, exceedingly pale feet, and blue veins, which stood out quite disconcertingly. She felt exposed – she might as well have been naked. She felt his eyes travel over her as though he was searching for something. She didn't know what to do, her mind was still sluggish, but he said in a voice far more gentle than usual:

'Let's have a nice cup of tea.'

She stumbled upstairs to put on her housecoat. Gosh, her

head was spinning. She couldn't find the belt – Patricia had been playing cats with it the other day: cats with long tails. She'd have to manage to hold it together. This was typical Julian! He must have swaying his way home after a few glasses at the Shilling Arms and thought he'd poke his nose in. It was aggravating. Or was it helpful to have some company? Everyone had been negative, even when they were trying to be positive; you could see it in their eyes – that was one thing you could say about Julian: he was an optimist. And why not? A charmed life makes you that way.

He sat down in the kitchen, pulling a school tie from down the chair with some curiosity. Yes, he was squiffy, which was unusual because, although he drank an awful lot, Julian usually held his drink well. Maybe it was good he was squiffy; Clara really didn't feel like herself either.

'I'm sorry, I upset you,' he slurred.

'Oh, that's Trevor's tie,' she remarked slowly. 'Well done. Thank you for finding it.'

'Your wish is my command.'

Despite his inebriation – or perhaps because of it – Julian was agreeable company, and Clara let herself succumb. She made a pot of tea, one-handed, holding her housecoat together, and he made jokes, and it was the distraction she hadn't realised she needed. He was an old friend in some ways. He was one of the first people she had met in Lavenham. That meant something.

She got the best china cups out for him.

Then he asked her what the police had said regarding Ivor.

'They don't know anything,' she said.

'There must be something they can do...'

Tears prickled at her eyes. This was mortifying, she had no self-control. Julian stood up, removed a handkerchief from his breast pocket and gave it to her with a magician's flourish. She took it, but her emotions wouldn't be contained in that cloth square. Soon she was sobbing. She had held the tears in when she was with Mrs Horton, Miss Webb, Anita, Dr Cardew, yet now look at her! She hated being a weeping willow, but the handkerchief was soon sodden.

'Come here,' Julian said, drunkenly or gruffly. Goodness, she was probably embarrassing him. He would no more want to be the comforter than she wanted to be the comforted –sometimes needs must. As she got up clumsily, the chair nearly fell over behind her.

She went into his arms like she was falling into place. Like a teacup slotting into a saucer. He clutched her and she let herself be held. He smelled of expensive alcohol and expensive lifestyle. He wasn't much taller than her, he fitted against her differently than Ivor had, but it was instantly familiar – it was as though her body remembered what to do.

He spoke into her hair. 'My darling girl, let me look after you.'

She was woozy because of those sleeping pills, although perhaps not as far gone as him, but she quickly sensed that something about the way he was stroking her back wasn't quite right. It was too much. Something about the way he was squeezing her to him, so that there was nothing between them, was too close. He wasn't her man.

'It's always been you,' Julian murmured into her ear before he placed his hand on her bottom.

'Julian! NO!'

'Oh, come on,' he mumbled. Teacup overwhelms saucer.

'I said...'

'Get out,' someone else said.

Suddenly there was a clonk and Julian collapsed in her arms, then slid down clumsily onto the kitchen floor.

26

Julian was out cold. Over his body, Clara saw who had done it.

'I heard a noise – I thought Ivor was back. And then I realised... I'm sorry.'

Trevor was standing there, trembling, holding Maureen's tea tray. Frank was just behind him, cowering with his hands over his mouth, in pyjamas that were, she realised absurdly, much too short for him. He was growing fast.

Clara tried to lift Julian up into the chair, but he was a dead weight. The boys somehow manoeuvred his bottom into it, his legs stretched out like stabilisers to the front. He was groaning as he came to. 'Oww... Uh – wha!'

'Go upstairs,' Clara hissed to the boys. 'Now! Quickly.'

They had to disappear. Clara knew exactly what Julian was like. They didn't come much more vengeful than him, the foxhunting tax expert.

He was blinking and groaning. As he revived, she knelt at his feet. Like Mary Magdalene, she thought. Oh God. This was terrible.

'Uh, I actually saw stars,' Julian was muttering.

'Stars?' said Clara brightly. 'Wow. What was that like?'

'Someone hit me...'

'You just had a tumble.'

'I didn't. I felt a crack on the back of my head.'

He looked around him, feeling his skull. *He's broken his crown*, thought Clara.

'And there's the malicious implement!' He pointed gleefully at the tea tray on the table. The etching of Queen Elizabeth and possibly a corgi innocently looked back at them.

Clara snorted. 'That's not a malicious implement. It's a tea tray I got last Christmas!'

She picked it up.

'Look, it's got...'

Julian was up now and angry. He was still not sober though. Perhaps he was still seeing stars. It was possible he would forget all about this by tomorrow morning. Surely he had bigger fish to fry than them?

'It was one of your feral beasts. I always said they were ghouls.'

'Julian!'

'They're not going to get away with this.'

Or maybe not.

Frank was asleep – he had a great capacity for that, a child's way of escaping – but Trevor was awake, staring at the ceiling and shivering. He didn't look over at her but Clara knew he was aware she was there. Clifford and Jonathon were snoring the other side of the room.

'I had to defend you,' he whispered.

She could have handled it herself, she was almost certain, but she didn't want the boy to think his actions were futile.

'Thank you, Trevor,' she whispered. 'Your intentions were honourable.'

She thought of the way Trevor played chess. 'You've got to be aggressive – that's how you win.' His knights, his pawns were always lined up ready for the fight. No one was going to get to his queen.

'Am I in trouble?' His lower lip was trembling. And Trevor never cried. 'What about being head boy?'

There had to be the right words for this somewhere. Floundering, Clara plucked some blindly.

'I'm going to fix everything,' she said, and he pulled up the covers so she couldn't see his face.

Now Clara was awake, wide awake, and it was nearly one o'clock in the morning.

One man clonked over the head with a tea tray. And another – the important one – still unaccounted for. Ivor would become memories and photographs and what-might-have-beens and what-should-have-beens. And all the things they never got to do and never managed to say and didn't get to share. She thought of a beach where small dogs barked at big horses, and countless conversations in his workshop in the glow of the lanterns, and his face, the way he listened.

Ivor's workshop would be shut up and sold up. Perhaps they'd put a garage in there, or turn it into a house. Julian was always on the hunt for property to invest in. She swallowed. The prospect of Julian living there was too much. He wouldn't, would he?

The thought that she wouldn't have a role in Patricia's life broke her heart too. Slowly but surely, she had formed a great affection for the little one, but she couldn't see how Patricia would stay with her. It was too complicated.

She tiptoed downstairs again; this time, she went to the parlour. She selected a cigarette end from an ashtray and lit it. A filthy habit but it felt appropriate. She felt like she was the worried wife in a war film and any moment now Ivor would walk in through the door, take her in his arms and...

Clara thought of other deaths she had experienced and it almost felt like it was obvious she would lose Ivor too. She was bad luck, she was bad blood Mother, Michael, Judy, Father, now Ivor. And yet, she knew she would endure. She would get the children up and she would make them their breakfast. She would pick them up from school and sign their forms and clean their sheets and check for nits and distract them at the dentist. She would shout at them about their teeth, 'wash your hands!', encourage them to practise, that wouldn't change – but she also knew that inside, she would be shattered. She would be in tiny broken pieces. She would be ruined.

She stared out of the window at the white light of the moon like Jane Taylor, who had lived here once, might have done, like all those people in trouble had done before her, like all those people in trouble would do again.

Someone, she thought, *help me*.

27

Someone was shaking her. A voice spoke urgently in her ear.

Clara snapped awake. She was surprised to discover that she was on the sofa in the parlour. Light was creeping through the curtains.

'Ivor?'

'It's me, Maureen.'

'Is there any news?'

'No, sorry...'

How long could Clara go on like this in purgatory? All she wanted was an answer, one way or another. *If it's the worst, let me know.* Anything rather than the unknowing. Clara swung her feet off the sofa and then steadied them on the cold floor. She tried to smile at Maureen, but it felt like she was grimacing.

'I went upstairs, and you weren't there,' Maureen said. 'It's half past six.'

Already? Okay, so she had overslept.

'There's a woman here.'

'What?' *Ruby, it has to be.* She had come after all.

'She said she's come to do your hair.'

All right, so not Ruby.

Pulling her housecoat around her – which reminded her of Julian's God-awful visit – Clara hurried to the kitchen. Beryl was smoking, hunched over the sink. Her face was tired and drawn and she was wearing an incongruous leather coat and high heels.

'He's gone missing, has he? Your handyman?'

Clara wouldn't have called Ivor that, but she nodded.

'I heard the news last night. Couldn't sleep a wink. But can't have you looking like that for when he walks in the door – he'll have a fright, he'll turn round and walk back out.'

Clara chuckled; she couldn't help it. Beryl was single-minded.

'So I got my kit together and came straight over. Thought I'd do you before the babies get up.'

Clara submitted and Beryl tilted her over the kitchen sink and wet her hair.

'There... if you look better, you feel better.'

Clara usually found this unconvincing, but today thought there might be some truth in it.

'What star sign is he then?'

And usually, Clara found Beryl's obsession with astrology excruciating but now she rather welcomed the distraction. There was still hope.

'He doesn't know...' she said, smiling at the idea of Ivor discussing his star sign.

Beryl guffawed. 'Tell me his date of birth and I'll tell you!'

'No, I mean – he doesn't know his date of birth.' Like little Peg too, she thought. Her darling foundlings.

'Oh, in that case,' Beryl said, 'he looks to me like a Leo. Or perhaps an Aquarius. I bet he's a Sagittarius rising. Either way, I know he's going to be okay. He's a born survivor, that one.'

Beryl spoke about Ivor with such certainty that it was lovely to hear. Today was a day for collecting absolutes even if they were baseless.

· · ·

The children got ready with Maureen's assistance. Breakfast, teeth, hair, face.

'Your school tie is on the chair, Trevor.'

Where Julian found it.

'And there is egg on your blazer. Wipe it off, please.' Clara patted the boy's shoulder. 'And don't worry about the other thing. I'll deal with it.'

Gladys told Beryl and Maureen that she loved them. Then she listed, 'Hunstanton, Holland, Hungary,' and Frank yelled at her because Hunstanton wasn't a country and they argued if the rules specified town or country – 'What about Norfolk then? Can I have that for N?'

'No,' the other children chorused.

Peg didn't want to go to school. But, again with Maureen's help and encouragement, the children all went off. Even Jonathon looked relieved to be out of the house. Trevor said shyly he'd tell everyone about him being a hero and Jonathon winced and said, 'Please don't. It wasn't like that,' and Trevor mumbled that it was.

'You won't, you know, disappear again, Jonathon?' Clara said as she went to close the door, and he ducked his head as though he were afraid.

'I'll come home,' he said lightly.

She didn't know if she believed him.

It wasn't until later that she thought to check Jonathon's bags and coat for clues as to why he had run away. She hadn't really thought it would produce anything of interest, but to her surprise, there in his pocket *was* something – a newspaper article. She couldn't tell which paper it had been taken from, and it was ragged from damp, but although only half of it was legible, all of it was impactful.

Her fingers were trembling. She smoothed out the creases and read.

University Reader put on probation to have organo-chemical treatment

Alan Mathison Turing (39) single university reader of Wilmslow described as one of the most profound and original mathematical minds of his generation.

Clara couldn't read the next paragraph, and she was unsure about the next bit too.

What is going to happen about all this? Isn't there a Royal Commission meeting to legalise this?

A witness said Turing was particularly honest and truthful.

Submit for treatment by a duly qualified medical practitioner at Manchester Infirmary.

Alan Turing, being male, had committed an act of gross indecency with a male person.

At first, Clara wondered if it was a study for school. A project on scientists perhaps? But why would Jonathon choose this article about a criminal who had become a security risk? Was there a Manchester connection in his life that had drawn him to Turing, maybe?

Maybe this wasn't anything to do with Turing himself. Maybe it was just paper for... for the lavatory or something.

But although it was wet through, it was carefully cut, scissored not torn, and carefully folded, not scrunched – and her heart beating fast was telling her something too.

She went through his files again, looking for clues. Jonathon's late mother was from Bournemouth and his much-decorated war hero father was from Portsmouth.

And then she went back to the article. She couldn't help it. She did have a weird feeling about that last line. She couldn't pretend she didn't. It was a niggle, a tension, a tickle in her gut: *an act of gross indecency with a male person.*

28

The police were coming up the path. It was ten o'clock in the morning; Maureen was out shopping and Clara was cooking something with cauliflower, although she wasn't quite sure what.

This had to be it. They had to finally have news about Ivor.

It was the same two men as yesterday: Sgt Worsley and PC Banks. Or Tweedledum and Tweedledee, as Mrs Horton might say. Clara's heart was thumping wildly, nineteen to the dozen; she saw their sombre faces, she saw the looks they gave each other. She grasped at the door handle, had opened it before they reached it.

'What is it? Tell me!' she demanded.

PC Banks had already taken off his helmet.

She knew it. And then he spoke.

'We understand that an act of assault was committed here last night.'

'What?' Clara's mind was so full she could hardly get any words out. 'You... *what?*' she repeated, outraged.

'We understand Mr White of 3 Shilling High Road was attacked here last night around midnight. We need to take a statement.'

They were in the kitchen, although she wasn't sure how they'd got there, she was in such a daze. She put the porridge pan into the sink and remembered to run water into it. *What was this?*

'Is there...' she said weakly. 'Have I got this right? You haven't come about Ivor, Mr Delaney?'

The two men looked at one another. 'Sorry,' Sgt Wolsley said quietly. His expression seemed to say, *I knew this was a mistake.*

As Clara made the tea, the police officers sat in uneasy silence. She could feel anger boil inside her – perhaps they could too. She dealt out their cups (not the best ones), then got out the jug of milk and slapped it down in front of them. She envisaged pouring it over their smug heads. She couldn't get over this. The cheek! Then she spoke again.

'You know I am... I am waiting to find out if my— Mr Delaney is alive or not, and you thought it would be an appropriate time to arrest one of my children?'

'Mr White has filed a complaint,' PC Banks said. He too had the grace to look guilty. 'The thing is – he wouldn't be put off.'

'We did explain the situation to him,' said his side-kick.

'I don't believe this,' Clara said flatly. Then, shaking her head, 'You're certainly providing me with a distraction. It's better than knitting, I suppose. Not that I would have chosen this.'

PC Banks pulled his notebook in front of him ruefully. 'Can you tell us what happened last night?'

Clara thought of Trevor's shocked, bloodshot eyes, and his fear. The first ever child from a children's home to be a head boy, the teacher had said. She thought of all he'd suffered in his many previous homes, and his home before this one, in Ipswich, where he had experienced lack of care, beatings, deprivation. He didn't talk about it yet seemed to have dealt with it healthily. He knew it was deeply unjust and unfair, but not his fault. He had somehow managed not to let it define him, to burst out from his past and to just concentrate on the things he loved. But the idea that he could be put in a dark place again was just unfathomable.

And all because of a chain of events that she herself had started...

'I... No, I can't.'

PC Banks played with the end of the pencil. He tapped it against his teeth.

'It's all right, Miss Newton.' Clifford came in and grabbed the teapot. He began pouring tea into each of the cups. 'You can tell them the truth.'

Bewildered, Clara stared at him. 'Wha...?'

He was wearing just a white vest – no shirt – and trousers. His chest was stuck out like a pigeon's. His hair was smoothed back and his expression was haughty. 'Tell them that I did it.'

It didn't seem unlikely that he might be part of a tray-wielding criminal gang.

'You?' sneered PC Banks.

'Yes, sir,' said Clifford proudly. He winked at Clara as she sat astonished. 'Little old me.'

29

It was late morning by the time the policemen left, and Clara and Clifford went out and sat in the garden. It was still biting cold, and they had had to wade through mud, but Clifford refused to put on a jumper or a coat. He didn't seem to feel the cold like normal people – or maybe he just didn't want you to think that he did.

Clara was feeling a lot of emotions all at once. 'Why did you say it was you?'

'Have you got a fag?' Clifford countered.

'No.'

'Don't worry, I have.' Grinning, he dug into his trouser pocket.

He had a lighter too – a Zippo, the same type that Michael used to have. He lit one cigarette and passed it to her and then took out one for himself. He held the lighter so close to his face she thought he might burn his eyebrows. Clara hadn't planned to smoke again but thought she may as well.

'Trevor's a good kid, isn't he?' Clifford interrupted her thoughts.

'Yes. He is.'

'Thought so.'

Taking a long drag on the cigarette, Clifford then stared ahead at the leafless branches.

'What's the point of him getting in bother then? Everyone knows I'm the ne'er-do-well here. Trevor's got a bright future ahead of him – I haven't. They'll just send me back to that Reform place anyway, won't they?'

The Reform School in Hunstanton was still shut – one positive thing about the flood, she supposed. The Reform boys were all being housed in nearby caravans, apparently. Clifford showed no inclination to return, but he couldn't stay with them for much longer.

Still, Clara disagreed with him. Told him it wasn't right. Clifford shouldn't take the blame for something he hadn't done. He had a lot going for him, loads even. He mustn't think like that. He waited patiently for her to finish and then he shrugged.

'It all depends on what Mr White decides to do, I suppose.'

Clara wished she didn't have a feeling about this, but she did. If it was left solely up to Julian, it was going to go very wrong for Clifford.

Back in the house, Peg and Gladys were running around playing 'It' in the parlour.

'You're supposed to be at school!' bellowed Clara.

Peg threw down her schoolbag and stormed off. This was an example of how quickly things fall apart when you're not paying attention.

'They've only come back for lunch,' Maureen explained mildly. 'I'll feed them and then take them back this afternoon. You look half-frozen, Miss Newton!'

Clara hadn't realised it was already lunchtime. Maureen had sliced the bread and was now arranging ham on a plate. The abandoned cauliflower sat in an unappetising cloud on the side. Plonking herself down on the chair, Clara felt as though she couldn't take many more surprises. Then she let out a shriek.

'Where's Patricia?'

'She's fine too. Nanny Norland came and collected her.'

Everything was under control, Clara told herself. She tended to think everything would run to rack and ruin without her. It wasn't arrogance but came from experience. Usually there was no one picking up the pieces behind her. Having Maureen there was a revelation.

'Spam fritters for dinner tonight, and I'm baking some apples for dessert,' Maureen said, and Clara was reminded how much she loved to cook. 'With raisins and cinnamon. You need to keep your strength up.'

Clara couldn't help but smile. When did this girl become so grown-up? She had an old head on young shoulders suddenly. Clara had had such trouble with Maureen at the beginning of her time at the home, and now Maureen was like her own fairy godmother. She knew where everything was and what to do, and she did it all without a fuss. She even made sure Stella was fed and de-flea-ed. Clara knew she needed to trust her.

'You know that's not her actual name, the nanny?' Clara asked.

'Isn't it? It suits her – Norland, Norbert. She's strange. She just said to me, "Every cloud has a silver lining."'

Clara laughed. It felt like the first time she'd laughed for a long while, and she felt guilty instantly. Ivor was pinned under some upturned bench or some roof beams or a fallen chimney stack and she was sitting in the warm, contemplating a baked apple and laughing.

Maureen said, 'Dr Cardew said he'll take you there this afternoon. If you want to go...'

'Where?'

'Hunstanton.' Maureen bit her lip shyly. 'You'll find Ivor, Miss Newton, I know you will.'

The faith Maureen had in her made Clara's heart ache. It was fifty-six hours since Ivor was last seen, rowing off into the unknown. But if Maureen still believed, then Clara could try to as well.

30

Just before one o'clock that day, Dr Cardew stood at the front door of the home with his car parked out in the road and a large coat draped over his arm.

'I already have one,' Clara said reflexively about the coat. She was wrapped up in an old winter perennial.

'It's for Ivor,' he said. And the thought, the very idea, that Dr Cardew still thought Ivor was alive, that Ivor would still have wants and needs, and a desire to be warmed up, made Clara's tattered little heart sing. Other people might try to reassure her that Ivor was okay, but Dr Cardew was a professional, an educated man, and he was rarely wrong about anything.

They got in the car and set off. Anita had packed supplies: Scotch eggs and salmon, and even her legendary marble cake.

'It's a picnic!' called out Clara in surprise when she saw the hamper on the back seat. There was a tablecloth and some serviettes on top.

'It's not just for us,' he said, which made Clara blush. Oh, of course. It was for the rescuers and the survivors there.

'Mrs Cardew felt desperate to do something. You know how she is.'

'Is she okay?'

Clara realised there would be ripples to this – whatever this was – and the ripples would be far-reaching. Anita and Ivor were old friends too, and Anita already knew more about loss than most people. A survivor of the Holocaust, she had fallen into the deep chasm of grief many times. She might look hard as steel sometimes (often), and she certainly came across like that, but Clara knew this fortress was constructed on shaky foundations.

'Evelyn's looking after her,' Dr Cardew said. 'You know Evelyn.'

Clara thought of kind-hearted Evelyn, who had been a resident of the home and then been adopted by the Cardews. She too had endured terrible trauma. After Evelyn had spent many years in care, her mother had returned, only to be killed in a car accident soon after. Fate could be cruel.

Dr Cardew was quiet for a bit, concentrating on the road ahead, and then he said with a faint smile, 'Aren't we lucky to have such lovely children in our lives?'

All the way there, the sky still felt swollen with water. Clara tried to think how she would describe it if she were writing a file or a letter: smoky white or off white. Or maybe grey/white – was that it?

As they drove on, Clara's thoughts returned to the home. Would Maureen remember to collect the children from school? She was mature and yet she was still untested. Clara remembered the strip of paper that Maureen kept in her coat, the LMNOP, because she got her alphabet confused. The way she was easily seduced by bad men... But she had to let Maureen have a go. And anyway, Miss Webb was coming to the home that afternoon. Mrs Horton was only a telephone call away. They were a community, weren't they?

And Clifford was there, and he was showing maturity too,

wasn't he? What he was suggesting – taking the flak for Trevor – was hugely selfless. Clara couldn't even begin to process just how kind it was. And Jonathon would be home from school, and he was usually sensible – at least when it came to others, if not himself.

They drove past fields and green hedges and Clara remembered how Ivor would talk about this, his home county: 'I like the flatness. I like hills and mountains too, of course, but there is something about the way you can see miles into the distance that is such a magical thing.' If she ever got the chance, she would tell him she agreed.

Nearing their destination, Clara grew increasingly nervous about what Hunstanton would be like, and she kept going back to the question she had now asked herself over a million times: Where was Ivor?

Jonathon didn't know what time he had last seen him – but if it was around 4 a.m as he guessed, it was now approaching sixty hours that Ivor had been unaccounted for. How long can a person last? *How could anyone survive for that long?*

But Ivor had survived one of the fiercest battles of the war. A flood wasn't going to get to him – was it?

They finally approached Hunstanton and Clara couldn't hide the shock on her face. The destruction of the place was biblical. It was epic. She felt ridiculously naive since she hadn't connected the word 'flood' with all this devastation. It was overwhelming to see – a world awash with water, water where it shouldn't be. It looked all wrong, it felt all wrong; she felt like she was a tiny person trapped in an upturned cup of tea.

Random things were floating past in the streets that had turned into canals. Newspapers. A black bag of rubbish – only it wasn't rubbish, it was someone's home, someone's precious things. Clara reached out the window and grabbed a photo frame but the picture was too misty to see. She suddenly found herself trying not to gag at the smell, a bad-egg smell that must have been blocked drains

There were roadblocks everywhere she looked. Sandbag road-blocks, road signs. Shades of the war. She couldn't help but remember the Blitz – only then it was fire and rubble, and here it was water and rubble.

Dr Cardew steered them through the roadblocks and the obstructions. Whenever people stopped him, he wound down the window and said, 'I'm a doctor, coming through,' and it was like he was a wizard on a broomstick; no one questioned it – actually, one man did, but Dr Cardew smoothly said, 'We're part of a search party.'

A *search party* – the phrase sounded like something they'd do at Lester's birthday.

She remembered the day of the air-show disaster – the day her father died. She had been driven around by Dr Cardew then as well, and in a way it had bonded them. She felt sick. Was this really history repeating itself?

Everywhere was grey and rubbishy; a few boats were being rowed up the end of one street, another was abandoned upside down.

'Danger of contaminated water,' Dr Cardew said briskly. The more upset or worried he was, the less he sounded it. 'They'll clear this up quickly, otherwise we'll have a cholera or typhoid outbreak on our hands.'

She thought they'd go straight to the hospital, but Dr Cardew suggested they go to the police station first, a small dark building set back from the main road. The water was receding here, but the reeds in the garden were all flattened, and a small wall was broken at both ends. When she saw a half-drowned mattress, she thought of the place in Ipswich where Frank and Trevor used to live.

Dr Cardew offered to go in on his own, but she wanted to get out of the car. In some places, the water was up to her knees; it felt swampy and wild.

'We're after a missing person,' Dr Cardew announced to the policeman behind the desk.

Ivor had gone from unaccounted for to missing without her realising.

She had a photograph of herself and Ivor, taken last Christmas in front of the tree. Mr Horton had borrowed a camera from his bowls pal. He was supposed to use it to improve his technique, but Mrs Horton had insisted on photographs of the children and then Mr Horton had taken one of the two of them.

Clara was camera-shy – not only because in this one she was sweaty from hauling the Christmas chicken out of the oven but because secretly she thought nothing ever good came of having your photo taken. But that day, she remembered, Ivor was looking at her like she was the plum pudding and the prize coin.

Just before they left today, she'd scissored through the picture, cutting herself out. She was not missing. Now Ivor was standing alone, proud as punch, smiling lips-closed. Clara could remember that as the flash went, Ivor, who had his arm round her, had tickled the small of her back and she had burst into laughter. Mr Horton had said he'd get better at it, and for some reason that made them laugh some more.

The policeman put a pin in her half-photo and stuck it on the corkboard, which was crowded with other pinned photos: elderly faces, someone's mum, someone's uncle, all suspended in mid-air. And two children with their arms round a cat. It was unbearable. She had to focus, she had to remember to detach. Accept the things she could not change, change the things she could.

'Apparently, he went back for a dog,' she told the policeman, but the heroic sweetness of this story did not appear to win him over.

'I see.' He was preoccupied with his pen. He shook it, then pressed the nib onto the blotting paper. The blue spread from the middle, blurting out everywhere and turning his fingers blue. She thought she saw a boat-shape in the ink.

She imagined Ivor floating in the wide-open sea. Would a fishing vessel pick him up? Or perhaps a couple of day-trippers? She pictured the horror of children playing in the sand dunes, finding her man washed up on the beach.

How would she explain this to Patricia? Maybe it wouldn't be her job any more, maybe Ruby would do that?

They left the station. Back outside, they watched as cars were pulled on tow-ropes and boats were dragged up and down streets. People in sou'westers were shouting through megaphones. Again, the sandbags and whistles took her back to the war.

She felt passive, like a nuisance, a child in the way, and she felt sluggish too – perhaps it was the effect of watching the sludgy movements of the vehicles around her. Perhaps it was more of the slowing down of her brain since she had first heard about the flood. Perhaps that's what the mind or the body does to protect itself from horror.

Clara suddenly realised her feet were wet. Her wellington boots were ill-fitting and ripped. She never had the right equipment; it was something she and Ivor laughed about once.

Where was he? He'd gone back for a dog. Perhaps if she'd got him a dog sooner, he wouldn't have tried to rescue this one. If the person hadn't called about Clifford. If she'd not asked him to go. If she hadn't had Clifford put in the Reform School. If if if.

Dr Cardew looked at her kindly. 'We still have the hospital to try, Miss Newton.'

THE NORFOLK DAILY

Tuesday 3 February 1953

More Stories of Heroism

Stories of heroism as the emergency services and members of the public rallied to help those in urgent need. There were so many individual human tragedies.

Mr Ted Bangle of Meadow Way, (Jaywick), whose wife is feared to have drowned, saved his three-year-old grandchild, Terry May, by clinging to a barbed wire fence. 'As we pushed open the door, the full force of the water hit us. I was up to my neck. My wife, who was a semi-invalid, just disappeared under the water.'

Maisie Norton of Hunstanton joined two teenagers and a man to rescue five families from the roofs. 'Then the man went back for the dog and we haven't seen him since.'

31

Even at the hospital, the water had crept in stealthily. Puddles on the way in, and puddles inside, creating a grey-black floor that a caretaker in sandals was fruitlessly trying to sweep. The sound of the broom going back and forth reminded her of the metronome that Anita used: *Slowly, not that slow, Rita, your timing needs work.*

Everyone looked stoical. Nothing about their expressions, their clothes or their conversations told you how they were feeling inside. People are incredible, thought Clara.

She talked to the tired woman at the front desk. Ivor was not a patient here. And no, they didn't have anybody who they weren't able to identify, and no, no patients who had lost their memory, and no, they didn't have a list of people who had been brought in from the floods and who had already left, because no one had.

Dr Cardew went to see if he could find out anything else or be of assistance. Clara was left in a large waiting room with children's chairs along each wall.

A woman with a patterned headscarf tied tightly under several chins asked Clara if she was waiting to see Dr Chadwick.

When Clara said she wasn't, the woman blinked, pleased: 'Looks like I'm next then.'

Clara asked what she was here for – she wouldn't normally enquire but the woman looked like she wanted to chat – and, to Clara's surprise, she raised the hem of her skirt and showed enormous bruises and gashes over both heavy legs.

'When I went back to my house,' she said. 'My own fault, I should have waited. Glass everywhere. Windows shattered.'

'I'm sorry,' Clara responded. She could hardly take her eyes off those legs, they looked painful.

'Don't be,' the woman said. 'We made it – which is more than you can say for some.'

Dr Cardew came back, shaking his head.

'Do you want to stay longer?' she asked.

'It's under control here. It's mostly elderly people with hypothermia. A few broken limbs. One fella crushed by a bed frame.'

'I should call home,' Clara said, feeling defeated.

She hadn't heard from them for four hours – anything could have happened. She thought suddenly how, in her first year at the Grange, she didn't have a telephone, and how she had begged for one. Thank goodness she had.

'Shilling Grange – 078484.'

Maureen must have been taught to answer the telephone like that at secretarial college. Her voice was breathless and Clara was reminded that it wasn't only her who was desperate to hear Ivor's voice; all the children were too.

'It's only me,' Clara said. She kept picturing the woman's gritty scraped legs. The image seemed to stick the more she wanted it to disappear.

'Anything?' Maureen said before Clara could go on.

'No, nothing.'

Maureen sounded desolate, and Clara knew if she was desolate, then she herself couldn't be. They couldn't both be desolate, not at the same time.

'No news is good news,' Clara, said channelling the Norland Nanny. 'Bad news travels fast.'

'Mm,' said Maureen as though she didn't agree. And Clara was reminded that, when Maureen was a little girl, she had covered her mother's fatal wounds with tissue paper – the police, when they came, couldn't understand what had happened.

Clara thought of how talking to Marilyn the other day had given her strength and comfort. She tried to remember what she'd said: 'Whatever happens, we will cope, we absolutely will.'

Maureen sniffled a bit.

'How are the children?' Clara asked, suddenly feeling guilty for leaving the girl to look after them all.

'Tolerable,' Maureen said in a tone that suggested the opposite.

'What's going on there then?'

'We're playing Newmarket. Clifford is cheating.'

But Clara couldn't be anything but grateful to Clifford from this day on. 'Tell him to stop.'

'I'm not!' Clifford was yelling. 'Just because I'm better than everyone else doesn't mean I'm cheating.'

Maureen huffed. 'Jonathon is out running again. Does he ever stop?'

Clara thought of the sad newspaper cutting as her finger hovered over the dial. She wanted to be back with the children now. Shilling Grange was where she ought to be.

'No, he doesn't...' She paused. 'It's okay, I'll be home soon.'

32

Dr Cardew was back at the steering wheel and Clara was next to him in the passenger seat. Some ducks were slowly waddling across the road in front of them. Clara wished he would hoot or something, but he seemed mesmerised by the sight of them. One by one they crossed, on their pretty webbed feet, one after the other. Only when the last baby duck reached the other side of the road did Dr Cardew restart the engine.

Clara was thinking: she would start cancelling the wedding tomorrow. She had to now; she didn't know what hope she had left. She had lost the deposit on the Cloth Hall, she supposed. And she would have a discussion with Anita: the music they were going to play at the church and the party – perhaps they could use that for Ivor? Nothing should go to waste. And the wedding guest list would become the guest list for...

'Are you all right, Miss Newton?'

'Just making plans,' Clara replied sombrely.

'Let me know if you want to talk.'

Clara nodded, glad they had started to move again. Maureen was capable of holding the fort but thank goodness Mrs Horton or Miss Webb would be there soon.

Dr Cardew glanced at her out the corner of his eye. There was even less traffic now, but occasionally a car's beams would dazzle them and they would have to shield their eyes.

Dr Cardew cleared his throat.

'You've been a good friend to Mrs Cardew, Miss Newton.'

Hardly.

'When Baby Howard was ill, and when Evelyn's mother died. Don't you remember? You even helped her give birth!'

'That was just...' Clara remembered the panic in her kitchen as Anita went into labour. She wasn't sure 'helped' came into it. 'She's been a good friend to me.'

'If you ever need anything, you know you only have to ask.'

They drove on and on. Clara stared out of her window at the fields – you wouldn't think dying in a flood was possible here. A biblical thing in this green and pleasant land. What was all of this without Ivor? What was she without Ivor? Nothing.

She could not go through this again.

But this phrase was meaningless; she might have to.

Norfolk became Suffolk and Dr Cardew asked her if she wanted something to eat but Clara had no appetite for the sandwiches and the cake. She remembered her fuss over caterers for the wedding. At least she hadn't made a payment to Julian's cook yet.

She also thought of the policemen coming over, and tried to understand why Julian was pursuing this. He was lonely, she supposed, since his break-up, and men like Julian aren't kind when they're lonely. It's as though they need a woman to soften their hard edges. She would have to speak to him again, she decided. Beg him to let it go.

She fell asleep, back pressed uncomfortably against the seat, blanket over her knees gathered around her ankles. Her handbag was digging into her, but there wasn't room for it elsewhere. She dreamed she was in a council meeting in front of all those people.

'We can't be separated,' she was saying, but not about the children; it was about her and Ivor. 'It's inhumane. We've been through so much.'

But she was speaking not to Mrs McCarthy, but to Ruby.

She woke with a start. *Why did I call Ruby? If only it had been a wrong number!*

The landscape had changed again, the way it does in early February. Now it was dark and shiny, glossy even. The windscreen seemed tearful.

Dr Cardew looked over at her again. His driving gloves were light on the wheel. He had been saving some lemon sherbets in the glove compartment, he said. These she could eat. Here in hell, it was a taste of heaven.

The wipers were screeching to a huffy rhythm and she was going to make a comment about them when he said, 'I'm sorry, Miss Newton, I think we might have to prepare for the worst.'

Dr Cardew, her trusted friend. The educated professional who knew best. He was telling her it was over.

'I am prepared for the worst,' she said, and it was true. Without realising it, Clara had been preparing to accept the inevitable for days now.

The home was lit up like a bonfire as they approached. Each window blazed yellow. The street was black as coal and yet the home was emitting a golden statement of light.

The children should be in bed, for goodness' sake. It was a school day tomorrow. What on earth was Maureen thinking? She was too young – Clara told herself grimly – for such responsibility. Clara shouldn't have left them with her. She couldn't rely on anyone but herself.

'I don't believe this,' she said.

As Dr Cardew pulled up, the front door of the home swung wide open. A little silhouetted figure was in the frame. Peg? It was like a painting somehow.

'What on earth is going on?!'

Dr Cardew turned off the engine. 'I'll just see you in.'

Yanking at the passenger door, Clara almost fell into the road. She picked herself up, then galloped towards Peg. Drawing closer, she saw Peg's eyes were huge and wild. Clara's heart was beating nineteen to the dozen.

For the first time since she'd heard Ivor was lost, she could feel a new sensation: the rising of hope.

Peg was mouthing something. And then the words came out, not quite distinct but loud, as if she were using a loudspeaker. Peg spoke. Not only did she speak, Peg shouted. For the first time in all her years, Peg used her voice.

'Ivor is back.'

33

And there he was, making his way towards her from behind Peg. Her Ivor, her darling, was home.

Nothing felt like that moment. That feeling when he put his arm round her, his chin over her head, locked her against his body. Ivor. He smelled of bath and sea and aftershave. It was hard to believe it was real.

'I'm sorry, I'm sorry,' he murmured over and over again, and she cried hot tears into his shirt. She made it soaking, a thousand emotions, a thousand thankfulness, prayers, the relief, the relief, the relief.

They were both sobbing. Patricia and some of the other children were clutching them too, some crying, most laughing.

She pulled away to look at that face, that dear kind face she loved so much.

'You really would do anything to get out of doing the invitations,' she said, as their tears merged into laughter. Clara pulled Peg to join them in the embrace too. Oh, this was lovely.

'Did you just speak, Peg?' asked Ivor. 'Or was I imagining it?'

Peg nodded her head up and down against Clara's stomach.

'It took that...' Clara said, still weeping and laughing.

'Say something else, Peg,' Ivor encouraged her.

But Peg just laughed through her tears and shook her head. Clara ran her hand through Peg's hair, her other arm locked round Ivor's waist. She was never going to let him go.

'You don't need to say anything now, Peg. We've got all the time in the world.'

And then Peg laughed and pulled away. She had a gleeful grin on her face when she said, first in a little voice and then much louder: 'Kiss! KISS!'

'You cheeky devil!' said Clara and went to kiss her – but Peg pointed at Ivor. So Clara kissed Ivor's salty lips until his eyelids fluttered shut, then turned back to Peg, who was now hopping up and down with glee. 'You're a clever girl, that's what you are,' Clara said, pulling her girl in for one more hug.

Soon enough they were settled in the kitchen, and, as Clara went to ask the first of a million questions, she heard what sounded like a bark. But it couldn't be a bark, could it?

'What on earth?' Clara asked, looking in the direction the sound had come from.

'Ah,' Ivor said, rubbing his forehead and looking contrite. 'That's another thing.'

The cause of the barking was indeed a dog. And not just any dog – this was the dog that Ivor had rescued. The dog had long ears, a black nose and a shaggy tail, and it sauntered into the kitchen like it was already familiar with the layout of the house. Stella, on Gladys's lap, was studiously ignoring it. Frank was fascinated by it and Clara could already feel that he was on the same trajectory of obsession with the dog as he was with planes.

'It's done two poos in the garden,' Frank said, tugging Clara's sleeve. 'Is that all right?'

'Better than in the house, I suppose...'

Jonathon got up. 'I'll sort it, Miss Newton.'

'But two...' Frank continued doubtfully. 'If he does that every hour that would be forty-six.'

Trevor punched him in the arm. 'Forty-eight, prat!'

'That would be a lot,' said Clara with a laugh. My God, Ivor was back. Everything was funny, everything was golden. Dr Cardew had come in too, and within minutes Ivor was sent to the sofa, under a blanket and under strict instructions not to move. He was a patient and must be treated as such. Ivor had been back about one hour, apparently, and Maureen had immediately made him get in the bath. She had also run over to his workshop to get him clothes and, when she couldn't get in, she'd got some of Jonathon's stuff for him instead. The children were still milling around in shocked delight.

'And a hot-water bottle if you please, Maureen,' Dr Cardew said.

'On its way.'

'And you've had hot drinks, Ivor?'

'Many. Florence Nightingale here has been looking after me.'

Maureen curtseyed. Clara busied herself pushing Ivor's hair back from his sweaty forehead. God, she loved this man. Was he real? This wasn't another dream, was it? The children used to end some of their made-up stories with 'and it was all just a dream,' and Clara had explained to them that that was a let-down.

Don't let this be a dream!

The dog was one of those dogs that demanded attention. Clara eventually tore her eyes from Ivor to indulge it, and stared at the sweet doggy face. Its eyes were like a man's. Even its nostrils seemed cute. It seemed like a wise dog who had a lot of interesting things to say.

Ivor was calling it Max.

'Why Max?'

'I don't know,' Ivor said, scratching the dog between its ears. 'I called him that and he answered.' He paused. 'That's not a sensible reason, is it?'

It didn't seem scientific. Gladys looked a little put out. 'I wanted to call him Timmy,' she said, pouting. 'After the dog in 'The Famous Five.'

'He looks like a Max, though,' Clara said. She would have agreed to anything Ivor said at that moment in time.

'I hate to tell you but it's a girl dog,' pointed out Clifford.

'How do you know that?' Gladys asked, eyes narrowed.

'He doesn't have a willy,' Frank screeched.

The children were in uproar. This was almost as exciting as Ivor's return.

'Then it's Maxi,' said Ivor. 'Everyone agree?'

Everyone agreed.

Ivor had his arm round Patricia, who, Clara noticed now, looked wan and exhausted – the last few days had taken their toll on her too. After another round of tea and biscuits, Clara felt it was time for the children to go to bed.

'Properly this time!' she warned, trying to sound strict but unable to stop smiling.

She didn't know where Ivor and Patricia were planning to go. Gladys had never stayed up this late before and was almost asleep on her feet. Jonathon and Clifford seemed to think they were adults now; they were playing gin-rummy.

Ivor was too exhausted to move from the sofa, which kind of settled what to do with him, and Patricia was soon snoozing gently, head resting on his chest. Clara offered to take the sleeping child up to bed but Ivor mumbled, she was fine, she could stay next to him.

He was muttering his thanks, too. She brought down another blanket and another pillow and by now he was so deep in sleep, she had to raise his head – and it was heavier than it looked – and stuff the pillow under him, and he *still* didn't open his eyes. And she put more blankets and cushions on the floor just in case Patricia rolled off.

There were seven – no, eight – children in the house, Clara

realised. Good grief, it was just like the old days. Only this time she didn't feel like the old lady who lived in the shoe. She felt like Snow White after her prince had just woken her up. She was revived, reborn, and she would let nothing and no one come between them again.

34

Clara was emotional as she made breakfast the next morning; every time she saw Ivor, she wanted to cry. Or rather every time she heard him: he was snoring like a trooper in the parlour. He had never stayed the night in the home before and it felt like a dam had burst.

She had crawled into bed and imagined she'd go over the events of the day – a day that had begun with her thinking of funeral songs, taken her through the desperate sight of Hunstanton underwater and ended with the greatest news. But she was so wiped out, she snuffed out immediately, like a candle, like a milk-drunk baby. Children may have come and gone from her room in the night, but she had been too oblivious to notice.

The next thing she knew, watery February sunshine was streaming through the curtains and there was the slam of the front door – and the pitter-patter of Jonathon's running shoes on the path, and the sound of a – what was *that*? – something scratching and whining at the bedroom door. She suddenly remembered the dog. Maxi wanted to go out and explore the garden. Frank said he'd take her because they worried that she'd get herself lost or manage to squeeze through some gap in the garden hedges.

Clara fried fat sausages that spat in her face, and sliced the bread until it crumbled. She scrambled eggs and sliced tomatoes. The butter was hard and a little messy to spread, but it didn't matter. This was a celebration breakfast: Ivor was home.

When Maxi came back in, she watched Clara cook with a religious intensity. Jonathon and Clifford laid the table. Clara was surprised that Clifford was assisting, before realising it was a ruse to impress Maureen. Maureen raised her eyebrows at Clara, though, and said, 'You've got the knives and forks the wrong way round.'

'I need a teacher,' he said, his eyes plaintive.

Patricia, much refreshed this morning, was drawing pictures of fishes and singing to herself. The children drank tea or milk and knocked their glasses together, calling out 'Cheers!' Peg didn't join in but Clara had decided she wouldn't draw attention to it. She seemed more than happy.

The telephone was ringing off the hook. Clara had called Mrs Horton first thing. After a yelp of pleasure, Mrs Horton had told her off.

'You should have called sooner. Last night, I knitted two pairs of mittens with worry.'

'It was very late,' Clara said. She was exaggerating, but the truth was she hadn't had a moment to think.

Then Marilyn called, wept with relief, said she knew it all along, and then in the next breath insisted she was sending life jackets and money for swimming lessons. And Clara leaned against her wall with the curly telephone wire between her fingers and felt nothing but gratitude.

There was too much going on; Clara's head was spinning. She tried to organise her thoughts. One thing that she was still going to have to deal with was Clifford and the Julian White debacle. Another was Jonathon. She still hadn't managed to talk to him about the newspaper article. And another was Peg – her speaking and her possible adoption. Then there was Maxi the dog, and of course the other secret dog that Clara had planned for a wedding gift... And then there was Ruby.

But before all that, there was Ivor. Ivor was accounted for.

The children wanted to take a day off school: 'It's a momentous occasion!' argued Trevor.

'A. Ivor is home, and B. we have a dog!' said Frank, 'and C. Peg spoke!'

'I haven't told Ivor I love him yet,' insisted Gladys, 'and he's sleeping.'

But Clara remained firm. Ivor would be here and awake when they got home. 'Shoo-shoo now.'

Maureen offered to walk the younger ones in again. Then she said she'd pack up a few of her things and take the train to London, and would be back in a few days.

'Unless you want me to stay?' she proposed shyly. Clara would have cuddled her, but Maureen hated a cuddle.

'Of course I do! If it's all right with you. What about your college work?'

'I'm all up to date,' Maureen replied immediately.

'We love to have you,' Clara said, squeezing the girl's hand gratefully.

'So would I!' added Clifford.

'Shut up, Clifford,' Maureen said. She wasn't falling for him and Clara was glad to see it.

Clara put a belt round Maxi's neck and fashioned a sort of collar, confident that Ivor would create something better when he had recovered. She walked her just for a short while, long enough for her to do her business – and ducked down a side street when she thought she saw Julian White strutting the other way.

Ivor slept on, his snores reverberating around the home. The children had gone to school by the time Dr Cardew dropped by, this time with a vat of chicken noodle soup.

'Mrs Cardew doesn't make this for just anyone...' he began. Clara set it on the stove. She stopped smiling when she saw his expression.

'Do you know anything about... what happened?' he asked. He had gone into professional mode again.

'Not yet,' she said. 'Why?'

Dr Cardew shifted his legs. 'He may take a while to recover, Miss Newton.'

'He'll be fine now he's home,' Clara told him, and, at that moment, she really believed it.

35

Ivor woke up about eleven, attacked some porridge like a starving man, asked after Patricia, then went back to lie down again on the sofa. He was still asleep after lunch, so Clara left him with the dog curled over his feet and went to Frank's friend Lester's house. This wasn't a pleasant task and Clara felt as guilty as she imagined a prospective adoptive parent reneging on a deal. Lester's mother, Mrs Greene, was scrubbing her doorstep and welcomed her heartily, which made her feel worse.

'Frank must come round again!' she said, and Clara mumbled something about Lester having to come over soon too. She hoped she wasn't about to drive a tank through Frank's one and only precious friendship.

Suki was wandering around the front garden, her long mournful face even longer and more mournful than Clara had remembered. She came over heavily and nuzzled Clara's hand. She probably smelled Maxi on her fingers.

'Oh, I just knew you'd want to see how she's getting along,' Mrs Greene said, beaming.

Clara swallowed. 'I'm afraid it's not that – we've had a change in circumstance,' she said guiltily.

Mrs Greene's face dropped. Suki's might have too if it weren't already very droopy.

'The person I was getting it for has unexpectedly acquired another dog, you see.'

Pained as she was, Mrs Greene seemed to find this reason palatable. She asked all about Maxi and then stroked Suki, who lay down, offering up her swollen belly.

'You see, girl, you'll all be friends.'

'Like Lester and Frank,' said Clara, still nervous.

Mrs Greene squeezed her hand. 'Like Lester and Frank. Now, is Frank free later? Tell him to come and knock.'

This time when Clara got back, Ivor was up and dressed and making tea in the kitchen. A fine sight he was too, in his unbuttoned shirt and braces. She always felt ridiculously like pinging those braces. He made her heart gallop. She was glad – and more than a little relieved – that he was up. She didn't know how she could take care of everyone and everything, all at once and on her own, for much longer.

Maxi was curled up on the only sunny bit of floor and Ivor was feeding her crusts of toast. Poor little dog. Somehow, Maxi really did remind her of the children when they first came to the home. The way she startled at the slightest noise. Once Maxi had worked out there was no more toast, she went and hid behind the sofa in the parlour. (It was too late to say no dogs in the parlour, Clara realised; that ship had long sailed.)

Ivor grabbed her hands. 'Thank you for looking after Patricia so well.'

'No need,' Clara said. Ah, they were doing formalities now. She added, 'My pleasure.' She thought *so well* might be an exaggeration: she should have done better.

'It must have been awful,' Ivor said, shaking his head.

Clara gulped. It was always difficult balancing her needs and the children's. The children's needs should come first – but they hadn't last week. She'd been pulverised by it all. She needed to make it up to them, she knew. They needed her time and attention now more than ever before.

'Worse for you, I expect. Out in the cold and dark,' Clara gently pushed, desperate to know more about what had happened.

He nodded. His expression said he didn't want to talk about it.

She thought of Ruby's two voices on the telephone. The sophisticated lady-of-the-house and then the young girl from Shilling Grange.

'Ivor,' she began and she was just about to launch into her call to Ruby when Clifford burst in – she had almost forgotten he was still in the house – and started on about West Ham, and then moved on to some other news story about some failed bank robbers. Those were the things Ivor wanted to talk about now, not Ruby, it wasn't the time for all that.

36

Ivor ate tea with the children when they came home from school and then promptly fell asleep on the sofa again. The puzzle of the *Titanic* was still in the middle of the parlour floor, and everyone had to walk round it or the girls would yell at them. Peg still hadn't spoken again, but she was grinning like a Cheshire cat. Jonathon seemed to have sunk into his normal polite but disengaged self. Patricia was overexcited, or 'overtired', as Mrs Horton liked to say. She was screechy and stubborn, but it was lovely to hear her laughing uproariously again.

But Ivor? He was sleeping a lot, wasn't he? Clara felt like calling Dr Cardew back – was this normal? – but she resisted. It was probably to be expected. It was early days. Dr Cardew had said it would take time. Ivor had suffered a shock. A trauma.

It was still too cold and wet to play outside. Frank rested his hand on Maxi's silky head and said that A. He'd always wanted a dog– Clara interrupted, 'She's not ours, Frank.' But he insisted that since Clara and Ivor were getting married then she might as well be.

The children played the alphabet game. Today, their arguments were over whether 'Bugbear' was a real bear or not and if

'España' could count as an E word. Clara decided never ever to let this lot play Monopoly: it would only end in violence.

Then Peg – *Peg!* – said yes, it was, and Clara was so happy to hear her speak again, it would have been churlish to correct her.

The wedding invitations sat in tantalising piles on the sideboard, Clara's guest list in between them. Okay, they'd get them out soon. Ivor was safe, that was the important thing.

Ivor slept on. Clara was surprised when, later that evening, Patricia trooped up to her bed upstairs rather than staying on the sofa with him.

'Daddy snores,' she said, and giggled, and then, before Clara knew it, Patricia leaned in to give her a kiss. That was a first; usually Patricia allowed herself to be kissed but was never proactive. Clara was too surprised to say anything, which was probably for the best.

Clara was locking up the back door for the night when Clifford appeared in the shadows next to the stove. She squealed, her hand fluttering to her heart.

'Clifford! You gave me a fright.'

'Sorry...' He curled his lip. His hair was overstyled. Somehow, he made even old clothes look fashionable – he had an instinct about which button to button and which to leave.

He asked if anything was going to happen: if anything would happen to him, he meant, of course. Clara knew she had to be honest with him. She hadn't heard anything yet. To be honest, with all that was going on she hadn't given it much thought. But Julian White was unpredictable. *And* he had a grudge against Clara.

'We'll just have to wait and see,' she said apologetically, and he smoothed back his hair.

'I thought so,' he replied, and nodded stoically, making Clara wish she could make this whole sorry affair disappear for him.

. . .

Everything should have been perfect, but that night, Clara dreamed that Ruby was an octopus and with one of her tentacles she was pulling Clara underwater and holding her down. She heard Patricia screaming, 'Want Daddee, not you!' – then she woke up. She was relieved it was just a dream, but why did it feel like she was in purgatory?

Even though Ivor was home and safe, it still felt like an in-between bit, like she was just waiting for something else to happen.

She had two nocturnal visitors and she had to get up to let the dog out twice or maybe three times – she lost count. The next morning, Ivor said he was recovered enough to go back to the workshop with the dog and Patricia. Maxi would be happier with the quieter household, he said. Clara felt bereft at the prospect of his departure – had she not taken care of him enough? She knew she didn't do the nurse or the devoted girlfriend as well as she might, but it was all there, in her heart, in her intentions.

Ivor kissed her cheek. 'It's fine, sweetheart,' he reassured her. 'I need to sort things out at home. I can't stay here forever.'

Clara fluttered her eyelashes at him in a comical attempt to convince him to stay, and he chuckled.

'All right, all right. We'll do the invitations soon.'

'I'm not worried about that,' lied Clara.

'I promise you,' he said. 'Everything is going to be okay. We'll be back to normal in no time.'

He hugged her and it was a joy to lean into him, but then Clara felt grey suddenly. Last night's terrible tentacled dream came back to her – it had been horribly vivid and lifelike. There was no point mentioning Ruby though... Or should she? Should she put it on the table? But no, Ivor was exhausted. They both were. What would be the point? The point was, she had done something bad and she needed to set it right. For a moment, she wished she had a Clifford who would jump in and say it was all his fault. But she didn't have a Clifford; this was all on her.

She decided she would tell Ivor about Ruby at the weekend. After all, there was nothing really to tell. There was no urgency about it. Far more important, over the next few days, was to get him fit and strong. Dr Cardew had spelled it out to her, in case she was in any doubt – he said Ivor had to rest, which meant no physical exertions – and no *nervous* exertions either. The issue of Ruby would just have to wait.

37

Two days after Ivor came back and the first thing Miss Webb said when she came round was to enquire if Clara had taken the children to the church to thank the Lord for his survival.

'I have not,' Clara admitted. 'I've had a few other things on my plate.'

'You should! It will aid their spiritual recovery too.'

Spiritual recovery? wondered Clara, feeling quite worn down. Just how many recoveries was she expected to oversee?

Fortunately, Miss Webb had other issues on her mind too. She sat and talked about the Easleas while Clara washed up the breakfast dishes and cleared the table around her. The Easleas were determined to adopt Peg as soon as possible. And Miss Webb was thrilled.

'It will be splendid for our figures. A much-needed boost for Suffolk's childcare service.'

Miss Webb pushed a graph across the table and Clara could see the line going upwards, which Miss Webb insisted was as it should be. Clara thought it was a gross simplification, but she didn't say. Evidently, Miss Webb had worked hard on this.

'Oh, and splendid for Peg too, of course,' Miss Webb added, reddening a little. 'Which is the, uh, most important thing.'

When the cleaning was done, Clara made a pot of tea, put some macaroons on a plate, then sat down. She felt as though she was fizzing with agitation but she knew it wasn't Miss Webb's or the Easleas' fault. Stella jumped onto Miss Webb's lap. Stella liked the woman and, although cats weren't necessarily the best judges of character, Clara thought they weren't the worst either.

Miss Webb asked how Peg was, and Clara told her that Peg was –hesitantly – speaking a few words a day. She now said, 'Good morning', 'Bad dream,' 'Good night,' 'Sleep Tight' and 'Don't let the bedbugs bite'. Actually, Clara realised that was more than a few words – gracious, it was incredible. It had been a long wait to get to this point, and now her progress seemed incredibly quick.

Rather annoyingly, Miss Webb attributed this advancement to the visit of the Easleas.

'There we are then,' she said, puffed up and arms crossed. 'I just knew that once we managed to get Peg a proper family, she'd come on leaps and bounds.'

Clara pondered whether to say anything to that. It felt like an insult but it was probably unintentional, so she decided to hold her tongue.

'Didn't you think they were a match, Miss Newton?' Miss Webb asked, and Clara said they were but she thought it sensible to move forward cautiously. 'For Peg's sake,' she added, because she knew Miss Webb suspected it was for her.

Miss Webb took a macaroon and crunched loudly. 'Anyway, they adored Peg.'

'They only saw her for two minutes.' Clara tried not to sound curmudgeonly or as though she were against the match – she wasn't – but Miss Webb could be so insensitive.

'Whose fault was that?'

Clara took a breath. She and Miss Webb just came to things with a different perspective, that was all.

Treacherous Stella was purring like she was in kitty heaven.

'I have been meaning to ask – will we have any new children soon?' Clara said.

Miss Webb put yet another macaroon into her mouth, and it seemed to Clara she was doing it because she didn't want to speak. It gave Clara the chance to continue though.

'There haven't been any since last winter. And once Peg goes, we'll be down to only four. You said a while ago you had a couple of children you might need to place.'

As Clara said it, something added up – or rather it *didn't* add up. It felt like the mysterious algebra the children sometimes asked for help with.

'I like this,' Miss Webb said, patting the tea tray – or, as Clara now privately called it, 'malicious implement'.

As ploys to change the subject went, Clara thought this was poor.

'What is going on?' she persisted. It wasn't that she wanted new children right that moment – God forbid, there was enough going on to keep her busy until Christmas – but she wanted some clarity.

Miss Webb started coughing. She kept coughing. She went on so long that Clara stood up, ready to thump her childcare officer on the back if necessary, but Miss Webb hissed, 'Water.' Clara dashed to get her a glass, which Miss Webb swallowed gratefully before apologising.

Everything was calm again, although Clara was more determined than ever to get answers. Something was in the air.

'The thing is...' Miss Webb started.

And just like that Clara could feel her anxiety rising again. It was like climbing up a helter-skelter – she didn't want to get to the top, but it was too narrow, too awkward, there were too many children behind her, to reverse.

'What is it? What is *the thing*, Miss Webb?'

Poor Miss Webb. She was quite red in the face. 'The thing is... you're leaving, aren't you?' Miss Webb said finally.

'I'm *not* leaving!' said Clara indignantly.

Miss Webb looked mystified. She swallowed and then broke the remainder of her macaroon into bits.

'Then what will you do once you're married?'

'What will I *do*?' repeated Clara.

'Well,' said Miss Webb uncertainly. 'You know...'

Clara did know, but she pretended she didn't. She hadn't put what she would do on her list because it felt so far away from where she was. Really the question belonged at the top of the list – but instead, because there was no likelihood of a satisfactory answer, she hadn't put it on at all. She was a cheat.

The thing was, she didn't know what to do once she was married. She didn't want to give up her job or the home. Being a housemother was not a nine-to-five job, it was a twenty-four-hours-a-day job. And that wasn't because of the council, but her own moral integrity. You couldn't do this less than wholeheartedly. So how could she combine her two worlds? Being married to Ivor *and* working at the Grange?

She and Ivor had largely avoided talking about it, preferring to 'cross that bridge when we come to it'. But would they? Was this a bridge they should load up with explosives? Or a bridge they should tiptoe across? Should they avoid the bridge altogether and look for a different method of crossing?

And they would be facing the bridge pretty soon.

'I am not giving up my job,' clarified Clara.

'What about...' Miss Webb leaned forward and whispered like she was uttering sacred texts, 'starting a family?'

It was always *Starting* a family. People made it sound like starting a race. Ready Set Go. Firing pistol. Dig a hole for the shoe. Everyone seemed to think she was at the pulling-up-her-socks stage, when she hadn't even got to the stadium yet.

'I have my family here,' she said, gesturing at the macaroons. This seemed odd, so then she pointed more vaguely at the ceiling. 'This is it.'

'But you'll want your own?' asked Miss Webb, clearly mystified by Clara's answer.

They were her own family, why didn't anyone get that? Family was more than blood. And did people say it to Ivor? Had anyone EVER said it to Ivor? No, they had not.

Clara had made the decision a long time ago – she didn't want children of her own. She wanted to care for lost children. Ivor knew this – Ivor accepted this – why did she have to declare it? Should she put it up on a sign? She remembered the pleasure the children had taken in tearing down the sign in the front of the Grange, the sign that had declared to the world that the occupants were orphans. There was no point *hiding* what you were – but there was no point announcing it, advertising it, labelling, declaring before you were ready, either. And the fact was: if everyone knew you were an orphan or a childless woman – everyone had opinions on you.

Clara hoped her silence would chill the room, but Miss Webb didn't seem chilled.

Then Miss Webb surprised her.

'I hope to marry and start a family soon.'

'Oh!' said Clara. She hadn't expected this – neither the confession nor the substance of it. 'Did you have someone in mind?'

'Maybe.'

As Miss Webb looked away, she was blushing again. Still, at least they had moved on from the discussion of Clara leaving – for now.

38

Later that afternoon Clara had another visitor, and this time it was Mrs Mount. Last year Mrs Mount had been about to adopt Frank, Trevor and Gladys when her husband left her, and the adoption had fallen through. Clara was fond of her and they had stayed in sporadic contact. She didn't know anything about the floods or that Ivor had been missing and, as they sat down for tea, Clara decided not to tell her. The near-tragedy had dominated Clara's every thought for the past two weeks, naturally, but the idea of not talking about it for a couple of hours was rather refreshing.

One of the first things Mrs Mount said when she walked into the home was, 'I'm over Monty,' (her errant husband), which inevitably made Clara think that perhaps she wasn't.

Mrs Mount was as beautiful as ever, but she was more relaxed now, which made her – in Clara's eyes anyway – even more compelling to look at. She carried herself so finely, her clothes were all fitted and modern. She was also wearing a beret, which made Clara wonder how she would look if she wore one. (Ridiculous, probably.)

Stella did not jump on Mrs Mount's lap but she did walk

around the legs of the chair, as though she were another one impressed by Mrs Mount's fine porcelain skin.

The contrast between them was great and Clara couldn't help but feel bedraggled. She had been deliberately avoiding the mirrors but, when she did catch sight of herself, she thought it was amazing how quickly she had deteriorated. In less than ten days, virtually everything about her had started to look haunted. And this morning she had found not one pair of stockings that didn't have a ladder in them.

'Did you hear that he is engaged?' Mrs Mount said dramatically, as if she had rehearsed it. 'And I couldn't give a fig about it.'

Another one engaged. Clara felt another weird, and childish, prickle of envy. It was not as though she thought she was the first one or the only one – it was just – *everyone* seemed to be doing it these days.

'I didn't think Miss Cooper wanted to settle down,' Clara said, naming the woman she assumed Mr Mount was engaged to.

Mrs Mount froze. 'How do you know who she is?'

Clara had forgotten she hadn't told Mrs Mount about the connection. Miss Cooper was Clara's previous childcare officer – the one before Miss Webb.

'I just worked it out,' she said cautiously. She thought of Miss Cooper, who she liked, who had helped with Maureen's troubles, who had assisted her with lots of things. She hoped Mrs Mount wouldn't be too angry with her.

'Tart,' said Mrs Mount acidly. 'She's welcome to him.'

This would make the guest list awkward too. Mrs Horton said Miss Cooper should be invited. 'After everything she did!' But Clara felt Mrs Mount should take precedence. They had become friends.

Ideally, she'd have them both there, but she couldn't be sure now that they wouldn't wrestle each other to the floor.

Clara rinsed the sink of burnt toast scrapings and deliberated over the invitations again. If they had sent them out before, then she wouldn't have to worry about this now.

'I'm thinking of fostering,' said Mrs Mount, changing the subject suddenly.

Clara realised belatedly this wasn't a social call; or rather it wasn't just a social call: Mrs Mount was on business. A less worn-out Clara would have cottoned on to that straight away.

'What do you think?'

'This has come as a—' started Clara.

'I have the house. I have money. I have principles. Most importantly, I have...' she choked back a sob, or else the tea had gone down the wrong way, 'lots of money.'

She said it like the money would make up for the lack of husband. Maybe, Clara thought, it did. Rich people didn't adhere to the rules, they simply hurdled over them as though they didn't exist.

'They gave me the go-ahead once. Why wouldn't they do it again?' asked Mrs Mount hopefully.

'I'm not sure – you know there are stringent regulations.' Clara had never used the word 'stringent' before, but it seemed appropriate here.

'There must be a way round those,' Mrs Mount said airily with the entitlement of her class. Stringent regulations were minor inconveniences, nothing more. 'I'm an upstanding citizen. That must count for something. Besides, if the Council say no, there must be other ways.'

She turned her deep violet eyes on Clara, and, worn out though she was, Clara suspected that she was being nominated as one of those 'other ways'.

Clara didn't see Ivor that night, but some of the children went over to the workshop and reported that he was still resting. Gladys said, 'He sleeps a lot for a grown-up,' and swore that when she was an adult, she would never waste her time merely sleeping. Clifford opined that he 'looks rough as an old goat'.

Clifford had also eaten the buns Clara had been saving for the weekend, *and* upset Trevor by calling chess an old man's game.

He asked her if she'd managed to see Julian yet, and Clara realised she had been unkind to the boy by letting the incident rumble on. But the prospect of begging Julian to back down was not a pleasant one.

On Thursday, a long thin envelope arrived, with the address typed wonkily. It seemed to have doom written all over it and Clara opened it tentatively, only to find Mr Sommersby was requesting that she attend his office next week. This was not auspicious news. Clara tucked it out of sight and then, once the children were at school, she popped into the workshop to speculate about it with Ivor. Perhaps she shouldn't have been surprised to find him still in bed, but she was. Maxi woofed at her and then came over to show off one of Ivor's socks, held between her teeth.

'Patricia is with the nanny,' Ivor apologised. 'I've got so much work to catch up on but...'

'It's all right.' Clara felt sad that Ivor felt he had to explain himself to her. He got up though. He went to do his 'ablutions', as he said, and while he was in the bathroom, she opened the window because the room smelled rather stale. Then she tugged at Maxi's sock for fun. Maxi growled, thoroughly enjoying the battle.

When Ivor came back, he looked better. 'I'm not very...'

'Very what?' she teased him. It was silly, but she loved him more than ever. He rarely showed her his vulnerable side – he would say he did, but he didn't really.

'Appealing. An attractive prospect. As a groom, I mean.'

'I find you appealing,' she said in a little voice, but he didn't seem to have heard.

She was going to ask him if he wanted to talk about what happened on the night of the flood, but she decided not to. Hopefully, he would tell her when he was ready. *If* he was ever ready.

39

The children were playing 'It' and screeching, and Clara went into the parlour to escape from the noise. She didn't usually feel the urge to hide, but right now the need was pressing. It had been a painful few days and she couldn't help but feel that more pain was ahead. The Ruby issue had not been resolved and it seemed to grow and grow every time she looked away from it. She still hadn't told Ivor.

Breathing deeply, Clara leaned against the wall opposite the window, her lower arm over her forehead. And then she saw: the wall was covered in black marker-pen marks. There were squiggles, snake-like lines, tidelike shapes and loops. Clara couldn't believe her eyes. She tried to rub it off with her finger, but the markings wouldn't go away. She always told people that 'very little shocked her' but actually it wasn't true. This certainly did. Few children would dare anything as anarchic as this. In her parlour, her sacred and calm space, and on her lovingly wallpapered walls?

Clara stormed into the hall. 'I want to know who was in the parlour today!' she shouted. It could only have been today surely, since she would have noticed it otherwise?

'I was in there,' said Frank. He was trembling. For all his bravado, he hated being shouted at. 'Why?'

Clara reminded herself to calm down.

Trevor also appeared. 'What's going on?'

Patricia wobbled at the top of the stairs. 'I did NOT draw on walls,' she said in a baby voice with her arms crossed.

Her children – trauma survivors, victims of assault and torture – had not done this. Patricia, who had everything, had. It wasn't just scribble, it was an act of wanton destruction.

Clara didn't ever like to tell Patricia off – the little girl was not hers – but this was too much.

'Patricia!'

The little girl disappeared into the girls' room and the door slammed after her. The other children came to examine the wall and Clara could sense that under their horrified exclamations, they were impressed.

By the end of the week, Clara was very concerned about Ivor. He wasn't back to normal – no, he wasn't even approaching it. How long was this weirdness going to continue? She expected him that evening, but he didn't come. The next morning, she let herself into the workshop and called out for him. It was already nine o'clock, yet he was still in bed. This time he didn't get up.

'It's all right,' he mumbled. 'Patricia is with the nanny.'

She sat on the end of the bed next to Maxi, who looked as mournful as Clara felt.

'It's you I'm worried about.'

'No need. I'm just exhausted, that's all.' He closed his eyes. She felt left out.

'Let's do the invitations tomorrow!' she said in her most sparky voice. 'I'm having awful quandaries about who to invite or not. I need you to be stringent.' The word 'stringent' seemed out of place. 'Strict,' she amended. She thought, *I can't do this myself.*

He turned onto his side, so he was facing away from her.

'What hurts?' she asked uncertainly.

'All of it,' he said.

'Ivor,' she said loudly. 'There's something else I need to talk to you about.'

He looked up, shocked, yet weary, and she found she couldn't bring herself to say what she had planned to say. She couldn't bring Ruby up and into this room, not while he looked and felt like an old goat.

'What's happened?'

'Oh, nothing...' said Clara, feeling herself retreat.

'Tell me,' Ivor pressed, but half-heartedly.

Clara assembled her thoughts. 'Patricia scribbled over the parlour wall.'

Ivor covered his face with his hands. 'Nooo. How bad was it?'

Clara told him, but she played down how destructive it seemed. Instead, she made it into a sweet tale.

'I'll have to paint over it, for you,' he said. 'When I feel up to it.'

'That's not why I'm telling you.' She kissed his forehead. 'I'll move the dresser for now, I just thought it was funny.'

He closed his eyes again.

40

Clara knew she also had to do something about Jonathon; she just didn't know what. She remembered that the psychologist she had met last year, Dr Morgan, had advised 'sharing something,' with hard-to-reach teenagers. She found some *Sherlock Holmes'* stories in an old pile of Florrie's books that she thought they might read together, but Jonathon said he did enough classics at school, sorry, thank you. That made Clara miss bookworm Florrie. It had been fun going to the library with her. And she missed Billy and Barry, the twins who couldn't keep still and whose minds seemed as far from neurosis as is possible to be. Except when it came to their beloved Arsenal football team.

Jonathon didn't want to do baking together either, which Clara could, of course, understand. And he already did plenty of chores, but he did them by himself, or with the other children, and always quickly and efficiently. There was never an opportunity for 'a talk'.

Then one afternoon, quite by chance, Clara found a pair of Maureen's old school plimsolls in the toybox. She put them on and, although they felt unnatural, they fitted okay. This was something they could share perhaps.

She approached him after he got back from school.

'Thought I might come running with you today.'

He gaped at her. She kept her eyes on the funny plimsolls.

'Uh?' he said. 'Why?'

'Oh! I used to like running at school.'

This was not even remotely true. She'd preferred running to throwing things, but only slightly. She had never been a sporty one. She had never represented her school, nor even her class. The only physical activity she quite enjoyed was football, and girls weren't allowed to do that.

Jonathon shrugged. She thought he would creep off without her, but he waited at the back door.

'Do you, uh, want to warm up first?' he asked.

'Already have!'

Another lie. She didn't even bother to cross her fingers any more.

Jonathon took Clara on his usual route, to the paths by the fields, alongside the wildflowers. She liked the idea of the two of them, running, like cartoon characters. The thought that it would be dark soon didn't make her go faster, but it did frighten her; what if they got lost? Ivor wouldn't be able to help this time.

She loved the feeling of the cold air tingling on her cheeks, but she hated almost everything else about it. She felt like she couldn't breathe. It was terrible. Her left ankle wobbled. It was not often her body felt fragile, but it did now. She was afraid she'd trip herself up and her back hurt *and* did she need the lav?

A few hundred metres further and she thought she might die, and Jonathon would have to drag her body home and everyone would say, 'What on earth was she thinking?'

Still, it might shake Ivor out of his stupor, she thought nastily, and then hated herself for it.

They went through some nettles; they sprang back into her face. Jonathon was a distant blur. She stopped. He wound back to find her. And for some reason, far from the house, while she was catching her breath, she decided this was the right moment to talk.

'Jonathon – I wanted to say – I found a newspaper cutting in your blazer. About Alan Turing.'

His cheeks were already red from running and the wind, but Clara was sure they reddened more. He was breathing easily though, unlike her.

'Put your hands on your knees,' he said, and she did. 'That's it.'

'Okay. What was it doing there?' she asked, and the effort both to seem casual and to recover from the run was tremendous.

'I'm interested in what he did in the war,' he said nonchalantly. 'And he knew my father.'

'Alan Turing did?'

'Yes.'

She knew he was lying, and he knew she knew.

'If there was anything at all, you'd tell me?'

He nodded. 'There isn't anything. Do you want me to walk with you?'

'No, you go ahead if you like...'

And off he sprinted.

She limped slowly back. The ankle twinged. That hadn't worked and she wouldn't attempt it again. Some people are built for running, she thought. She was built for a cup of strong tea, a biscuit and a cigarette in the garden. There was a cup of tea ready for her when she got in, still warm, *and* a ginger biscuit, but Jonathon had already disappeared upstairs.

41

The butcher was chatting about Ivor and how lucky he was, and what a hero he was – they don't make them like him any more, etc., etc. – when the doorbell clanged and Julian came in. He was wearing a flashy wool coat over a pinstriped suit, and he looked his usual debonair self again.

'I wondered when you'd make an appearance,' Julian said, after he and the butcher had greeted each other. But under his hat, he still had a bandage round his head. Clara couldn't help thinking it was disproportionate and then she remembered the almost comical way he had plonked down, and it almost, but not quite, made her want to laugh.

Clara ignored him and went over to the butcher's other counter.

'Why are you walking strangely?' Julian asked.

Nothing got past him.

'It's fine.' Clara blushed. It wasn't that her ankle hurt so much as she was never more aware that she had an ankle. It was as though a siren was going off in her leg.

There was blood on this counter, and fatty meat. Clara was not squeamish, but she suddenly felt off-kilter. Tipping his hat at the butcher, Julian said to Clara significantly, 'I'll wait for you outside.'

'No nee—'

'Oh, I think there is,' said Julian, cutting her off.

The butcher took his thick knife and sliced into some meat. Clara winced.

'Tell Ivor I've got the chops he likes. You'll be wanting something for the mongrel too, I expect.'

Everyone knew about Maxi already too. The Lavenham grapevine. It was heart-warming if everyone was nice. Horrifying if everyone was not. She remembered fondly the newsletter the children had made with Joe – what was it? The *Shilling Grange News*? Maxi would have been front page, back page and centrefold.

Clara took a long while over paying. Hopefully Julian would get tired of waiting and give up on her. The butcher said kindly in a low voice, 'Don't worry about Mr White, he's all gristle, no meat.'

Unfortunately, Julian *was* still outside, sawdust on his shiny shoes. The wind was picking up.

'We need to talk about your feral boy – Clifton, is it?' said Julian, clearly not wanting to waste any time.

'What do you want to say?'

Clara hadn't slept well for days, and now the adrenaline and the elation from Ivor's return had worn off; and after the terrible run, she felt bone-tired. And Ivor hadn't returned, had he? Not properly. It was like something had chipped off, been left behind there in Hunstanton: His self-esteem, his sense of self. When she thought of him saying he wasn't an attractive prospect, it made her want to cry. The contrast between the hero in the butcher's story and the man who wasn't getting out of bed recently felt great.

The bag she was carrying felt too heavy, too much for one person. And she had a metallic blood taste in her mouth.

'I'm going to press charges,' Julian said brightly, like he was announcing a win at a raffle.

Clara thought of Clifford's kind offer and Trevor's fears. She thought of the chance Clifford would have – in court, in jail, in the future. The odds were stacked against him anyway – and now this. But otherwise, Trevor's opportunities would be ruined. She was stuck between a rock and a hard place. She didn't feel sad or surprised, she just felt fury at Julian – he always had to be at the heart of their turmoil.

'Right,' she said. 'That's your choice.'

Her cheeks were burning but she was surprised how steady her voice sounded. 'If you think orphans don't deserve second chances then that's... that's...'

This was not the closing line she had hoped for.

'He's had more than two chances,' Julian said.

'Do what you like...'

Clara started to storm off down the street, but her ankle refused to oblige. Nevertheless she limped on, shaking her head to herself. Damn him. Julian was the worst kind of person to be involved with: charming yet unpredictable, vengeful.

But he had caught up with her. 'Unless... I was just thinking – you could do something for me.'

'Oh no, Julian,' Clara responded furiously; he was lucky there wasn't another tea tray in the vicinity, 'that's not right. I am disgusted you would even...'

Julian laughed. 'Heavens no, don't flatter yourself, Clara. I was drunk the other night, that's all.'

'Right,' she said, humiliation now drowning out rage. 'Go on then. What were you thinking?'

'Remember that book I got you, some Christmases ago when we were... intimate?'

Of course she knew what he was talking about. Her Jane

Taylor book. Once the best present in the world.

'Which one?' she said, like there were a million in her arsenal.

He grinned, wolf-like. 'You know which one I mean, Clara.'

She couldn't pretend for long, never could with Julian. He would have been good at torturing special operative agents.

'If I give it to you, you will leave the children alone?'

'It's worth a few bob apparently.' Julian grinned his cocky lopsided grin.

It was her favourite book ever, but of course nothing was more important than the children. If this was it, *if,* then they'd have got off lightly.

Julian accompanied Clara back to the Grange and waited in the hall while she went upstairs to collect the book. She handed it over to him without emotion. She knew the poems from memory anyway: 'The Violet', 'The Poppy', 'The Star'. She knew the illustrations that accompanied each of them. She didn't have to have the thing to love it – years of working with children had taught her that. And she was happy to get rid of it if she was getting rid of him. She didn't want Julian's things any more. If this was all it took to get him out of her and the children's lives, then it was a massive weight off her mind.

'You don't mind?' he asked.

'Not at all.'

'Friends again?'

He held out his hand. Beryl would say he was a tricky customer, the sort who wouldn't be happy with any shade of blue. She'd say he was a typical Scorpio. Clara shook his hand as normal, but like the children, behind her back, she kept the fingers of her other hand crossed. Thank goodness for Jane Taylor, she thought. Marilyn was right: *Take all offers of help.* Jane Taylor might be over a hundred years dead, but it felt like she was on Clara's side.

42

Clara looked for Clifford upstairs, and out in the shed, but couldn't find him. *He's run away*, she thought. But although Clifford was another unpredictable one, it didn't take Clara long before she worked out where he might be.

Anita invited her in and then led her to the living room. Clifford was leaning against the grand piano like Sammy Davis Jr. Most of the large, elegant room had been turned into a railway line. Howard was on the floor, legs in a V-shape, chewing a train but no doubt pondering an engineering feat that would put Isambard Kingdom Brunel to shame. Evelyn was at school; the only sign of her was a book on a coffee table full of tiny squares and even tinier red ticks. The Norland Nanny and Patricia were at the swings, apparently.

'Let's try again,' Anita said to Clifford. She wouldn't let the silly fact of a visitor – Clara hadn't quite forgiven her for calling her 'unimportant' – get in her way.

Anita sat on the piano stool with her fingers spread over the keys. 'One, two...'

When Clifford sang, it was beautiful. Even more beautiful than how he used to sound. There was more pathos in it, perhaps, as he'd grown up. He was like Johnnie Ray. He was such a different child here in Anita's house than he was at home. Clara wondered why that was. Anita treating him like he was an idol, or perhaps that he was not competing with other children for attention? Who knew?

'What do you think?'

Clara didn't realise Anita was addressing her until she said, 'Good enough for your wedding?'

Clara couldn't have said no, even if she wanted to – but she didn't want to.

'We'd be honoured.'

'Although I still haven't got my invitation yet!' Anita said.

'I know!' Clara snapped, exasperated. She thought of poor Ivor, horizontal and with those exhausted eyes. *What hurts? All of it.* 'No one has yet. We'll do them soon.'

Anita said she'd go and make some tea. While she was out of the room, Clifford looked at Clara, and she knew what he was going to ask.

'Are they going to arrest me then?' he asked, his tone defeated.

'I think it's going to be okay,' she said. 'Julian has made a deal.'

He raised his eyebrows at her, grinned, then stopped himself.

'But I've got to go back to the Reform School?'

'Maybe not.'

This time his face lit up. He clearly hadn't expected that. 'Then where?'

'I might have found somewhere else for you to live...'

'Is it here?' he asked, his eyes hopeful. 'With Mrs Cardew?'

That stung.

'No, but it's with someone very nice indeed, and they've already been checked. I just need to make a few phone calls first,' said Clara, pleased with the plan she was hatching, but aware that it was yet another thing to put on her to-do list.

43

It was Sunday, which meant Sunday School again – that came round quickly! – and the children were excited and chirruping all the way there. 'B – Bread, bacon, brown-chocolate – nooo, you can't have brown-chocolate – it's the only chocolate I like.'

Once they were deposited, Clara hurried over the road to Ivor's workshop. He hadn't got up yesterday, but she had a better feeling about today. He wasn't at his workbench but, amazingly, he wasn't in bed either, which Clara decided was progress, definitely.

Patricia was on the floor, building houses with cards. Maxi was asleep, oblivious, next to her, several small socks scattered around her like petals.

Every time the houses fell down, Patricia shouted, 'Sod, sodding cards.'

Clara made a face at Ivor at the swear words, but he was busy boiling the kettle and pretending he hadn't noticed.

It wasn't until after they'd had coffee and chatted about Peg and the Easleas, and her ankle – 'just a silly thing' – that Ivor told her about going to see Dr Cardew, and then all he said was: 'Please, don't make a fuss.'

Clara tried to swallow back her concern. She wasn't making a fuss; she wanted to know what this was. She thought then that she had to tell him about Ruby. That panicky telephone call in the midst of it all was beginning to dominate her every waking thought. Under the circumstances, she reassured herself, contacting Ruby was a normal thing to do, as normal as paying your milk bill.

'I'm not fussing,' she said eventually. 'I'm just worried about you.'

He screwed up his face.

'I know. It's just since the flood.'

'I see.'

But Ivor didn't elaborate further. Clara couldn't leave it there.

'What is "it" exactly?'

'Oh, the pain – my arm, my shoulder... my neck too.'

Of course the hypothermia, the exertion, the exhaustion had had an impact. It had to have. And, to be honest, she still got sore ribs from the air-show disaster, and her ridiculous bicycle crash shortly after. But sometimes, in a strange way, she liked the pain in her ribs because it reminded her of her father. And *then* her ankle sprain the other day. It was only in films where you could nearly die and be skipping through the tulips the next day.

Ivor already had aches and pains from his war injuries. Although aches and pains didn't seem to do justice to what he experienced.

'What should we do?' By 'we', she meant *me*, what should *I* do?

Clara adored Ivor – he was the love of her life – but she knew he liked to keep some things back. She knew that, especially when it came to his arm, he didn't like to tell her – perhaps he saw it as a burden, as a weakness, or something else – whichever way, he liked to play his cards close to his chest.

'I'm not to have any distress.'

Clara half-laughed. 'Which means?'

'I'm to take some more time off work.'

In all the years Clara had known him, Ivor had never not been working. Even a weekend away; that was what he was. Cotton for veins, cushions for his heartbeat. It was a joke between them. The only downtime Ivor permitted himself was Patricia, Clara and the children and stargazing. Even then, if he could combine them with some measuring or cutting or stapling he would.

'Will you?' she asked softly.

'I don't know how,' he said. 'But Dr Cardew seems to think I'll have to sooner or later, so it might be better to jump rather than be pushed.'

Clara thought for a moment. It was her fault he had been in Hunstanton, after all. It was her fault he was suffering; she had to provide a solution. She looked around her wildly.

'Should you – get rid of the dog?'

Ivor was appalled. 'Put down my Maxi?'

'I didn't mean get rid of her like that! I meant find somewhere else for her. She could live over the road with us,' Clara said recklessly.

'Oh, I see,' he said, chuckling, but his face was serious. 'But Maxi is no trouble – she makes my life easier, if anything. She saved me.'

Was it wrong to feel a pang of envy for a dog? Yes, it was, Clara reprimanded herself.

'How about you don't make my wedding dress then? I know you need the paid work. You can't really afford fifty hours, can you...'

Ivor considered this, but she had the feeling that it wasn't his first time thinking about it. He had, she realised, already decided and had been waiting for her to suggest it. Why was she so slow? She should have noticed. It probably weighed heavily on him.

He cleared his throat. 'I'd be letting you down though, wouldn't I?'

'No, you wouldn't.'

Although she loved his dressmaking, Clara was more thrilled that she could do something for him. She was only too grateful to have some way to free him from his distress. It was only a dress, after all. She'd think of something or someone else.

'How about you get one and I'll do the adjustments for it?'

'It's a deal,' she said.

'I'm sorry,' he said in a strangled voice.

She didn't have the heart to mention the invitations that she was longing to send out, and she didn't have the courage to mention Ruby. She couldn't add to his bother – not now, when he seemed to be finally unloading all his burdens: they would have to wait. But the conversation left Clara with a nagging fear. She couldn't work out why he was so sad – and she wished he would confide in her.

The children came bouncing down the Sunday School steps full of joy. Oh, to be a child, thought Clara enviously, or actually anyone without the world on their shoulders.

'What did you learn today?'

Usually, Frank or Gladys would yell some nonsense. 'A. Adam and Eve and the snake.' Or, 'You can turn water into wine, Miss Newton, but not into milk, so it's no good for the children.'

Today, Peg replied, in her careful untested voice, 'It is easier for a camel to go through the eye of a needle than for a rich man to enter the Kingdom of God.'

And Clara was so shocked to hear Peg doing whole sentences now – she scooped her up: 'Well done, Peg,' – that she didn't think much about what the words could mean.

44

Mrs Horton offered to drive Clara to the meeting with Mr Sommersby at the council offices.

Clara felt uneasy with this being babied. Nevertheless, a lift was a lift. *Take all offers of help,* she thought.

Mrs Horton slammed through the sleepy Suffolk roads like she was racing at Le Mans. When she asked how Ivor was, Clara was gripping hold of the passenger-side door handle and her knuckles were white. She didn't tell Mrs Horton the full story – *what is the full story?* – but just said that Ivor was exhausted, and Dr Cardew had told him he had to slow down.

'Slow down?' yelled Mrs Horton, her foot on the accelerator.

'I mean take it easy, rest... He's exhausted.'

'You seem pretty wound up too,' observed Mrs Horton as they took another corner, tyres screeching. 'Are you sure you don't want to cancel Mr Sommersby?'

'Nobody cancels Mr Sommersby!' Clara said, shivering at the thought. She knew he wasn't happy with her. He was never happy with her. What she didn't know was what she had done to make him unhappy with her this time.

She told Mrs Horton that Ivor was no longer making her

wedding dress. At first Mrs Horton was despondent, and then she cheered up and suggested, 'Why don't we go dress-hunting afterwards? There's a lovely shop in Bury!'

'Be good to have something to look forward to,' agreed Clara. She tried not to think of Ivor's 'I'm sorry'. As if she cared about the dress – all she cared about was marrying him!

Mrs Horton parked up by the council building and then went off to source some Wensleydale cheese. Clara walked in the opposite direction. She sat in the familiar odd-smelling reception area of the council building and waited. A family – Mum, Dad and three children – sat in silence opposite her. An old man picked his nose. Clara had read most of the magazines there, but there was a newspaper on one of the tables and self-consciously, she went to fetch it. There were grainy photos of floodwater and boats and things that were not boats being used as boats. It made her feel nauseous to see it and she put it back down again.

She was summoned up the stairs to Mr Sommersby's office. Her ankle still twinged but compared to other people's woes – Ivor's woes – it was nothing. Mr Sommersby appeared in fine fettle, puffing on a cigar like a movie mogul. 'I hear your friend was missing, but like Lazarus, he miraculously came back to life?'

'He did...' Clara forced her lips into a smile. Although this office was large, the largest in the building, it was still smoky enough to make her eyes red. He had a photograph of his wife on his desk now – Clara was sure it wasn't there before – it was a close-up of her in contemplative pose, her chin resting in her pretty fingers. It seemed to be a statement somehow, but Clara wasn't sure what of.

'That must have been hard,' said Mr Sommersby, tilting his head.

'It has been an interesting few days, yes.'

Interesting, she thought. This was typical British understatement. Everyone did it though. It was expected of you. If you said what it was – it had been *bloody awful* – eyebrows would be raised.

Yet Mr Sommersby was looking at her so sympathetically that, for a moment, Clara had to remind herself that this was Mr Sommersby, leader of children's services, a man who had never previously had her best intentions at heart.

Perhaps he'd changed? Perhaps that was what the genial family portrait represented?

'So you must be wondering what you're here for, Miss Newton.'

'A little...'

'Let me put you out of your misery – what we've been thinking is this: we can waive the usual notice period and you can leave us as soon as you like!'

Or perhaps not.

'We can relieve you of your duties immediately, let you concentrate on your friend. He must need some attention!'

He said it like he'd delivered her a big bouquet of flowers. Like he expected her to coo, 'Oh, Mr Sommersby, you *are* marvellous, thank you!'

'Pardon?' said Clara. She couldn't believe this. Mr Sommersby wasn't overly fond of her but he wouldn't just sack her, would he?

He got up and poured whisky into a glass. The sound made Clara cross her legs.

'I mean – I accept your resignation, if you wish.'

'I'm not-I'm not... *resigning*,' stammered Clara. This camel was going through that needle. She and Mr Sommersby didn't see eye to eye, but she hadn't realised it had got this bad. 'And I don't know why you think I would!'

'You're leaving in May anyway, aren't you?' continued Mr Sommersby brusquely. His tone was full of recrimination. 'What's a few months?'

'Huh? Nothing of the sort has been decided,' Clara responded, exasperated.

Mr Sommersby snorted. 'Miss Newton, everyone and his brother is talking about your impending nuptials.'

'Yes, but—'

'How were you thinking you would manage? You'll want to start a family.'

He didn't even say it as a question, it was a blank fact.

There was a silence. Clara swallowed. He puffed.

'We haven't decided on next steps,' Clara responded stonily. *How dare he?* She was fed up of walking on eggshells on this issue. These eggshells were long broken. 'I don't know who told you that.' *Miss Webb probably. Bloody woman!*

Mr Sommersby's expression was as sour as the air. 'We don't have *any* married women working as housemothers.'

'Then I'll be your first,' she wanted to say. Instead, she said, 'I understand that, but I'm not even married yet.'

And the rate things were going with Ivor, Clara was beginning to wonder if she ever would be.

'You'll be pleased to hear we have a replacement in mind.'

Pleased to hear?

'Really?!' Clara folded her arms and glared.

'She's an excellent worker – years of experience. In fact, she worked at the home before.'

'What?'

'So, she is familiar with protocol and procedures – and Lavenham, of course.'

'Who on...'

'I don't think you'll have met her – she's one of the nuns.'

'Sister Grace?!'

'Sister Eunice—'

'Noooo!' yelped Clara, her face aflame. 'Absolutely not!'

That woman! That woman who used to whip and beat the children, that woman who made them eat silently and sleep silently, and locked them up. That woman who made Peg speech-less, who shamed Maureen, who caused untold miseries, that woman who sat on every exuberance, that woman who Clara imagined would have 'plucked her nipples from boneless gums and dashed its...' *That* Sister Eunice?

For once Mr Sommersby looked surprised.

'Er, yes. You do know her then?'

'Over my dead body is she coming back,' Clara said. She didn't care what he thought any more. 'You can put that right out of your mind, Mr Sommersby. I will not be leaving Shilling Grange any time soon.'

Mrs Horton was waiting outside in the car. She moved her shopping bags from the passenger seat to the floor so Clara could get in. At the top of the bag there was a paper bag and a wheel of cheese, and next to it was another cheese. All cheese bases were covered.

'I've sorted out some food for the next couple of days, so that's one less thing to worry about – Mrs Horton senior is demanding, Clara. I can't do anything right by her!' She smiled at Clara as if only just remembering why they were there. 'How did it go with Mr Sommersby?'

'It was... interesting,' said Clara guardedly. She couldn't bring herself to say anything about it yet. Right at that moment, it felt like the whole world was conspiring against her.

Sod, sodding, sod, as Patricia might say.

'Right, dress-shopping it is!' Mrs Horton slapped the steering wheel.

'I'm sorry,' Clara said, 'not today. My head is aching.' It was. 'I'd rather just go home.'

45

Peg was going to spend the weekend with the Easleas. Little Peg. It was the best thing – it was the worst thing. A life, a normal family life, would be hers, and not just for the rest of her childhood – forever.

Clara had talked to Mrs Easlea on the telephone a few times. Mrs Easlea was happy to listen – it was something Clara liked about her.

She felt sick at the thought of not seeing Peg's little face every day, of not watching her grow up. Seeing her flick through her notebook, play the drums, arrange her shells. But this was what life at Shilling Grange was – transient. Temporary. It was supposed to be a stepping stone. A ladder. A halfway house. It was not, Clara told herself, the final destination.

We do the best we can, but it's a second best. It's a replacement. It's a make-do-and-mend, she told herself. It was the philosophy of wartime – no wonder she had fitted in so well at the orphanage. She was forged in the fire of the Second World War; it was what she knew – managing – keep your chin up – don't know when we'll meet again.

She folded Peg's small white vests, and the grey skirts and the socks. The trouble they had with those socks! She rolled up the jumper and the cardigan. She didn't need a lot for one weekend; it fitted snugly in her school satchel.

Clara looked out of the window at the sun setting over the garden, a flaming sun – it would take just minutes for it to disappear – making a playground of colour of the sky. And then darkness until tomorrow. There was the lawn with the mud, there was the small, unsuccessful vegetable patch, there was where the roses used to be, the shed with its burn marks up the side, the piano that no one ever touched, the drum kit, skipping ropes. All of these things holding a million memories of the children who had lived here over the years.

'Can I take the drums?' Peg asked loudly, bringing Clara's attention back to the present and making her smile.

'Not this time, but yes, when you go for longer.'

'I thought they belonged to the house.'

There was an argument that they did, thought Clara. But: 'You'll take them if you want them,' she told Peg.

When the Easleas arrived, Clara watched the interaction between them. He was grumpy, that special kind of grumpy that might come from being in pain, but he was kind too (that also might have come from being in pain). Mrs Easlea was hardworking – she was one of those women who never seem to stop – but she was not downtrodden.

When it came to time to leave, Peg disappeared. Clara ran up to the bedroom, but Gladys said she hadn't seen her. She wasn't in the parlour, the kitchen or the bathrooms. Trevor worked out she was in the shed. Clara could hear the drums – ba boom tish. It must have been cold in there – it was cold out in the garden. She could see her breath.

It is difficult negotiating with someone who won't speak – it's even worse when they are in a different room.

'Peg,' called Clara in a sugary voice, 'it's time to go, sweetie.'

After some time, a note was pushed under the shed door.

'Dont want to see nobdy.'

Clara had to proceed carefully. 'Would I ever send you anywhere you wouldn't want to go?'

Eventually, she heard the pencil scratching on paper, and another note came out.

'No.'

H-okay, that's progress.

'I will always listen to you, but I would like you to give these people a chance. They've come a long way.' Clara didn't actually know if they'd come a long way today. But what if they had?

'And they do seem nice.'

They did.

'What if my muver comes back though? she won't know where to find me.'

Clara took a deep breath. She didn't know Peg had these thoughts about her mother – although why shouldn't she? Mothers did come back. Rita's had. Evelyn's had. Florrie's father had.

'She will be able to find you because I will tell her – I will make sure if she does, she will find you.'

'Will you be here forever then?'

Tears filled Clara's eyes. 'I'll be here for a long time, yes.' She shouldn't make promises she couldn't keep. 'And if I'm not, the council will tell her...' she added tentatively.

Peg edged open the shed door and Clara knew that the battle was halfway won.

'What do you say, Peg?'

'I don't want to leave,' she eventually said. 'What about the wedding?'

'You'll come. Of course.'

Peg seemed to relax slightly. She let Clara take her hand. 'What about Gladys?'

'You'll always be friends,' Clara reassured her.

'I just don't see the point. You're my family.'

'The point is, it's permanent.'

'Nothing is permanent.'

Clara smiled. 'The more people who love you the better.'

Peg screwed up her nose. 'Not into big numbers. One or two is enough for me.'

When they walked back into the kitchen, the Easleas' worried expressions dissolved and Clara couldn't help but warm to them, the two lovely guinea pigs.

'Oh, Peg!' said Mrs Easlea. 'We hear you're talking now!'

And Peg smiled. 'A little.'

'Talk or not,' added Mr Easlea, and Clara realised it was the first time she'd heard him say a whole sentence, 'we just want you to be happy.'

46

After Peg had left, Clara went to see Ivor in his workshop and found him still asleep. She didn't have the heart to wake him with her problems again. She washed up the cups, wiped the sink and emptied the ashtrays. There was no sign of any work under way. The workshop had a melancholy air – but that might have been Clara's imagination.

She went upstairs. Her steps seemed loud and invasive.

He was lying still, awake now though, and staring at the ceiling.

'I'm off, Ivor,' she said, standing in the doorway to his bedroom.

No reply.

'I've done the dishes and some bits.'

'You shouldn't have, I'll get up now.'

Clara swallowed. She couldn't leave him like this – he looked so down-hearted. She thought about mentioning Peg and the Easleas but thought it best to stick to something cheery.

'I thought we could get the invitations out soon,' she suggested brightly.

A few weeks back, his eagerness had irritated her – now she wanted that enthusiasm back more than anything.

He said it was just weariness, Dr Cardew said it was nervous exhaustion, but what if it was more than that? What if he didn't love her any more?

'For God's sake, Clara,' he said, turning away from her in his bed. 'Really?'

Tears came to her eyes. She couldn't help it. Ivor and Peg were both slipping away from her. She knelt at his side. 'What is it, Ivor?' she pleaded, just wanting answers, whatever they may be.

'Just go ahead, do it without me,' he finally replied in a small voice.

Clara felt despondent. She didn't want it to be like this. The event she was excited about – she felt as though it was a burden to him. *She* was a burden to him. 'I will need your list though...'

'I'll do it later,' he said and there was no joy in his voice, just weariness.

'You don't have to,' she said and then she fled down the stairs, desperate to get away before they fell out any further.

Mrs Horton came round and, as soon as she saw Clara's teary face, she offered to mind the children so that Clara could go off to Beryl's Brushes. She didn't have an appointment and she wasn't due another do – although Beryl would probably say she was – but she did need to get away for a short while. Home felt a strange combination of empty and suffocating.

She would not cry again, she would not. Fortunately, Beryl was too preoccupied with her last customer, an elderly woman who had the temerity to complain she had been given the wrong shade of blue, to notice Clara's state of mind at first.

'There is no wrong shade of blue,' Beryl was insisting to the woman.

Clara wondered what Ivor would say if she came back from Beryl's with any shade of blue. Probably nothing. She had never known such apathy. Between his malaise and Peg moving on, it felt like her whole world had tilted on its axis.

It wasn't until Beryl hovered behind her with the mirror and it was the moment to admire the back of her head that Beryl brought up Peg.

'You don't know when she was born, do you?' she wondered. 'She looks to me like a Pisces. It's the big eyes, see. Always a give-away.' She placed the mirror down and got the broom.

Clara let out a sob. 'I don't think I can do without her.'

Beryl looked astonished. Clara's breakdown was most out of character. 'There, there,' she said, leaning on her broom and surveying Clara, slack-mouthed. 'It's been an emotional few weeks.'

'An emotional few weeks' was one way of putting it. Rather more apt than 'interesting'.

Peg was going to leave. She couldn't think there'd be a reason the Easleas or the council would say no. And Clara knew she would put on a brave face. And a new Peg would come. A new child with new agonies and new ways of dealing with those agonies that would probably need to be undone too.

And what about her and Ivor? Were they over? She couldn't make him get married, and he seemed indifferent to everything right now.

'You're a brave girl, aren't you, Clara?' Beryl said and it was such a motherly thing to say, it made Clara want to cry more.

She sniffed. 'Not very.'

'To give and give to someone without hoping they'll give anything back. Without expecting to get anything back – that's brave.'

Beryl swept up the curls on the floor into the dustpan.

47

Peg had an excellent weekend at the Easleas. She didn't tell Clara much about it, but apparently there was a park nearby, and she wrote down a convoluted story about a neighbour with a rabbit who did not like carrots.

The day after she'd got back, Clara was setting out the plates for tea when Peg burst in the back door.

'Ivor wants you.'

It was still so peculiar hearing Peg speak that Clara found herself sometimes marvelling at that and not hearing what she was actually saying. She still couldn't quite adjust to it. Peg had a voice! You might expect it to be hesitant or sound inexperienced, but in fact it was direct and usually clear.

Clara dried her hands. Was he going to apologise for the other day? Had he done his list?

'Did he say what it's about?'

Peg shrugged. She blew her nose on her handkerchief and then stroked Stella. She seemed surprised to see that Clara was still waiting for more information.

'Oh, I don't know.'

When Clara was in her last year at school, there was a fashion for playing with a Ouija board. You put your fingers on a glass and the glass moved to spell out letters, which made words, which made messages. Invoking the devil, her father said – his belief system still within her – and for the next few weeks, months, she had thought the devil really was everywhere, even after one of her friends – Marianne – had admitted moving the glass.

She felt that now. While obviously she and Ivor were still engaged, the terrible prospect of Ruby reappearing was all about her. Her head told her that it was okay, *calm down, it's not real*, but the rest of her was in a constant state of anxiety: it's the devil! It must be what it's like taking a slow-acting poison and just waiting, waiting for the disaster to strike.

And now she was having dreams not only of Ruby and her tentacles but of Sister Eunice and her whip too. She felt trapped between them.

Clara had decided that she would tell Ivor about Ruby as soon as he was back to normal. She'd start with Mr Sommersby's horrendous suggestion – *Sister Eunice!* – and then she'd throw in the Ruby issue almost as an afterthought. He would be so incensed about the first that the second would hardly leave a stain.

The workshop door was wide open and several glass bottles teetered on the step. Patricia loved her milk. Even from the other side of the road, Clara could see Ivor was at a machine, although not working but leaning back in his chair, still looking exhausted. She could see a bottle and a glass on the bench – it looked like whisky. He looked up at her as she approached, and gave her a half-smile. It was only as she drew closer that she saw that, for the first time she'd seen in a long while, his eyes were full of tears.

The bad feeling swept back in. The climbing-up, fizzy feeling in the gut. It was a feeling she had come to recognise as 'Ruby fear'.

'What on earth's happened?' she was asking even before she was inside. In her mind, she was fleshing out the absolute awfulness of it. She *knew* what had happened – she had made what happened happen.

'You look like you've seen a ghost.'

He shook his head.

'What is it, Ivor? Tell me.'

She was almost paralysed with worry. The expression on him – he looked hollowed out. He'd found out, she knew it.

He got up from his bench. He was shaking his head, *too late*, and then he came over and took her into his arm. He had alcohol breath, and that was rare. She was rigid with horror.

'They took Maxi,' he whispered into her ear.

Maxi?

'Maxi the dog?' Clara had to recalibrate herself. It was not Ruby. It was not her. It was the dog.

'What?! Who did?'

'Her owners have been looking for her all over the place. They came to collect her today.'

'Oh, Ivor.'

Her heart was beating like a steam train. She could hardly catch her breath. She felt like little explosions were going off inside her. This was not right, this was not normal.

But nothing about Ivor and Ruby and her was normal.

'It's a good thing,' he said bravely. 'Maxi was thrilled to see them. Her name isn't Maxi – well, obviously – it's Blue.'

It was not Ruby.

Clara had to say something. 'She doesn't look like a Blue.'

'I know. Stupid name.' Ivor made a sound, half sob, half laugh. 'No, it's not stupid. It's just not her. I don't know why I got attached. She was just a...'

Ivor, who almost never drank, drank some of his whisky, gulped loudly. Grinned at her, with his lovely teeth, his eyes still shadowy.

'Dr Cardew says it's perfectly normal – a shock-trauma reaction.'

Clara stared at him. He'd already seen Dr Cardew then? Before he'd asked to see her. She felt slighted again, which was ridiculous.

'What else did he say?'

'The best way to get over it is to get drunk and spend time with beautiful women.'

Oh, Ivor.

'One out of two isn't bad,' she joked. Would she ever stop shaking?

'Your hair looks lovely,' he said tenderly. 'Beryl?'

'No other,' she said.

She could have done with a strong drink too.

He reached for her again. He stroked her and buried his face in her shoulder, and then he pulled away.

'Do you mind leaving me for a bit? I'm not merry company today.'

'You are to me – but no, of course not. Whatever you want.'

'I'll be better soon. This is just a rough patch. You'll wait for me?'

'Of course. Forever.'

He had no idea what she'd done.

She had to tell him about Ruby.

But she couldn't tell him *now*.

48

Clifford and Clara took the train to London. Julian had taken his pound of flesh, but Clara still couldn't trust him not to change his mind. And Clifford deserved a brighter future. Underneath his delinquent exterior, he was a hero of the flood. She could get him a better place than the brutal Hunstanton Reform School for Boys.

She offered to look after his ticket, as she did with all the children, but Clifford insisted on hanging on to it. She didn't quite trust him not to lose it.

Outside the window, the fields raced past. The carriage smelled of polish and stale socks. A little girl got on with her mother, carrying a cage covered in a blanket, and the mother said, 'We're going to release it, aren't we, Cecilia? Far from the house.'

Lip curled, the mother looked at Clara and Clifford. 'It's a mouse. She wouldn't let me kill it. Sentimental old thing.'

Cecilia didn't seem too impressed with the releasing-into-the-wild idea either.

They got off at the next stop, Cecilia still grumbling. Her mother was increasingly brisk with her. 'Come now, Cecilia, it's what we agreed.'

Once they'd got off, Clifford and Clara laughed.

'*Come now, Cecilia, it's what we agreed*,' Clifford repeated, reminding Clara what a brilliant mimic he was.

When the conductor came, Clifford pretended he'd lost his ticket and Clara nearly blew a gasket, but he was joking. He produced it from up his sleeve and the conductor shook his head like he dealt with this kind of errant behaviour all day long and clipped it as though he'd prefer to clip Clifford round the ear.

Clifford had a light moustache and fur on his chin but, even without that, he looked older than his age. Hard times did that to you, thought Clara. She felt she looked forty recently. So much for the blushing bride. She'd be the blighted bride.

'You never really liked me, did you?' Clifford said once the conductor had stamped his way out of earshot and they were alone. He blew out a smoke ring.

'What? Of course I do,' Clara said. She really needed to concentrate more. Dolly-daydreaming about the wedding wasn't fair on anyone.

'Not really,' Clifford challenged lightly.

'I found you difficult, that's all,' she admitted. And Clara felt ashamed that she hadn't hidden that from him better. She should have risen above her frustration. It disappointed her that she hadn't.

'I know that,' he agreed factually. 'It was obvious.'

'I'm sorry. I hope I didn't make you feel bad.'

'You didn't,' he said cheerfully. 'I was a sod, wasn't I? And I wasn't aware of how it affected the people around me.'

As he looked out of the window, a shadow crossed his face. He was the least emotional child she knew, but she saw a tightness there. The events of recent days had taken their toll.

When he next spoke, he was fighting back tears.

'It was dark and cold. I've never been that cold in my life. But Jonathon was full of courage. He kept our spirits up and then... When we saw the boat, it was him, he wanted to keep going. Keep looking for people. I wanted to get back to safety.' He looked at Clara with his flinty eyes. 'I was starving, I hadn't eaten for ages. I would have given anything to stay back. But Jonathon, he said it – we'd go on.'

Clara put her hand to her face. It was terrible to imagine what they'd gone through.

'We didn't know what was what at first. Neither of us had rowed before. But Ivor knew how, so he taught us. My arms were aching like hell. And then when we found this first family, they were so grateful, and me and Jonathon had to bring them in – I mean Ivor was tough and all, but you know his arm... and I didn't think we'd have the strength yet Jonathon was like a warrior. I'll never forget it.

'And then I rowed us back. Maisie, the girl, couldn't do it any more, bless her, and so... And then we did it again and again. I lifted two old ladies, and an old man.' He said it proudly, and then his eyes darkened.

'And then they said they heard a dog. I couldn't hear it. And I refused to go. You have to understand, I was exhausted, I'd never felt anything like that in my life.'

He rubbed the window with his thumb and the pane of glass made a squeaking noise.

'Ivor will be all right,' he said, sounding years older than he was.

Clara nodded, but she was thinking, *How would this boy know?*

'I know he's down now but he will be – he's crazy about you and the babby. When we were out there, he talked about you all the time – how he admires you. How he can't wait to be your husband. And he's tough.'

Clara stared out at the telegraph poles as they stood solid and strong against the fields. Ivor was tough but he wouldn't ask her for help, and she felt useless. It wasn't just the invitations, of course not, but they symbolised it. Ivor wasn't interested, Ivor didn't care.

'I hope so,' Clara agreed, before adding, 'thank you.'

'You don't give up on people easily, do you?'

'No.' Clara smiled. That was a big compliment, maybe bigger than Clifford realised.

'I like Jonathon,' he said.

'So do I,' replied Clara.

'You know he's a homosexual though, don't you?' he said, abruptly, but in a hushed tone. 'Jonathon, I mean?'

Clara's head sprang up. She remembered the cutting from the newspaper about Alan Turing. She had vaguely sensed something like this but now Clifford put it in words, it crystallised for her.

'I-I wondered. Maybe.'

She leaned back in her chair, feeling the hairs on her arms stand on end. She had no idea what Clifford was going to say next. In a strange way, she had no idea what she thought about it either. It ran through her fingers; it slipped through her teeth. She loved men – and desired men – the idea that someone would be attracted to men was perfectly logical to her. But it frightened her too. Would men hurt Jonathon? It seemed it opened him up to a world of risk – in a world that was already horribly risky. Many other men were bigger than Jonathon – and other men felt strongly about it.

It was a new thing for her. She knew of homosexuals, of course, but none personally. She knew what her father thought about them. She had a memory of her father saying, 'Hello, sailor' in a funny voice to Jonathon, and Jonathon looking even more sheepish at that than usual.

The sad thing was that she actually thought they'd been making progress. No, that wasn't *the* sad thing. There were a hundred sad things about this. The thought that he had been trudging along all this time with this secret made her heart break. Why should he have to – and why hadn't she realised it before?

Jonathon, dear Jonathon.

He just wanted to be able to love freely and be loved in return. But he knew society wouldn't let him.

'Did he tell you that?' Clara asked finally.

'I just knew he was different.' Clifford grinned and then flicked his ticket from one hand to the other. It took willpower not to tell him to stop. 'He's not girl-mad like me.'

'There is a middle way,' Clara pointed out primly. And Clifford laughed again. He was in such high spirits today, it was like he'd come up for air.

'I told him it don't matter, not to me anyways. Less competition.' He grinned, showing his sharp teeth. 'For the ladies.'

There is that, Clara thought ruefully.

'So you told him you knew?'

'Maybe not as directly as I just told you but yeah, he knows I know. We're going to stay in touch anyway. He's my first proper friend. You know, I like him. And we went through all that together in Hunstanton. That's got to count for something.'

She felt a huge affection for this boy who sang like Sinatra and who seemed to be able to negotiate the world better than most people. But it was true she hadn't always felt this fond. And she felt a great relief, knowing Jonathon had someone to talk to, that he wasn't alone in this any more.

'You're a good boy,' Clara said impulsively.

He straightened his tie and collar self-consciously. 'I don't think you've ever said that to me before.'

'Well, you are. A very good boy.'

He grinned and his fingers jangled on the table. 'You might change your mind when I tell you something else – I asked out Maureen.'

Clara shook her head. He was incorrigible.

He continued. 'But don't worry. She said no.'

'Ah. She is a bit older than you.'

Clifford chuckled to himself. 'She's going to introduce me to her friend Joan.'

'Which one?' There were two Joans. Big Joan and Little Joan, and so far as she knew, they were very different characters.

'I'm not fussy.' Clifford shrugged.

He was honest, you could say that for him.

At the next stop, people got into their carriage and noisily put their luggage in the overhead compartments and Clara knew the conversation was over for now. They looked out of their respective windows again and she wondered what he was thinking.

Once they were out in public Clifford became a performer again, forever sneaking glances to see who was listening or watching. Clara hurried him along the platform – past the man selling spoons, past the woman selling flowers. What if it didn't go to plan, what if this was all a ridiculous idea?

Then there she was, dashing out the station towards them. Mrs Mount had a funny way of galloping – on anyone else it would have been ridiculous, but not her. With her black fitted suit and her red lips, she looked like she was on a film set, or like an angel cloud-hopping. She was so smartly turned out; she was mesmerising, and Clara saw that Clifford was mesmerised.

Clara had persuaded the council to send him to Mrs Mount instead of back to the Hunstanton Reform School for Boys. It helped that the Reform School was still closed due to floodwater damage. Mrs Mount was going to be his landlady for six months, until he was old enough to be set free. But she would do more than that, Clara was sure of it. She would keep an eye on him. She would help him knuckle down. She had a lot of love that needed to go somewhere. And he was another young man who needed to be loved.

They were already chatting nineteen to the dozen.

'And there's a youth club down the road, and I've already told them you sing.'

Clara found she couldn't keep up with them, but she knew it didn't matter. Clifford would be okay. And Jonathon? Things would be hard for him – these were dangerous times for homosexuals – but he had a solid friendship with Clifford, and although he mightn't trust her yet, she would do all she could to support him too.

She let them race ahead, patting her pockets: where had she put her ticket?

49

Although the female voice booming down the phone line the next morning sounded familiar, Clara couldn't place it at first.

'Congratulations,' it said. 'I have been meaning to talk to you, Miss Newton!'

It was only six weeks since the extraordinary council meeting, yet in that time Clara felt like she had travelled to the other end of the universe and back.

'Can we meet face to face?'

'I... pardon?'

'Otherwise, things can be misconstrued,' Mrs McCarthy boomed down the wire. They arranged to meet outside the Guild-hall. They could potter around the amateur painting exhibition that was on, she said. They would meet outside at midday. There was no 'I'll get there when I can' about Mrs McCarthy.

'Perfect,' said Clara nervously, with crossed fingers. She had no idea what this was about.

Clara got on her bicycle and wobbled her way towards the centre of town. She didn't often cycle and, when she mistakenly arrived twenty minutes early – cycling was faster than walking! – decided to go inside. There were seascapes and countryside views. Clara was especially taken with a picture of a dog and a boy. She remembered an art exhibition Victor had taken her to once – she couldn't remember the name of the artist, but she had loved the portraits of motherhood.

Here, there was nothing so adventurous. There were lots of aeroplanes – lots of Spitfire pilots to avoid. She understood why they were popular, but that didn't mean she liked them; and this dated to before Michael and her father had died in air collisions.

Before too long, Mrs McCarthy was at the door, small yet larger than life, walking cane and frosty hair, winter coat buttoned up to the collar even though it was quite a warm day.

'What a terrific speech you gave to the council,' she began brightly.

Clara blushed. Ivor said she was not good at receiving compliments, and it was true.

'I know it's only been a few weeks, but I should have let you know sooner – we agreed it was excellent.'

'Thank you... I'm glad...'

'I'm working on many of the points you raised. Keeping siblings together, keeping parents in contact where possible, and the idea of bags. We're implementing changes. You know, we all need a kick up the backside now and again.'

Clara would have said Mr Sommersby needed a kick more than most but, although she liked and admired Mrs McCarthy hugely, they were not friends or equals.

'And transparency – and better filing systems. Honestly, Miss Newton, you've been a breath of fresh air in Suffolk and we are all the better for it.'

These were lofty ambitions but Clara couldn't help but doubt that the council staff would be doing as much as Mrs McCarthy imagined. It was more likely they would be engaged in elaborate cover-ups. And then Clara chided herself – maybe she shouldn't be so cynical about bureaucrats – she didn't used to be.

They stood in front of a painting of a nativity scene. Peg would like this. There were shepherds and wise men surrounding a baby in a manger. The baby had its arms raised as though wanting to be carried. Clara thought it was one of the better paintings there.

'Anyway, that wasn't what I wanted to see you about.'

'Oh?' Clara turned away from the stable scene.

'Mr Sommersby said you were leaving us...'

The idea that Sister Eunice was waiting in the wings, ready to saunter in, was just unthinkable. Clara wouldn't let that happen. It mustn't. She thought to herself she'd rather call off the wedding than allow this.

'I'm not leaving,' Clara hissed loudly. *How dared he?*

Two people who were examining a sloppy painting of a German tank looked over. One of them tsked.

'I didn't think you were,' Mrs McCarthy responded coolly. 'And between you and me, I know Sister Eunice is entirely unsuitable for the role and I will block any attempts at a return.'

Clara felt a rush of relief. Having Mrs McCarthy on her side meant the world to her. It was like when you listened to Churchill's speeches – you knew you were in safe hands.

'But you are marrying your handsome neighbour?' the older woman continued. 'The one who came to champion you? Dishy chap with the dark eyes? He made quite the impression on me that time.'

Clara couldn't help but smile. Accurate description! She was glad Mrs McCarthy didn't say the obvious 'No arm' about Ivor either.

'Yes,' Clara said, although secretly it still felt up in the air, and would do until they got the sodding invitations done.

At this Mrs McCarthy actually clapped. 'Wonderful. But you're not planning to split from the council?'

'It had occurred to me,' admitted Clara, 'but I don't think it will work.'

She and Marilyn had discussed it. The council's lease was for another few years and a breakaway just wasn't tenable.

'So, what's the plan?'

'Well, we're going to keep on keeping on much as we are now. Everyone appears to find that objectionable, but Ivor – Mr Delaney – is prepared for that.'

'He's a rare chap.'

Clara smiled. Ivor was exceedingly rare, yes. Her thoughts turned, strangely, to Jane Taylor, writing her poems by candlelight with no hope of recognition. This is what you did. This is what you had to do.

And Clara felt herself strengthened in the company of the older woman. 'There is no way Sister Eunice is returning – I would not let her either, but frankly, I have no other plan.'

'Well, I do!' said Mrs McCarthy loudly. And again, tsking man stared over, annoyed. This time Mrs McCarthy glowered back at him and he slipped away. Clara wondered that anyone would do that.

'You'll just go part-time, won't you, Miss Newton?' Mrs McCarthy continued.

'Uh...?'

'One week live in, one week live out. Why not?'

Clara gaped at her. Was she joking?

'I don't...'

'I thought you were the bold *ideas* girl? Innovative house-mother? You mean to say you hadn't thought of this? It's all the rage in London.'

No, I haven't thought about this. 'Uh, I'm open to all options,' she stuttered. Mrs McCarthy wasn't joking! 'Food for thought,' she finished.

'More than just food,' insisted Mrs McCarthy 'We don't want

to lose you, Miss Newton, just when you've found your feet. I would like your input on council policy too.'

'Oh, I don't want to be a childcare official.' She couldn't do that. She wasn't sure entirely of her strengths, but she knew it wasn't those.

Mrs McCarthy laughed. 'That's not what I'm suggesting. I'm saying – let's continue to put some of your commendable policy ideas forward and see what we can do regarding the shaping of systems.'

Clara gulped. This felt enormous. And exciting too.

'Let's find a compromise. A third way, yes? Use your imagination.' Mrs McCarthy stopped suddenly, and her face lit up. 'What do you think of this one?'

It was a bleak and grey painting of a large, battered ship coming through a raging sea in the fog. The sails were torn and you could see tiny figures at the oval windows.

Clara was torn between two adjectives: 'amateurish' and 'interesting'. She chose the latter. Moments later, she was glad she did.

'It's mine,' said Mrs McCarthy. 'My first seascape. Not too bad, is it? The ship is ravaged by the storm but not sunk, you see – symbolic, yes?' She grabbed Clara's hand. 'As ever, the important thing is to have a go.'

Part-time? thought Clara as she hung out the sheets on the line later that afternoon. She had a gazillion things to catch up on – she had only meant to be out half an hour, but somehow it had turned into three, and in that time she had also managed to invite Mrs McCarthy to the wedding. Mrs McCarthy said she would be honoured to come! She'd add her to the list.

Job-share? she thought as later, she ironed Trevor's shirt, Gladys's socks and Peg's apron for cookery class. It was an idea. *One week on and one week off?* she pondered as she mopped the kitchen floor. *Or what about four days on and three days off?* She could move into Ivor's workshop and then move back out again. But how would that work? Stella did similar, but she wasn't a cat. She didn't just go where dinner was. Wasn't it ridiculous?

It *was* ridiculous. It was ludicrous. But it was also brilliant.

50

Giving a talk at the Jane Taylor Society was just about the last thing Clara wanted to do and for the umpteenth time she wished she'd said no when she had had the opportunity to do so.

The children needed her, Ivor needed her more than ever, the house and the garden needed her and, instead, what was she going to be doing? She was going to the library to blether on about a little-known poet of the nineteenth century.

Clara didn't imagine she'd attract a crowd. The Jane Taylor Society meetings usually got ten to fifteen visitors at most, the majority of whom were largely tempted by Mr Dowsett's wife's famously delicious cakes. And that was when the weather was unremarkable. It was still bleak and windy, although mercifully the torrential rain had eased off.

But on the day a crowd did arrive, and Clara counted them as they filled up the library chairs – thirty – thirty-two – thirty-four! She stood nervously behind the lectern, and then she asked the audience where they had come from. Several had travelled in from out of town, two were from Colchester, one all the way from London. Some professed a deep love for Jane Taylor, and this was both good and bad – yes, they were interested but also, yes, they probably knew more about Jane than she did. Three years ago, Clara had never heard of Jane Taylor, and now she was giving speeches on her – that didn't feel right...

Nevertheless, there was no turning back. Clara knew she had to get stuck in.

Clara recited her favourite Jane Taylor poems, 'The Violet' and then the classic 'Twinkle, Twinkle Little Star' – because she didn't want to disappoint anyone and it was a crowd-pleaser. Then she talked about Jane's life, her struggles and about her sister, Ann. It was an overview for new members and a recap for old members and it seemed to be going down well. Mr Dowsett had recommended she end the talk with something positive, a happy ending, but she hadn't remembered that, so here they were.

'Jane died of breast cancer on the thirteenth of April 1824.'

The audience contemplated. They didn't think she'd finished. Clara realised Mr Dowsett was right after all; Jane's untimely death wasn't the note to end on. She continued. 'For too long, "anonymous" has been a woman. There's always something more important than crediting women with their work. But that's why we're all here, to change that – let's remember the great yet forgotten women who changed history!'

At that point Anita came in late, mouthing, 'Sorry!'

'And that concludes my talk. Do feel free to ask questions.'

Everyone clapped. Anita clapped the loudest.

'Did Jane Taylor never marry?' asked one of the women from Colchester.

'No,' Clara said. And she suddenly felt terribly sad. 'She did not.'

'Why not?' asked the woman, her eyes like saucers. 'I thought everyone did, back then.'

Clara tried to answer. 'We don't know for sure.'

'How can you not know? You're the expert!'

Clara looked at the woman in surprise. She could hear Anita

tutting, on her behalf hopefully (although with Anita, you could never be sure).

The woman's neighbour tried to help. 'Maybe she didn't meet anyone she wanted to marry.'

The woman nodded. 'Or maybe they died.'

Her neighbour raised her eyebrows at Clara. 'Mrs Perry can be morbid.'

Another audience member, the one who'd come from London, raised his hand.

'I had been reading and I found this and....'

He seemed to go on interminably. For about the same time you could hold your breath underwater for. Was there a question? Clara wondered. Would he ever get to it, or would they all stay suspended in this moment in time forever?

'It was just an observation really,' he said at the end of his monologue.

'Are there any more questions?' Clara said, hoping they understood that this was code for *it's time for tea.*

But there were no codebreakers in the Jane Taylor Society meeting that morning. Another man's hand was in the air.

'Do you think Jane Taylor would have written so many poems and books if she had married?'

'Her sister did. And she continued her activism, despite having many children.'

'Yes, but,' insisted the man, 'she might have wanted to give up.'

Another man had his arm in the air. There were only three men in the room, yet incredibly, each one of them had a question.

'Go on,' said Clara, although she had only one thing on her mind now: cake.

'When Jane Taylor wrote, "how I wonder what you are", I understand it to mean she was saying, *I know what you are, I am just wondering what formed you?*'

'An interesting observation,' observed Clara, thinking the

opposite. She raised her eyebrows at Mr Dowsett and he, fortunately, understood this to mean, *fetch the tea trolley.*

The other woman who had travelled from Colchester asked Clara what it was like living in the Grange, seeing as it was formerly Jane Taylor's home, and Clara was stopped in her tracks. She hadn't anticipated this question, and it threw her.

'I suppose... I-I feel like I'm a caretaker in some ways.'

'A custodian?' corrected the woman.

'Yes, that's it. I feel a responsibility to honour her, and to make sure we preserve her legacy.'

Clara looked after the orphaned children and the house, yes, but also, she did have a responsibility to Jane's history, her story. It hadn't occurred to her to see it in that way before and she was suddenly taken aback.

'I like "The Poppy",' said a woman in gardening dungarees.

'Oh, so do I...' Clara said fondly.

'I like "Honest John",' another woman piped up. Clara bit her lip. Anita used to say Honest John in the poem was like Ivor. Clara agreed he was like Honest John, but recently had started to fear that she was Dishonest Clara.

'I liked *Pride and Prejudice* best. But my second favourite is *Sense and Sensibility.*'

'Ah,' said Clara, 'I think you may be conf—'

'We have time for one more question,' Mr Dowsett interrupted mercifully.

A woman from Ipswich asked what it was that Clara admired most about Jane.

Clara paused, then said, 'She defied the conventions of the time. To write, to campaign, to stay unmarried – this wasn't the done thing for women of that era. She was really brave.'

'She was, wasn't she?' agreed the lady.

'I think it shows battles aren't won in a day – or even a few years – it takes generations and generations of people to effect change. For Jane it was God that provided her with the fuel to keep going against the constraints of the time.'

'For others' – Clara saw that Mr Dowsett was nodding away approvingly – 'it might just be that you want to make a positive contribution to people. Whatever is your fuel, I would say use it to make a difference.'

Clara hadn't expected it but, after the meeting, she felt uplifted – and it wasn't just Mr Dowsett's wife's cream puffs. It was this bringing together of people, this sharing of ideas; this positivity was exactly what she had needed and she hadn't realised it. She recalled the laughter and the warmth of the people in the library, and she thought if Jane Taylor could do it – whatever 'it' was – she, Clara, could have a go too.

And she felt heartened, and more certain than ever that she and Ivor would come through this rough patch, stronger than ever.

51

The next day, Ivor called in just as Clara was washing up after lunch. He was freshly shaven, and his shirt was smooth and ironed, but his expression was serious.

'There's something I need to talk to you about...'

Clara gulped; when she had seen him arrive she was delighted, but this didn't bode well. He wasn't calling the wedding off, was he? Just when she had figured out a way they might be able to move forward together.

'What is it?' she asked tersely.

'About the flood.'

The flood? Not us, not Ruby...

'If that's okay?' he continued, oblivious to her turmoil.

'Of course.' Clara dried her hands hurriedly. 'Now?'

'It's as good a time as any.'

She had the bottle of whisky the Hortons had left her. She wouldn't usually – no, she would *never* drink in the afternoon, but somehow she felt the need for a glass. As she poured one each, she couldn't help thinking: if Ivor was emptying his heart to her, was this the time to reveal what she'd done too?

They sat opposite each other at the table; she took his hand between hers. A beautiful hard-working hand. She braced herself. She had always wanted him to talk about his experiences – in the war and now in the flood– yet when at long last he seemed ready, she wondered if she really was.

'We'd got Clifford – and then Jonathon heard some other people. I don't know how. They were on a roof, but the wrong side, and their way off was trapped. We knew we could take two – the boys did it.'

Clara stroked his wrist. She could have lost him, she kept thinking. He could have died.

'We did those three more times, apparently. I lost count, but that's what they said. Rescuing old people. It was incredible. The boys were incredible. And then once we were back, we lay there, in relative safety I suppose, and then one of the children said they could hear something. We thought it was a bird at first.'

Clara admired him so much. She held on to his hands as though afraid she would lose him again.

'Clifford said it was nothing, he was half-asleep, but Jonathon said maybe it was a dog, and once he said that, it kind of fitted into place. I knew it was a dog and that it was trapped. Jonathon offered to come, but you should have seen him, Clara, he was shattered.'

'I bet you were shattered too.'

'Oh, I was,' Ivor said and he drank some more whisky.

'I rowed – but with one arm, you know, it was slow. I kept going in circles at first.'

'I can't imagine.'

'I could hear it making these piteous cries, and I knew I had to get to it. But Clara – I saw some terrible things before I did. I don't know...'

'Tell me.'

Ivor swallowed, took a deep breath, and then said: 'Bodies just floating there. Facing up. Facing down. It was like Dunkirk. I remembered scrambling for the boats then – and... It was awful. I grew confused. I thought I might be dead too.'

'Oh, Ivor.'

'Maxi was my guiding star. I got there, found her on some rickety old shed roof barely higher than the water, surrounded by trees, I held on to her, then got her into the boat. She was reluctant at first. With good reason, I realise now – seconds later, I saw the branches coming, the tree shifting, and then I must have been hit. I was knocked out for hours. And then I woke up in the middle of nowhere. Maxi was on my chest, licking my wrist. We'd drifted out to sea. It must have been Sunday night. I had to find someone, anyone. We rowed some more... Then we found a cottage – I tied up the boat, clambered up a load of steps, but there was no one there. I broke in. No telephone, of course. I took some mouldy bread and some cheese then fell asleep in a chair. It was dry and warm. I must have travelled miles. When I woke up, still no one there.

'I had better go back and replace the food I stole. I hope they don't mind, but Maxi was starving. We both were.'

Ivor shook his head. He could hardly believe it himself.

'I just thought, I've got to get back to you. And so from there, we went inland, and I just walked and walked. We must have walked ten or twelve miles. And then I hitched a ride – chap doing deliveries didn't stop talking – the car smelled of smoke... and then I got back to you.'

Ivor came round the table and put his arm round her. Clara leaned into him and she thought he was the cat with nine lives and she was the luckiest girl in the world.

Later that afternoon, Clara walked up the high road to the Greenes' crooked house. The birds were singing; it felt as though they were encouraging her on. There were many reasons to do this – and one secret reason that she wouldn't even admit to herself was that, if she did more and more nice things for Ivor, then Ivor would obviously have no choice but to forgive her for the Ruby thing. At the same time, Clara had resolved to put Ruby behind her. She wouldn't tell him because it wasn't important and why should she disturb their new and beautiful equilibrium? They'd come through their rough patch and she could get on with looking to the future.

The crooked house looked different with the sun reflected off its windows and making its walls glow. She heard Suki bark a warning, or a welcome – she didn't know which.

Mrs Greene opened the door and laughed. 'Miss Newton! Changed your mind *again*?'

'I'm not too late, am I?'

The lovely Suki sloped out, heavier than ever.

'Not at all. Suki, come and say hello, girl.'

That night was the first night in a while that Clara didn't dream of either Ruby or Sister Eunice. Instead, she dreamed she was on a ship navigating high seas, blundering through a storm. It was hard work – the waves washed over the sides, and the sails tore – but it was exhilarating and invigorating, and at no point did she feel she couldn't go on.

52

The next morning when Clara left the house to go shopping, she found a boy standing in her way down the path. A large boy, around sixteen years old perhaps, with a face she vaguely recognised. Clara blinked, trying to make sense of him.

He was in a dirty damp shirt, shorts and knee-high socks – and he was wringing his hands. There was a small grey duffel bag next to him and his shoes were old and muddy. He looked tired, like he'd been on the move for some time. She was just about to say hello when he spoke: 'You said I could come.'

He had escaped from somewhere, she thought – he had 'runaway' written all over him. Suddenly Clara knew exactly who it was; it was the potato-faced boy from the cruel family that had fostered Trevor and Frank. She had rescued the boys and felt bad leaving him there. And she had told him he could come, hadn't she? Any time.

She had lots of questions, but the one that demanded its way to the front was: 'But why now?'

He nodded like he'd expected that. Then he raised that shabby discoloured shirt to reveal his chubby chest. It was full of marks, slices. It looked like... it looked like an image of Jesus on the cross.

'He whipped me,' he answered.

Clara ran the boy a bath. She made him a dusty hot chocolate and he gulped it down. She had a marble cake made by Evelyn in the cupboard that she'd been saving, and he ate a healthy slice of that. She made him a sardine sandwich. It was all in the wrong order but, when she had asked if he was hungry, he had said no.

He looked around him with wide eyes. She knew the Grange – for all its faults – was vastly different from where he had been living, and she felt for him that he hadn't had a comfortable home.

'It's not how I imagined,' he said. 'It's really special...'

Clara remembered the rubbish in the yard and the buzzing of the flies at his father's house in Ipswich. 'Thank you. I'll register you with the council. We'll get you sorted.'

She needed to know his name. She couldn't exactly call him *'potato-faced boy'*.

'Hugh,' he said, 'Hugh Johnson.'

'Hugh.' She repeated. She offered him her hand to shake, and he did so, limply.

'I'm Miss Newton. And I'm going to help you.'

Miss Webb had a day off. Mr Horton was out on a nearby call, so he came by quicker than he usually would. Clara was glad it was him rather than Miss Webb. It felt serendipitous.

She introduced Hugh to him and Mr Horton asked him questions and scribbled in his notebook and Hugh looked more embarrassed than ever. After they were done, she sent Hugh into the parlour so she and Mr Horton could talk privately.

'He seems a pleasant enough kid,' said Mr Horton.

'Doesn't he?' agreed Clara. He hadn't been, but people

change. She remembered a line from her old favourite Dr Spock parenting book – love and attention, that's what children needed (and not just children, she thought).

'Bad news,' Mr Horton said. 'There's no emergency care. We're helping with the flood regions. We've got over six new orphans in Suffolk alone. I've got three siblings at the house today, waiting for placements.'

'Mrs Horton senior must be going mad.'

'She likes it. She's telling them about how she won the Great War single-handed.'

Clara smiled wryly.

'So, what shall we do with him?'

'You know what I'm going to say,' Mr Horton said between gritted teeth. 'Just until we determine what to do next. Could be days, could be weeks, could be months at this rate... Things are moving at a snail's pace.'

Clara nodded. 'The bed is already made up.'

Clara walked to the shops with Hugh. She saw the pretty buildings and the historical houses, the hanging baskets, through his eyes and she thought how wholesome Lavenham looked. This was an agreeable place to live. She was glad of him, glad that she was *doing* again. This was her job and purpose. She would not leave children out in the cold. When she wasn't doing, she was left thinking, and when she was left thinking, she took herself down dark and miserable roads.

And perhaps there was something about having a new child that nailed her to the home. Mr Sommersby and Miss Webb still thought she was leaving soon. Well, she wasn't – and Hugh Johnson was an illustration of why she wasn't. She really was needed.

'Different to Ipswich?' she said.

'Pretty much the opposite,' he said.

She returned some books to the library and let Hugh choose some on her card. He was slow at first, but eventually chose *The Thirty-Nine Steps* and *The Day of the Triffids*. Clara didn't like to think of the boy getting any ideas, but it seemed unlikely he could develop a poisonous sting like the plants in the novel. And he looked pretty pleased with his haul.

'We don't have to pay?'

'Not at a library, no.'

When they were back on the high road, Mrs Garrard waved Clara over.

'I wanted to ask you about flowers for the wedding. Oh, who's this?'

'New boy,' said Clara, which she supposed he was.

And Mrs Garrard said, 'Oh, another one? You *are* wonderful, Miss Newton,' and Clara couldn't help but feel a shiver of – what was it... pride? Yes, probably. It *was* something to be recognised.

And the postmistress said, 'Who's this then?' and gave him a lolly on a stick, and although he was fifteen, Hugh's face lit up like a child half his age.

People were generous. Everyone deserves a second chance, she thought fondly. It wasn't like Hugh was a Triffid. He was just another one for the guest list.

Hugh was peeling turnips and Clara was frying beetroot when the younger children came back from school. Gladys was giving a long, drawn-out explanation about a teacher being locked in the cupboard. 'Accidentally,' she kept saying. She was too busy talking to notice Hugh at first, but Peg did.

'Who are you?' she asked in her serious voice.

And he responded nervously, 'Hugh.'

Peg, determined to get it right, said, 'Hugh are you?'

Smiling, Clara put down her knife. 'No, Peg, you got it first time. This *is* Hugh. He's going to stay with us for a while.'

'Not another boy,' said Gladys, then laughed. 'All right. I love you, Hugh.'

Peg wrote down in her book, 'Is he replacing me?'

And Clara said, 'No one could ever replace you, Peg!', which made her smile.

Gladys said he looked like a grown-up. When, chortling, he explained that he was fifteen, she said, 'Exactly,' with eyes like saucers.

'Miss Newton is old – she knew Queen Victoria and the match girls.' They had been studying that at school. 'Isn't that right?'

'Not exactly!' Clara exclaimed.

They all laughed.

The back door opened again, and this time Frank, Trevor and Jonathon came in. Trevor was telling Jonathon that he was faster than any of them, Jonathon was laughing. And then the brothers stopped dead.

'What the hell?!' Frank was the first to speak.

Clara expected him to make his usual new-boy jokes. 'Looks a bit old...' But Frank was near-spitting with rage. 'What are you doing here?'

Trevor had picked up the chopping board. 'Don't you dare!' he shouted. 'Not here, not my Miss Newton.'

Clara jumped between them. 'Whoa there. Put it down, Trevor.'

Trevor put the board down but his eyes never left Hugh's petrified face.

'Stop this. Hugh is—'

'We know who Hugh is,' said Frank dramatically.

'He's our guest.'

'No!'

Trevor rushed towards him – if it wasn't for Jonathon holding him back, he would probably have punched him in the face.

'Calm down!' shrieked Clara.

'It's alright, Trev,' whispered Jonathon. 'Let's talk about this.'

Hugh stood there with his head down and his hands in his pockets, his face full of woe.

'Either he goes or we do,' said Frank.

'Simple as that,' added Trevor. For once, the bickering brothers were united.

At that, Hugh made for the back door.

'No, wait,' said Clara, intercepting him. 'I didn't mean for any of this to happen.'

How could she not have considered what had happened to the boys? She had been so intent on being loving and being kind and giving second chances to a new child that she had forgotten to be kind to the children already in her care. She had under-estimated how angry they were.

They were her priority here, not Hugh.

'Wait. We'll come to an agreement, we'll find a compromise.'

'He used to do terrible things,' said Trevor, keeping his eyes on Hugh as though at any moment the larger boy would pounce.

Gladys started yelling too. 'Then I hate him too.'

Peg was staring in horrified wonder.

'We all need to calm down,' said Clara, although her voice was not at all calm. *What have I done?*

She sent Hugh once again into the parlour, saying, 'I'll be with you in a minute.' And he went off, chin on his chest, ashamed, the stick of the lolly sticking out of his pocket.

Trevor had grabbed Gladys and wrapped his arms round her protectively.

'You'll just have to stay out the way of Hugh for a bit,' Clara said to them all.

'He's Hu-ge,' said Gladys with dismay. 'He's like the giant in "Jack and the Beanstalk".'

'He's not sharing with us,' said Trevor. 'And he can't share with the girls either.'

'That's fine,' promised Clara wildly. 'I'll take care of everything.'

She may have wanted to be distracted – but this was proving one hell of a distraction.

She got back on the telephone. As she explained, Mr Horton sounded exasperated.

'This is complicated, Miss Newton.'

She could put pressure on the boys, she could just override their wishes, but it would be wrong. She couldn't offer kindness on someone else's behalf. That *wasn't* kindness. And they were entitled to boundaries and safeguards themselves.

She had thought Sister Eunice was the main threat to the children right now. But there were other threats – and she had invited them in.

'I appreciate that,' Clara confirmed. 'But it's impossible...'

Mr Horton sighed again.

' I'll be there first thing tomorrow.'

Clara thought of Frank's terror and Trevor's despair. The boys had come on leaps and bounds. She couldn't hurry them and she couldn't betray them. And that's what it would be if Hugh stayed – a betrayal.

'I think you'd better come now.'

In fact, Hugh hadn't gone to the parlour; he had gone outside to the street and was sitting on the kerb, big feet in those tired old shoes sticking out into the road.

'Small problem,' Clara said as she went and sat next to him.

'I thought so.' He didn't look up. His hands were tucked between his thighs and his head was low.

'The children are uncomfortable with you here.'

'Do I have to go?'

She almost wished she could say he could stay. In just four hours, she had grown fond of the boy. She didn't see him as a bully, or a tyrant, just a frightened child. But just because he was a victim didn't mean her children were any less victims. She had to be their – what would Ivor say? – *advocate* first.

Ten minutes later, Mr Horton's car pulled up in front of the home.

'I'm sorry, Hugh.'

'I understand.' He shrugged. 'I do.'

And maybe, she thought, maybe there was hope for the boy. Shilling Grange wasn't the place for him but Clara would see to it that he went to a place of kindness. Everyone deserved that.

53

Ivor said he was getting over Maxi and that he was (almost) glad she was reunited with her people. He said he was feeling better too; his aches and pains receding like the floodwater. Whether it was the new painkillers, the reduced workload or the enforced rest, or perhaps all three, the old Ivor seemed to be on his way back.

'Have you really cut down on work?' Clara asked. He always seemed to be upholstering or measuring or cutting when she saw him.

Ivor pretended to be offended. 'Yes. I'm determined to be in best condition for our wedding.' He chuckled. 'Once I've trapped you, then I'll let myself go.'

The children were in bed, although not yet asleep, and she and Ivor were cuddling on the sofa in the parlour. Once again, the relief that he was safe and nearly back to his old self was overwhelming. It was so good to be reunited that, if Clara had been the type to write poetry, she would have. Instead, she joyfully wrote things on her lists and then ticked them off.

'Nothing else is wrong – other than your health, I mean?' she asked gingerly, that concern that he had cold feet still niggling at the back of her mind.

'No, there's nothing wrong other than that,' he reassured her. Ivor's health – tick.

She nestled into his chest. This was where she belonged.

He kissed her. 'Loving you saved me.'

'The other day, you said it was Maxi who saved you.' She laughed. 'I distinctly heard you.'

'Did I? I get the two of you confused sometimes. There are many similarities.'

She kissed him quiet and watched the beautiful way his eyelids fluttered shut. She kissed his eyebrows and the bone beneath his eyes, and he was kissing back and smiling. She could not hold back from her adoration of him, she worshipped him in that moment. And then she remembered, like a crack of a whip: *Oh God. Ruby had better not get in touch.*

It was such an intrusive idea, it spoiled everything. Not only was it vivid but it felt painfully realistic; Ruby, head tilted, arms crossed, accusing her, pointing her finger at Clara: '*She* got in touch with me, Ivor. She was the one who told me to come back.'

'I can't wait for you to be my wife,' Ivor crooned into her hair.

'Me too. Husband, I mean. Do you think we can get the invitations out soon?' Clara couldn't walk down the high road without people asking where they were. And perhaps then at least, if Ruby came back, there'd be nothing she could do.

She decided she wouldn't tell Ivor about her conversation with Mrs McCarthy just yet, because she didn't want him to get too enthusiastic and then for it not to work.

And then of course she still had to find someone to share the job with – and, whoever they were, they had to be the perfect for the role.

· · ·

A few days later, Ivor said he was ready to send out the invitations. Their talk must have done him the world of good. It was over six weeks later than they'd planned but oh so much had happened since then.

The wedding felt like a photograph, fuzzy and indistinct at first, but now – not before time – becoming much sharper and clearer. At last, she could picture it happening.

Clara spread out the invitation designs on the kitchen table. 'My favourite is this.' She picked up one of them.

Ivor peered. 'Why butterflies?' he asked, bunching up his face.

Clara scowled. Did Ivor have to question everything? Could he not let her organise something?

'They're symbolic.'

'Of what?'

Clara made a vague gesture. 'Because they start out as something plain and turn into something beautiful.'

She wanted Ivor to say, 'Aw, like you and me?' but instead he said cynically, 'By eating a lot?'

She wished she were the kind of person who stood her own ground. Instead, she too looked at the sample invitation, and thought, *why on earth did I choose butterflies?*

'What do you want instead?' she challenged.

He shrugged. 'How about a dog?'

'A dog? Why?'

'I like dogs.'

Clara sighed.

'Or why not keep them plain?' he suggested.

Plain invitations had been her original plan, but then subsequent conversations with Mrs Garrard – 'Ooh, won't that be depressing?' – and Anita – 'You definitely need a feature of some kind!' – had convinced her otherwise.

Trevor walked in and grabbed an apple. He was growing

lately and eating more. Every week, he seemed to gain an inch. Frank came in next. He had turned into Trevor's shadow recently, much to Trevor's chagrin. They both studied the invitations gravely.

'What do you think, boys? You like the butterflies?'

'Can you do a fish?' suggested Trevor.

'A dead fish,' shouted Frank.

'Everyone's got an opinion.' Clara said, grabbing Frank and tickling him.

Ivor pretended to contemplate. 'A dead fish, huh? That's not a bad idea.'

'Enough, all of you!' Clara laughed. 'We're having butterflies whether you like it or not. I've waited long enough on this.'

Ivor shrugged. 'Fine. Butterflies it is.'

Ivor's guest list had twenty people on it, all from work: collaborators, clients, people he knew from the upholsterers' society.

'There's a society?'

Clara's list had over one hundred names on it. They began signing, away from the butterflies. For this occasion, Clara was using a fountain pen, although she let Ivor use her Bic. After a while, he sat back, shook his wrist and watched her.

'Is Donald Button on your list?'

Clara swallowed. The TV presenter who had taken her out and made a clumsy pass at her so she had to run away from him was most definitely not on her list.

'I think he'll be busy presenting.'

'Shame,' he said guilelessly. 'You were friends, weren't you?'

Clara snorted instead of answering.

Maureen couldn't help getting involved too. 'What about Big Joan and Little Joan? Can they come?'

'I don't see...'

Clifford would be pleased.

'And what about their boyfriends?' she went on.

Clifford would have to get over it. 'Big Joan is seeing Larry and Little Joan is seeing Richard...'

What about the man who stamps your tickets and the woman you wave to from the train?

'Ah, why not? I'll put them on my list.'

She, Gladys and Peg went to post the invitations. The girls linked their arms in hers.

'Will people actually want to come?' Peg said, displaying the same existential fears that dogged Clara sometimes.

'I hope so...'

Since the conversation about him with Clifford, Clara also felt better about Jonathon. She brought it up with Ivor too, now he was well enough to be her confidant again.

'I think Jonathon is homosexual,' she said – quietly, otherwise, big-ears Patricia would be bleating 'Jonathon is a homosexual' every day until Christmas.

Ivor lit a cigarette, took a deep breath.

She had to go on. 'And I think he's unhappy with it.'

'It's not surprising he's unhappy with it,' Ivor said, 'when it's illegal.'

'Mm,' Clara agreed, unable to fathom how loving anyone could be deemed illegal.

'If you want my advice,' Ivor said slowly – and Clara said she did, she always did – 'I think it's important he knows that there's nothing wrong with him. Men have been homosexual since...' He cast around. 'Forever. If he loves men, he loves men. There shouldn't be a stigma or shame about it. Love is love.'

Clara nodded, relieved that Ivor was understanding. In fact, he probably went further than her; Ivor thought that it would be legal within his lifetime. Clara wasn't as optimistic that the world would change so quickly.

54

Within days, invitations were landing on doormats throughout Lavenham and beyond. Or fluttering, corrected Ivor, who was still laughing about butterflies.

And soon after that, the RSVPs started coming back to the home.

The younger children loved collecting and counting them.

'It's the four one this week!'

'Thank you, Peg, can you say fourth?'

Gladys said it was all becoming very real, and Clara thought the same. She and the children put the replies in a yes-pile and a no-pile.

Sir Alfred Munnings was one of the first to respond. He said he would be delighted to attend. And for a present he was hoping to give them an oil painting. He didn't mention that he'd been at her engagement party to Julian a few years ago. Maybe he was being kind, or diplomatic, or maybe he'd simply forgotten. Clara was certainly trying to forget it too.

Mr Sommersby and his wife wrote a note declining. They had a trip to Bath planned. Clara jumped in the air when she heard they weren't coming.

Judy's mother and father declined, which was also somewhat of a relief. She loved Judy and her family but it would be hard work having her 'old world' mingle with her new world on her wedding day. Their reason was that Judy's brother had had a baby, so they were busy with their first grandchild. Clara's heart stung at that – *poor Judy had missed such a lot* – but she wouldn't let herself dwell and she wrote that she would visit them in the autumn.

Peg and Gladys were worried about the growing no-pile but Clara explained that it was fine and just to be expected. Gladys thought for a moment and then enquired dubiously, 'You invited them but you didn't want them to come?'

'Not at all,' lied Clara.

Clara realised she still hadn't invited the postmistress or her assistant – poor postmistress, sending all those letters and yet being ignored! She had to find out their names and then do that. And she hadn't invited the Easleas, another oversight, especially since they were on Peg's mind a lot.

Other invitees replied in person which, while lovely, didn't help Clara with her paperwork. She was at the market one afternoon, buying oranges, when the milkman said he would be coming, along with his boy and his mother. Another time, Clara had come out of the lavatory in the library to find schoolteacher Miss Fisher wanting a word. 'Thank you,' she said. 'I don't need to bring anyone, do I?'

'Not at all,' Clara replied. 'It was just if you wanted to.'

They had put 'feel free to bring a guest' or 'plus one' on some of the invitations. But the questions didn't stop there. Drying her hands, Miss Fisher said, 'I hope you don't mind me asking – what will you be doing next?'

'Uh, I'll be taking the children – and their books – home?'

'No, I mean, after you marry...'

'I'm staying on at the Grange,' said Clara. The tap at her sink was broken and the water wouldn't stop. She winced. 'Thank you for your concern though.'

Then Clara was at a flute grading for Gladys in the Guildhall. A woman she didn't even know, except that her son played the Snake Song dreadfully, leant over to say they were delighted to be included and had Clara got their RSVP?

Clara hesitated; she didn't recognise the woman – but then she said her husband was a supplier. *Of course, Ivor's people. But are these the Adams or the Richardsons?*

The Norland Nanny said, yes, and she would bring a plus one, thank you, how thoughtful of you, Miss Newton.

The plus ones had been Ivor's idea – but Clara didn't say so.

Another time, she was in Dr Cardew's waiting room (Frank had pushed a dried pea up his nose – A. Frank didn't know why he'd done it and B. Could Miss Newton not ask again) when the temporary nurse said she was coming, she couldn't wait. Clara thought, *that can't be right* – they'd never met before – but then she remembered she was the daughter of Ivor's favourite customer and he had invited the entire family.

'You'll be sad to leave all this behind, won't you?' the nurse remarked as she extracted the offending item from Frank's nose.

'I won't be sad,' said Clara abruptly. 'Because I won't be leaving.' She held out a handkerchief. 'Frank, if you put anything else up your nose, I will not be responsible for my actions.'

Clara could share with Ivor these worries about what she would do about work once they were married and the spectre of the hated Sister Eunice, but her other worry – the possible reappearance of Ruby – she most certainly could not.

She dreamed that Ruby turned up at the wedding, was waiting for her at the church. She imagined that when the vicar said: 'If anyone has any reason why—' Ruby jumped up, shouting, 'I do. He stole my baby!'

When Ruby had said, 'I'll get there when I can' it had just sounded flippant, uncaring. Now it sounded ominous – she'd come when she was ready. In her own time.

Clara should have told Ivor, she really should have. But the longer it was since she'd spoken to Ruby, the harder it was to tell him.

She felt like Ruby was circling the house, waiting to pounce.

When Gladys said a pretty lady in the street had asked her for directions, Clara went on full-scale alert. Ruby would obviously know the way to the home – she had lived there for more than thirteen years, after all – but still, could this be her?

When out the blue, Frank asked, 'Are rubies red or blue?' Clara was nearly catatonic with fear.

And when Peg said, 'I'll miss Patricia,' Clara nearly jumped out her skin. Panicking, she asked, 'Why?'

Where do you think Patricia is going?!

'When I go to live with the Easlea family of course,' Peg said, wide-eyed and confused.

'Oh, yes, absolutely!'

Clara knew she had made mistakes in life but mistakes this catastrophic? Never. Every night, she debated whether or not to tell Ivor. Sometimes she forgot about it, and didn't think about it for whole days; other times, she thought she'd ruined everything.

55

Do What Women Do Best – Caring
    Female 20–40 responsible and sensible. Stimulating job,
accommodation provided in an attractive location.

A long time ago, August 1948 to be precise, Clara had answered an advert in the *Evening Post*. The wording of the advert had appalled her – she didn't think caring was the thing women did best, and she had met women who weren't caring – but nevertheless she had applied because there was no other job in the paper that she was eligible for.

Now there was one person who Clara thought would be perfect to share her job with – someone she had always thought of as caring, responsible and sensible. The pair of them may have had their disagreements – in fact, they definitely had – and she was over the age-limit but she had the patience and the common sense, and her detective skills were second to none.

Clara invited Mrs Horton over for tea and Mrs Horton brought cheese scones in a paper bag. Clara wished they were plain scones, but she didn't have the heart to tell her. She had been planning to give a long preamble but instead, she just launched in:

'Can't I job-share with you, Mrs Horton? I think it would be brilliant.'

'Clara!' Mrs Horton looked shocked.

'Hear me out – it means you'd get away from Mrs Horton senior – no offence, but she is challenging, isn't she? And it would be good to mix things up so we'd benefit from your lovely child-care experience and wisdom.'

Remembering the rule of three, Clara wanted to add something else, but she couldn't think of anything. 'Mr Horton could do his bowls more often...' And then she thought of something else to tempt her. 'And I'll make sure we always have plenty of cheese.'

'Cheese?'

Clara realised this didn't sound right.

'Anything you like... What I mean is, you'd be a real asset.'

After this speech, which didn't come out exactly as Clara had hoped – as an orator, she thought, she was more Chamberlain than Churchill – they both fell silent for a moment. Then Mrs Horton chuckled and repeated. 'You'll make sure there is plenty of cheese?' and Clara laughed too.

'You would be perfect though!' she said, slightly abashed.

'Perhaps if I were twenty years younger,' Mrs Horton admitted, sipping her tea, 'but I'm content now. Although I complain, especially about Mrs Horton senior, my life is harmonious... And I have no desire to mix it up. But I'll certainly look out for someone.'

At first Clara felt gloomy. No 'someone' could possibly be as suitable as Mrs Horton. No one could complement her in the ways Mrs Horton did. Where Clara was weak, Mrs Horton was strong. Where Clara tended to drift from her mission, Mrs Horton kept focused. But then Clara felt happy for her friend – Mrs Horton was content as she was, and that was the important thing.

Clara had a second favourite lined up though. This one was Ivor's idea, and she was appalled with herself that she hadn't thought of it sooner. The next day, she rode her bike through town. She was getting so much better at cycling that it was hard to remember how scary it used to be for her. At the gates of the nunnery, she jumped off her bicycle and wheeled it up the long gravel path, feeling self-important. The nunnery was a beautiful, grey stone building with lovely grounds. Clara thought it might be tough to give up this place of serenity, but then she had thought all along that Sister Grace did not belong in a nunnery.

Sister Grace provided holiday cover for Clara, and much more. She loved spending time with the children, reading to them, singing to them and cleaning. Clara didn't see how it could not work. Sister Grace had a keen sense of mischief, and a delightful interest in fashion and films. She would probably be a keen cyclist too, given the chance. And she was coming to the wedding.

At first, Sister Grace was pleased to see Clara – *how fetching you look!* – and then concerned.

'I wasn't supposed to be at the Grange today, was I? Oh, Miss Newton, I do get caught up in my tomato plants.'

'No, not at all.'

Clara explained the story. She explained that she couldn't completely give up the home, didn't want to ever give up the home, but everyone expected her to when she got married, and after some consideration she'd decided that it would be better all round if she could share her role with someone wonderful.

Sister Grace said that seemed a sensible move.

'And?' said Clara, nearly hopping from foot to foot with enthusiasm.

'And?' Sister Grace was mystified.

'And...' Clara continued excitedly. 'That's where you come in!'

When finally the penny dropped, Sister Grace was astonished. 'Oh, no, Miss Newton,' she said, grabbing hold of the wooden cross round her neck as though Clara was a vampire. 'This is most irregular... whatever made you think I would?'

'You could grow vegetables in the garden at the home,' suggested Clara hopefully, but to no avail. Sister Grace said she would pray for her.

Miss Webb insisted on doing the job advertisement herself. She said ads were all a similar format, but that she had updated it a bit for today's *modern* housemother.

'You didn't put anything about *what women do best?*' Clara asked warily. She didn't trust Miss Webb to get this right.

'No, I didn't. Miss Newton, please don't worry.'

'Miss Newton, please don't worry,' meant 'Miss Newton, stop interfering.'

Before too long, Miss Webb had also sifted through the applications and selected four to come to be interviewed. Clara was a little put out that she had gone ahead and done it all without her.

'I will be the one working with whoever we choose,' she pointed out.

'It was to save you time,' Miss Webb said sulkily. She didn't take criticism well.

Whatever the other woman's motivation, Clara felt aggrieved. What if the ideal candidate was out there in the reject pile? She and Miss Webb might be after someone with different qualities. Miss Webb valued bureaucracy and prayers above all else; Clara thought the qualities needed were more nuanced.

But then, as long as it was not awful Sister Eunice, Clara thought, she would be happy.

And then Miss Webb unilaterally decided the interviews should be held not at Shilling Grange but at the council offices.

'It's more neutral, you see.'

Actually, Clara agreed with her on this one; if the interviews were at the home and the children saw them happening, they would be anxious. But she hated that by the time she found out it was already a fait accompli.

Another thing they agreed on was that only after they had decided on their preferred candidate would they submit their choice to Mr Sommersby.

'Do you think he'll say yes?' pondered Clara.

'I have no idea,' said Miss Webb. At least she was honest.

Clara found she was looking forward to the interviews, and not only because it would make a nice change from laundry and cooking. On the train to the council building, she imagined lots of hypothetical questions she could ask. Years of enjoying the quizzes in *Good Housekeeping* had made her an expert on those:

How would you like your home to be run?

a. Stringently!

b. Let the children run wild.

c. With love and rules.

d. I'll do whatever I'm told by my seniors.

(Obviously C with a touch of D was what they were looking for!)

Clara went up to the office on the first floor of the council building. She thought they had an hour to go through the applications together, but Miss Webb didn't want Clara to see the applications in advance.

'There's no time anyway,' she said.

'What? The first candidate is not arriving until eleven!'

'Oh, didn't I tell you?' said Miss Webb guiltily. 'She's coming now.' Right on cue, there was a knock on the office door.

The first candidate, Miss Franks, reminded Clara somewhat of Mrs Dorne from Sunday School. She was quietly spoken and keen to have it known that she was a regular churchgoer. Clara quickly gathered that she and Miss Webb were friends from that regular churchgoing and that Miss Webb had encouraged – nay pushed – Miss Franks's application. She also gathered that Miss Franks had no experience of children, none whatsoever, although she thought the idea of them was 'precious'.

Clara had had no experience of children before she started at the home, so she could hardly hold that against her; but Clara also took an instant dislike to people who used the word 'precious' about children. She told herself not to be judgemental; goodness, if she ruled out all the people in the world who used words she didn't like, she'd be down to just about Ivor and Peg.

However, there were other reasons for hesitancy about Miss Franks. One was that Miss Franks herself didn't seem that certain that she wanted the job – which was kind of crucial – and two, and this was just an instinct but Clara thought the children would make mincemeat of her. She came across as rather soft or timid. Clara could imagine Frank, Trevor and Gladys ganging up on her. It wasn't that they were bullies exactly, but, combined, they could be quite a force to be reckoned with.

There was no doubt though that she was Miss Webb's preferred candidate.

The second candidate telephoned ahead and cancelled, citing transport difficulties.

'Hmm,' said Clara. That showed a distinct lack of gumption. Could she not get a taxi or cycle or something? What else might she cancel at the drop of a hat?

Clara thought this would be a good time to read the other applications, but Miss Webb didn't want to – she wanted to go downstairs and make weak tea and talk about the weather. Clara acquiesced. She had a feeling that this process was like Goldilocks porridge – the first was too hot, the second too cold, but the third would be *just right*.

So Clara was feeling quite optimistic – until number three walked in. It was her ex-childcare officer, Mrs Harrington. The two women stared at each other and the hostility in the air was immediate and palpable. Mrs Harrington pulled her cardigan around her and then held on to her pearl necklace as though she thought Clara would grab it and run off.

'Have you met?' said Miss Webb, bewildered. 'Miss Newton, Mrs Harrington used to work at the council.'

'We've met,' said Clara. All she could think was how Mrs Harrington had weaselled her way into Ivor's life two years ago and that this might be a ploy for her to do so yet again.

'It's always been a dream of mine to work at the Shilling Grange Children's Home,' Mrs Harrington gushed. Gosh, thought Clara, she was exactly what Florrie would have called 'a phoney'.

'And when I heard you were leaving, Miss Newton, I thought... I know those are big boots to fill, but I thought I would have a go.'

From anyone else 'big boots' would be a compliment; from Mrs Harrington it sounded like Clara was some kind of hoofing giant.

And Clara could bet she would. Mrs Harrington would jump not only into her big boots, but into the rest of her life as well, given half a chance. She felt sick. This third porridge was not just right at all – it was poisonous.

'I'm afraid there's been a mix-up – I am not leaving,' she said.

She took out her fountain pen and flicked it into the blotting paper and there she could make out a big blue heart.

Mrs Harrington looked between the two of them. Miss Webb shuffled papers and made a grimace with her mouth that seemed to say, 'I'm staying out of this.'

If Mrs Harrington was in any way like Goldilocks, it was because she broke into other people's houses and stole their food, chairs and beds or boyfriends.

Once Mrs Harrington left, Clara gave Miss Webb a brief outline of their history together and Miss Webb said, 'Oh dear.' And 'How unfortunate.' But then she brightened: 'I suppose we'll simply have to offer it to number one then. Dear Miss Franks. I do think she'll be precious.'

'We've still got one to interview next week,' said Clara, although she couldn't help feeling like she'd been stitched up.

56

Gladys, Trevor and Frank seemed happy enough, Jonathon was his usual subdued self and Peg – Peg with the prospect of adoption – was now blossoming.

She tugged at Clara's sleeve. 'Can I have your wedding dress after you get married?'

'You know Ivor is not making my dress any more, Peg.'

And she still had to find time to go shopping for one. The idea filled her with dread.

Peg shrugged and then said, 'I don't mind.'

'Okay then, yes, if you like. I'll save it for you, I promise.'

Peg held out one finger: 'Pinky promise.'

Lavenham Primary were having their first Easter bonnet parade since before the war. Clara had mixed feelings about it. Hurrah for the return of the parade, but boo for the extra work it inevitably entailed.

Clara had spent the last few evenings bonnet-making, so, when she went to the high street to watch the procession, she was feeling pretty confident that the children's bonnets might not be the best, but they weren't the worst there either (she had seen the milkman's lad rush by with a bottle tied precariously on his head with a ribbon).

The daffodils were in full bloom. Clara always thought of them as rather an awesome triumph of nature over modern life. It was considerably less inspiring to see Julian White leaning against one of the pillars of Robinson, Browne and White, smoking a cigar and looking for all the world like the parade was just for him. He waved at Clara and, when she ignored him, he called out.

'Miss Newton – why no Easter bonnet?'

Clara gave him a withering look. 'You aren't wearing one either, Mr White.'

He chuckled, and even his laugh was superior. It irked her how friendly he was after having tried to stomp all over her.

'My girlfriend made me some bunny ears, but they're not for out in public.'

A girlfriend? There was always a lady with Julian, bubbling under the surface like a breakout of teenage spots. She wondered if that was why Margot had left him. Or if the girlfriend were Margot, back for round two. Stranger things happen.

'How long have you been courting this one?'

He smiled. 'Wouldn't you like to know?'

Clara meant to say 'Oh,' but it came out as 'Ho'.

She wondered if it had started after the malicious implement incident – no, it was probably before, she thought.

Clara waved at the little ones under their bonnets at the head of the parade. They really were exceedingly small. Some were still toddling. Most had gone for either chick or egg themes, unsurprisingly.

'Oh, and thank you for the invitation. I can't wait.'

'Pardon?'

'The wedding,' he said.

'I know you mean the wedding,' she said, 'but you are not invited.'

'I'm a plus one.'

You're a minus one, she thought. 'Whose plus one are you?'

And here were Peg and Gladys, marching proudly by, beaming. Clara waved enthusiastically. 'Girls! I'm over here!'

Then she turned back to Julian. 'Well?'

He tapped the side of his nose. 'That's for me to know and you to find out.'

'You're not coming.'

'Oh, I am. I will be smirking at the back.' He leaned in. 'Or the front?'

'No.'

'Don't let me put you off. I thought we were quits – you protected your monster and I got my asset back. You'll need someone to dance with too, won't you? I know you love a little cha-cha-cha.'

'Julian, you're NOT coming to my wedding.'

Miss Fisher walked past – at least it might have been her; she was in a massive hat with a paper tiger coming out of the rim. Clara shook herself. She felt like she was in a parallel universe.

'Darling, you know I can't resist a party,' Julian said in an infuriating drawl. He dropped his cigar to the ground, where it glowered menacingly. 'Can't dally.' And he was off.

How could he possibly think he'd be welcome? After all he'd done!

His cigar was still glimmering when she stamped on it. She waved at the children but inside she was feeling murderous.

Anita was holding Baby Howard's hand. He was wearing a hat piled with fruits and he did look rather regal. Anita loved an English custom and threw herself into them wholeheartedly –

anyone would think her family had been making Easter bonnets for generations.

Clara wouldn't usually have confided in Anita, but she was too incredulous to keep it to herself.

'Men behave differently with different women,' Anita said. 'I know Mr White was a rake with you, but that doesn't mean he'll be a rake with everybody.'

Clara scowled. Anita seemed to be insinuating that she brought out the worst in Julian. She didn't think that was the case. He *was* the worst, he didn't need bringing out.

'What's the matter, Miss Newton?' asked Gladys, who was wearing a Christmas paper crown with some extra tin foil.

'Everything is marvellous,' she said with her fingers crossed behind her back. She was furious.

Frank was wearing his usual woollen hat but with a daffodil stuck in one of its holes while Trevor had gone for chess- rather than Easter-themed. Peg looked adorable as usual but the cardboard daffodils kept flopping over her face so she couldn't see where she was going.

Frank's bonnet won fourth prize, and Clara wondered if someone was being sarcastic, but Frank celebrated in all serious-ness. Only first to third got to stand on the podium though, which was a relief since a man from the press was hanging around, wanting to take photographs, and the last thing Clara wanted was another story in the newspapers. In her experience, they were nothing but trouble.

The prize-giving had just finished when Lester's mother, Mrs Greene, came over to Clara, wearing such an elaborate outfit that Clara didn't recognise her at first. She appeared to be covered in papier mâché flowers from head to toe. Lester was wearing a far more low-key dog mask.

'Do you want an update on Suki's condition?' One of the papier mache flowers seemed to whisper.

'Always...'

Suki had given birth last night, to eight beauties. Mother and pups were all thriving. So one thing, at least, was going according to plan, thought Clara. She finally had Ivor's present ticked off the list; and she felt confident that he would adore it.

57

A few hours later and Clara was still burning about the conversation with Julian and his smug insinuations. She went to Ivor's workshop, where Patricia was drawing Easter bunnies at the speed of a machinist on an assembly line.

'I love that fluffy tail,' Clara said, looking for something specific to compliment.

Patricia agreed, serenely. 'It's good, isn't it?'

Ivor was not gossipy, especially when it came to Julian. 'I don't care about him and I don't know why you do either,' he would often say. But when she told him that Julian had somehow connived his way to their wedding, he was as furious as she was, if not more.

'This is a joke?'

'Uh, no, that's what he said.'

Ivor's face was flaming red. 'You sure you didn't invite him, Clara?'

'Of course I'm sure! You saw my list!'

'Then how?'

'He stood there and said bold as brass (when was Julian not bold as brass?) he's coming as a plus one.'

'Who the heck would invite him?'

'Who the heck?' repeated Patricia.

'That's what I don't know,' said Clara, but her mind was racing. To her knowledge, they had sent out only five plus ones. That meant there were five possibilities...

And suddenly Clara could bet she knew which one it was.

They still had the fourth interview to do, but Clara had more than the new housemother on her mind when she stormed up to Miss Webb's office.

Miss Webb was typing at speed, cheeks sucked in and her shoes off.

'I need to talk to you about... your thing with Julian White.' Clara was mindful that after talking to children most of the day, she could sometimes get the tone wrong when talking with adults. She could instruct the children, she could boss them. She hoped she wasn't doing that now. Miss Webb was looking at her as if she was crazy.

'My thing?'

'Yes.'

'With Julian who?'

'Mr White,' Clara said impatiently. It was infuriating that Miss Webb was pretending not to understand. She kept typing but Clara could see that her fingers had slowed down.

'Of Robinson, Browne and White. The solicitors. The tax specialists.'

Miss Webb had been looking for love in Lavenham, Clara had remembered. She couldn't imagine a less likely couple than the high-minded, churchgoing childcare officer and the cynical lawyer, but there was no accounting for taste.

Miss Webb burst out in peals of high-pitched laughter.

'I don't see what's so funny,' Clara said haughtily.

'Noo. It's not... He's more than double my age, Miss Newton, urgh.'

'Oh,' said Clara, shocked – and yet also slightly put out that Miss Webb was so vehement on the age thing. Julian was repulsive but it wasn't just his age that was the problem.

'I'm absolutely not walking out with him. Perish the thought.'

'But you are walking out with someone?' Clara could give Mrs Horton a run for her money when it came to detecting skills.

'Not that it's any of your business, but yes, I am...' Miss Webb tittered.

Clara glowered at her, not quite sure whether to believe her or not.

'It's PC Banks,' Miss Webb went on. 'We met at yours the night after the floods. You didn't know?'

Clara's hand flew to her throat. She remembered that they had both been in the kitchen for a while, and Miss Webb had had a peculiar flush afterwards; but she often did, and yes, she was laughing her high-pitched laugh quite inappropriately, under the circumstances – but she often did that too.

'I had no idea... ah, congratulations.'

'Thank you,' said Miss Webb coolly, but then she couldn't keep the coolness up and went on eagerly: 'It's early days but I do think we might have a future together. He is a God-fearing man...'

It was funny how some people's relationships ran straight from A to Z, while others went all around the houses. Over the last few years, Clara and Ivor had been up and down and round and round, in her lady's chamber, but Miss Webb had met PC Banks and was now walking out with him – no drama, no secret babies, just boy meets girl.

'I-I see...' Clara stammered. She felt like an idiot.

'I hope you don't mind. He told me that you were fond of him at one stage.'

Fond of PC Banks?! Clara scowled, but a voice inside reprimanded her, *it's not worth it.*

'PC Banks, hey,' Clara said as neutrally as she could. 'How nice for you, Miss Webb.'

Who was Julian courting then? Or rather, who on earth was Julian courting that was coming to the wedding? Should Clara warn off whoever it was? While sometimes Julian could be sugary-soft, at other times, the big bad wolf wouldn't look quite so big or quite so bad next to him.

It was time to concentrate on the other task in hand. The more important task. Clara tried to compose herself. She was wearing an old dress suit of Anita's that she hadn't worn before and she felt ridiculously overdone.

'Who've we got in today then?'

The fourth candidate's name was Mrs Schofield. She looked pretty suitable on paper – and when she arrived, warm and energetic, on time and with a confident handshake, she seemed pretty suitable in person too.

Clara was rubbish at guessing ages, but she would estimate around thirty-six, maybe? Mrs Schofield had an impressive bust, which made her look no-nonsense somehow. A cross between Mrs McCarthy and a hospital matron perhaps.

Miss Webb asked her why she wanted the job and Mrs Schofield said that, as she'd explained on her application, she hoped to be a live-in housemother because when she was a teacher, she had felt that a lot of problems started at home, and if you got to the children at home then you could help them earlier.

Everything seemed to be going quite smoothly until Miss Webb asked Clara if she wanted to ask questions.

'I must ask you – some of the homes use capital punishment...'

'Capital punishment!' Mrs Schofield squawked, and Clara realised she had got it wrong again. Bloody words. 'Corporal, I mean!'

Mrs Schofield thought for a moment and then responded: 'I

am against it for several reasons. It can escalate, you lose the moral high ground, you create a culture of fear, and Dr Spock says that it's a last resort.'

'I absolutely agree,' Clara said. To have found a candidate who was a disciple of Dr Spock –this was, dare she say, precious?

They smiled at each other, and Clara felt, ridiculous notion that it was, that they were kindred spirits. Beryl had told Clara that a Virgo would suit the home – perhaps Mrs Schofield was one?

'We also have a cat,' Clara said. 'Named Stella.'

Please don't have an allergy, please, please, please.

'That's unusual,' Mrs Schofield said, eyes narrowed.

'Isn't it?' agreed Clara, unsure whether she meant having a cat or the cat's name.

Mrs Schofield said she was more of a dog person – 'Oh, so am I!' agreed Clara, determined that this fish would not be thrown back.

Mrs Schofield laughed and supposed she might get used to it, and Clara was hugely relieved that Stella was not a deal-breaker.

Mrs Schofield said she didn't have any more questions because 'you covered everything beautifully.' Clara preened; and then, when Mrs Schofield said that she was keen to start as soon as possible, she felt she could hug the woman.

Clara was nervous about Miss Webb's reaction – she had been deathly quiet during Clara's questions – but perhaps love of a good policeman had softened her icy heart for, once Mrs Schofield had left the room, she beamed at Clara.

'I suggest we offer the position to Mrs Schofield before she gets snapped up by someone else.'

'I agree,' said Clara, relieved. 'I think she'll be terrific. But what about Miss Franks?'

Miss Webb made a face. 'She's decided to become a verger instead.'

'Ah, perhaps that's for the best...'

When Clara had imagined working closely with someone, she had thought it might be awkward or difficult, but now she had met Mrs Schofield the prospect didn't seem half so bad as she had thought. She was certain the two of them would get on splendidly.

Miss Webb was still shaking her head. 'I can't believe you'd think I'd ever get involved with someone as repulsive as Mr Julian White.'

Clara kept her head down low and then muttered an apology.

58

Queen Elizabeth was visiting some of the areas affected by floods and there was going to be a special programme about it on the television. Anita invited Clara to watch it at her house. It was on too late for most of the children, but Clara was pleasantly surprised when Jonathon asked if he might come. She still hadn't managed to have 'the conversation' with him – she just couldn't seem to find the words.

Maureen came to sit with the other children. She was coming back and forth from London a lot at the moment. Clara asked her how she could afford the fare and Maureen said she jumped the barrier. Clara didn't know what to say to that.

Evelyn answered the door wearing an amazing hand-knitted sweater. In one hand, she was holding a textbook called *Parlez-vous Français?* and in the other a pencil that had been sharpened to a fine point.

'Mum said to come straight through. I'm revising.'

Evelyn was always revising.

Anita was just putting Howard to bed. Unlike Patricia, Howard Cardew was never seen downstairs past seven. Ivor told Clara that Howard would turn into a pumpkin if he stayed up late, and Clara said, 'turn into?', which made Ivor guffaw and then guiltily tell her off. Unlike Patricia, Howard never said, 'sod' or 'what the hell', not in front of grown-ups at least.

Evelyn was a whizz at working the television. She knew exactly which buttons to press.

'You really know what you're doing!' Clara said admiringly.

'Oh, it's simple, once you're used to it.'

Evelyn explained how long it took to warm up and what to expect. Jonathon was taking it all in, but the television made Clara feel like she was old and past it.

They were enjoying the opening credits to the documentary when Anita swept in and poured herself a drink.

'Is Donald Button presenting?' she said, with a pointed glance at Clara, who ignored her.

Evelyn, expert on programmes too, said he wasn't.

'What a shame,' Anita cooed. 'He's such a skilful presenter, such an everyman.'

The presenter was the actor James Mulroney, a much better choice, Clara thought privately. He was a swashbuckling hero straight out of *Robin Hood*. He looked far swishier in a mac than Donald Button, who wore a toupee and – don't ask how Clara knew – ill-fitting false teeth. Clara thought this actor had a touch of Ivor about him too. Anita sighed and said Clara thought every handsome man resembled Ivor, which was probably true.

And here was the Queen.

'Doesn't she look amazing?' said Anita, who was the Queen's biggest fan in Lavenham – although it seemed Jonathon came a close second.

'She has a strong personality,' he piped up.

'Such a trooper.'

'Isn't she?'

'And look at that outfit!'

'She can afford nice —' began Clara before thinking that made her sound like she had a chip on her shoulder. 'But, it's certainly kind of her to go there.'

Standing close to the screen, Anita was staring so intensely that Clara thought she was in danger of becoming the thing she was always reminding Howard not to be: 'Square-eyed'.

'She is never not impeccable. I would love to know what colour that coat is. Olive green, possibly.'

'My grandfather said that the Queen had a great sense of humour,' Jonathon said in a low voice.

'Oh of course, your family knew her. Ah, this is special then.'

The show didn't just focus on the Queen though. It looked at the devastation caused by the floods and there were interviews with some of those affected. The people of Canvey, Hunstanton and Felixstowe told their sorry tales and Anita cried. Evelyn put her arm round her and Jonathon said solemnly, 'I hope the people know how much we think about them.'

Clara swallowed. She wasn't sure watching this programme would be a good idea, especially for Jonathon, who had gone through so much. However, although he was gripped by the television, he didn't seem upset.

There was some more talk about flood defences and heroism, then Anita told Evelyn to switch it off.

'Will Ivor and the boys get anything, do you think?'

'How do you mean?' Clara responded.

Jonathon looked at them both, chewing his lip.

'An award or recognition?' said Anita.

'Good grief, I doubt it.' Clara laughed. 'Things like that don't happen to people like us. The most people like us get is a bill for damages and a clip round the ear.'

Anita shrugged. She wanted to move on to talking about the wedding plans. She was ridiculously pleased to hear that Clara had arranged for Mrs Wesley from the next village to do the food. But then when Clara said that Ivor was no longer making her bridal dress she grew concerned.

'What? Then what will you wear? I know – you can have something of mine!'

Clara adored Anita's outfits: they were invariably slick, sophisticated, and 'Continental'. But for once she didn't want Anita's hand-me-downs. It wasn't that she didn't want anything second-hand – she loved second-hand, who didn't? And it wasn't that it would be unlucky somehow, Anita and Dr Cardew's marriage seemed, from where Clara was standing, something to aspire to. It was just – she didn't want to marry in Anita's dress, not with Anita there. She couldn't explain why exactly, she just didn't.

Nevertheless, Clara thanked Anita – was there ever such a generous friend? – and said she was in the process of sorting something out, which she was not but she hoped she soon would be. Maybe next week Mrs Horton would be free for that shopping trip in Bury?

She and Jonathon were just leaving when the Norland Nanny came home. She was wearing a swishy dark dress and a pill-box hat. Clara hadn't realised she was out. She looked different in her going-out clothes, a charming mixture of glamour and eccentricity somehow.

'Evening, everyone,' she called. She really was in high spirits. 'Red sky at night, shepherd's delight...'

From the top of her bag, a familiar-looking book was peeping out.

'Hoh?' said Clara. A terrible idea had just occurred to her.

Nonchalantly, the nanny took off her coat and hung it up; she was all smiles for Evelyn and Jonathon.

'Uh, have you been out?' asked Clara, blinking.

Clearly she has!

'The cinema and then for tea. A bird in the hand is worth two in the bush – I don't work Thursdays,' she added. 'Is there anything amiss, Miss Newton?'

'Na-uh,' managed Clara. 'That book in your bag...?'

Now the nanny blushed.

'Oh, my friend lent it to me. It's full of the most splendid poetry. You'd like it, Miss Newton. It's by a woman called – what's her name? I always forget—'

'Jonathon, get your coat,' Clara blurted out. She couldn't stand there listening to the young woman a moment longer.

Clara burst into Ivor's workshop the next morning. 'It's the Norland Nanny!' she said. She was incredulous with the possibility, incredulous and maddened. She had tossed and turned all night long, weighing it up.

Ivor must have been shocked too; he was sewing by hand, and he stuck a needle into his lower arm. A bright red dot appeared, and then a thin line of blood.

She'd never seen him injure himself before. 'Ivor!' she said, not sure if he'd realised or not.

He jumped up. Blood was trickling down his finger He grabbed a handkerchief and dabbed it.

'Bloody hell,' he said when he turned his attention back to Clara.

'I know!' Clara agreed. 'I don't know if there's anything we—'

'Wait there...' Ivor stormed out of the workshop.

After the flood, Clara had wondered if Ivor would ever volunteer to do anything for her or the children again. He might think it only ever led to calamity and perhaps he would prefer to stay out of their affairs altogether?

It seemed she needn't have worried. When Ivor came back, from wherever he went, he gave her a big kiss on the cheek but then said he didn't want to talk about it.

'Is he coming to the wedding?'

'Doubt it,' Ivor said. He smiled, broadly, but wouldn't elaborate.

The next day, Anita said that the nanny had split up with her chap and she would not be bringing a plus one to the wedding after all.

59

Marilyn had sent some money for renovations, but Clara stripped the parlour wallpaper herself. Then she got Anita's workman in to do the rest. And he got put on the guest list too.

The parlour looked much fresher; the children said it looked like a real home, which was their best compliment and always pleasing to hear. Frank added that A. it looked like Lester's lounge – (it didn't). and B. if he scribbled on the bedroom walls, could he have a renovation too?

'No, Frank, that's not how it works.'

Trevor lost his first chess tournament *and* his bicycle and, according to Frank and Gladys, he had asked out his crush, Hettie Legget, chess champion from the girls' grammar school in Ipswich. Clara lent him her bicycle and it made her heart ache to watch him wobbling away to see her. He was growing into a fine young man.

Gladys was invited to her first birthday party. This was especially well timed because Clara wanted her to stand on her own two feet now that Peg was going. The two were inseparable. Not that Clara doubted Gladys's ability to cope. She was a loving and joyful little thing. The birthday girl, her new best friend, had just moved into the village.

'I love her.'

Out of the mouths of babes, as the Norland Nanny might say. The Norland Nanny, who, incidentally, was courting again! Clara, who hadn't thought there were many/*any* single young people in Lavenham, was impressed. The girl was clearly resourceful and had resilience and energy. Later, Clara found out it was Sgt Worsley, and Clara was even more impressed for he was more eligible than most. They made a charming couple.

The children didn't talk about the appearance of Hugh Johnson for a while and Clara wasn't going to bring him up, but one day when they were washing up, side by side, Trevor said, 'Thank you, Miss Newton, we appreciated what you did.' She asked what about, and he said, 'You know – that boy,' and she was going to launch into a long justification of her actions, but instead she just said, 'You're welcome.' And that seemed to be enough.

There was one month to go until the wedding. Clara still had to get a dress but other than that, all was going splendidly. Mrs Schofield was almost definitely going to be her job-share; just a few details to sort out and everyone had replied to their invitation. There were a lot of ticks on Clara's lists.

It was time for Peg to go to the Easleas, for good this time. The Easleas were eager – Mrs Easlea said they hadn't slept for days – and Peg was excited too.

At the council meeting early in the year, Clara talked about how the children didn't have suitcases for when they were moving. Peg didn't have a suitcase of her own. And Peg had acquired quite a lot of stuff, not only her collection of shells, skipping ropes, her drums, but also piles and piles of notebooks, some filled with art but most with words.

'Do you want to take them all?'

Peg shook her head, and then said, 'Just the one. I don't need the others no more.'

Clara had promised herself not to cry.

Getting into the attic was like a military operation: you had to stand on a chair on the upstairs landing and then reach above your head to remove a board. Clara rarely went up in the loft because even once you got in, it was perilous: picking between the rafters was like walking a plank over shark-infested seas. If the younger children knew it was there, they'd be forever wanting to go up so she waited until the children were at school.

Navigating the rafters, Clara quickly spied the large suitcase she was after and dragged it clumsily towards the hole. She didn't know how she would get herself and the suitcase downstairs in one piece. Finally, she just dropped it, making a huge dust cloud rise on the floor beneath her. She had worked out that she could give Peg the suitcase and put her own old stuff in a black sack.

Easy. Only it wasn't easy, it was quite emotional.

Her father had brought this suitcase to the home once, when he was staying at Beryl's. She had opened it and seen it was full of her mother's clothes, letters, books, but rather than go through it, she had put it in the loft so she didn't have to face any of it.

Now, she picked out the things which she would also continue to leave until she was ready. She had almost decanted everything from the suitcase when she got to the box, a long rectangular box that gave the suitcase a kind of fake floor.

Inside it, wrapped in tissue paper, was her mother's wedding dress.

60

Peg chose the dinner for her last supper – pancakes with cheese. Miss Fisher was invited, and she came, stoical as ever as she handed Peg some presents for her new life – a pretty bookmark and a velvet drawstring bag for bits and bobs. How she managed not to cry, Clara had no idea.

Peg chose the game they would play after supper: Newmarket, naturally; and later on, the story – a *Secret Seven* book. They read four chapters together – they weren't short chapters either – yet Peg still didn't want Clara to stop.

'Your new mummy will read it to you,' said Clara. Much as she cherished these moments, it was nearly nine, the dishes were still soaking, and the chores were calling. 'I will write it in the notes.'

At about midnight, a knock came on the bedroom door and Clara sprang up, her first thought that someone was sick.

Peg crept in and turned back the cover.

'One last time,' she said, and it wasn't up for negotiation.

'One last time,' Clara agreed. She couldn't sleep but watched the little girl. It occurred to her that this speechless child was the

one who had turned her into – not a mother but a grown-up, a
protector, a lioness perhaps – and she owed her so much for that.

It was before six when Mr Horton's car pulled up the next
morning. Half-asleep, the children all scrambled up, ready to
wave Peg off.

Jonathon and Trevor had hung up some bunting on the
outside walls and it flapped gently in the breeze. Bunting was
becoming a Shilling Grange tradition, although Clara associated
the decorations with hellos more than goodbyes. The weather was
just perfect for a send-off too. Blue sky, no clouds – a day for a
fresh start – although the crescent moon was still hanging around
in the distance, keeping a watchful eye.

Clara hoped she was giving Peg a sense of occasion and a
joyful one at that. But Peg was very unemotional that morning, in
big contrast to Gladys, who was weeping and then apologising.
Clara had had a talk with Gladys about being as encouraging as
she could, and she could see the girl was trying her best.

Peg ate her porridge quickly and kept checking her bags. Mr
Horton raised his eyebrows at Clara, then picked up the luggage
and walked Peg outside. There wasn't time to think. One minute
Peg was beside her, the next looking tiny; she was all alone on the
back seat.

It was all happening too fast.

As Mr Horton started up the car, Peg wound down the
window. She was doing her best to be brave. Clara could see it.
Gladys blew kisses and the boys shouted: 'See you at the
wedding,' 'See you soon,' 'We'll miss you!'

Clara tried to speak but nothing came out her mouth, nothing
at all, and then Mr Horton accelerated away and her littlest one
was gone.

· · ·

'Hurry up and get ready for school,' Clara told the remaining children, even though they had plenty of time. She wasn't going to cry in front of them, but when Frank muttered, 'I don't think she wanted to go, did she?', she had to gulp back the tears.

Gladys was in floods. 'She didn't, she really DIDN'T.'

Jonathon put his arm round her. 'I think she did and she didn't,' he said softly.

This one's hit me hard, Clara said to herself as she filled up the kettle. It felt like that first cup of tea after the all-clear siren had gone and you could get back in your home. She felt slightly unhinged by it all.

She had children she admired, sympathised with, had a lot in common with. She had children who intimidated her, fascinated her. With Peg, it was just... she loved spending time with the girl. She was easy to be with. She was a great companion, a partner, a friend.

The lucky, lucky Easleas.

Clara had gone through this experience several times before. She had shed tears over Rita and Peter. Both of them had moved on to better things, both of them were happy in their new situations. Peg would be too.

'All's well that ends well,' she reminded herself as she blew her nose. She imagined Peg in her new room in her new house, with her drums, a garden to play in, and then she blew her nose some more.

'Miss Newton's got a stinking cold,' she heard Frank say.

'She's just sad,' Jonathon explained, 'about Peg leaving.'

'I'm sad too,' said Frank, 'but I'm not going through all my hankies.'

'People deal with things differently.'

Frank snorted.

. . .

On her bedside table, Peg had left her favourite shell, the one her mother had left her with at the church ten years previously. There was no note.

Clara had told herself to hold out for at least a week before getting in touch with the Easleas – she didn't want to be a bother – but she didn't make it through the day.

Mrs Easlea didn't appear to mind and said Peg ate beautifully – 'although there's nothing of her' – and was currently eating a boiled egg with soldiers. Cousins were coming to visit in the evening. They were going to look around the high school tomorrow.

'Would you like to speak to her, Miss Newton?'

'No, that's fine. Oh, um, we were reading…'

'*The Secret Seven*, I know. We're up to chapter nineteen. I think I know whodunnit.' She chuckled.

Clara put the phone back on the cradle and sank down against the wall. She thought maybe she wasn't cut out for this life after all.

61

'Oh dear,' Ivor said the next day, at the sight of Clara's bloodshot eyes and red nose. She'd had a bad night. The bed had felt empty without her usual nocturnal visitor.

He put his arm round her and let her sob into his shirt. Spontaneously, Patricia offered her a blue-green marble. Clara knew it was her favourite one.

'It's for you, Aunty Clara,' Patricia said in an uncertain voice, and she looked at Clara with wider eyes than usual. Clara knew how children hate to see an adult in distress, so she quickly pulled herself together.

'This is special' – she closed Patricia's fingers over the glass ball – 'perhaps we can share it.'

Patricia nodded, relieved. Then she stood on tiptoes in her shiny buckle shoes and kissed Clara on the cheek before running ahead to the workshop.

'Patricia talks about you all the time,' said Ivor gruffly. 'I think you've won her over.'

Clara wondered if maybe, just maybe, it had something to do with the fact that Peg had gone.

Two can't occupy the same square in chess.

.   .   .

Later that day, Clara went to the workshop and gave Ivor her mother's wedding gown to work on. Ivor didn't comment on the shape or the material, but Clara felt certain he approved; and if anyone could make something of it, he would. Ivor liked 1920s style too, she knew that. The engagement ring he had taken back to the shop last year would have been a beautiful match, she thought ruefully.

They were a team, and something she hadn't realised before, in all her worry, was that it was good to model a happy relationship to the children. For children to see people in love, to see people support each other through thick and thin, was a good thing.

While Clara would always be pleased she had managed to reunite the Gluck siblings – and rescued the boys from their horrible foster family – she always wondered if they would have had a better chance of being adopted if they had remained separated. Certainly, Gladys would have, she was sure of it. And so she did wonder if, because of her obstinacy, the children might forever be deprived of a family.

A few days after Peg was adopted, Clara talked to Gladys, Frank and Trevor. Trevor was now the proud head boy of Lavenham High School and had a metal badge proclaiming just that. He'd already lost it twice; any hopes Clara might have had that his position of responsibility would stop him losing things had evaporated. He did take his role seriously though, and often gave talks in assembly.

'Would you like to be adopted?' she asked them.

'Not particularly,' said Trevor. 'I've got a lot going on at school and I'm teaching Jonathon to play chess and he's helping me with my Latin...'

'And he's got a lot going on with Hettie,' giggled Gladys.

'He loves Hettie,' teased Frank.

He shrugged. 'I like Hettie. She plays chess and she's intelligent, unlike you two.'

'How about you, Frank?' Clara interrupted.

'Not bothered. A. I've got Lester,' said Frank, scratching his hat. And B. I've got Stella. And C. You know what?' He winked at Clara.

Of all the children to share the secret of Ivor's present with, Frank might have been the worst. He loved being 'in the know' and could not stop taunting the others about it.

There was one more answer she needed to hear: Gladys's.

Gladys kissed Clara's hand. 'I love you,' she announced. She could never resist saying that. 'I don't want to go anywhere else. All my family is here in this room and that's all I ever wished for.'

A couple of days later, the children and Patricia were playing Old Maid in the kitchen. Clara was warming up some chicken soup when Patricia wandered over to her and grabbed her hand. Her blue eyes filled with tears.

'Mama,' she said. It was the first time Patricia had ever said that. Clara didn't know what to reply, but she didn't need to. Patricia puckered up her lips for another kiss. One kiss might be an accident, Clara thought, but two, two couldn't be ignored.

62

The Master of the Household has received Her Majesty's command to invite: Mr Jonathon Ainsley Pell of Shilling Grange, Lavenham to receive the George Medal – For bravery in peacetime at Buckingham Palace.

Miss Clara Newton of same address is invited to accompany him.

The boys were going to get something, they really were! This was unbelievable. Unbelievably marvellous and magical, Clara thought as she clutched the letter to her chest. She couldn't imagine how delighted they would be.

And then she read on.

at 11 a.m. 30 May 1953

Oh no, no, no.

Clara ran over to the workshop but Ivor was out visiting a client. It wasn't until later that evening, after a frantic day of worry, that she found him. He was at his usual place on the bench, head down, pins in his mouth.

'Did you get one too?'

He looked up, pulled the pins from between his lips, raised an eyebrow.

'One of these?' insisted Clara impatiently, flapping the card.

'Oh, I haven't open it yet...' he said, remarkably relaxed for someone who had just received a letter from Buckingham Palace.

'You're not going to believe it!'

Of all the dates, in all the world, it had to be the day before their wedding.

'You, Jonathon and Clifford are going to be given the George Cross!'

'Yes?' he said mildly.

'On 30 May!'

Ivor looked at her with narrowed eyes. She couldn't tell if he realised the significance of the date or not.

'What's wrong with it?'

'It's THE DAY BEFORE THE WEDDING!' Clara shrieked before collecting herself. 'The actual day before we get married...' she repeated.

Ivor swung back his chair in a way for which, had he been eight years old, she would have told him off.

'So it is,' he said after a moment. 'I'll write back and say we can't go then, shall I?'

'Nooo... We can't cancel this, Ivor. It's Buckingham Palace!'

'Then you want to cancel the wedding? I don't know if we'll get the deposits back...'

'I don't want to do that either,' Clara said, exasperated.

'Then we'll just have to crack on with it. It'll be a busy couple of days, that's all. We'll manage.'

Clara sank down. She was feeling stunned. Less than a month to go and this felt like another huge obstacle. Why couldn't it have been in June or July?

She was considering that when Ivor asked if she wanted to back out of the wedding.

'No! Not at all. It's just the dates are less than ideal, that's all,' she said.

'You're not worried about tying yourself to a man with a disability?'

'Good grief,' said Clara, genuinely surprised. 'I thought we were past all that?'

'I'm just checking. These past few months have reminded me I'm not like other men.'

'You're certainly not like other men. And these past few months have reminded me how much I love you for it,' Clara said, thinking how lucky she was that Ivor was nothing like ghastly Julian or PC Banks.

'Truly? You're not just saying that because the invitations are out?'

Clara snorted. 'I'm not just saying it.'

'Do you have time for some stargazing then?' Ivor said, getting up from his chair.

'Is that what you call it these days?' Clara winked. 'No, I'd better get back, but soon I'll be living here every other week!'

Clara had finally told Ivor all about the no-nonsense Mrs Schofield who would hopefully be living in the home and looking after the children every other week. Ivor thought a job-share was a great solution. (She had not told him about seeing Mrs Harrington at the interview. Some things are best kept under your hat.)

It wasn't just moving in part-time to Ivor's workshop that Clara was looking forward to now, she was also excited about getting her hands on Ivor's accounts. She felt Ivor would increase his work output if she could modernise and streamline his book-keeping. Ivor laughed at her ambitions but admired her too. He liked to say, 'If you were in charge, the war would have been won in weeks.'

He got up to see her out. 'I can't believe that you'll soon be Clara Agnes Delaney – you know that makes you a cad?'

'I do, and I like it.'

He put his arm round her.

'You'd better let the Palace know we're coming then.'

63

Two days before Buckingham Palace, Mrs Schofield came to have
a look around the home before making her final decision. Clara
was reminded of how much she liked her and thought again what
a good fit she'd be.

Again, Clara couldn't help being impressed by Mrs
Schofield's almighty bosom. She thought Frank would be equally
awe-struck; he was a little – how do you say? – obsessed with the
birds and the bees recently. Even Mrs Dorne, who prided herself
on her tolerance, was complaining about his interest in certain
passages in the holy book.

Clara introduced Mrs Schofield to each of the children.
Jonathon demonstrated his usual impeccable manners and Mrs
Schofield congratulated him on his forthcoming medal. Trevor
and Frank weren't rude either, which was pleasing. Gladys
declared she loved her and asked was she coming to the wedding?

'I'm not, dear,' Mrs Schofield said firmly. But Gladys said, 'Oh
I'm sure you can, you can be a plus one. There are loads of
those—'

'I'll show you around,' interrupted Clara. This was getting
slightly out of hand!

Clara felt proud leading Mrs Schofield from room to room. The house gleamed. Clara told her about the history of Shilling Grange, making sure to include their most famous ex-resident, the poet Jane Taylor. Mrs Schofield looked suitably impressed. Clara explained about the council leasing the home from Marilyn Adams, their American benefactor. Mrs Schofield said she was already aware and 'whatever works!', which struck Clara as a particularly positive and open-minded reaction.

'There are only four children living here?'

Clara thought of her missing Peg enjoying gardens, drums and cousins elsewhere. She swallowed.

'At the moment, yes. There will be more soon – once we have everything settled. There's no shortage of children who need care.'

'I always feel that five is optimal,' Mrs Schofield said, which was something Clara herself liked to say. She grinned, almost giddy with relief. Mrs Schofield surpassed expectations.

'And where will you be going?' Mrs Schofield asked. Her tone was light, understanding, so the question didn't sound as confrontational as when other people asked. 'After your marriage?'

Clara took in her kind eyes and smiled. 'Ah, nowhere.'

'I don't understand,' Mrs Schofield asked with a confused look on her face.

'I'm not going anywhere.' Now Clara paused. 'Didn't Miss Webb explain?'

'Explain what exactly?'

'It's a part-time role, a job-share thing. The council have agreed it.'

Mrs Schofield stood up. She was much taller than Clara. She took off her glasses and then put them back on again.

'I wasn't made aware of this.'

'What?' Clara asked, slowly feeling her intricate arrangement slipping through her fingers.

'No one said.'

'What? The advert didn't?' Clara desperately tried to cling on to any hope that this was just one of those misunderstandings that could be fixed.

'It didn't mention anything of the sort,' Mrs Schofield said. 'How on earth would that work?'

'We haven't gone over it exactly. I'm adaptable, though. We can find a way round this,' Clara said, still pleading although she could already see that this was a lost cause. Damn Miss Webb!

'I need full-time work, not part-time. I'm dreadfully sorry,' Mrs Schofield apologised. 'There must have been a mix-up. I really can't do it.'

And Clara watched Mrs Schofield stand up and walk away and watched her hopes for staying on at Shilling Grange leave with her.

64

On the day of the palace trip the morning sun was streaming through the curtains while Clara lay in a bed for a while. This was the calm before the storm; she may as well enjoy it.

She had worried about sleeping the previous evening, but when it came to it she had been out like a light. The children had too. It had been a rare night without interruption or incident and Clara felt strangely rested.

It was coming up to five thirty when there was a sound of a car horn outside. Clara got out of bed and waved out the window. Then she dressed hurriedly and dashed downstairs. Jumping in the Cardews' car, Clara nearly landed on a bag of mints.

'Mind!' yelped Anita.

Clara patted her hand. 'You know how much I appreciate you, don't you?'

They had an early appointment with Beryl.

'Buckingham Palace, eh? Your father would have been proud of you,' Beryl said as they walked through the door of the salon.

Clara felt peculiar receiving these platitudes from Beryl, but hoped she did not let it show.

Beryl had an occasional assistant, Doris, who was doing Anita's hair today. Anita was rather bossily directing her. They sat leaning back with their heads in the sinks and Clara could just make out them discussing the current attempts to climb Mount Everest.

'I just don't believe they will do it,' said Doris cynically. 'And anyway, who'd know?'

Anita sounded impatient. 'They will put a flag there.'

'And you know that, how?'

Beryl threw questions at them both. She insisted that Clara's marriage would be a long one because of the alignment of the stars. It was an auspicious date too.

Anita snorted. Clara could sense her friend's blood pressure rising even without seeing her. When she was upright again, she smiled at her and Anita made a face back.

'I'm only not arguing because it's your special day,' she whispered.

Back at home, Clara whipped upstairs to change. She put on a favourite dress, the dress she'd worn to Hunstanton the first time they went, when Ivor proposed.

The children were eating breakfast – thank goodness for Maureen – but they came to the front door to see her and Jonathon off. Jonathon was wearing his school uniform – the only smart thing he had – but, whereas Frank and Trevor made an outfit look worse, Jonathon had a talent for making it look more special.

Frank had a question before they left. 'Miss Newton? MISS NEWTON?'

'What is it, love?'

'What happens on your wedding night?'

'Frank!' Clara blushed to her newly tinted roots. 'What do you mean?'

'Do we go to the party or come home?' Frank asked, confused as to why his question had garnered such a reaction.

'Oh!' Clara composed herself. 'There's a party and then we come home, Frank. Is that okay with you?'

'Fine,' he said. 'Will we play Sleeping Lions?'

'Uh, it's not that kind of party, Frank.'

'Will there be dancing?' asked Gladys.

'Absolutely...'

'Will you and Ivor dance?'

This was a more difficult question to answer. There would be dancing, Anita had organised a band for them, but Ivor was uncomfortable dancing. Clara had hoped to persuade him but he insisted he wouldn't, and she knew it wasn't the joking kind of insistence, it was the insistence of an immoveable rock.

'Maybe. Now, be good, everyone – and we'll have a celebration when you're back from school.'

'Can we play Sleeping Lions, then?'

Clara considered. 'Maybe...'

Gladys whispered to Frank, 'Maybe means no.'

Jonathon and Clara walked up to Lavenham station with Ivor – who looked even more handsome than usual – and met Clifford at Green Park underground. She wanted to instruct the boys on decorum, on not picking their noses (Clifford) or chewing their fingers (Jonathon), on not making eyes at the ladies-in-waiting (Clifford) or not looking like they'd rather be anywhere else in the world (Jonathon), but she didn't. It was their day; why should she try to make them feel inadequate? Plus, it was too late now – if they really didn't know how to behave then last-minute commands probably weren't going to help.

They were all excited. Ivor held her hand but, like Jonathon, he didn't say a lot; they were both nervous. Even though there'd be food at the palace, presumably, Ivor bought them all tea and a Bath bun, since it was a special occasion.

'I could get used to this,' joked Clara as she tucked in, and Ivor winked. 'Only the best for my girl.'

'I can't believe we're getting married tomorrow!'

'You'd better believe it, darling,' he said. 'It's been a long time coming.'

Is there anything better than the walk up to Buckingham Palace on a sunny summer's morning? Clara suddenly remembered the photo that she had taken here a long time ago – with Michael, and his friend Davey and his girlfriend Nellie. How good it was that the country was no longer at war! Once, she had thought Britain would never recover, but it had – and so had she.

The flag showed that the Queen – how strange it was to say that: Clara was more used to saying King! – was in residence.

They were met by a man in a dress suit and tall top hat. Now even Clifford was rendered speechless. They were led down corridors, on carpet so thick her heels dug in and she worried she'd leave tiny holes. Kings and priests in oil paintings and gilded frames stared down at them. In one painting, though, there was a girl holding a puppy, and Ivor whispered that maybe that was the young queen herself. Clara irreverently thought of her tea tray and had to suppress a giggle.

More corridors. Ivor and the man were talking in hushed library tones. She felt proud of him as she hurried to keep up. The man was saying how busy it was, preparing for next week's coronation – they were expecting millions of people around the world to watch it on their television sets for the first time ever. And Clara thought preparing for a wedding for a hundred people was bad! It gave her some perspective.

Clifford needed the bathroom – it was nerves – and then there was more waiting, and other people joined them to wait. It wasn't too long, though, before they were led into another room. This room was not as large as she'd imagined, but it was definitely as grand, and there were paintings of soldiers and horsemen, magnificent ornaments, Chinese-looking jugs; and she wondered what Ivor thought about the soft furnishings. He was looking around him appraisingly, and she thought, I like Ivor's curtains more, which made her laugh to herself. She had turned sentimental.

They had front-row seats. A lady showed them to their place, and whispered that today's ceremony would be short and sweet. Clara thought these might be her favourite words. She thought of how she would describe this in great detail to Peg one day. Her relationship with Peg wasn't over, she realised suddenly, it was just different. There would be letters, drawings, gifts and stories. She would tell her about the painting that might have been of the Queen as a young girl with a puppy.

And then the Queen arrived and, up close, she was smaller than Clara expected and also more smiley than she appeared in the photographs in the newspapers or on the television shows. She looked quite amused. Clara couldn't wait to tell Anita and Marilyn about this. Anita was always claiming that the Queen was six foot tall, and it was just the television that made her look weeny.

And then it was time for the awards. They were the last. Before them were a line of people who had performed Extraordinary Service: a policeman, a nurse, a mother of three, an ambulance driver, two fishermen. And then it was the turn of Clara's men. They got up, Ivor brushed himself down, Jonathon put his fingers to his mouth, Clifford strode to position.

'This is Jonathon Pell, ma'am,' introduced the woman who may have been a lady-in-waiting, Clara wasn't sure. There was a lot going on.

The Queen spoke. 'I understand I met your father on several occasions.'

Her voice was a bit like Mrs Mount's. It was posh. Not movie-star posh but plummy, that was the word.

'You did, ma'am.'

Oh, but Jonathon was impeccable. He was graciousness personified.

'You must be proud,' the Little Queen said.

For once, Jonathon couldn't stop grinning. He was the Cheshire cat as he took his seat again.

Next up was Clifford. Clifford was unpredictable but had she thought about it, Clara could have predicted this – he loved performing, and he was performing the role of hero to a T. He bowed. He accepted his medal. He was friendly yet deferential. He didn't overstep the boundaries.

'You did well,' the Queen said.

'Thank you,' he said, ducking his head. And Clara thought with astonishment that he too sounded almost plummy.

'I wish you the best of luck in the future.'

The Clifford Clara used to know might have come back with a cheeky riposte: 'I don't need luck, sweetheart!' but this Clifford – Clifford Mount – lowered his eyes and said, 'Thank you very much,' and moved on without a fuss.

And then it was Ivor's turn. The woman whispered to the Queen and her face brightened further.

'Is it true you are getting married tomorrow?'

And Ivor, shy Ivor, nodded, and then pointed directly at Clara. 'There she is. That's my intended over there.'

Clara didn't know why she did it but she stood up and curtseyed. She could remember curtseying at school and the teacher telling the girls, 'You need to know how to do it, in case you meet the King...' and everyone had laughed because what were the chances?

'I expect you are proud of this man,' the Queen – *the Queen!* – called out to her.

Clara's mouth was too full of saliva to reply straight away. She swallowed and then managed, 'More than... more than I can say.'

'Good luck tomorrow.' The Queen smiled.

'You too,' Clara said reflexively. 'And with the coronation and... everything.'

Dear God! What was she doing?

She almost said, 'I love you!'

Then Ivor took his medal and moved on. She could sense his happiness; it was written through his whole body like a stick of rock.

After the medals, there were speeches – this was one of, oh, plenty of reasons why Clara did NOT envy the Queen – and Clara tried not to twist Ivor's arm to look at his wristwatch. If they said they'd be done by eleven, they would surely be done by eleven – these things ran like clockwork.

Crackers and cheese were offered on silver trays. Canapés meant it was over soon, surely. Clara grew anxious again. There was still a lot to prepare for tomorrow. The boys tucked in though. 'You can't turn down free grub,' Clifford said, eating with his mouth open. They had been well-behaved for a long time, Clara thought, it wasn't surprising that they couldn't keep it up much longer.

And then there was a last speech, by the top-hat man, and they were thanked for coming and no one knew quite what to do until someone opened another door that Clara hadn't even noticed.

She put her arms round her men, her medal-holders.

'Let's get going.'

Mrs Mount was waiting to meet them outside. She looked splendid and Clara wondered if Ivor would have a reaction to her. Most men did, even if they thought they were hiding it. But Ivor was just chatting with Jonathon and laughing with Clifford. It transpired that Mrs Mount had been to dozens of medal ceremonies before so she wasn't aggrieved not to be included in this one.

They all walked to the underground together, down the tree-lined Mall towards the great grey buildings around Trafalgar Square, and Clara still felt as though she was floating. She had just met the Queen! She had just wished the Queen good luck! She tried to bring herself back to earth as they waited to cross the road. A double-decker bus went by and the people on the top – tourists maybe – waved.

They were teasing each other and joking – the Queen was so small, *almost as small as you, Clara!* – those jewels must be worth a few bob. And did you notice those chandeliers, the size of a house? And the paintings...

'She was more attractive than I expected,' Clifford remarked.

'Good grief, you didn't make a pass at her, did you, darling?' Mrs Mount said, shaking her head. 'You are a nuisance.'

'Course I didn't. I like an older woman, but she is twenty-five.'

'She is twenty-seven,' corrected Clara, who followed these things.

Mrs Mount and Clifford were coming to Lavenham early tomorrow. Clifford was singing in Anita's choir in the church, naturally. Mrs Mount said that she wouldn't miss it for the world and since Miss Cooper had declined her invitation – recurring shingles – Clara felt she could relax about that too.

'How are you enjoying life with Clifford?' Clara said when the boy was out of earshot.

'It's not just life with Clifford,' Mrs Mount said. 'There are always young people coming and going. Girls crying on the doorstep early in the morning., boys getting ready to go out after supper. There's never a dull moment!'

'And Clifford is knuckling down to his work?' (Clifford was helping a local builder)

'He's doing rather brilliantly,' Mrs Mount said. 'He'll do his National Service soon. And between you and me, Clara, I might look into fostering other teenagers. I feel that's where my strengths lie.'

Hugh Johnson! Clara thought instantly. She'd try to arrange it. It wasn't his fault the adults in his life had let him down.

'That's wonderful,' said Clara. They were still waiting to cross the road – the stream of London buses, trams, delivery vans and bicycles felt endless compared to sleepy Lavenham – when Mrs Mount took her hand and whispered in her ear, 'And it's all thanks to you.'

And then it was just Jonathon, Clara and Ivor alone on the train again. Ivor held her hand and Jonathon closed his eyes and gripped his medal tightly. The conductor came round and clipped their tickets and gruffly pointed his clipper at their medals – 'You just got that?' and 'Well done, son,' to Jonathon.

Ivor went to the buffet car and Jonathon smiled at her. 'I'm going to enter some running races,' he said.

'Really?'

'Trevor's going to train with me sometimes. And I'm going to look at studying biology at university. Dr Cardew is going to help with the applications.'

'This is great news...' Clara was just about to ask what had changed when he spoke up.

'I don't know why,' he said. 'I just don't feel so bad about myself any more. It feels like something has lifted.'

'You shouldn't feel bad about yourself. Ever.'

And she realised that, although it was probably pleasant to hear, her opinion wasn't that important to him any longer; his peers, boys like Clifford and Trevor, they were the ones who had made the difference. Even so, she had to say it.

'You are perfect just as you are.'

He nodded. 'I even like being a Pell now,' he said. 'It's like I'm part of something.'

Clara was beaming with pride. She knew Jonathon's life wasn't going to be easy, but this honour would help. It was a safety net, a reassurance, and it was well-deserved.

Ivor came back with tea. 'Happy?' he asked.

She told herself to remember this moment forever. Jonathon and Ivor knee to knee, the grimy window beyond them. Her, slightly apart.

'Very.'

They were talking about that evening, and Clara told him that, although they were having a celebratory tea at the home, just a little one, Ivor had to go back to his workshop before six.

'Superstition dictates we spend the night before our wedding apart...' she explained.

'You do pick and mix the rules, Clara!'

'Doesn't everyone?' she laughed. They watched London recede and the countryside beckon. The land was so flat; it was just as Ivor said: you could see further from here than you could from anywhere else. The place of the big sky – the place of her home and soon the place of her marriage.

'Early night tonight,' she said, more to herself than Jonathon or Ivor, 'tomorrow is another big day.'

As they walked down the high road, Clara was mentally going through all the things she had to achieve before tomorrow. There would be ticks on her lists! Ivor was telling Jonathon about Jesse Owens and the 1936 Olympics; and then suddenly he fell silent. Outside his workshop was a big black Bentley so shiny you could see the shape of the trees reflected in it and so big it took up half the road. Clara was bewildered at first. *Who has such a fancy car?* She thought maybe it was something to do with the awards, or PC Banks.

Then she thought, *could it be Marilyn?* It would be just like her to arrive like this. Marilyn didn't do small or unobtrusive visits; but Marilyn had been apologetic when she explained that she couldn't make it until tomorrow.

And then Clara finally realised. It was her worst nightmare come true.

From the passenger side, a woman's slender knees swivelled out, and then the rest of her followed. It felt like it was happening in slow motion, like dropping a pudding or losing a kite. A purple hat with netting – who wore purple? – a smart cream suit. Cream – it was almost bridal. No one dressed like that in Lavenham. Everything about the woman screamed money.

Clara recognised that walk. Even if she hadn't recognised the person, even from one hundred yards away, she would have known from the gait – it was all in the hips. It was deliberate, exaggerated.

Ivor's face was white as chalk. 'What the hell?' he said. And then he looked around him with eyes narrowed. 'What is she doing here?' he snarled. 'This is the last thing I need.'

'Ah,' said Clara, her heart beating nineteen to the dozen. Ruby would tell him anyway, so it was better coming from her first. Maybe. Or maybe it was too late for anything. She wrung her hands.

'I might have something to do with that.'

Ivor was shaking his head; his lips formed a thin grim line like a crack in concrete.

'It was when you were missing,' she told him quickly. She was shaking, and her voice didn't sound like hers at all. She should have told him earlier – why didn't she tell him?

'I was worried, and I didn't know what would happen with Patricia...'

And then she was up close. Ruby, impeccable, fashionable, stylish. Cover girl – destroyer of dreams.

And she had Patricia's bright blue eyes. Clara swallowed. Patricia was the spit of her after all. The idea that Patricia resembled Clara in any way was just a big game of Let's Pretend.

People say not what they really see but what they think you want to hear. People had their fingers crossed behind their backs the whole time.

Patricia was the image of her mother. And didn't Ivor love Patricia?

She had never seen him look so horrified.

'You took your time,' Ruby called out, familiar.

Out of the side of his mouth, Ivor said to Clara, 'What have you done?'

65

As they stood in the street, Clara tried again to explain, but it felt like her reasons were excuses and Ivor's patience had run out.

'I didn't do anything. I just... I just called her when you were lost.'

But he was so focused on dealing with Ruby that she doubted he even heard her defence. It was obvious that he didn't want her there.

It was Jonathon who tugged on her arm: 'Let's go, Miss Newton.' And it was Jonathon who pulled the keys from her handbag and let them in. He was the one who made the pot of tea, added the sugar for shock and told her to get it down her.

Her head was fuzzy; she felt feverish. If she didn't know otherwise, she would have thought she was coming down with the flu.

It was a terrible mistake to contact Ruby. *What had she been thinking?*

He'd lose Patricia and she'd lose him. And for what? Her

stupid, misguided sense of duty. Her compulsion to interfere in other people's business. Her arrogance...

She had been the same with the Norland Nanny and Julian coming to the wedding. But the Norland Nanny and Julian were nothing compared to this, that could be sorted out with an exchange of words; this was disastrous.

When the children came home from school about an hour later she was still sitting there, her head in her hands. They had been expecting a party or some bunting or a celebration cake. The least they were expecting was a story about the palace, a display of the medals, an anecdote about the Queen.

And Frank was expecting Sleeping Lions.

'Go and lie down, Frank,' Clara told him flatly. 'You're out if you move.'

And bless him, the boy did go and lie on the parlour floor – until he grew fed up and went upstairs, roaring as he went.

At least there was cake. Mrs Horton had brought it round when they were out. Clara cut it down the middle and then again several times. Each slice felt like she was parting her and Ivor over and over.

'I thought Ivor would be with you.' Sweet Gladys never missed a trick.

'He's got to sort out Patricia,' said Clara. It was true in one way. She hoped no one noticed her red eyes. If they did, she would say it was Stella-induced (although what a surprise, disloyal Stella had trotted off to Ivor's).

Jonathon looked over at her sympathetically. He reassured her he didn't mind, he hated a fuss. Maureen came back from the shops and Jonathon must have told her what was going on, for she was quiet as she put the things away.

'Can I go over the road? I want to show Ivor my drawing,' Gladys said.

'You can show it to me,' Clara suggested weakly.

The picture was of a man kneeling at the feet of a woman

wearing a crown as she placed a chain round him. It must have been how dear Gladys imagined Ivor and the Queen.

'It's beautiful, one to keep forever.'

'I want to give it to him now.'

'NO.'

Gladys was so surprised that Clara raised her voice that she plopped down into the chair, open-mouthed. Oh gosh, Gladys was going to cry. Trevor sprang up and put his arms round her and looked accusingly at Clara.

'Sorry, no. Ivor's busy right now. Why don't you do another one, this time with the boys in it as well?'

Gladys squinted at her. 'I love you.'

'Thank you. I love you too.'

'I might draw Jonathon later,' she pondered.

'Let's play the alphabet game,' Trevor suggested.

Maureen shouted, 'Duck-billed platypus!'

Even Jonathon joined in. 'Dragonfly?'

'Miss Newton – what's your D word?' Trevor prompted.

Clara couldn't let them down. 'Dog,' she suggested croakily.

That was another thing she had to sort out before tomorrow: the arrangements for Suki's puppy.

'I was going to say that!' Gladys squealed.

'Duck then?' Clara said hastily. It felt as though everything was on edge and about to tip over.

She would let Ivor come to her, Clara decided. In the years they'd known each other, they'd had as many arguments as there were stars and they had got over each and every one of them. They'd disagreed on the home, on friendships, on children. They'd been angry, jealous, suspicious and weary. This was not new.

Yet, there was something about this that was far deadlier. Clara knew this. Perhaps because, all along, Ruby had felt like something poisonous, like a slow-seeping gas. Other issues came and went, deadly as bullets, but this, this was invisible and omnipresent. This mattered. Perhaps because it wasn't an argument but a threat. What Clara had done – even with the best intentions – would have hurt him very much. Whether he would forgive her or not, she supposed, depended on what Ruby did or said next. It was not pleasant to think that her fate was in that woman's hands.

66

Clara made tea. It was a different atmosphere in the home that evening to the one she had anticipated and Ivor didn't come over.

The children were so careful with her that Clara felt like one of those china dolls with the slowly blinking eyes. Maureen served up parsnip soup and when Frank complained, 'Do we have to polish our shoes again?' Jonathon said, 'Miss Newton would be ashamed of a mucky pup who couldn't be bothered.'

Anita called and Clara said that the day at the palace was wonderful, yes, the Queen was charming, yes – yes, but it had taken it out of her and she should rest otherwise she'd be in danger of a migraine tomorrow. She was missing out some vital information, but it was plausible.

She heard Trevor speculating, 'I think Miss Newton and Mr Delaney have had an argument.' Then Frank asking, 'Are they not getting married then?' and all the children hushing him, Maureen the most vociferous, 'We don't know what's happening yet,' and Jonathon's more measured, 'We'll just have to wait and see.'

. . .

There was a part of Clara that had always sensed she wouldn't get married. She'd always thought she might have that in common with Jane Taylor and that she was single to her bones. If it were a quiz in *Good Housekeeping*, she would probably have got mostly D's: 'Old Maid: You're a spinster, not for lack of trying, but just bad luck – if you were born in a different era maybe things would have worked out for you, but being a young woman in a time of war can be complicated...'

There was a part of her that confused a 'maybe' with a 'no'. That always knew she didn't deserve the happy ending. It wasn't that happy-ever-after was a myth, it was just that it only applied to certain people. The straightforward ones. The normal ones. People like her got the twisted-ever-after or a bumpy-ever-after.

She wasn't Cinderella – why had she overestimated herself? She was the pumpkin turned into a coach – and then bong, what happens after the clock strikes twelve and the party's over? The pumpkin is just a pumpkin again.

What would be going on in the workshop right now, she wondered as she washed up. She had told Maureen she would do it by herself and when the girl hesitated, she'd snapped, 'Please, give me some space!' Maureen had looked woebegone but backed away and Clara had immediately apologised: 'It's not you – I just need a moment to think...'

She carried on alone, wiping the dishes and the cutlery. She could hear Maureen organising the children upstairs, getting them ready for bed. Thank heavens for that girl.

Clara's thoughts returned to Ivor's workshop. Ruby would be demanding, toe tapping, because that's what Ruby did: 'Ivor, do we have a deal?'

Perhaps Ruby was packing Patricia's things? Ruby wouldn't even know which things were Patricia's favourites. Clara knew.

Her Polly, her mallet, her collection of cardboard tubes, her borrowed black marker pens, her marbles, the *Ladybird Book of Nursery Rhymes*.

Maybe as Ruby packed up her toys, she was scolding Ivor: 'You couldn't even keep yourself safe, how am I expected to trust you?'

Possibly Ruby hadn't packed Patricia away. Perhaps Ruby had rocked her to sleep. Patricia probably subconsciously knew her mother's voice and knew intuitively not to whack her round the head with her mallet.

And Ivor would have watched this scene, and tears would have filled his eyes and maybe, when he saw Ruby and her glowing skin, her alluring cleavage, he'd think she didn't look run ragged like Clara, she looked like she was a movie star.

Perhaps they'd set Patricia down under her blanket and then together, carefully, giggling to themselves, moved up to his room. Over there, right now, might be a lovemaking scene worthy of the cinema. Ruby would be rolling down her suspenders, and Ivor would be looking at her in awe, admiring her in that surprisingly hungry way he had, pulling her close impatiently.

Or perhaps he was holding Ruby to him as she watched the stars through the telescope. Watching the night sky, *their* night sky. 'We're stardust, darling.'

Clara didn't know which scenario made her heart ache more. The jealousy pulsed through her at the thought of him whispering sweet nothings into Ruby's ear: Orion. The Great Bear. The moons of Jupiter.

Perhaps he didn't love Ruby more than Clara, but perhaps he put them on the scales – the scales he sometimes used for his work – and on one side was Clara and the wedding – and on the other was Ruby, and perhaps the scales were equal until you added in the other chips. Patricia. Patricia's well-being. Patricia now, and Patricia's future. Maybe he didn't fall for her exactly, but he calculated this could work, we three, it would be easier, and anyway, Clara has her work, Clara has her children. Clara hasn't even sorted out what's going to happen regarding the home...

Who had Clara been trying to kid?

He loved Ruby more. He always had. Look at the fact that he didn't want to get married on her birthday!

She would have to cancel everything, the church, the hall, the caterers, the band... No, she would maybe get Maureen to call them all, she was strong like that.

Everyone would wonder what happened: everyone would have a theory – they would throw up ideas, they would get it right sometimes, without knowing they'd got it right. They would guess he dumped her.

Then there would be new analysis. The reinvention of history.

'They were never quite right, were they?'

'I always thought it was odd: He was a celebrated hero and she was a nothing.'

'You know she was engaged to that Mr White once. And then there was the professor. She goes through them faster than a dose of castor oil.'

'If you ask me, Ivor had a lucky escape. She's like a black cat.'

'She does have bad luck, doesn't she? Lost her father, her friend.'

Clara knew suddenly, with an overwhelming certainty, that the reason bad things happened to her was because she was bad. Her partners got wiped out of the sky. Her friends got murdered. Her mother got forgotten. Her father got eviscerated. A woman was mown down in the street in front of her. They all nearly drowned. What did they have in common?

Her. Clara Agnes Newton.

It was not death or grief that she carried around her, that shrouded her like the London smog. No, it was failure, the stink of failure. Each of those endings could be traced back to her:

Didn't Michael insist on working more so they'd have more money?

Didn't Judy beg her to let her adopt?

Didn't she stop writing to her mother?

Didn't she fail to welcome her father?

She could go on forever, but this was the biggest failure of all, coming at her like a ten-foot wave, like an area with no flood defences: didn't she call Ruby – didn't she invite this storm into their lives?

She would move from Lavenham. She would enquire about other children's homes. Maybe approach Norfolk Council or the London ones? There were enough of them there. She wouldn't leave them straight away – goodness no, she'd make sure everything was all right – and she would make sure it wasn't Sister Eunice she handed over to. In fact, she would call on Mrs Schofield – 'Oh, a full-time position has just become available...'

In the meantime, Ivor would avoid her, she presumed; she'd had the cold treatment from him before. Perhaps he'd go away again. She wouldn't be able to bear to see him and Ruby living in the workshop together. He wouldn't expect her to, surely.

Yes, she'd have to move. She'd have to build her life up again. She still had one suitcase, the one she'd taken to Hunstanton, and she'd borrow boxes from the flower shop. She'd pack up the contents of her life, and she would marvel at how small and mobile they were – how she was. She was not a person of material things. You could pack all of her up like a week's food shopping. She'd take the wedding dress, but only because it was her mother's. She'd leave the bicycle, the piano... she'd find a position somewhere, that she didn't doubt.

She'd make new friends – a new music teacher, doctor,

teacher, flower shop manager, friendly nun; Stella would have to come... No, perhaps Ivor would have her. Ivor loved Stella, and everyone preferred Ivor in the end.

The house had turned quiet. The children must be sleeping. Clara rested her head on the kitchen table and wept.

67

'Miss Newton?' When Clara jerked awake, she was slumped over the table and the room was in darkness. Gentle Jonathon clicked on the light, and she saw it was gone ten. She had escaped into sleep for an hour, no longer. The Order of Service for the following day was in front of her, mocking her. That was another thing that would have to be cancelled.

'Do you need anything?' he asked.

'No, thank you.'

'The children are in bed. I read Gladys *The Little Prince*.'

The sweet boy. He was all lip-chewing concern.

'I bet she enjoyed that.' She sniffed. It should have been her reading to them. Why was she always so preoccupied?

Jonathon looked at her kindly though.

'Why don't you go over there?' he asked, his voice gruff. 'It's not too late... To Ivor's, I mean?'

'I don't think I can,' she said and the boy who had struggled, who still struggled, seemed to understand.

She had stood up at the extraordinary council meeting and said, 'Mothers need to have access to their children.' She had been thinking of Peg, and Florrie too. She hadn't been thinking of Patricia. She *hadn't* thought of Ruby. What a hypocrite she was! Was that the right word? Yes, probably – or maybe she was self-righteous. Pious. Inexperienced. Or naive.

'We need to support parents of children in care far better, so that if at any time they want to come back, if they are ready, they can.'

Her words.

'I would like a system whereby parents can get back in contact with the children in care whatever has gone wrong before.'

Her words again.

Yet, it wasn't black and white. There she had been advocating that parents might be able to swoop into children's lives without punishment or judgement, and yet here it was happening to Patricia and it felt unfair.

She looked across to Ivor's workshop, as she so often did. The open doors were an invitation – or were they? The lighting was golden, but she didn't feel the contentment she usually did. She had to face this – no, she had to face *them*. She combed her hair, powdered her nose, and put a slick of plum lipstick on. She wouldn't argue with Ruby or attempt to reason with her, she would just listen.

She had begged the council to take the interests of birth parents seriously. And now look at her. She felt – what was it? – 'hoist by her own petard'. She had been too simplistic, too pat. It wasn't as straightforward as she'd thought.

But she did still have to see Ivor. She had to know for sure that the wedding was off. As she walked over the road, all of her was apprehension, and the fear was as real and tangible as her footsteps on the cobblestones. It was quiet and it felt like she was marching towards the gallows. She thought randomly of Derek Bentley, that poor feeble-minded half-man, half-child, and her heart bled for him – and also the man who was shot.

Ivor was still at his sewing machine – did he ever not work? – and he didn't look up at first.

Where was Ruby? She might be in bed, or maybe she was having a post-coital cigarette out the back. She might be cooing over Patricia's things. Clara wanted to weep. Had Ruby taken Patricia away to live with her and her new husband? Patricia would have such a different existence than the one she had here. Ruby could probably afford to employ a nanny now. Maybe it would be better for Patricia? Those were the unquantifiable things.

Next to Ivor on one side were stacks of material waiting to be done and on the other side, the ones he had completed.

'Knock, knock,' she said awkwardly.

'Who's there?' he responded.

Rubbing his eyes, he looked up at her. The machine slowed and then stopped. He looked exhausted. He didn't look like a man who was getting married in the morning.

'It's me,' she said in a small voice.

He made a funny shape with his mouth and his eyes pooled with tears. She felt the lump in her throat harden.

'Where's Ruby then?' she finally managed to ask.

'Gone,' Ivor confirmed, roughly wiping at his cheek.

Gulp. But the next question was the big one. 'And Patricia?'

'Asleep.'

'Upstairs?'

'Yes.'

Clara's legs wobbled. She could have collapsed. He stretched out his arm towards her. Steadied her onto the bench.

'Or maybe not asleep, you know Patricia.'

'Ivor, what happened?' Clara wanted him to be honest with her now. To be completely clear. There mustn't be any room for misinterpretation.

He was nodding at her, smiling beneath the tears.

'So... I'm officially adopting Patricia. Ruby wants that to

happen. She was going to wait but she's... she's met someone. And she doesn't want them to know about Patricia. She doesn't want to have a relationship with her. I'm sorry I shouted at you, Clara.'

The relief caught her. He still had Patricia. Ruby was not the big bad wolf. It was going to be all right.

'No, *I'm* sorry – for everything.'

He grabbed her hand and squeezed. 'I know you are.'

'Forgive me.'

'Nothing to forgive,' he said. He kissed the tip of her nose. 'Now, I thought I wasn't meant to see you tonight? You said it was bad luck?'

She shook her eyes, tears still ready to fall. 'It doesn't matter...'

And then Ivor was rummaging for something by the rolls of material. He produced a note and handed it to Clara.

'Ruby asked me to give this to you,' he said with a faint smile at the corners of his mouth.

She saw it was scribbled in haste and was just a few short lines.

It said:

Take care of them both, they need you.
　　With infinite gratitude,
　　Ruby

Clara vowed to herself there and then that she would; she would take wonderful care of them both for the rest of her life.

68

Finally, it was her wedding day! Clara woke up before six. She didn't want to wake the children, so she crept past their doors, but she could already hear rumblings from the girls' room. Fortunately, Maureen – who had been a blooming godsend and deserved a George Cross herself – was shushing them. Maureen had had a convoluted plan of changing all the clocks to fool the children into sleeping later, but Clara hadn't agreed to it.

Marilyn arrived about seven, and there was hugging and presents for the children and much excitement. Clara half-wished she hadn't arrived on this day because Marilyn was a major event, a circus in herself; but Marilyn was sensitive too. She said she was popping back to the Shilling Arms to get ready.

'I'll stay out of your way, Clara, and when we've got time, we'll catch up properly.' She was also determined to give Ivor her present from Scotland: a kilt.

'He'll be delighted,' lied Clara.

The telephone was ringing, the doorbell was going non-stop. Clara made sure the children had their porridge – nothing worse than a whinging child in church – and, while they were scraping their bowls, Dr Cardew and Evelyn turned up. They'd brought along Evelyn's signature 'Marble' cake. 'Because we don't want the children to get hungry...'

They were chatting in the kitchen when Frank ran in, his hair all over the place, his shirt untucked, delighted to see his favourite person.

'Did you hear the news, Dr Cardew?'

Dr Cardew looked up, surprised. Clara's heart sank again. News was not welcome. Not today. Would nothing ever run smoothly for her? She had worked hard on organising her wedding. She knew she couldn't anticipate every eventuality, but she had contingency plans and checklists and was fairly confident she had most things covered. She wanted to clamp her hands over her ears and sing la-la.

'What's happened now?' she asked in a voice full of dread.

'Is the wireless on the blink?' Trevor asked.

'I don't think so, why?'

'Put it on,' insisted Frank.

The New Zealander, Edmund Hillary, and the Nepalese Sherpa, Tenzing Norgay, have become the first to reach the summit of Mount Everest on the Nepal–Tibet border.

The two men hugged each other with relief and joy but only stayed on the summit for fifteen minutes because they were low on oxygen. Then they began the slow and tortuous descent to rejoin their team leader, Colonel John Hunt, further down the mountain at Camp VI.

When he saw the two men looking so exhausted, Col Hunt assumed they had failed to reach the summit and started planning another attempt.

But then the two climbers pointed to the mountain and signalled they had reached the top, and there were celebrations all round.

Col Hunt attributed the successful climb to advice from other mountaineers who had attempted the feat over the years, careful planning, excellent open-circuit oxygen equipment and good weather.

In the kitchen, everyone hugged each other with joy and, certainly in Clara's case, relief that it had nothing to do with her wedding.

'See,' she said, laughing. 'You can achieve anything with careful planning.'

'And excellent open-circuit oxygen equipment and good weather,' added Dr Cardew, laughing too. 'Who would have thought it? We humans aren't just good for war and destruction, we can do great things too.'

'What an achievement,' he continued. For him this was the big news of the day. 'Good old Edmund Hillary. He dreamed he would do it – and he did it.'

Evelyn scowled. 'He did it too, Dad. The other one. Sherpa Tenzing.'

'He did.' Dr Cardew cuddled his girl. Evelyn was so grown-up now.

'*Both* men were astonishing,' he said. 'What a feat of ingenuity.'

'Feet?' repeated Frank.

'We'll put a man on the moon before too long,' Dr Cardew continued, winking at Clara. 'If we can get Mr Delaney and Miss Newton married without incident – then it just shows ANYTHING is achievable.'

'I like incidents,' said Gladys, cheerfully cutting herself a thick slab of cake.

It was time to get ready. Clara's heart was singing as she went upstairs. She heard Peg arrive. How generous of her new parents to bring her back so soon after she'd left. It was taking a risk, but the Easleas trusted her and they trusted Peg. A short while later, she thought she heard Peter's voice and the children shrieking a welcome. It made her smile.

When she had told Ivor she had asked Peter to walk her down the aisle and to give her away, he'd said, 'Oh no...' and sat with his head in his hands.

'What's wrong with that?'

Ivor wasn't going all traditional on her now, was he? Peter wasn't her father but he was family... But Ivor had laughed. 'Thing is... I was going to ask him to be my best man!'

At that they both had laughed. 'Great minds...' he said.

'Ha, I got there first,' said Clara triumphantly. Peter had been delighted to be asked. They had both shed a tear or two.

'That's fine,' Ivor said. He had winked at her. 'I have another idea.'

Clara did her make-up in a hand mirror. Oh, it was a relief to have some peace and quiet. She suddenly remembered Judy's wedding. *Oh, Judy.* She should have been here today. And she remembered Mrs Horton's wedding too, another happy occasion.

She wondered what it would have been like if her mother were here. But if her mother were alive, she would never have come to Lavenham, and she would never have found Ivor...

Would her mother have approved of him? Clara liked to think so. And maybe, like her father, she would have mellowed. People do – people did, if they had the chance. That's why being robbed of the chance to find that out was particularly painful. Memories of her mother were becoming less distinct; they were more lists of words than actual tangible things to hang on to.

She remembered coming out from school one time with the handwriting pen she had won for neat handwriting and her mother really taking time to look at it, and then patting her head. 'You've got a knack for that. Just like Grandma Jean. She was good at anything on paper too.'

It was such a sweet, bittersweet memory; she could picture herself trailing after her mother in her dark wool coat and dark heeled shoes. The paper, the pen, her mother's approval washing through her. The way she told her father, 'Clara had an achievement today.' But then it was like a television switched off and there was nothing more. She tried to tune in again.

Her mother had loved sewing. She and Ivor would have had that in common. She could picture her mother and Ivor in the workshop at their machines, side by side. Her mother could be competitive, in a friendly kind of way; they might have had races. She would have been here today. She would have helped Clara do up her dress. She would have made her a veil. She would have helped her put it on and adjusted it, checking it was straight. She would have looked into her eyes, and she would have said, 'I'm proud of you.'

Maureen was knocking on Clara's bedroom door, then she stuck her head round it, a bit like Maxi the dog used to.

'Frank's been sick.'

Oh God. She'd known something had to go wrong.

'He's fine though,' Maureen continued. 'It's the excitement.' She entered the room and squinted at Clara: 'Have you done your make-up?'

'Yes!' said Clara, unsure whether to be offended.

'I thought so,' said Maureen reassuringly. 'You look lovely.'

Maureen was chief bridesmaid. Her hair was white and curled up at the ends. She did it herself.

But what is the girl wearing?

It was a tight skirt with an even tighter blouse and a kind of tie like a bow. She looked years older than she was.

Clara wished she'd got Ivor to make her an age-appropriate frock. 'Are you wearing that?'

'Me? Oh yes! Big Joan lent it to me. How do I look?'

'You always look wonderful.' Clara swallowed. 'I'm proud of you.'

Frank followed her in. He looked a bit peaky but insisted he'd be all right if he could have some honey tea.

'Someone's stolen my tie!' yelled Trevor from the boys' room.

'It's under the wardrobe,' Clara reminded him. 'Where you left it,' she added under her breath. Neither brother had wanted to be a pageboy – 'that's for babies' – but they had agreed to be ushers at the church, which was more than she had expected and sweet of them.

Gladys was going to be a bridesmaid with Peg, but she was permanently worried about who was holding the ring.

'You're not holding the ring,' Maureen explained patiently for the umpteenth time. 'You can forget about it.' And for a minute, Gladys looked relieved; and then her eyes narrowed again. 'But who is?'

The best man presumably, and Clara still didn't know who that was.

Now Gladys stormed into Clara's room, complaining. Her dress wouldn't do up at the back. It wouldn't budge for Clara or Maureen either. She couldn't have grown in the two months since they'd got it, could she?

Usually, Clara would tell the children to rush over to Ivor's to get help with clothes, but Clara knew he would have enough on his hands sorting himself and Patricia out.

'Oh, hang on, Anita will do it. Or Evelyn. Someone take Gladys up the road, please... Maureen?'

Gladys scowled. 'I can go by myself.'

'I expect you can.' Gladys was becoming an independent thing. 'Okay then, and hurry.'

The children left the bedroom and Clara took a last look at the photos she had of Michael. They were taken so long ago, it felt like a different lifetime. A moment frozen in time. He was such a dear selfless boy. It was unjust that he had been deprived of a future. She looked at the photo of him as a baby, the photo of them together outside Buckingham Palace, and the one of him with his beloved plane – the last one.

'Thank you,' she told the Michael behind the glass. And she pressed her lips to where his once were. She would always be grateful for the time they had together. And Michael had taught her such a lot: that relationships could be joyful, that the good in the world outweighs the bad but you have to fight for it and that you should throw yourself in and let yourself love and be loved.

69

When Clara finally went downstairs in her mother's wedding dress, her sense of *look at me, don't look at me* self-consciousness felt overwhelming. Ivor hadn't had to do much. He had let out a bit at the sides and taken it up at the hem – Clara was broader and shorter than her mother – and it was perfect.

The boys had gone ahead in the first car with Marilyn. There was only Peter, Maureen and Gladys left. Gladys was back from Anita's house, red-faced and out of puff, but mercifully with her dress safely done up.

'I love you,' Gladys said, 'You look like a princess.' Then the remaining children proceeded to discuss who Clara resembled more: Princess Margaret or Queen Elizabeth. (They decided Elizabeth.)

'Very nice,' said Peter approvingly. How wonderful he looked, all grown-up, in his RAF uniform. It suited him. He held out his arm and she looped hers through it.

'Are you ready, Miss Newton?'

'She won't be Miss Newton for much longer,' screeched Gladys. Clara, who felt all mixed-up about changing her name, liked it when Peter said with a shy smile, 'She'll always be Mum to me.'

It was a surprise to find Maureen's ex-beau Joe was driving the car. Mrs Horton had offered but Clara knew she had enough going on since she was in charge of corralling all the children. Joe said this was a new business venture he was trying and that Clara was only his third client. She told him she was honoured and patted him encouragingly on the shoulder when she realised how nervous he was.

Gazing out of the passenger window, she was astonished to see that people stopped to wave at them. One car, then another and another hooted. People stood outside their shops and clapped. (Had she invited them?!) Now she really did feel like a princess. The don't-look-at-me feeling remained strong but it was now trumped by her excitement at seeing Ivor, at marrying Ivor. Not long now!

She saw Farmer Buckle, purple-faced, running down the road towards the church in his suit – he scrubbed up surprisingly well – and then Miss Webb in a long dress, stumbling out of a car driven by PC Banks. She saw Joyce hobbling along with her parents – she looked in at Clara and waved so vigorously, she nearly toppled over.

It was only when they were nearly at the Church of St Peter and St Paul that the old doubts began to surge like floodwater. What if Ivor had changed his mind? What if he was still angry? What if he didn't come?

And then they were outside. The sun was shining – but it was not too hot – she couldn't have arranged the weather better if she had tried. Weather, oxygen and careful planning. They had it all.

Hurrying round, Joe opened the passenger door for her and whispered, 'Best of luck, Miss Newton, you deserve it.'

'Thank you, Joe.'

She and Peter walked together towards the church. Peg joined Gladys and Maureen at the gate and Clara could hear Maureen hissing something at them to get them to behave. They were each holding a posy. Clara tried to think where and when they had sorted that out. She supposed a lot had been going on behind the scenes that she was unaware of. Her head felt full but in an unexpectedly delightful way.

She heard Gladys whisper, 'Who *is* carrying the ring?' and Maureen shushing her. 'You'll see...'

The church door was open – Clara noted for the first time, it was a beautiful-shaped door – the church really was a magnificent place, whether you were religious or not – and she was suddenly thrilled to be marrying here. And there directly down the aisle was her love. Her love and his teeny tiny best man – best girl: Patricia Delaney. And Patricia was wearing a lovely lacy white dress that somehow – Clara didn't know how he did it – seemed to be a perfect match to Clara's own. Ivor's talents never failed to impress her.

Take care of them both, they need you was ringing in her head. It felt like a blessing.

Ivor smiled broadly at her, and she smiled back. He raised his eyes, as though telling her she looked pretty, and she hoped that by her eyes he understood that she thought he looked wonderful. He was wearing the suit that he wore on all important occasions – the one he'd rescued her from the council in, the one he wore to the palace.

And oh, oh, that music. It really was the Shilling Grange Children's Choir. Re-formed, for one day only, for this special occasion. Maureen slipped into position with Gladys; and there was Denny, sweet little Denny had returned – Clara waved – and there was Clifford of course, Maureen, Peg and Gladys; and they sang – a beautiful medley of songs that only Anita could make work. Only Anita would know how much Clara loved these ones: 'We'll Meet Again' and

'Shine on Harvest Moon' and 'Keep the Home Fires Burning'...

Do not cry.

Standing next to Ivor, it felt to Clara as though the rest of the world disappeared and the *don't look at me* feeling faded to a small dot. They were here finally and Clara wanted to giggle – here was her Everest. She was going to plant her flag on him – the only place she'd want to be.

The dark fears of the evening before had vanished. This was their wedding day.

The vicar welcomed everyone and then said, which she hadn't expected, 'There are three recipients of the George Medal here today,' and everyone clapped and cheered, and that broke the ice, and Clara was relieved. She couldn't stand a stuffy or formal ceremony – they weren't stuffy or formal people, after all.

Under the stained-glass windows, of colourful fishermen with their nets and the farmers with the wheat, she let herself deliberate on the vicar's words.

'In richness and poorness,

In workshops and children's homes,

'If any man can show just cause, why they may not lawfully be joined together, let him now speak, or else hereafter for ever hold his peace.'

In Clara's worst imaginings, Ruby had intervened at this point, so she held her breath here. She couldn't help herself. She could hear Frank querying in his booming tone, 'Why can't they be awfully joined together?'

And Trevor's snapped retort: 'You're awful.'

'No, you are.'

Jonathon's more patient voice: 'It's lawful, not awful!'

Clara might have turned round and said, 'Children!' or 'Shush,' but she couldn't, not on her wedding day, not in church. She could tell from his expression that Ivor too was trying not to laugh. And so was the vicar.

'Do you, Ivor Delaney...'

She may have heard Peg say, 'I thought he was a Humphrey?' And then it may have been Maureen who said, 'Sssh' followed by an 'Oi!' at something else.

'Do you, Clara Agnes Delaney...'

She *definitely* heard some giggles at the 'Agnes'.

'I do.'

Patricia jumped to attention, but for once she did not smack Clara with her mallet or wail about napping. She had an incredibly serious expression as she presented Ivor with a small velvet box.

Ivor gently took the wedding ring out of the box and took Clara's hand.

The ring squidged down her finger and then she and Ivor kissed, a clumsy, shy people-are-watching kind of kiss. And then they walked down the aisle at last, man and wife, and it felt like the most natural thing in the world.

Outside, the children threw rice over them, too much rice, a waste of rice, and she could hear Frank complaining, 'A. it nearly went in my eye and B. I want to throw some more.' Maureen was telling him to be careful and was that Alex telling anyone who would listen about the wives of Henry VIII?

As rice sprayed all over her Beryl-set hair, Clara was bursting with happiness and relief.

Thank goodness that was over. Now the fun could begin.

70

Mrs Horton, Miss Webb and Anita had surpassed themselves: the Cloth Hall looked amazing. They had been organising and decorating until late last night, apparently, and again early this morning. Clara had been banned from 'helping', so when she did, finally, get to see it, it felt like she was walking into a magical kingdom – or a precious land of the Faraway Tree. There were tapestries on the walls and bunting criss-crossing the ceiling. The tables were covered with gleaming white tablecloths and Mrs Garrard's flowers were in glass vases everywhere you looked. The guests who'd got there before them already had glasses in hand and were chatting happily. They greeted Clara and Ivor warmly and told her the ceremony was wonderful, and that she looked beautiful, and she proudly thanked them and to those that asked, she explained that it was her late mother's dress. It felt special to say that. She felt like she was part of something; a long line of brides had gone before her and her mother was with her.

She was reunited with adored ex-residents and their adoptive parents, old and new friends, and Ivor's hand – her *husband's* hand – came and went on the small of her back, reminding her that he was there.

. . .

In the few minutes before the food, prepared wonderfully by Mrs Wesley from the next village, was served, Clara decided to give her wedding present to Ivor. Her eight-week-old present. She had visited the Greenes' home a couple of times since Suki gave birth, and the puppies were all lovable, but one had stood out. He wasn't too forward yet he wasn't too anxious. He was just right. He had sauntered over and climbed onto her lap. He had dark streaks down either side of his eyes that looked like tears. Wasn't he just made for them?

Now Frank walked out of the hall holding Lester's hand on one side and Mrs Greene on the other, which was the agreed signal, and Clara went over to Ivor, who was being heartily congratulated by Dr Cardew and Anita, and told him he had to come outside.

'I thought we were about to sit down and eat?' he asked.

'I need to show you something,' Clara said.

'What's going on?' Ivor was mystified – which was great since Clara had thought the game was up on several occasions, not least when Frank had said in front of everyone, 'A. I love dogs and B. Oh no, I can't say that.'

'It's my present to you. You didn't think I'd forget, did you?'

Ivor was laughing now too. He let himself be pulled to the front door of the hall. Anita and Dr Cardew followed.

'What's going on?' Ivor kept asking, and, 'What did you do?'

The children crowded around them. Clara had a sudden memory of the time they had got the cat for Rita and the joy Stella brought to the children's lives (sometimes). She remembered them watching Stella climb on the windowsill to stare at the birds. The way Denny might cuddle up to her after a surge of painful memories, or Joyce might after a bad day at school. The way they stroked her, casually or carelessly sometimes, but reassured she was there.

Ivor was outside now. When he shook his head, bits of rice dropped to the ground. He still didn't suspect a thing, Clara was sure of it.

There was Frank, her small smiley boy, holding a cardboard box not much bigger than a shoebox. He peeled back the flaps of the lid and, when Ivor didn't appear to know what to do, he himself plucked the puppy out. It was all legs and tail and licky tongue.

'He's for you!' said Frank and handed him over to a bewildered Ivor.

And just how utterly handsome did her husband look, holding a sweet puppy in his arm? His face seemed to go as soft as butter.

'You didn't!' he kept saying, while the dog nuzzled against his chest. He was irresistible, Clara thought, smiling to herself – and the puppy wasn't bad either.

Patricia was on tiptoes, squealing to have a hold. Very carefully, Ivor let her take a turn, and then he turned to Clara.

'You know me too well,' he said in his low voice that would never not make her heart beat faster.

'I should hope so,' she said as she kissed him again.

'What's going to happen about work?' Mrs Horton asked after the excellent starter course of celery soup. She had a skill at bubble-popping. 'I hear Mrs Schofield let you down.'

'She didn't let us down as such, it's just we weren't what she wanted.'

'What does it mean for the home?'

'I'm not sure, but for now we'll continue as we are.'

'You haven't found anyone else?'

'Not yet.'

It was disappointing, but it was also all right. Clara was nervous of stepping back from the home but it would happen one day. It just wasn't happening yet – it had to be the right person. She and Ivor were patient people, they'd learned to be.

And there had to be someone out there who would want to do it – perhaps a student or a housewife or a—

'I have an idea,' interrupted Mrs Horton 'Look over there...'

Clara followed where she was pointing to see Maureen was lugging Patricia over to the children's table. Patricia was squealing, her face flushed, Polly bear flopping at her side. But Clara didn't understand what she was being told to look at them for.

'What?'

'*Maureen* is looking for a part-time job.'

'Maureen?' Maureen, the sulky girl, the one who played house, who cooked and cleaned, the one who listened. Maureen working in the home had never occurred to Clara before – which now seemed a ridiculous oversight. She considered it for a moment or two, and then, as Maureen carefully set Patricia back on the ground, asked Mrs Horton: 'You think she's ready?'

Smiling broadly, Mrs Horton nodded. 'I do, I really do.'

Clara remembered how Maureen had been in those upside-down days after the flood. How she had quietly and unobtrusively looked after the house while Clara was all over the place. She had collected children, she had *comforted* children. Maureen *was* ready – the shocking thing was that Clara hadn't noticed it until now.

Clara went over to her. Maureen was kneeling down by Patricia, talking as though she were Polly. She looked up and smiled. Hadn't Clara only yesterday thought she was a godsend?

'You look beautiful today, Miss Newton! That dress is perfect.'

And she was good at giving compliments too.

'Maureen,' Clara began. And yet she couldn't find the words. She tried to think of Ivor's advice when she was speaking to the council. *What is it you want to say? What is it you want them to feel?*

'Would you consider working in the home with me as a kind of job-share?' The words came out in a rush. 'I think you would make a brilliant housemother – you're wonderful with the children, you're great in the kitchen and a whizz at paperwork. I would be honoured if you'd consider it— Oh, sweetheart!'

Maureen had burst into tears. Clara scrabbled around for a handkerchief. She couldn't hear the girl through her sobs, so she had to wait and then ask her to repeat herself, a few times.

'I've... sob... been... sob... waiting forever for you to ask.'

'I had no idea,' Clara said.

'I couldn't wish for better,' Maureen continued. 'Thank you.'

And then, because Clara didn't know what on earth to say next, she drew Maureen into a big hug as the young woman wept some more.

Ivor wasn't going to give a speech and Peter wasn't going to either since they both loathed public speaking. Clara had privately hoped one of them might give in in the end and get up to say a few words, but at the same time she thought good on them for standing their ground. And then, quelle surprise as Anita might say, Clifford got up. He had nominated himself. As he rose, for the first time today Clara noticed he was wearing his George Cross on an expensive-looking blazer – Mrs Mount had the budget for such extravagancies. He was now acting toastmaster and tapping his fork on his glass.

Where did Clifford get his confidence from? He had the air of someone completely at home in the world. He thanked everyone for coming, then said, 'I'm not going to make a joke about Miss Newton – sorry, I mean Mrs Delaney's cooking,' and everyone laughed, 'but thank you to the caterers. You might just have saved our lives today.'

'Ain't that the truth?!' Marilyn shouted, clapping.

Clara rolled her eyes. She was wary of what else Clifford

might come out with, but actually she had no need. He had been trained impeccably. Mrs Mount sat nodding her lovely head on one side of him and Anita was mouthing along with him on the other.

Clifford thanked absent friends and read a list of telegrams and messages from those who were unable to make it, including sweet Florrie and dear Terry. Clara wiped away the tears at the one from Judy's mother and resolved to visit her soon. She laughed at the one from lovely Rita, who wished she could play a song for her and Ivor but sadly she had committed to doing a piano recital for the King of Denmark instead. 'Will see you next Christmas,' Rita promised.

And then, voice growing more serious, Clifford said, 'People don't know what "home" means to kids like us. I wasn't one of Miss Newton's best residents' – he laughed – 'I probably was one of her worst.'

He smiled at Clara, who smiled back, thinking, *he* was *the worst.*

'But she always made me feel accepted and she made me feel safe. I think people from normal backgrounds with normal loving families don't understand what it's like to be us, how precarious everything feels. We know that everything can be snatched away from us in seconds. It means you don't trust people. You just grip hold of things to keep your balance and sometimes, they're the wrong things. That's why we sometimes...' he paused, '*often* get it wrong. And then I came here...'

Did he wink at Maureen then?

'And I still got it wrong. But Miss Newton helped me. She introduced me to people too – people like Mrs Cardew, Mr Delaney and Mrs Mount here. Safe people – people I can trust – people who keep their promises – because I think sometimes that's all you can do, get the good people together and that somehow one of them will get through to you and help you turn your life around.'

Now, everyone was clapping. Ivor was smiling at Clara with love and admiration in his gentle eyes. And suddenly, Clara knew she had to get up and give a speech. It wasn't the done thing for a woman, it especially wasn't the done thing for a bride, but she felt full of emotion right then. It was as though the words had to spill out of her whether she wanted them to or not.

So Clara stood up and, briefly, she thought of her mother and her father and what they would have thought of her today. Her father had of course met Ivor and he had already said, 'You have my blessing,' and she did indeed feel blessed. And she knew her mother had loved her. Whatever else had happened, whatever else had gone wrong – and a lot *had* gone wrong – what a thing that was: to be loved.

'I just want to say a few words before we tuck into our main course – as Clifford said, we had a talented cook prepare all the food today, it is not only safe.' The guests gently chuckled again. 'I think you'll agree it is exceptional. And this let me get on with the things I am better at. For example - I thought up a little ditty for my new husband:'

> *Twinkle, twinkle, Ivor Delaney*
> *How I wonder you drive me barmy*
> *Hard at work, you look smart*
> *Like a diamond in my heart.*

Clara was grateful when everyone laughed. She continued. 'There are three things I love about Ivor...'
The best speeches use the law of three, she thought.

'He has always been there for me. He has the kindest face,' Clara laughed self-consciously, but he did! She couldn't leave it out. 'He cares for all the children with all his heart, including his own daughter, Patricia, of course. He's my hero.'

Patricia was beaming. Polly bear and her mallet were set on the tablecloth in front of her.

'That's four,' shouted Jonathon, his medal glistening, and the guests cheered. Clara couldn't quite believe it was him. What happened to the boy who wouldn't say boo to a goose?

'I could go on about Ivor, but I won't – I'll just say I can't wait to share the rest of my life with him!'

And she leaned over to kiss him and Patricia puckered up for a kiss too. Clara happily obliged before returning to her speech.

'It's been an amazing few years. When I first arrived here in Lavenham in the dark days of 1948, I had no idea what I was letting myself in for. And it was difficult at first, adjusting to a new job, a new town and new people...'

Clara felt a lump in her throat – but she had to go on.

'I was grieving and... I felt very alone. And unequal to the task ahead of me.'

Clara swallowed back the tears; looking out at the sea of smiling faces in front of her, she continued.

'But thanks to you all, this place has become my home and this community has become my family. You mean the world to me. Thank you for your open arms and your warm hearts, Lavenham – you've made such a difference to me and the children. We wouldn't be here without you. Here's to all of us!'

The guests raised their glasses and repeated, 'To all of us.'

After the roast chicken and strawberry tarts, which were indeed one hundred times better than anything Clara could have produced, Anita's grown-up band were picking up their instruments. It was time for dancing.

'Clara' – Ivor held out his hand – 'will you do me the honour?'

But Ivor hated public dancing almost as much as he hated public speaking, so, as Clara rose to her feet, she felt mystified. He wasn't going to dance today, was he?

The lead singer looked over at Ivor. 'Are we ready? Come on, everybody.'

Now it was Clara's turn to ask, 'What's going on?' as Ivor led her to the centre of the hall. Then the band struck up a familiar song and the children all raced over to join Clara and Ivor.

Clara laughed. 'No, not this one, really?!'

And then she was grabbed by the arm and the children and some of the adults had formed a large circle. Their first dance was the hokey cokey. The lead singer grinned at them from behind his microphone.

'You put your left arm in, your left arm out. In, out, in, out, you shake it all about.'

Still laughing, Clara kissed her new husband for the umpteenth time that day. 'You know that I'm *all* in with you.'

'And that,' Ivor said as he kissed back his glowing bride, 'is what it's all about.'

Later, Clara shared a cigarette outside with Peter and Clifford. She let Maureen borrow her lipstick in the ladies' and thanked Mrs Wesley from the next village again. Mrs Wesley said she'd had a jolly time too.

Then Clara looked around that big, beautifully decorated hall complete with friends, residents and ex-residents, and her heart felt full.

There was Mrs Horton laughing at something Mr Horton had just told her – about bowls, most likely. There was Anita wiping Baby Howard's chubby cheeks – he'd got himself into a right old mess, while thinking about Aristotle, probably – and Dr Cardew was folding a cloth serviette into a duck-shape for Evelyn, who was watching closely, a big smile lighting up her serious face. And her dear Marilyn, her almost mother-in-law, was pouring the vicar a glass of sherry and he was miming smoking a cigarette. And knowing Marilyn, she would be saying, 'Oh, I couldn't possibly... Oh, all right then, just the one.' And Beryl was gazing around, open-mouthed, as though trying to work out who was rising

Aquarius and who was a pitiable Sagittarius, and Farmer Buckle was trying to catch her attention. Mrs McCarthy and the man known only as ShabbyHut were deep in discussion with Sir Alfred about oil paintings. (ShabbyHut was not a great fan apparently.) Sister Grace was nodding earnestly at something Mrs Mount was telling her. The two policemen and their girlfriends were on their own table nearby and she could hear the Norland Nanny saying something about something borrowed, something blue,' and PC Banks responding pompously, 'We all know what borrowed means, don't we?' And Miss Webb's high-pitched laughter at that.

Little Peg was waving at her and chatting – *Peg was chatting!* – to sweet Terry with her short hair and flowery shirt. Billy and Barry were in smart suits – they'd grown so tall – and were laughing at something, or talking football, and Alex and Frank were earnestly chatting or competing about school and their results while Trevor was explaining something to Bernard about chess and Ivor was holding the puppy while Jonathon and Denny were waiting for their turns and Joyce was trying to take a photograph of them all. Maureen saw her watching and blew her a kiss.

Clara did not have her mother or father there, and she was no one's mother, but here were her family – her orphan family – and they were every bit as precious. These were her lost children – and they had been found – and in finding them, she was lost no longer.

THE SHILLING GRANGE FAMILY –
WHERE ARE THEY NOW?

RITA JANE WITHERS

Rita joined the Vienna Philharmonic Orchestra as pianist and spent many years touring the world with them. Throughout her illustrious career, she released fund-raising records for Barnardo's, and she appeared on *This Is Your Life* in 1998. She lives in Switzerland and occasionally teaches the piano.

TERESA 'TERRY' SERAPHINA CARTER

Terry worked as a gardener at various locations throughout the UK. She was the head gardener at Hyde Hall in Essex for over ten years. She was the first woman in England to marry, wedding her long-term partner Gillian Harris when the law changed to civil partnership in 2013.

Terry died suddenly in 2015.

MAUREEN AMY KEATON

Maureen was housemistress at Shilling Grange for over ten years, before moving into children's services. She is currently in charge of children's services at Essex County Council, a role which combines her love for child-care and administration. She still keeps a strip of paper with the letters LMNOP on it in her purse. She married Harry Carpenter in 1956 and they were divorced two years later. In 1963, she married her childhood sweetheart, Joe, in St Peter and St Paul Church in Lavenham, where they live today. They have three children including Joe's child from his first marriage, Vincent Parker, seven grandchildren and a great-grandson.

BILLY COULSON

Billy worked his way up to football coach at his favourite club, Arsenal. He married Claire Coulson née Brown in 1958.

Proud father of Barry Peter Coulson, who played for Arsenal and England in the 1970 World Cup, and daughter Louise Clara Bryant, who works in catering at the Emirates Stadium.

PROFESSOR ALEXANDER 'ALEX' DAVID NICHOLS

Alex married Professor Alice Higgins of Magdalene College, Cambridge and they have five children and three grandchildren. Alex wrote a popular book called *The Two Princes* and appeared on *Christmas University Challenge*. (His team answered questions on Cromwell, the Fauvists and the Theory of Relativity but failed to beat the team from the University of Warwick.)

JAMES 'PETER' DOWNEY

Peter married childhood sweetheart Mabel in 1955, after National Service that saw him serve in Korea and Germany. They have one daughter, Helen, and two grandchildren. Peter returned to a career in comics in London and his cartoons have also been published in the *Daily Telegraph* and the *Observer* newspapers.

Peter curated the exhibition 'Orphans in Comics' at the Victoria and Albert Museum. On retiring, Peter and Mabel moved to Lancashire. Peter died of lung cancer in 2005.

BARRY COULSON

Football fan Barry never missed an Arsenal match. When he was not watching football, Barry was a warehouse manager in Stoke Newington. Barry was killed in a motorcycle accident in 1962. He is much-missed, especially by his many friends, co-workers, adoring girlfriend Sherry and twin brother, Billy. A minute's silence was held at Highbury to commemorate his death and the warehouse football team that he used to play for in defence was renamed 'The Barrys'.

PEG CHURCH/EASLEA

Peg was the drummer in the 1960s pop group, the Lorelies. They toured in England and America and had a number-one hit in Japan.

She married architect Martin Halfpenny in 1965 and had three children, Keith, Simon and Sharon. After her adoptive parents the Easleas died, and with the encouragement of her children, Peg tried to find her birth parents. In 2012, Peg approached the ITV programme, *Long Lost Family*, for help. Sadly, they were unable to trace either her mother or father.

Peg has recently started drumming again.

EVELYN MARGARET WYATT-CARDEW

A midwife and lecturer, Evelyn Wyatt-Cardew was a renowned campaigner for better maternal provision. A strong advocate for home birth, she co-wrote *Stay Home – A History of Out-of-Hospital Birth Experiences*.

She married Mark Cope in 1959 and her daughter, Anita Cope, is also a midwife and campaigner for women's rights. She was very close to her four grandchildren – grandson Aaron Kyle was the first winner of talent show *Popstars* in 1999. Evelyn could be seen in the audience waving.

Evelyn died in 2017 after a short illness.

JOYCE HALL

Joyce became an art teacher at an inner-city London school. She remained a keen photographer and was runner-up in the Wildlife Portrait of the Year in 1983 and 1987. Joyce married Phillip Hargreaves, an art teacher. Now retired, Joyce enjoys caravanning and is planning an exhibition on collage.

DENNIS 'DENNY' PATRICK REED

Denny studied engineering at Durham University. He worked for Holst Engineering and was a founder member of the Lincoln engineers' choir. When he was forty, Denny suffered a mental health breakdown and decided to step back from work. He and his wife, Sandy Clarke, became foster carers and have looked after over forty children. Denny often talks about the impact the Festival of Britain had on his life.

CLIFFORD 'CLIFF' NELSON HARVEY

Clifford became a firefighter. In 1970, he was saving three children from a tower block when the floor crumbled, and barely survived. Clifford was later invalided out of the service. He has been married four times and is proud grandfather to nine, great-grandfather to five and great-great-grandfather to a little boy, Noah. He remains close friends with Jonathon Pell and is a fierce advocate of gay rights.

GLADYS GLUCK

After a successful career in marketing and sales, Gladys took a degree in counselling and now practises in CBT in a clinic in Islington, London. She married businessman Richard Deacon in 1970 and has three stepchildren and several step-grandchildren, who she loves very much!

FRANK GLUCK

Three times married, Frank worked in airline fitting production in Letchworth. In his free time, he was a proud plane-spotter and dog-lover. He died of Covid in April 2020 and is much-missed by his wife Kate, seven children, twelve grandchildren and their many pets.

TREVOR GLUCK

Before he retired, Trevor worked on the London Underground as a driver and was active in the union. He stood in election against Margaret Thatcher – and only lost by 200 votes. He has been a very popular Labour councillor in Essex for the last ten years. He still runs a local chess club and enjoys cruises with his wife, Hettie.

PHYLLIS 'FLORRIE' MACDONALD

Florrie became a fashion model and a campaigner/ambassador for healthy foods. She was featured in a wide range of publications, including *Woman*, *Woman's Own* and *Good Housekeeping*. After she gave up modelling, she worked in a library and later revealed that she had struggled with an eating disorder for much of her life. She adored books and ran library book clubs for teenagers and adults. She also set up several nursery rhyme story sessions for toddlers; each session began with 'Twinkle, Twinkle, Little Star,' and Florrie would proudly relate how she once lived in Jane Taylor's house. She died of heart-related issues in 1997.

JONATHON AINSLEY PELL

Jonathon represented England in the 1960 Olympic Games in Rome and gained the bronze medal in the 1500 metres. He went on to write sports columns in the *Guardian* and *TIME* magazine. He wrote a memoir, *In My Father's Shadow*, which won the 2004 Samuel Johnson Prize, with one of the judges saying it was one of the finest sports memoirs of all time. The book was dedicated to his best friend, Cliff Harvey. In 2006, he came out about his homosexuality after an ex-partner went to the press. He lives with his long-term partner, cycling gold medallist Neville Stewart.

PATRICIA DELANEY/HAWTHORNE

Patricia is the CEO of award-winning international fabric and design company *Buttons*, which designed several of Princess Diana's dresses. Patricia married the designer Gerald Perrin in Paris, France, and they had three children but were divorced in 1974. She married second husband, banker Nigel Hawthorne, in 1978. He died in 2001. Patricia travels all over the world but is never more at home than in Suffolk. She bought and modernised

Sir Alfred Munnings' property in 2004. She is a grandmother of twin girls, Erika and Laure.

CLARA NEWTON

Clara married Ivor Delaney in May 1953. She continued to work at Shilling Grange as a part-time job-share and was also involved in policymaking for Suffolk County Council. Bags for Orphans, Better Record-Keeping, Siblings Stay Together and Transparency are some of the policies that were attributed to her.

She gives speeches and writes on the importance of child-centred care and, in later years, helped several of the British children sent to Australia find their birth families. In 2005, she was invited to write the foreword to a reprinted edition of Jane Taylor's poems and she collaborated with the daughter of the late Mr Dowsett on this.

Clara retired in 1989.

Clara and Ivor have one daughter, Patricia Delaney. Ivor was unwell for some years and died in 1997 of pneumonia. Patricia has been a great comfort to Clara and the two enjoy book clubs, magazines and travel together. In 1998 they went to Sub-saharan Africa, where they found Clara's mother's grave and even some people who remembered her. Clara loves spending time in Switzerland with Rita, or with her three grandchildren and her great-grandchildren in Lavenham.

A LETTER FROM LIZZIE

Dear reader,

Thank you so much for choosing to read *An Orphan's Wish*. If you enjoyed it and want to be kept up to date with all my latest releases, just sign up at the following link. Your email address will never be shared and you can unsubscribe at any time.

www.bookouture.com/lizzie-page

Well, it's over! That's a wrap. The Shilling Grange series is all finished.

Clara and Ivor are married and the children in the home are safe and happy – and I can't think of a better way to end the story than that!

This started out as a three-book series, but I loved writing it so much that I asked to write two more. It's been an absolute blast to immerse myself in post-war England, in Lavenham, in Clara's life, and especially in the lives of the children. Each of the children in Shilling Grange is very real and special to me. I know Peg perhaps has the most fans, for her sweetness and her struggles, yet I really did love all of them, even the difficult ones, and one of my biggest joys about writing a series is being able to show how children grow, change, develop and, in some cases, redeem themselves.

Close readers will probably have guessed that Peter has a special place in my heart too!

I know lots of people had their favourite children (yes, yes, I know we shouldn't, but it *is* fiction!), and I'd love to hear which ones touched your hearts the most, so do get in touch. I'd also love to hear which storylines interested you most, and why.

It's hard for a book to get noticed these days – more and more we rely on lovely readers like you to spread the word for us. If you have enjoyed the Shilling Grange series, and if you feel like it, reviews and recommendations are much appreciated.

You'll probably have read at the back of this book the stories of the children's lives after Shilling Grange. I found this section quite emotional to write! In some cases, I knew how the children's stories would turn out; others came to me later. I think they all did rather well – testimony not only to Clara's love for them at the home but also to their own strength and resilience.

Researching and writing about children's homes has led me to a place of greater compassion for all those with painful childhoods. As a society, it's imperative we look after our abandoned young ones – and have empathy for them still as they grow up, when their wounds are less visible.

As usual, I have woven real-life events into this historical fiction. The North Sea floods of 1953 were devastating to many areas of the UK as well as Holland and Belgium. I hope readers get a sense of how communities suffered during that time, only eight years after the end of the Second World War. There is also mention of the new queen, Derek Bentley, Alan Turing, and the conquering of Mount Everest. This is to add a flavour of the time, and illustrates an age where people were moving away from the dark post-war years into a time of problems, yes, but also of greater optimism and a sense of hope. Whether we like it or not, we are all affected by current events, and I wanted to show how Clara and children were too.

Where to now? I'm working on a three-book series about the evacuated children of the Second World War, their families and their host families. I guess there are some themes that will always interest me, themes that I like to explore in different ways –

displacement and how that affects us in later life, the search for belonging, the responsibilities and rewards of parenting, etc.

I hope you will enjoy this new series too. You will hear more about it if you sign up to my newsletter or me on any of my social media accounts or follow me on Amazon.

Once again, a huge thank you for coming on this journey to post-war Suffolk with me, Clara, Ivor and the children.

Keep reading!

Love Lizzie xx

ACKNOWLEDGEMENTS

There would be no Shilling Grange series without editor Kathryn Taussig – I'll always be indebted to her. There would probably be no Bookouture books without Kathryn either. She was the first editor to want to publish my first novel, *The War Nurses*. She also has great ideas for great stories. I remember clearly the Zoom conversation (it was early lockdown) when Kathryn, my agent Thérèse Coen and I wrestled – not literally – our ideas into shape.

'You write children very well,' Kathryn said, 'let's do more of that.'

By the end of that Zoom meeting, I knew I wanted to write a series that would sit somewhere between *The Durrells*, *Virgin River*, *Call the Midwife* and *The Sound of Music*. These were great reference points that have served me well – keeping my stories in shape and giving me a kind of structure, not only of subject matter, but of tone or feel too.

I have lost track of which editor helped with which edits where, but huge thanks also to the lovely Rhianna Louise, who inherited me from Kathryn and bravely stepped in to be my editor for Book Four, *The Children Left Behind*.

Claire Simmonds came in as my new editor while we were finishing up Book Four and was the midwife to Book Five – and what a brilliant experience it has been. It must have been hard for her to come in so late in the series, but I can't speak highly enough of all the work she has done on this book. She knows the series inside out (better than me, I think). She has a most beautiful turn of phrase, and I am learning such a lot from working with her. Thank you, Claire, looking forward to the next series!

This is the fifth set of acknowledgements and I'm afraid they will be quite boring – but I do need to thank everyone at Bookou ture. They've been brilliant to work with. Yes, we don't always agree with titles and covers, but ultimately, I feel so valued by the team and able to produce my best work and able to get that work to the largest number of readers possible. I am a happy writer, thanks to them.

I am hugely grateful to copy-editor, Jacqui Lewis, and proof-reader, Jane Donovan. It's been brilliant working with them throughout the series. They both have an extraordinary eye for detail, for continuity and their edits improved my work immeasur-ably. Any mistakes that have slipped through are all my own.

I always need to thank the awe-inspiring agent Thérèse Coen at Susanna Lea Associates. She is the best. She is encouraging, supportive and communicative. (Another reason I am that perhaps rare beast, a happy writer!)

Oh, and so much gratitude to the wonderful audio narrator, Emily Barber. I feel lucky that her beautiful voice has been here throughout the series. She could narrate a tax return and make it sound interesting.

Okay, who else?

This is a weird one – I feel I need to acknowledge Jane Taylor. A strand of her, her poetry, and of course her home, has run through this series, helping to hold it together and also being a kind of inspiration to me. Women throughout the ages have had to battle to be recognised. We shouldn't forget that – and we should try to remember those we can.

So, thank you, Jane. I'll keep on banging the drum for you.

I think I have some of the best readers. Really. If you're still reading this, hello, that's you! From your generous reviews to your Facebook messages and recommendations and your supportive words, your reading and championing has meant the world to me. I do read my reviews – and I do listen to your ideas.

It's only by knowing many lovely children that I was able to create characters who, I hope, hop, skip and jump off the page. So to everyone who has inspired me, thank you.

Thank you, friends, for our coffees and conversations. I would go insane without you, I know it.

Finally, to my family – you are my sunshines. Don't ever forget it.

Printed in Great Britain
by Amazon